PRAISE FOR AMANDA PROWSE

'Amanda Prowse is the queen of contemporary family drama.'

Daily Mail

'A tragic story of loss and love.'

Lorraine Kelly, *Sun*

'Captivating, heartbreaking and superbly written.'

Closer

'A deeply emotional, unputdownable read.'

Red

'Uplifting and positive, but you may still need a box of tissues.'

Cosmopolitan

'You'll fall in love with this.'

Cosmopolitan

'Warning: you will need tissues.'

Sun on Sunday

'Handles her explosive subject with delicate care.'

Daily Mail

'Deeply moving and eye-opening.'

Heat

'A perfect marriage morphs into harrowing territory . . . a real tear-jerker.'

Sunday Mirror

The Girl in the Corner

OTHER BOOKS BY AMANDA PROWSE

OTHER NOVELLAS BY AMANDA PROWSE

The Girl in the Corner

AMANDA PROWSE

LAKE UNION
PUBLISHING

Text copyright © 2018 by Lionhead Media Ltd
All rights reserved.

Published by Lake Union Publishing, Seattle

www.apub.com

Amazon, the Amazon logo, and Lake Union Publishing are trademarks of Amazon.com, Inc., or its affiliates.

ISBN-13: 9781503904996
ISBN-10: 1503904997

Cover design by Rose Cooper

Printed in the United States of America

I used to be the girl in the corner. I still am sometimes; I often think I don't quite fit – and I don't think I am the only one. I dedicate this book to all the women who know what it's like to feel the churn of nerves in their gut at the thought of putting themselves forward, who would rather cling to the wall than dance alone in the spotlight. I would say this to you: if not now, then when? When is it going to be your time? Take a deep breath and take the plunge and hopefully another girl in a corner will be watching, cheering you on!

This is how we gain confidence: by supporting each other instead of tearing each other down, by having each other's backs instead of talking behind them. Women supporting women – what a wonderful, wonderful thing!

ONE

Find a partner . . . are you kidding me?

The tall woman from administration smiled at each and every one of the hundred or so new students now gathered in the rather musty gymnasium, the sporty odour only barely masked by the liberally scented cloud of Paco Rabanne's Pour Homme and The Body Shop's White Musk that hung in the air. She handed out large sticky labels for them to write their names on and pop on their chests. She then told everyone to find a partner.

The instruction was added almost casually, something so incidental it required no more build-up than that; whereas in reality the very idea of trying to seek out a partner among these strangers was enough to send sixteen-year-old Rae-Valentine into a spin. She leaned back against the wall and tried to hide her nerves, though she felt like throwing up.

'Anyone will do,' the tall woman yelled, encouragingly. 'Don't over-think it, just grab someone, anyone! Shake their hand and introduce yourself and share some fun facts!'

The college induction was turning out to be one of the worst days imaginable. Grab a stranger? Shake their hand? Exchange fun facts? She was certain Debbie-Jo, her gregarious older sister, would thrive in this environment, probably pirouetting around the room and delivering her fun facts through the medium of song. But Rae wasn't sure which part filled her with the most dread – touching a stranger or trying to *think* of fun facts. Either way her heart beat loudly in her throat and her legs felt like jelly.

It was Debbie-Jo's words that came to her now, uttered on a dull afternoon over a decade ago.

'There are only two sorts of people, Rae,' Debbie-Jo had informed her, as Rae sat on her bed, watching her big sister, who, with their mum's make-up mirror propped on a stack of books, brushed her thick, dark hair, practising how to twist it into a tight bun for when she was a prima ballerina. 'Those who are memorable and those who are not. It is important in a sea of people to be the one everyone remembers, the one who stands out in the middle of the room, the star; otherwise you might as well be like furniture, the girl in the corner. And who wants to be that? No one. That's who.'

The words had crystallised in Rae-Valentine's mind, forming a frag-ile platform on which her confidence would teeter for a lifetime. As she clung to the wall and eyed the sea of people, she spied the exit and wondered if she could make it without being approached. She was in half a mind to grab her bag and run, to simply go home and tell her mum and dad she had had a change of heart and that college might not be for her after all.

She watched as people darted about in front of her, running this way and that, seeking out those who had earlier caught their eye. Pretty, fashionable girls now linked arms with their lookalike counterparts, gig-gling with relief that they were among their own, manicured kind. One self-assured, good-looking boy with a New Romantic-style haircut and a smidge of kohl around his eyes sauntered up to a confident-looking, trendy girl wearing a bunch of Madonna-inspired bangles, his hand extended. Rae couldn't help but imagine what their kids might be like: world leaders, probably, with long fringes, firm handshakes and eyeliner.

As she considered this she caught the eye of a girl with a shock of red, backcombed hair and severe make-up. She was striking, her features big, a fleshy nose, pillowy lips and wide eyes. Rae would not have described her as pretty, but she was certainly memorable and that, in her book, was just as attractive – and, according to Debbie-Jo's world-view, a lot more important.

The girl approached with an outstretched hand, against which Rae anxiously slid her shaking palm, and pointed at her large sticky label, which read simply 'Dolly'.

'My name is Dolly Latimer, I'm sixteen and you look like the only other person in this room who thinks this whole introduction thing is as lame as I do. I saw you looking for the door and so I picked you.' The girl was loud, and Rae blinked rapidly and stepped back in response. 'Fun facts: I am planning to lose my virginity within the next few weeks to the most gorgeous boy you have ever met. His name is Vinnie and he's twenty and has his own car. And another fun fact would be that during her whole welcome speech, I fantasised about taking lanky admin woman's clipboard and whacking it over the top of her head.'

Rae placed her free hand over her mouth to stifle her laughter and looked at the girl.

'Now it's your turn!' Dolly Latimer instructed. She gave a maniacal grin while still pumping her hand up and down.

'Oh! Okay, well, my . . . my name is Rae Pritchard.' Rae faltered. 'Rae-Valentine, actually, but no one calls me that, not really.' She cursed the dryness of her mouth, which was making her words sound sticky as they left her lips. 'I failed my O levels. School wasn't really my thing – I could never seem to get started on studying, even though I actually found the subjects easy – and time kind of ran out, so my mum and dad have told me to come here to learn typing. I wanted to learn to cook, but they said typing would be more useful.'

Dolly threw back her head and laughed loudly and Rae felt a flush of joy that she was capable of eliciting this response.

'Jesus, Rae-Valentine! Way to sell yourself! You *failed* your O levels? Good! O levels – in fact all exams – are shit! And be under no illusion:

this college is *not* the scrapheap for those of us who couldn't get to university,' she boomed.

'It isn't?' Rae asked softly, taken aback by Dolly's loud, loud voice and finally managing to extract her hand and looking around to see if anyone was listening in.

They weren't.

'Hell, no!' Dolly shouted. 'This place is the portal through which we enter as kids and leave as adults with tits, driving licences and typing skills – *and* we do it without pressure, because no one expects anything from us, meaning we can't actually fail. This place is fucking Nirvana!'

Rae noticed that Dolly already had tits; and as she looked around the room, taking in the wooden, multicoloured-tape-riddled floor with its myriad scuff marks, the polystyrene-coated, cream-painted ceiling tiles and the blue plastic chairs lined up around the walls, she had to admit it didn't look like fucking Nirvana. If anything it looked quite depressing; though she had the feeling that with Dolly by her side it would be anything but.

'You got brothers and sisters?' Dolly asked.

Rae was sure this hadn't been part of the task, but answered anyway. 'One sister, Debbie-Jo, who works on cruise ships. She's a dancer and a singer. Really pretty. And when she's not on the cruise ships she works in Woolworths, part-time.' She smiled at the image of her glamorous sibling, who sent photographs back home of her on a mini-stage with a plastic palm tree, wearing sequinned low-cut frocks and very red lipstick. Her mum propped them up on the shelf in the kitchen above the toaster.

Dolly laughed that rasping laugh again. 'Debbie-Jo and Rae-Valentine? Are your parents country and western geeks? Please tell me your house is strewn with gee-tars and that your dad plucks a banjo on the porch wearing a cowboy hat and a bootlace tie and your mum has full skirts with petticoats underneath, answers to the name Mary-Beth!'

Rae stared at the girl, who was quite unlike anyone she had ever met before. She thought about their little house in Purbeck Avenue with the paved driveway and her mum's collection of cement frogs, which lined the path. She pictured the front room, with its mustard-coloured Dralon sofa and two matching chairs and the bookshelf that instead of books housed a collection of glass. Bowls, cake stands, tumblers, all inherited from her gran or her great-aunt Millie or bought on the cheap by her mum from jumble sales.

Not a gee-tar in sight.

'No, my mum is called Maureen and my dad is called Len, short for Leonard, and they're not really into country. But they do like Simon and Garfunkel and Bread. They've got their cassettes.'

Again for some reason this struck Dolly as the funniest thing ever said. Rae liked the way she felt when Dolly laughed like this: elevated and interesting. This in itself was a rarity for a girl who was used to being in the background, sitting in the corner.

When the induction day finally came to a close, the two new friends sauntered to the bus stop. Rae-Valentine stood at the bus shelter and pushed her hands down into the pockets of her jeans.

'So,' Dolly boomed, 'let's get straight down to business.'

Rae stared at her. They had been friends for approximately six hours and already Dolly was making plans with an air of assumption that was as flattering as it was enticing.

'Have you got a passport?' Dolly asked, prodding Rae in the arm.

'A passport?'

'Yes! That little blue book that means you can leave this bloody dull country and go in search of fun in Majorca!'

'Yes, my dad's got it; he keeps them all in his folder in the wardrobe with our birth certificates and stuff.' Rae looked at her feet, worried that this snippet of information might be the wrong thing to say; afraid that she might be giving too much of an insight into the mediocrity of her very average home life, which she assumed to be in stark contrast to Dolly's.

'Good. That's the first hurdle out of the way.'

Rae would soon learn that this was how Dolly operated, working methodically through any potential problem until all she could see was a shining obstacle-free path towards achieving her goal. And her goal right now was apparently figuring out how she, her new friend Rae-Valentine, Dolly's brother Howard and his mate Vinnie, the boy with whom she had decided to lose her virginity, could go to her family's apartment in Majorca for a week without parents. Rae had been abroad only once: a day trip to Boulogne, on a ferry with her family, where they ate proper French bread and stinky cheese on a bench overlooking the beach and her dad did cartwheels in the sand to make them laugh, and all the francs fell out of his pocket and they had to scrabble around on the hard, wet sand trying to find them. She found many more than Debbie-Jo, who was sulking that day because she couldn't have her ears pierced and wanted to change her name to Barbara Gordon, the real name of Batgirl. Her parents had given a definitive *no* to both requests.

Going to Majorca felt like an audacious plan, if not impossible. Rae was not allowed to go into town without getting permission from her mum and dad, couldn't take a bag of crisps from the cupboard without asking, let alone head off to Majorca – with boys! But she went along with it for now, not wanting to be the one to put a damper on the discussion and rather enjoying the plotting, even if it was only pretend.

'I know!' Dolly yelled suddenly, leaping up as an idea formed. 'You could tell your parents that my mum and dad are taking us!'

'I . . . I'm not sure I could.' Rae hitched her book bag up on to her shoulder. 'They are quite strict on the detail; they'd probably want to speak to your mum and dad before deciding if I could go or not, and they'd want to come and wave us off, and would probably write a card to your parents saying "Thank you for taking her" and send sweets for the journey, that kind of thing.'

Plus I could never lie to them! Not about something big like that! Not about anything, really – lying is the worst. Supposing something happened while we were away; supposing they found out? I would not enjoy any trip that was underpinned by such a big lie. I'd be worried sick every single moment I was away . . . scared . . . She rolled her eyes at Dolly to show the crappiness of it all.

'God. Way too involved. Kill me now.'

'Yep, *way* too involved.' Rae liked this phrase and its use in this context; she stored it away to use with any other words and themes she might pick up from her confident, worldly friend, trying in her head to perfect the languid, indifferent, yet heavily negative tone that conveyed as much as the words themselves.

Rae decided she wanted to be just like Dolly – or more specifically, she wanted to be like the girl Dolly saw her as: funny and confident, the kind of girl who might just be capable of lying to her parents and gallivanting off abroad, to Majorca no less, with Dolly's brother and her brother's mate, Vinnie, so Dolly could have sex.

The reality of Rae's existence, however, was very different.

She might have been sixteen, but she was in fact the kind of girl who felt as if the whole wide world were a party to which she wasn't invited, a girl who sat between her mum and dad on the sofa, wearing pyjamas her mum had warmed in front of the fire. She was a girl who more often than not went to bed early with a good book. The kind of girl who liked nothing more than the Sundays when they visited her nan and grandad in Essex and enjoyed a roast dinner along with a good reminisce about the old days, poring over the yellowed pages of the photograph albums that contained snapshots of her heritage. Not that her family had done anything remarkable – there were no pictures of Great-Grandad Walter on top of Everest, and her great-grandma Alice had not been a suffragette. But Walter did play the spoons, and there *was* a grainy picture of them both on the back of donkeys: Weston-super-Mare, she believed, circa 1900. Proof that her ordinariness went way back. She could only imagine Dolly's reaction were she to find this out.

Kill me now . . .

'Where is that bloody bus? I am actually going to die if it doesn't come in the next five minutes!' Dolly threw her head back and closed her eyes.

'Yep,' Rae agreed with one word, while desperately trying to think of something interesting to say.

'Plus I swear, Rae, if I don't get to spend time with Vinnie I am actually going to kill myself,' Dolly announced.

Death, Rae noticed, seemed to be a bit of preoccupation with her new friend. She watched as Dolly took her slender packet of ten Marlboro Lights from her coat pocket and tapped one from the packet into her palm, lighting it with a nifty single strike of a match that must have taken some practice. Dolly took a long, deep lug on the cigarette and handed it to Rae, who hated smoking, hated cigarettes, hated everything about them: the smell, the taste and not least the terrible rasping burn it left at the back of her throat and in her lungs. She took it coolly between her fingers and sucked on it, hoping she hadn't sogged up the filter – a cardinal sin, apparently. Unable to take the smoke down and speak, like Dolly – a natural when it came to inhaling the noxious cloud – Rae held it in her mouth, trying not to gag; turning her head casually, as if she were looking out for the bus, she slowly blew it out in a plume above her head. She felt cool and she felt older, both things very much on the wish list of this sixteen-year-old girl whose parents were way too involved.

'Why don't you just tell your brother you like Vinnie and get him to ask if he likes you?'

'Are you actually mental?' Dolly looked at her aghast and Rae felt the flutter of rejection in her stomach. She didn't want to get things wrong, not in front of Dolly. 'That's crazy talk! If I told Howard I liked Vinnie, he would not only take the piss out of me, like, forever, but he'd also tell Vinnie, and the one way to scare a boy off is to tell him that you like him.'

'So how will he ever know, if you don't tell him or can't say?' It was a genuine question.

Rae watched as Dolly placed the cigarette between her scarlet lips and took another long drag, throwing her mane of Titian hair back in laughter. 'You crack me up, Rae. You are hilare!'

This, another word to be stored away, was apparently short for 'hilarious'. Rae smiled. It felt good to be hilare.

'He'll know, don't you worry. At least, he will if I can ever get him to Majorca! The sight of these puppies in a bikini and he'll be all mine.' She cupped her breasts over her T-shirt and the two girls howled. 'I mean come on, Rae, I might not have the face of Madonna, but I have immense bosoms.'

Rae shook her head in mock disapproval.

'What?' Dolly stared at her. 'A girl's gotta do what a girl's gotta do!'

Rae stared at the twin humps sitting snugly inside her friend's V-necked T-shirt and had to admit her bosoms were indeed immense. She hunched her shoulders forward, trying to create some kind of cleavage, but it was impossible; hers were . . . deflated.

'Bus!' Dolly called out and stamped her cigarette into the pavement with the pointed toe of her grey suede slouch boots. 'Right, double dare.'

'No! No! I don't want a double dare!' Rae caught her breath.

'Yes!' Dolly screamed. 'You have to say to the bus driver, "I want to have sex with your brother!"'

'No way. I'm not saying that!' Rae felt a blush rise on her cheeks. Her voice had gone up an octave or two.

'Come on, it's a dare! It's being brave and putting something out into the universe and good things will come back to you, like getting to go to Majorca!'

Rae failed to see the connection. 'I . . . I can't! Oh my God, Dolly! I can't! No way!' She placed her hands over her face, as if she might be able to hide from the challenge.

'Yes, you can! Come on, it'll be hilare!'

'No! No way! It won't be hilare!' She shook her head and fished in her pocket for her bus pass. 'I would actually die. You do it!' Rae felt brave, throwing the gauntlet back to her friend.

Dolly shrugged and hitched her khaki ex-army satchel over her shoulder, waiting on the kerb for the bus doors to wheeze open. She held up her bus pass and looked the elderly driver in the eye. 'Iwanttohavesexwithyourbrother, thank you!'

The first words, strung together and mumbled, were barely decipherable, but the 'thank you' was loud and clear.

'You're very welcome, dear!' The driver smiled, delighted by her manners.

Rae felt the laughter explode from her. With one part nerves and two parts amusement, she shook with tears in her eyes as she held up her bus pass. The driver looked at her quizzically as she scooted past and ran up the stairs to join her friend on the back seat of the top deck.

'Oh my God! I can't believe you just did that!' She collapsed into the seat and the two girls bent double, with their heads touching the back of the seat in front, laughing so hard they could barely catch a breath. The more they laughed, the funnier it became.

'Stop!' Dolly yelled, punching her friend on the arm. 'I am going to wet myself!'

'Me too! I'm going to wet myself!' Rae gripped her stomach, trying to think of sad things to stem the hysteria that held her fast.

◆　◆　◆

Over the next three weeks the friends fell into a comfortable routine, and now at the end of another giggle-filled college day they tripped across the pavement laughing, as they did at most things, because nearly everything in their world seemed hilare and it took no more than one word or a particular expression loaded with secret meaning to set them off. They lived wrapped in a giddy bubble of closeness that gave purpose to even the most boring of days and meant that Rae went to bed with a fizz of anticipation in her gut at the prospect of seeing Dolly the very next morning.

Being so very softly spoken herself, Rae thought it probably the plan of the universe to match her up with the very loud Dolly, meaning that the noise they collectively put out into the world was about level. Her mum often commented that she could hear her friend squealing from the moment they got off the bus and all the way to the front door. And Rae liked it, the way they as a duo punched a hole in the quiet, making her mark, she felt, for the first time ever. Part of a team, a twosome.

Best mates.

They walked closely in step, each with a pair of headphones plugged into a Walkman and listening to Black singing 'Wonderful Life' on repeat.

'I have decided I want you to meet my brother,' Dolly announced, her tone suggesting it was a rare privilege.

'Who? Howard?' Dolly had mentioned him the day they'd met.

'Yes, Howard! Well, it wouldn't be my other brother, Paul, would it? He's old and married.'

Rae shook her head, certain her friend hadn't mentioned Paul. 'I couldn't; I'd be too shy.' She pulled her friend's arm and looked at the pavement, embarrassed by the idea of meeting the wonderful Howard, whose many qualities Dolly regularly extolled.

Howard is so funny!

Howard is really good-looking!

Howard has met Simply Red, Bryan Adams and the woman who cuts Annie Lennox's hair!

Dolly made his life as the manager in their parents' Surrey restaurant sound very glamorous, a world away from roast dinners at Rae's nan's.

'Well, you need to get over the shy, because he is sniffing around Lisa Hopkirk, who is good-looking but dumb; like, really dumb. She is very hair-flicky and she laughs *all* the time; like, all the time, this little giggle that drives you nuts. I swear you could say, "Oh look, Lisa, your house is on fire!" and she'd do that bloody laugh! Or, "Oh, Lisa, your tits have fallen off!" Hee-hee-hee-hee-hoo-hoo-hoo!'

Dolly's description made Rae laugh and gave a new sense of urgency to the plan. She might be shy, but she didn't want the hair-flicking, giggling Lisa Hopkirk getting in there first.

'Anyway, I've already told him all about you.' Dolly smirked.

'You have not! Oh my God!' Rae gasped, horrified and delighted in equal measure. 'What did you say?'

'I said you were quiet, pretty and nice and that you were my best mate!'

This description was enough to make her heart swell. 'I'm not pretty.'

'You are! Dumbkopf!' Dolly rolled her eyes. 'You are beautiful.'

Rae smiled at her friend. 'What did Howard say when you told him that?' Dolly had her interest.

'He said he should probably take you out for a drink and I said he definitely should.'

'God, Dolly, you can't go making arrangements for me without checking first! Supposing I don't want to go out for a drink with your brother? Or supposing I do go out for a drink with him and he is just disappointed and things get messed up and he doesn't like me or I don't like him? Then it would make things weird between you and me. I would hate that.' Rae felt herself getting flustered, knowing that would be the very worst thing. This friendship was as precious as it was all-consuming.

'Things wouldn't be weird between us, no matter what happened – besides, I know you two are going to hit it off. But of course if you'd rather not . . .' She let this trail.

'I'm not saying that!' Rae answered with haste. 'I am not saying no; I am just saying you should check with me first.'

'I am checking with you now, you wally!'

'Well, okay then.' She smiled.

'So I'll tell him yes?' Dolly pushed.

'If you like.' Rae tried for nonchalant but both girls ended up squealing with excitement all the way up her mum and dad's front path.

Her mum opened the door and stood wiping her hands on a flannel dishcloth, sniffing the air. 'Oh dear, I can smell cigarettes. Has someone been smoking?'

'Someone probably has, yes,' Dolly answered instantly, with a pleasant smile and a well-spoken manner that Rae could see left her mum wondering if the girl was being sweet or taking the mick. Her mum shot her a particular knowing look and Rae knew her friend's behaviour would be discussed when Dolly had gone home. She was, however, thankful that her mum didn't say anything now, in front of her, as that would be the worst, way too involved. The girls raced up to the sanctuary of Rae's bedroom.

'So, back to Howard.' Dolly sat on the bed with her legs crossed and applied roll-on, strawberry-scented lip gloss from a bottle whose contents, once clear, were now decidedly murky, tinged with the residue of red lipstick. She continued with her matchmaking. 'It would be so cool if you went out with him, and then me and you and Vinnie and Howard can go clubbing together or whatever. I will marry Vinnie and you can marry Howard and we will be best friends as well as sister-in-laws and we can have our kids close in age and they'll be cousins and we will be one big happy family and it will be bloody brilliant! Then we can go to Majorca for sex whenever we want!'

'Yes, but if we are all married, we won't have to go to Majorca for sex. We will be able to have sex at home whenever we want to.' Rae kept her voice down; even saying *S. E. X.* when her parents were on the floor below felt awkward.

'Good point.' Dolly nodded. 'Seriously, though, you are going to love Howard – everyone does. He's wonderful!'

Rae felt like fireworks were going off in her stomach. She had yet to meet Howard, but the picture her glamorous friend painted more than excited her. It sounded like a wonderful, wonderful life, a million miles away from cement frogs and day trips to Boulogne.

It wasn't that Rae didn't love her ordinary family and their modest suburban home – she did. But she knew she was never going to reach the dizzy heights of Debbie-Jo, who worked on a cruise ship that sailed the high seas. They tended not to mention the off-season, when her sister worked in Woolworths; she dated her floor manager, Lee, and the two would spend the evenings on the sofa looking at pictures of Debbie-Jo aboard the cruise ship in her sequins.

Rae-Valentine knew she was different, one of life's observers. She had spent her first sixteen years on the planet keeping most of her thoughts to herself, never being one to take centre stage, preferring the darker, quieter corner of any room. At least that was what everyone thought; but there were times when she wished she could be a bit more like Debbie-Jo.

Her sister had, throughout their childhood, dressed in a leotard and footless tights with her hair in a side ponytail, singing into a tape recorder or practising her Oscar acceptance speeches in the mirror. Their dad would often have to shout at her to 'move away from in front of the telly!' Debbie-Jo would wail and explain, 'But, Dad, I need to practise my thank yous!' with a stamp of her foot. 'Heaven help us!' he would sigh, and turn his attention instead to his newspaper or simply cock his head and watch the inches of screen visible to the side of his eldest daughter, who with tears streaming down her face would

14

begin – 'I never expected this! Thank you! Thank you all so much!' – with a thoughtful, loving gaze at the rolling pin in her hand, a rather skinny Oscar substitute, followed by a grand sweep of her arm around the room, followed by more tears. 'I would like to thank my mum, my dad and my agent; my amazing boyfriend, David Cassidy . . .' Rae-Valentine noticed she never made the list. It didn't matter; Rae loved her regardless. In fact she loved her whole family very much. But Dolly's family? They were a whole new kettle of fish.

Rae's dad, Len, drove a Vauxhall Nova and worked for British Telecom. He was a man who lived cautiously with the central heating on a strict timer; his insurance/TV licence/car-tax renewals were red-ringed on the RNLI calendar on the kitchen wall and he refused to eat out in restaurants other than when on holiday, as it was 'a bloody waste of money'. Her mum, Maureen, was less cautious, but lived quietly and in judgement of anyone whose life differed too much from her own – and not just in the big things. Rae had seen her look bemused at her own mother when she expressed a desire for mashed potatoes instead of roast one Sunday. It was as if Rae could read Maureen's thoughts: *Mash? On a Sunday? What on earth is the world coming to?* It made Rae smile and made her sad; she didn't want to see inside the mind of her mum, who thought spaghetti Bolognese was the pinnacle of sophistication and who, like her husband, felt a flare of panic if there was a diversion to their routine.

Dolly's family, by comparison, lived in a large sprawling house – with a swimming pool, no less! They owned three restaurants, an apart-ment in Majorca . . . It wasn't only what they *had*, not only the stuff that impressed Rae; it was also how they lived. She had heard Dolly swear in front of her mum, Mitzy, saying 'shit', 'arse' and 'arsehole' on more than one occasion without her mum even raising an eyebrow. Why, this family, the Latimers, in comparison to her own, were rock stars – and Rae-Valentine, who didn't have the confidence to cheek a bus driver let alone say 'arsehole' in front of her mum, wanted nothing more than to be a part of it.

'We will need to plan when we have sex so our kids are the same age.' Dolly broke Rae's thoughts, drawing her back to the topic in hand. She pressed her lips together and smudged her lip gloss into place.

Rae looked at her and wrinkled her nose, still a little unsure about the whole sex thing; kissing with tongues still felt like a big deal, never mind anything more.

'Oh my God!' Dolly yelled. 'You will have to say "Iwanttohavesexwithyourbrother" for real!'

And just like that, at the mention of that hilare afternoon on the bus, the two were reduced to giggling wrecks, with tear-smeared, foundation-streaked faces, as they bent double and laughed until they cried.

TWO

Rae smiled as she brushed her hair in front of the bedroom mirror, thinking of her best friend; wondering if she had a crystal ball or was – as Howard often suggested – a witch.

It was hard to believe it was now 2014 and that that conversation on the bed in her tiny room was nearly thirty years ago, when sex was not in Rae's world. Not that sex was in her world that much right now, but that was only because she was usually too tired. She sighed and placed her hand on her tummy, trying to calm the nerves that sloshed around in there along with the three cups of tea she had drunk that afternoon and the three shortbread biscuits that had accompanied them. She knew it was crazy to still feel so anxious about a family event, but crazy or not – and even after being a Latimer for all this time – the thought still fired a quiet ripple of nerves right through her.

'Ooh, eggs for my recipe!' Rae reached for a notepad sitting by the side of the bed and below the words

Kettle descaler

Soap dispensers for Barnet restaurant

Mum's knee support

she wrote:

Eggs for bacon, courgette and pecorino tart

Rae loved lists. She couldn't rest until the chore, item or recollection had been jotted down – otherwise it would swirl in her head, growing louder and louder. Lists were how she kept order and, not that she readily admitted it, crossing something off her list gave her just about as much pleasure as anything else.

Two bouquets had been delivered earlier: one from each of the kids. They were among her very favourite things, flowers – second only to cooking in her cosy kitchen in terms of lifting her heart and her spirit. Her son George's bouquet was quite extravagant and she suspected his lovely girlfriend Ruby had had more than a hand in it. She was pleased George had found someone nice and hoped it might last with this confident girl who looked at her son like he was sunshine; hard to tell, though, when they were so young. Not that age had mattered a jot to her and Howard; at sixteen Rae had held his hand and by eighteen she had waltzed up the aisle. Hannah's bouquet was thoughtful – yellow roses, which her daughter knew to be her favourites.

'Thank you, darling,' she had said to Hannah on the phone. 'They are just lovely!'

'You're welcome, Mum. I am sorry I won't be seeing you today.'

'That's okay, my lovely. It's not like it's Christmas or a birthday; it's a wedding anniversary, and that's different, a bit more of a personal celebration for Dad and me. I didn't expect you to come home. Not at all. I know you are very busy – and Liverpool is hardly around the corner.'

Rae did this: issued verbal platitudes designed to appease everyone but herself. How she would love to spend time with her daughter! A coffee, a lunch or a quick chat over breakfast – any would do. How she would love to be made a priority in Hannah's life just for a day, or an *hour*! But it was not her way. She would never want her kids to feel like she was pressuring them, even when this was to her detriment.

'Yes, but twenty-five years! That's like a lifetime.'

'It is in fact not far off *your* lifetime,' Rae pointed out.

'Urgh. I am never going to get married, Mum.'

'You don't know that, Hannah. And I'm not saying you *should* get married; but I would like you to settle in a relationship. I think it would be good for you, make you happy. It's a nice way to live, when it works.' She smiled and thought of Howard, who was secreted in his study, no doubt preparing for the night ahead.

In truth, not only did she pray Hannah would find someone to love who loved her back, but she was also a little weary of her daughter's militant views on just about everything. It wasn't that she didn't want her to have opinions – of course she did: strong ones! – but Rae couldn't help wondering if she needed to be quite so angry about everything. She hoped it was a phase, thinking how much easier her daughter's life would be if she were a little more appeasing. That, and Sunday lunch might actually be enjoyable if she were able to dish up vegetables without a knot in her gut, waiting for Hannah to take umbrage at something and begin one of her rather shouty lectures.

'I do know!' Hannah spat. 'Marriage is outdated, restrictive and pointless.'

'But weren't you out marching in support of same-sex marriage only last year?'

'That is totally different, Mum! God!' Rae pictured her daughter's eye-roll across the miles. 'That was about the principle of it! The discrimination, not the actual marriage!'

'I see,' Rae said, even though she didn't, not really, but was choosing to end the debate there, not having the energy for further discussion.

It felt like a poignant topic, on this of all days, when she and Howard were celebrating their silver wedding anniversary.

It had been a day of reflection, much of it spent at the kitchen table as she thought about the slip of a girl who had traipsed up the aisle on the arm of her dad, taking in the glances of admiration and thinking, she was now ashamed to admit, of all the pretty beribboned, boxed gifts that were piled on the dining-room table of her lovely new home, just waiting for her to rip off the paper. Her eyes now flew to the wide cherrywood chest of drawers on which sat a small glass perfume bottle with a silver lid. This bottle was just one of the gifts she had revealed on her wedding night, pulling the delicate thing from its fancy box as she sat with the full skirt of her watered-silk wedding dress spread on the floor like a picnic blanket. Howard had lain on it, his head resting on her lap, smoking, as he did back then, and with a slender glass of champagne clutched to his chest, the base sitting inside the open shirt front, which was a little stained with red wine. He seemed uninterested in the presents that had come flowing from relatives far and wide – his, mainly, and therein probably lay the reason for her joy: Howard was used to this life of opulence; she, however, was still impressed by it all. She felt it gave her status that had been lacking in her life so far and this, in turn, raised her confidence.

'Twenty-five years!' she breathed. 'And it feels like yesterday.'

Rae had heard many people talk about the nerves of the big day and she knew better than most how anxiety could peel the joy from any event. Many were the minutes – hours – she had locked herself in toilet cubicles, trying to summon the courage to participate on other occasions. But strangely, on her wedding day, she hadn't felt nerves – maybe a flutter or two, but her overriding feeling had been one of pure, unadulterated happiness.

She had fallen for Howard on their second date.

The first had been a mild disaster, a double date with the newly coupled Dolly and Vinnie. They hadn't made it to Majorca without parents; not then. This was partly because Dolly's parents, Arturo and

Mitzy, had pooh-poohed the idea, but mainly because the trip felt a little redundant once her friend's impressive bosom, loud mouth and sass had landed her her catch at a nightclub in northwest London called Coco's.

Vinnie had watched Dolly strut her stuff on the dance floor to the Pointer Sisters' 'Automatic'; this, followed by a slow dance to Kenny G's 'Songbird' with that body pressed closed to his, and he was snared.

She and Howard were quite overpowered on that first meeting by Dolly shouting, fidgeting and being generally overbearing as she and Vinnie flirted up a storm, making Rae – and, she suspected, Howard too – feel like the supporting cast for the drama that unfolded. She recalled sitting in the pub with her hands in her lap, wishing her friend wasn't quite so vocal and wondering what she was doing there at all, so out of place in this setting with these people. There was, she'd decided, no way someone as handsome and confident as Howard Latimer was ever going to be interested in someone like her, the girl in the corner. With this thought prevalent, she cursed the fact she had persuaded her mum to buy her a new floral blouse with leg-of-mutton sleeves and wished she could fast-forward the clock to when she was climbing into her warm bed in that familiar room and the whole embarrassing ordeal was over.

She had stepped from Vinnie's car at the end of the evening with a cloak of disappointment weighing her down. As she'd pushed open the garden gate and stood on the cement-frog-lined path, Howard had caught her up.

'That was a terrible, terrible evening.' He spoke softly, with the crinkle of laughter around his blue eyes.

'It really was,' she agreed, her laughter born of pure relief.

'I don't think either of us managed to get a word in edgeways.'

'I think Dolly was just a bit excited,' she whispered, looking again at her shoes.

He took a breath and placed his finger under her chin, lifting her eyes to meet his properly for the first time. 'You are kind and far too nice to be my sister's best friend. She's a nightmare.'

'Come on, Howard! Get a bloody move on! Let her go in already! We are getting so bored I literally might drop dead!' Dolly shouted from the front seat. Rae felt the twitch of net curtains all around, as the neighbours heard her too.

'See what I mean?' He didn't take his eyes from her face and the interaction felt a lot like talking, even in the gaps between the words. It made her tummy flip. 'I think maybe we should go out again, but just you and me. How does that sound?'

'Sounds like it would be quiet,' she squeaked, biting her bottom lip and cursing the lack of confidence in her tone.

'And right now quiet would be good.' He smiled at her. 'I think we should go for a long walk and not to the pub. What do you think?'

She smiled at him. 'I think yes.'

Their second date had come only a week later. The two of them had fallen into step and walked the track around the lake in the local park with perfect rhythm. They chatted and it was far from awkward, far from nerve-racking. It was in fact perfect.

Rae smiled now and rubbed the top of her arms at the memory, feeling, as she sometimes did, so blessed. In truth she had fallen for him as they walked laps of the water, as if afraid to step from the path and break the magic. She needn't have feared. As the afternoon drew to a close and dusk bit, he had held her close to him, so close she thought he must be able to hear her heart beating, and kissed her sweetly on the top of the head before offering the casual promise to see her soon.

As he'd walked away, she had imprinted an image of him at the front of her brain and that was where he had stayed. Even now she might be shopping or changing the bed linen when a feeling of warmth flooded her – so powerful that she would stop and take a moment, giving silent thanks for her husband, her marriage, her kids and all that she held dear.

Rae glanced at her watch and fought the desire to pace. She wondered what the arrangements were this evening for her parents. Her mum and dad were slipping into the realms of the elderly and it was happening a little too quickly for any of them to find comfortable. It was sobering to feel that time seemed be flying by faster the older she got. She hoped someone had thought to ask about her dad's dietary requirements for the evening and that her mum wouldn't be asked to stand for too long. Although if Debbie-Jo, Lee and their boys Luke and Taylor were invited, at least she'd be on hand, which would make a nice change. She didn't want to be mean about her sister, but she still found it a little galling that the golden girl could only manage the odd trip home from Northampton, when Rae knew she practically drove past her parents' front door on trips into London to attend concerts, catch flights, shop in the sales . . . Rae thought it was unfair. But this too she kept to herself.

Her relationship with her sister was an odd one. She had tried over the years to get closer to her but had given up when they were younger, figuring that Debbie-Jo, with her life of glamour and aspirations of fame, did not want to mix with someone as everyday as Rae; but then, when Debbie-Jo's career had fallen flat and she had taken a full-time role at Woolworths, Rae had tried again, hoping that maybe, with a more ordinary life plan, her sister might have room for her. But still no.

It was Howard who pointed out – and she now noticed – that whenever Rae spoke of the kids' achievements or their next holiday, the new tiles for the bathroom or the opening of a restaurant, her sister lifted her chin, looked towards the heavens and let out a barely audible 'huff' that relayed her utter and complete disdain for whatever was being discussed. It made Rae quiet, with a sinking feeling that whatever she had to say was of no interest or, as she suspected, boring.

Not that she was going to let anything spoil her night. It was a difficult situation. This evening she was going to attend a surprise party thrown by Dolly in honour of their anniversary; she was not meant to know about it, but did, and in truth she was finding it all quite torturous. She carried all the stress of hosting a big event, but without any of the control or the means to allay her many concerns. Ordinarily it was her who quietly organised lifts, taxis, accommodation, food, but she was supposed to be ignorant of tonight's whole affair, so had been forced to sit back and hope everything had been thought of. Still, this was preferable to the party being an actual surprise; at least she had known to get her roots done and pick out a suitable dress. She hated surprises; even the thought sent her anxiety levels soaring.

Howard had told her they were going out for dinner. And she would have believed him, had it not been for the loud message Dolly had left on their answerphone, asking him to call her 'Immediately! Seriously, Howard, like right now! Call me on my mobile or at home or call Vinnie's mobile – just make contact. I need to give the final decision to the restaurant about cake design and balloon colour and it can't wait . . . I swear I am so stressed right now I might actually die!'

Rae had laughed at the message from her buxom buddy who was, as ever, so very close to death.

Right now was the calm before the storm and Rae stood at her bedroom window, watching. She ran her fingers over the khaki-gold, ribbon-edged drapes that half-hid her form, and looked up and down the street: the magazine-perfect street she loved, where grand houses stood proud, front doors shone and window boxes spilled red-bloomed flowers and variegated greenery down brick walls. It was dusk, her favourite time of day, when the cast-iron Georgian street lamps flickered to life, bathing the pavements in a honey-coloured tint. There was something very *Mary Poppins* about the whole scene, and she often half-expected to see the flash of a chimney sweep's broom up on the roofline. She had always rather liked the position of their house, right there on the bend in the road, affording her an enviable view of both ends of the crescent and all the houses opposite. This evening she looked at the lit windows of the tall houses, standing like sentinels in a proud curve, and wondered, as she often did, about the lives that went on behind them, picturing the people she nodded to or greeted during the course of the day.

Morning, Mrs Williams! . . . Yes, it is a bit chilly; stay warm.

Hello, Mr Jeffries. How are you today? . . . Oh, I'm so glad to hear it. If you need anything you know where we are.

Well, hello, Fifi – aren't you full of energy today! Rae loved to pet the cute little shih-tzu and would smile at Fifi's owner, the quiet young woman who never responded with anything other than a brief nod and a stony silence, her eye contact non-existent.

Yes, she wondered about the lives of these people, her neighbours with whom she lived cheek by jowl, bumping into them in their pyjamas as they put the bins out, listening to them row, cry, sing . . . She knew so many intimate details of their lives, but not their first names or their favourite colours or even why Fifi's mum was so painfully shy. It was a strange and wonderful situation and one that she felt was peculiarly British; she considered the possibility that if the residents of Lawns Crescent had slightly less stiff upper lips and more open arms, she might have answers to all of the above.

The sun had all but sunk on this autumnal evening, sending a rosy glow out over the parkland, which nestled in a grand sweep on the west side of the street. Beyond to the east sat the bustling, growing suburb of the north London postcode they had called home for the last twenty-odd years. She remembered her and Howard getting the keys for the first time and walking through the front door with the kids in their arms and wide smiles of disbelief and excitement. They trod the stairs and took in every room of this, their new house. *Our forever home . . .*

Rae leaned close to the multi-paned glass and felt the cool breeze of the evening filter through. These houses were beautiful, traditional – grand even – but one thing they were not was efficient.

She wondered what it might be like to live in a new home, like Debbie-Jo and Lee; in a neat square box of a house where the doors didn't rattle and instead sat neatly in their frames, and there were no chimneys to facilitate the breeze or suck the heat from a room in minutes. A house on a development in the countryside maybe, where everyone moved in at the same time; no old-timers, no new families, no hierarchy measured by length of occupation or size of backyard, just everyone in the same boat with a small square of lawn, easily mown. A house where each room was built to exacting dimensions, as if designed in collusion to hold nothing more than the identical flat-pack Swedish furnishings of your neighbour and their neighbour too, and a brand-new shiny kitchen where everything was squeaky clean to the touch. Not that she wanted such a kitchen, loving as she did the slightly worn centre of their house, with its gently rounded edges, smoothed over the years from the brush of her hip, and the almost imperceptible dip on the countertop where her hands had kneaded countless loaves of bread. The kitchen was her haven, where the scent of a thousand recipes lingered in the wood and the memory of each meal, prepared with love, danced in the air like the finest seasoning.

But yes: she wondered what it might be like to live in a house like that.

'What are you up to?' Howard's presence took her by surprise; the question, though, was asked with an air of mock accusation to which she was accustomed. He found it funny, almost as if he hoped one day to catch her out, his predictable, quiet wife.

She turned and smiled at him warmly. 'I was just thinking about new-build houses, on developments, and how different it would be to live somewhere like that. Not as grand, but probably cosy, neat.'

'It would be different, that's for sure. Cheaper, for a start!' He gave a forced laugh and she wondered if he was nervous too. She found the idea most endearing: a touch of groom-ish anxiety even after all these years.

It didn't surprise her, however, that his first response had been a financial one. After his family, money was Howard's passion. He loved making it and he loved spending it, often extravagantly.

She wasn't sure if he had always been this way or whether she had only noticed it in recent years, along with other traits of his that now drove her to distraction. Not that she loved him any less – of course she didn't – and she was sure that he too had a long list of things she did that drove him nuts, like leaving plugs of long hair in the bathroom, her apparently inefficient method of dishwasher-stacking, stealing his socks and of course her unhealthy obsession with lists. But certainly she noticed that as he'd got older there seemed to have been a recalibration in his tolerance levels. He was a little impatient with waiters and didn't lower his voice in public, no matter what the topic. She feared he might be in line for a bop on the nose one day. It was all well and good while at home to offer his tongue-in-cheek misogynistic claptrap, cheerfully lamenting the current freedoms enjoyed by women, declaring that the world had been 'a much better place when the men went out to work and the women stayed at home, keeping a nice house and raising the kids – everyone knew where they stood! Nowadays? Men are disenfranchised, confused, and it's not bloody right! Yes, call me old-fashioned, but it was a better place then.'

Better for whom, she would wonder, while reminding herself to write down the word 'disenfranchised' – to look it up – and, like her husband, waiting for Hannah to leap with tiger-like precision on his views, verbally shredding his point with her intellect and panting at the exertion. It was a game they played. And one Rae found quite exhausting, as well as distressing.

Howard walked towards her over the soft, biscuit-coloured carpet of their bedroom.

'You look very dapper.' She eyed his navy dinner suit and the neatly pressed collar of his white shirt, which showed off his dark complexion, a gift bestowed upon him by his Italian grandma but denied to the alabaster-skinned Dolly.

'And you look beautiful.' He swallowed.

'Bless you, Howard! Look at you, all misty-eyed, you old softie!' She ran her hand over the lapel of his jacket; this type of emotional display was rare from him.

She looked down at the tangerine silk kimono dress she wore over slender black trousers and pulled first one, then the other long, wide sleeve over her slender wrists.

'Not too much, is it? I don't want to look overdressed. For dinner. Wherever we are going for dinner, I mean; I don't know anything.'

Howard gave a small nervous chuckle. 'You, my darling wife, are a terrible liar! Okay, so how much do you know?' He fixed her with a stare.

She breathed a sigh of relief, realising that part of her tension had come from having to play along. She placed her hand on his chest and laughed. 'Oh, Howard, thank God! I don't know any detail, but I did hear Dolly on the answerphone a couple of weeks ago: a message asking about cake and balloons – so I know I am going somewhere where there will be cake and balloons and that is about it.'

The boom of his laughter, which spoke of relief, sent a quake through her chest. He placed his hands on his hips and exhaled, licking his lips, which were dry. It obviously meant a lot to him, not breaking his promise, keeping the surprise. 'That Dolly, she hasn't got the sense she was born with.' He shook his head and spoke with affection: 'Do me a favour – play along. Be surprised.'

'Well, I will be; I still don't know much. Are you sure this outfit is okay?' Rae never looked upon her reflection and felt anything other than doubt, her eyes darting straight to her many perceived flaws, her wide hips, narrow chin, mismatched eyebrows . . . the list was long.

'I told you, you look beautiful; but then you always do to me.'

She looked at her outline in the windowpane, a little fuzzy, her features indistinct; without the precision offered by a mirror, this image of her looked young, younger at least, and this in turn fired a spike of sadness through her core. It wasn't anything to do with vanity – Rae wore each wrinkle with pride. No, it was more the realisation that so many years had passed, slipped away unnoticed from her prime until now, everything moving a little too fast; and sometimes, despite being middle-aged, she still felt as if she were trying to get a foothold. She still felt at some level that she was waiting for things to start, waiting to figure out what she wanted to be when she grew up. It had been her dream to go back to college when the kids went to school; she wanted a qualification other than her typing certificate and had often thought about training as a chef. She loved food, loved cooking, and the idea of formalising what she had picked up over the years very much appealed. But Howard had been right – how would she have fitted it in while caring for the kids, keeping the house, waiting with her phone within reach for the next request that would keep the restaurants running like a well-oiled machine?

'I said I've got you a little something.'

She stared at him, sorry for having zoned out, watching as he beamed and reached into his inside top pocket.

'Oh, Howard, no! We said no presents!' She felt the slow sinking of joy in her gut, replaced by embarrassment run through with irritation: *we had agreed!* 'I didn't get you anything!'

'I know, I know, but I couldn't help it.' He ran his fingertips over her shoulder and handed her the flat black velvet box with a small gold button protruding from its side. She felt the tremble of his fingers against her skin and realised that this must mean a lot to have him so anxious.

'Go on then. Open it!' he urged, his face that of a child, excited.

She held the box that gave him the edge in the anniversary stakes and pushed the gold button. The lid slowly opened to reveal a beautiful necklace, a delicate silver chain with a neat teardrop diamond hanging from it.

'Oh, Howard! Oh my God, it's so beautiful!' She felt the excitement swirl in her stomach at being in receipt of such a gift; it really was as stunning as it was unexpected.

'I know twenty-five years should be silver, but it's white gold. Looks silver, though, doesn't it? Cost a bomb, but you are worth it. You really are.'

She stared at him, fascinated that he had no clue that his comment reduced the gift to something with a price attached; to collateral, rather than anything romantic. His tone and words were the equivalent of the chimney she had considered earlier, sucking the joy from the gift and leaving her feeling a little cold.

'I don't need to know how much it cost. I just love it because you got it for me.'

'Let me put it on you. Please.'

She was surprised by his tone of desperation. This milestone was clearly affecting him more than she thought. 'Really? You think I should wear it tonight?'

'Yes, of course!'

She turned in the obligatory manner, lifting her newly honey-coloured locks. Howard took the necklace and stood close to her, placing a single kiss at the nape of her neck, which sent a shiver of something close to desire along her spine as he positioned it on her chest and fiddled with the clasp until it was secure.

'Dolly suggested it. It looks lovely on you. You deserve the best, Rae.'

She ran her fingers over the shiny stone.

'Well, Miss Pritchard, what do you think of it?' he pushed.

She felt the shallow ache of sweet longing at the mention of her maiden name, remembering the quiet sixteen-year-old who had held the hand of her new and impressive beau and taken a step on to a path that had turned out to be a time machine, moving so quickly it had spirited her here – nearly thirty years later. And it had happened in the blink of an eye.

Rae studied her reflection again, with the teardrop-shaped bauble resting at the base of her throat.

'Well?' Howard urged, clasping his hands as he stood waiting for her opinion on this beautiful gift, seeking validation, approval.

She turned, smiled at her husband, the brother of her best friend, and planted a kiss on his cheek. 'Thank you, Howard. It's lovely. I love you.'

'I love you too.' He pulled her into his arms and kissed the top of her head and she remembered the first time he had done so outside her mum and dad's gate.

'I really do love you,' he repeated, 'and I would not change a thing about the last twenty-five years. In fact, I would marry you again tomorrow if I had the chance.'

'We are lucky.' She kissed the back of his hand that rested on her shoulder.

'We are. We are so lucky.' He held her hands and looked at her earnestly.

'Are you okay, darling? You seem very emotional!'

'I just love you, Rae, and I want you to know that, tonight of all nights.'

'I do.' She stood on tiptoe and kissed the tip of his nose. 'I do know that, and thank you.'

Rae had seen her confidence bloom a little in her role as his wife. She spoke a little louder, held her head a little higher; never more so than when she was at home with her family, away from situations that were unfamiliar. The kids had pointed out how the two of them constantly burbled, babbled, chit-chatted, their every interaction peppered with two things: a running commentary on their lives, and a stream of inner monologue from two people so at ease in each other's company that it provided the happy background music to their day.

I thought I might roast a chicken for supper.

Remind me to send George that cheque, Rae.

I do love spring. We have daffodils on the verge; did you see them?

Think I'll set a fire tonight – it's still a bit chilly of an evening.

How do you spell phen-om-en-al?

Did you see they've dug up the road by the lights again?

Oh, this bread is good!

Cup of tea, love?

They also had a need, a desire to remain physically in touch. Either or both of them, no matter what the situation, would with unforced regularity reach for the other's hand, rest a palm on a knee or touch their nose to the other's face, just for the sheer joy of contact. Rae always thought these little physical expressions were like a battery recharge. And she welcomed them.

'Right!' Howard clapped his hands now. 'If I don't get you into the car and off to our destination to arrive at a certain time, I will be in big trouble.'

'And nobody wants that. Not on our anniversary.'

'Quite.' He kissed her once again and looked as if he wanted to say more, but the moment passed.

As Howard locked the front door and Rae climbed into the front seat of the car, she saw Fifi and the young woman who owned her walking along the pavement. She waved, as she usually did. The girl gave a cautious, brief nod of her head and instantly looked away. Rae smiled; this felt like a breakthrough.

She glanced briefly at her husband as they made their way past the Crouch End clock tower.

'Fifi's mum just acknowledged me, for the first time ever.'

'Who?' he fired. 'Are you too warm, darling? It's very hot in here.' He was already fiddling with the heating controls on the dashboard as if she had answered.

She nodded. 'Fifi! The darling little shih-tzu who lives at the end of our street. Her mum. I worry about her – the woman, not the dog. She is always alone and she looks a little lost, a bit sad, and I think she's shy. I have tried to make contact, but she avoids me. But she just gave me a small nod. That's a breakthrough, right?'

'I guess,' he exhaled, 'but I think in all honesty if she wanted to be your friend, she would have responded to you before now. If she keeps herself to herself there will be a reason for it and I guess, as lovely as you are . . .' He smiled at her. 'You have to respect that. Plus you have enough people in your life.'

'Enough people in my life? How many is enough?' She laughed at this idea. 'I suppose you are right.'

She stared out of the window at a young couple laughing, the girl in a bobble hat, bent double, hanging on to her beau for support while happiness and giggles folded her over.

That's how it feels to be this happy with the one you love – and I know it; I share it. Lovely . . .

Not that life was always smooth or worry-free. Hannah, now in her final year of university in Liverpool, had been struggling to settle in to a new student house and Rae was, as ever, concerned about her, holding an image of her alone, sitting on a narrow bed in her soulless room. She hoped she could lose a little of her spikiness, thinking it was these barbs that kept others at bay and wishing that her daughter didn't have need of them. This thought kept her awake. Was Hannah okay? Lonely? Hungry? Struggling?

George too had started his first year at college, and lived in Guildford; while he was blissfully happy with his lovely Ruby, he was not coping too well with the change and the new pressure. This had also been keeping Rae awake at night – was George stressed? Would he study enough? Fail? Was he happy? Struggling?

Sometimes she wished she could run away and spend an hour or two with her phone unplugged, just to clear her head in a place where no one could reach her and no one could commandeer her time with all that ailed them.

She had worked for the business full-time when the kids were at school, and even now to a lesser degree, helping with the scheduling, hiring, decorating and running errands at the drop of a hat. She spent the best part of each day on high alert, waiting for the next emergency to become her responsibility, usually via a frantic phone call.

We need pound coins!

We've run out of almond milk!

A twenty-first birthday cake!

Mitzy's prescription!

Dolly has lost her car keys!

Rae is on it!

Offering assistance wherever she could and whenever called upon. It might have been Debbie-Jo who wanted to be Batgirl's alter ego, but Rae was like a superhero whose superpower was getting shit done when no one else could be bothered to try.

Her brother-in-law Paul was the accountant; his wife, Sadie-the-Gossip, as she and Dolly affectionately called her, helped with the interior design. Howard was the businessman, always looking at how to expand: the ideas guy. Vinnie, her brother-in-law, dealt with all the suppliers for the restaurants, and Dolly – wonderful, brash, funny, loyal Dolly – was the glue that held it all together, the energy: the girl with the can-do attitude. Yes, Rae loved her life, loved being part of the Latimer-tribe *rock stars*.

Howard slowed the car and looked across at her. 'Okay, so we might have arrived. Hope this is all right.'

'Whatever has been planned will be fine,' she offered with as much enthusiasm as she could muster – excited, yes, but trying to swallow the nerves that leaped in her stomach, while thinking at some level that it might have been nice to do something just the two of them, without the cake, balloons, pomp and fuss. Blinking now, she looked ahead. 'Okay, deep breath . . .' Rae tried to play her part as Howard indicated and pulled the Mercedes up outside one of their family restaurants, in Barnet. 'The Latimers Kitchen?'

'Do you mind?' He pulled a face.

'No, as I said, anything is lovely.' She pulled down the sun visor and checked her lipstick, fixed her hair. His attention felt a little overdone as he swooped around to her side of the car and opened the door with a grand gesture, holding her hand loosely as she stepped out on to the pavement.

She tried not to look into the glass frontage, thankful for the teal-coloured plantation blinds that blocked most of the view of the thousand-square-feet restaurant where the menus were scrawled on vast blackboards that took up large areas of the wall, where there was a fancy zinc-topped bar and mismatched vintage chandeliers that were all the rage, hanging over tables themselves fashioned from painted doors. The look was part-garage, part-loft, part-food truck, and people loved it. The Latimers had hit upon this winning theme, and with their winning food on top, their seven restaurants were going from strength to strength.

Howard pushed open the big double door and took a breath. 'Shoot!' He patted his top pocket. 'Sorry, Rae, I've left my wallet in my coat on the back seat. Do not move. I want to walk you in.' She couldn't tell from his nervous hesitation whether leaving her on the porch was part of the plan. She looked ahead at the double louvre doors and, closing one eye, focused on the tiny crack where they joined.

She saw a crowd huddled together along the back wall and in spite of her anxiety, this made her smile. She watched as Dolly, her generous figure squeezed into a cream lace sheath dress, put her fingers to her lips and grimaced at her son, Lyall, batting her hand in his direction as if swatting invisible flies. Rae knew her best friend well enough to know that she would have gone to too much trouble to allow his larking around to blow the big surprise now. Turning from Lyall, Dolly set her eyes on the front door, almost looking directly at her. Rae remembered the moment nearly thirty years ago when they had been in the same position, with Dolly marching towards her, her hand outstretched. *My name is Dolly Latimer . . . Fun facts: I am planning to lose my virginity within the next few weeks to the most gorgeous boy you have ever met. His name is Vinnie . . .*

Rae smiled again, staring ahead at Dolly and Vinnie surrounded by their family, her family, watching as Dolly shushed the giggles that came from Lark and Ellory, Paul's young granddaughters. She looked along the line at the expectant faces of her mum, dad, sister Debbie-Jo and her husband, Lee. Hannah, George, Ruby – they were all here. Her heart lurched with love for them and she cursed the tears that gathered at the back of her eyes.

I love you all . . . I love you all so much . . .

She watched Dolly reach for her phone, which vibrated in the semi-darkness: the text she had apparently been waiting for.

'They're here! They're here!' Dolly whispered excitedly.

The door opened behind Rae and Howard placed a hand on her shoulder, simultaneously telling her it was all going to be okay while trying to calm her. Like he always did.

He pushed open the double doors and the noise was deafening. There was a roar of 'SURPRISE!' along with cheers, whoops and the bang of party poppers firing narrow streamers up into the air, as well as a flash overhead as the main lights came on.

'Oh my goodness!' Rae placed her hand to her throat and, having worried about striking the right note of convincing shock and delight, was quite taken aback by the tears that sprouted; all at once she was overcome by the joyous proximity of her kids, her family and their friends in this atmosphere of celebration.

A banner had been strung across the room: 'Congratulations Howard and Rae – 25 Years and Counting!'

Dolly stepped forward and held her close, her words choked by her own emotion. 'I wanted to do something to mark this amazing day! I love you. You know I do. And you, Howard! I love you too.' She pulled the two of them together in a fierce hug.

'I love you too,' Rae tearfully offered.

Hannah, George and Ruby came forward and greeted her and Howard with kisses.

'Happy anniversary, Ma!' Hannah beamed.

'Darling, you came all this way!'

'I was already all this way when I spoke to you earlier. I was in Dolly's kitchen!'

'Oh my goodness!' Rae touched her fingertips to her daughter's face.

'We've been hiding out at Uncle Paul's,' George explained.

'Thank you all.' She felt a surge of love for these wonderful kids, and again her tears gathered.

'I told you she was going to be crying all night!' Hannah called to her auntie Dolly.

'Wait till she gets some booze inside her – then the tears will flow. She's always been that way. I remember her knocking back cider until she sobbed watching *Dirty Dancing*.'

'I was sixteen!'

Laughter rippled around the room. As if on cue, Paul shoved a glass of champagne into her hand. He held her gaze a second longer than he needed to and closed his eyes briefly, his lingering expression a sweet gesture of love that she appreciated. Of all the family members, Paul had always been the most aloof – not exactly unwelcoming, but as if he didn't think she merited emotional investment. Howard had told her she was being oversensitive. This, she knew, was possible.

Howard now stood at the bar with his mates gathered around him, holding court, and Rae took a seat with Maureen and Len, her mum and dad, in a booth.

'Will you look at them?' Her mum spoke with pride as all eyes turned to Debbie-Jo, who was dancing with gusto, and Hannah who was doing her best to keep up with her aunt's vigorous moves. 'She is still such a beautiful dancer.' Maureen smiled with a twinge of sadness to her voice, making it almost a lament.

Rae felt the familiar flicker of inadequacy and looked away from the dance floor. She disliked the lick of jealous flames in her gut and swallowed the ridiculous desire to remind her mum that this was her night.

Suddenly she remembered being six again, swinging her legs back and forth as she sat between her parents with a hot swarmy feeling on her skin, wishing she were elsewhere, the bare underside of her thighs sticking to the plastic seat with nerves, Miss Rawlings smiling sweetly at her mum on this, her parent/teacher evening.

'I think it's fair to say that Rae-Valentine does not have a big voice. Sometimes I am pretty certain that she might know the answers, but hasn't got the courage to raise her hand. Could that be right, Rae-Valentine?'

She'd felt the eyes of all the adults in the room on her face as it coloured. She'd given a subtle nod and Mrs Rawlings's mouth formed a wide smile with her lips tucked in, which to Rae seemed part kindly and part disappointed.

'I have tried to coax her,' the teacher then explained with more than a hint of exasperation, 'but this seems to send her deeper into her shell – and the last thing I want to do is put unwanted pressure on her. It's a fine line.' She sucked air in through her gritted teeth, the way Rae had seen her dad do when contemplating a problem; this was usually followed by a scratch on the head.

'It's just how she is,' her mum added matter-of-factly, gathering her handbag on to her lap with a sigh, like they were discussing something broken, or the weather – something non-negotiable and over which they had no control. 'She's always been quiet. Her big sister, on the other hand!' She chuckled with a renewed lift to her voice at this glorious change of topic.

'Oh my word, yes!' her dad chipped in keenly, to emphasise the extraordinary nature of Debbie-Jo.

'Ah, Debbie-Jo,' Miss Rawlings said. 'I teach her English, quite a little actress!'

'Well, there's no forgetting her, that's for sure. Our little future star – that's what we call her.'

Rae-Valentine had looked at the adults and wondered if she were actually invisible. This was *her* parents' evening and it had taken less than a minute to skip over her and move on to the subject of Debbie-Jo. She'd listened to the joyous singsong note in her mum's voice when discussing her older sister, and had realised with an ice-cold stab in her chest that she was not memorable. And if she was not memorable that could mean only one thing.

She was like furniture: static, forgettable.

The music picked up tempo and drew Rae to the present. 'You look lovely, Mum. You got your hair done.'

'I did.' Her mum patted her neatly coiffed do. 'I told Pamela it was for your silver wedding and she remembered doing my hair for your wedding day! Can you believe that?'

Rae nodded and smiled at this lovely example of the contented life her parents led. They lived in the same house, shopped in the same stores and used the same barber, hairdresser, doctor's surgery, post office as they always had. Never striving for the next thing. Happy. She felt a small flush of embarrassment that this was not her life, not the Latimer way, where it was all about setting the next goal and striving for it. She knew her parents must at some level judge their seemingly extravagant, fast-paced lifestyle. She popped the diamond necklace inside the neck of her dress.

'Twenty-five years . . . I remember when you first brought Howard home,' Len chuckled. 'You know, I wasn't too sure – thought he might be a bit of a flash Harry – but then I saw how he looked at you and he told me . . .' He stopped talking and caught his breath, his eyes bright and moist with tears. 'He told me he'd treat you as I would treat you and that was good enough for me.'

Oh, Dad, my lovely dad . . .

'Long time ago, eh, Dad?' She smiled at him and sipped from her glass of champagne.

'And look how happy you all are. We were worried sick, weren't we, love? Not that we let on.' Her mum nudged her husband, who sniffed. 'We had been saving up a wedding fund for you and Debbie-Jo for years. We had two Post Office savings accounts and each came with a little book and whenever I could, when there was anything spare, which wasn't often,' Maureen chuckled, 'I'd put a pound or two or even just fifty pence into one of the accounts and it mounted up nicely. Well, you were only young and Debbie-Jo was on the ships, so I thought I had all the time in the world to save up more. I couldn't believe it when you said you were getting married! I have to be honest – my first thought was, how in the world are we going to afford it?'

'You and me both.' Rae's dad joined in, his words striking the saddest note in her chest. The last thing she would ever want was to put her parents under financial pressure; she hadn't thought about it at the time, hadn't properly considered the cost, swept up in the whirlwind of planning, beyond excited at the picture Dolly and Howard painted as she selected fabric, chose a frock, picked bridesmaids, sniffed flowers and sampled cake.

'Anyway,' her mum continued, 'I remember one night you came home and you had wedding magazines and brochures in your hands and you were talking about all the things you wanted – the dress, the flowers, the party afterwards – and my heart sank, but I didn't want to be the one to burst that bubble of happiness. I had never seen you so full of joy or so confident. I felt sad, but not because you were getting married – of course not; I was pleased you had found your Howard.'

'Why were you sad, Mum?' Rae whispered. She studied her mother's face as, for a second, it took on a look of distress that cut Rae's heart like knives. 'Because of the money?' The word jarred on her tongue, like something awkward, uncomfortable.

Her mum shook her head. 'Not only that, but I think that's when I realised that this was the world you were entering. And it was a world very different to mine, where I could vacuum the whole of the downstairs of my house without unplugging once, a small world in every sense. And you were moving up to a family with swimming pools and fast cars.' She paused. 'I thought I might be losing a bit of you, because I knew we wouldn't be able to keep up.'

'It wasn't moving up, not at all. I love you, Mum – so much. I have always been so proud.'

'Oh, I know, I know, love.' Her mum cut her short, patting the back of her hand. 'But I remember we paid for the cake in the end, and it took all the money we had in both Post Office accounts. Luckily Debbie-Jo wasn't in any hurry – she and Lee weren't that serious then, and that gave us a few years to top hers up – but I looked around on the big day and . . . oh, it was beautiful!' She smiled with her hand on her chest. 'But I didn't really feel part of it. It was like you had been swallowed up by the Latimers. And in all the extravagance and wonder of the day, I was conscious that our contribution was that little cake.'

'It was a wonderful cake, Mum, and you *were* part of it – you are my parents.' Rae struggled to control the warble in her voice.

'Oh, I know that!' Her mum tutted, as she did when any display of emotion left her feeling exposed. 'Ignore me. I'm just in a reflective mood. And I shouldn't be; this is a celebration, right?' She lifted her tonic water in Rae's direction and drank.

'I was so young, giddy really, without a clue about most things,' Rae admitted. 'And if I could go back to that time, I'd do a lot of things differently.'

I'd make sure you were more involved, Mum, and not let Dolly take control. I would have a small wedding in the pub, like you two did, and I would not take Debbie-Jo's wedding fund to buy a tier of a cake I never even got to taste . . .

Debbie-Jo executed an elaborate spin and came over to the table, where she reached for her glass of champagne. 'Pass my bag, Mum.' She pointed to her brown leather handbag, stowed by her mum's feet. Rae watched as her mum struggled to retrieve it.

'Now . . .' Debbie-Jo balanced the bag on her raised thigh and foraged inside before producing an envelope. 'Me and Lee didn't know what to get you.'

'You shouldn't have got us anything. I'm just really happy you came all this way!' Rae enthused.

'Well, as I say, we didn't know what to get. It's difficult, right – what do you get the girl who's got everything?' She laughed and Rae saw the stiffening of her mum's posture, and the narrowing of her mouth, indicating that this might be a recurring topic she was sick of discussing.

'And we decided' – Debbie-Jo took a glug from her champagne glass – 'that the best thing we could do would be to give you an experience.'

'Oh, you didn't have to—' Rae began.

'Just open the bloody envelope!' Her sister sloshed her glass in the direction of the slim gift balancing on her palm.

Rae did as she was told and slid her finger under the gummed flap. Her eyes scanned the homemade vouchers, her eyes struggling to make out the fine print in the dim light of the booth.

Debbie-Jo leaned in. 'Lee's mum and dad have got a caravan in Devon, just outside Torquay, and they said you guys can have any week, out of season; just let them know the dates and it's yours . . .'

Rae looked at her sister and back to the vouchers in her hand. Her first thought was how much Debbie-Jo and Lee would benefit from a week away and guilt flushed through her veins. 'Debbie-Jo! Oh my goodness, that is so kind. It's brilliant! Thank you!' She pulled her sister into a hug and saw the happiness split her mum's face in two. This she understood: any closeness displayed between her kids sent a bolt of happy right through her.

'You're welcome, sis!'

It was a glorious moment, as the music blared, laughter danced on the air and champagne flowed; she felt the stays of kinship pull her and Debbie-Jo a little closer, and she liked it a lot.

Hannah came to the booth and grabbed her hand. 'Come on, Mum, dance with us! Come on, Auntie DJ! Back on the dance floor!'

'I'm rubbish at dancing!' Rae protested, hating the idea of anyone watching her.

'Then drink more champagne. I find the more I drink the closer I get to dancing and singing like Beyoncé,' Hannah confided.

Rae threw her head back and laughed, happy to see her little girl without the crease of tension on her forehead. She sipped from her glass and was surprised to find, as the evening progressed, that Hannah was right. The three of them danced with abandon and it was great – a wonderful, wonderful party where her nerves were replaced by joy.

People were generous with their compliments and they sang as they danced. Rae, now gasping for breath after her exertions, stood by the bar with Howard and looked around at the large family gathered here in their own restaurant. She saw the little kids in their best clothes running around the floor, George and Ruby smooching at a table in the corner, and felt a warm sense of belonging.

She and Howard looked at Dolly, who balanced on the small step by the bar and clapped loudly to get everyone's attention. The music stopped and everyone on the impromptu dance floor sighed their displeasure.

'Don't worry, we can turn it back on in a minute, but I just wanted to say before we all consume too much champagne and I forget to do this: Rae-Valentine, my beautiful friend, I have known you since we were kids – and in fact if it wasn't for me, you and Howard would not have got married in the first place, so really it should be me getting gifts tonight, not you, and I do need a new deep-fat fryer . . .'

Everyone laughed. Rae felt Howard step closer to her and stand at her back, his hand on her shoulder. His proximity brought comfort and reassurance, as it always had. She briefly tilted her head and rested her cheek on the back of his hand.

'Howard and I got our heads together, as he wanted to get you something really special for putting up with him for twenty-five years—'

'Should have got her a bloody medal!' Vinnie shouted across the room.

Dolly shot him a look of disdain, despite everyone's laughter. 'Shut up, Vinnie! That's him on the couch tonight.' She was playing to the home crowd and everyone, herself included, loved it. The laughter and applause was loud and heartfelt. 'As I was saying . . .' She sipped her champagne. 'Howard, my wonderful brother, wanted to do something really special and I think he has.' She beamed at her friend. 'Howard has booked a holiday to Antigua! Fun fact: you are going to the Caribbean, baby!'

Rae turned to her man. 'You are kidding me!'

'Nope, just you and me. Two weeks of sun and sea and sleep . . .' He smiled at her. They both laughed, knowing that only a few years earlier it would have been sun, sea and sex that held such allure.

'I am so lucky.' She reached up and kissed him. 'I love you, Howard.'

'I'm the lucky one. Happy anniversary, darling. Never forget how much I love you.' His pressing tone bought a tear to her eye.

Rae caught Debbie-Jo's eye. She looked crestfallen, and was making her way out of the front door, probably in search of air. Lee followed at an urgent pace, as if it was all a little more than they could cope with.

THREE

It was a little after 1 a.m. when they arrived home from the party. Howard headed for the TV room while Rae slipped her high heels from her feet and flexed her aching toes against the cool tiled kitchen floor. It had been some while since she had danced, and even though sleep pawed at her she was reluctant to bring an end to the glorious night. She now pottered in the kitchen, arranging the stunning display of anniversary cards, putting the house to sleep and tidying things away. She still carried with her the warm afterglow of celebration, smiling to herself as she recalled the event in slow motion: Dolly making her laugh, her dad tucking into a plate of tapas, holding up morsels as he tried to identify them and eating them nonetheless, Howard dancing manically at the end of the night with his tie around his head, his jacket discarded, the kids and their cousins swaying arm in arm with Dexys Midnight Runners playing . . . Happy memories.

On opening the fridge door she eyed a misshapen lump of Brie and a small dish of syllabub, half-eaten. She felt her mouth salivate, wanting to eat both, but closed the door, knowing she wasn't hungry, just greedy. Her willpower gave her a small buzz of self-satisfaction. She wanted to try to shift a pound or two from her tum before they left for Antigua in four weeks' time. *Antigua!* Her stomach bunched in excitement.

She had waved the kids goodbye as they headed to a club and knew their happy faces meant a good night's sleep for her, content that there was no emotional fire that needed extinguishing – not tonight. Dolly had texted her to once again remark on what a fantastic night it had been. Maureen had whispered, as she left on Debbie-Jo's arm, that she needed paper towels, bacon and hand soap. It made Rae smile that, despite the evening of merriment, her mum still had half a mind on the contents of her kitchen cupboards and tomorrow's lunch. Debbie-Jo and she had shared a clumsy goodbye hug, where once again Rae thanked her for the vouchers.

With her booze glow now faded, Rae picked up her pen and jotted on her list:

Paper towels

Bacon

Hand soap

Mouthwash

And crossed through

~~*Water tubs*~~

~~*Turn compost*~~

Then added

Lose weight for Antigua!

And underlined it.

She would do a shopping order for her parents in the morning and get it delivered.

Howard had closed the door of the TV room, probably to watch a documentary with cars, motorbikes or police in it, possibly all three; either way it was noisy and shouty, the kind of thing that didn't really appeal to her. She loved this time of the night and it was rare for her to be up and about. The air felt calm, as if the whole city had sighed, finished its chores and was sleeping soundly. Rae thought of her kids and thousands like them who would be doing anything but.

She switched off the kitchen lights and cleaned her teeth, removed her make-up and blissfully shrugged off her bra before slipping her nightdress over her head. She wondered if it might be a night for sex. It had been a little while and it seemed only fitting after such a glorious evening and on this, their anniversary. Despite her increasing sleepiness, she sprayed her décolletage with perfume and decided to read until Howard appeared. She had Jessie Burton's *The Miniaturist* on her bedside table and was looking forward to diving back into her world.

Having climbed between the freshly laundered sheets, she looked up out of the window towards the west end of the street, fascinated, as she always was, by the light peeking through drapes and blinds, where people like her settled in for sleep. Her community: closely packed together in this pretty street and yet all separate like fish in tanks, their whole world defined by the four walls in which they swam. She placed the book on her lap and rubbed hand cream into the backs of her hands and between her elegant fingers, the scent of geranium a joy to inhale.

Rae looked up as her husband stood in the doorway. He loitered, as if he couldn't decide whether or not to come in.

'Hello, you. What a night! I keep replaying it over and over in my mind. Thank you, Howard; you and Dolly did a great job. It was wonderful.'

She stared at him, a little confused, as he looked straight through her.

'What have you forgotten, darling?' She smiled, knowing that she too was at an age where she would run up the stairs and forget what she had come for. 'I've locked the back door and switched off the kitchen lights,' she added, knowing he sometimes stood and tried to recall whether he had performed his nightly security check.

'I . . .' He placed the flat of his palm on the doorframe.

'What, you waiting for an invitation?' She laughed, pulling back the duvet a little and, waggling her eyebrows, striking the most seductive pose she could muster now that tiredness was catching up with her.

Later she would think that this had been the last laugh that came easily, a noise and gesture full of confidence because she lived with certainty of her place in this family and her place in this world.

He took a step closer and she saw his face had taken on a greyish hue. He looked sick, and her gut leaped in concern.

She sat up straight, sobering. 'Howard, what's wrong? You don't look at all well. Can I get you anything?'

He shook his head and took a seat on the end of the bed with his back to her, his shoulders hunched over.

'Are you okay, my darling? Speak to me!' Thoughts rushed through her head: was he ill? Did she have stomach medication? He had knocked back the booze all evening and had done so on a fairly empty stomach. Or maybe . . . maybe he was properly sick and had got some results, which he'd waited until now to tell her! She had dreaded this scenario so many times. *Oh my God! Be strong for him!* But surely he would have said something sooner? Maybe Hannah had called from the club; was there a crisis? Did they need to hotfoot it up to the West End and bring her home? Were George and Ruby okay? Had they rowed? The poor love. If this was the case, what could she do to ease her son's anxiety? Bring him home for some hot milk, a lavender pillow? Her mind whirred.

'Howard, what is it?' She was getting a little scared by his silence, more so when she realised, to her horror, that he was crying. 'Oh my

God! Howard! You're frightening me now! What is it? Has something happened? Are the kids okay? Is someone hurt? Is it my parents? Your parents?' With a pounding heart she scrambled from the mattress and came to rest on her knees on the carpet in front of him. He had locked his hands together and now rested his elbows on his thighs. His tears fell straight down, dripping from his stubbled chin and falling in little round blobs where they darkened the soft pale carpet.

'Howard, you are scaring me,' she whispered now, feeling a little lightheaded, as her breath came in shallow gulps with all the terrible, terrible possibilities racing around her head, which she tried in vain to translate from this language of tears.

He shook his head; she could see he was struggling to get his words out.

'It's okay,' she cooed, rubbing his leg and trying to get him to calm down. 'It's okay, my love; just talk to me, darling. What's going on? Take your time,' she encouraged, while inside her head she was screaming, *Hurry up! Hurry up! Tell me! Tell me now!*

Seconds passed that felt like minutes, until eventually he lifted his head and looked above her, unable to meet her eyes. He made no attempt to wipe away his tears.

'It's okay,' she coaxed once more, softly. 'It's all going to be okay, my love.'

Howard exhaled and sat up straight. He rubbed his face with the palms of his hands. 'Rae,' he began, breaking off again under the weight of emotion. He breathed out and tried again. 'Rae, there is something I need to tell you. I don't know how to say it, but I know I must.'

She held her breath, waiting for the knowledge of whatever had occurred and, despite the tremor in her limbs, knowing instinctively that she needed to brace herself, to give his words a steady platform on which to land.

'I love you,' he said. 'I love you so much. I do. You know I do.'

She stared at him and it was as if a penny dropped: if this was his opening line then it was unlikely that the news was about her parents, or even the kids, and probably not the business. Intuitively she removed her hands from his legs and placed her palms on her thighs as she knelt in front of him, feeling the heat pulse on to her skin through the thin cotton of her nightgown.

'I love you.'

So you said . . .

'But something has happened.' He broke away to allow a fresh batch of tears to fall. 'Oh God! Oh my God!' He spoke loudly. 'I can't! I can't!'

Rae gazed at him, numbness now being ushered in by fear.

Howard swallowed and sat up straight. 'The new restaurant, in Shepherd's Bush . . .' His voice had an odd quality, stretched thin.

'Yes.'

He swallowed again, as yet more tears fell. 'We took on a girl, a waitress . . . I'd not met her before the launch.'

Rae felt the chill of premonition at what might follow and thought back to the night of the opening, about six weeks ago, when she had stayed home and helped George go through his reading list before she cooked dinner and then helped him organise his bag for the move to college . . .

'You go without me,' she had insisted. 'I think I'm of more use here – plus, you know, love, it's not like it's the first launch and it won't be the last.'

'Only if you are sure?'

'I am. Go already!' She had shooed her dishcloth at him.

He had reached over and held her face in his cupped palm. 'Can you call Dolly and let her know you won't be coming? You know what she's like.'

'I do indeed. Good luck!' She had kissed him on the mouth and waved him off.

Howard's noisy sob focused her attention. 'I had too much to drink. Everyone did. You know what it can get like. That was it and that was all it was. A booze-filled decision, nothing more.'

'What . . . ?' She was struggling to make sense of his words; despite hearing them clearly, they arrived in her mind jumbled. 'I don't . . .' She shook her head.

'And then it kind of spiralled for a week or two. No more, I swear.'

She fixed her gaze on him, waiting for him to join the dots, confirm the words that were beating a path around and around inside her skull. Her gut now bunched with the desire to vomit.

'I slept with her. In the restaurant.' His voice shook.

'You . . . ?' She needed it repeated, as the idea was so ludicrous, so unbelievable.

'We had sex, when everyone had gone; in the restaurant.'

Her heart constricted and her bowel spasmed as she thought back to the night they had opened in Battersea all those years ago. The kids were young, at home with her mum, tucked up, and she and Howard had waved everyone off and started kissing. They had sex in the restaurant. On that one occasion, drunken and exciting. It had been their secret. Their thing.

Until now.

'Who was it that you . . . ?' She couldn't get the words out.

'Some girl, a new waitress.' He sobbed again.

Rae fell backwards towards the cherrywood chest of drawers. As she bashed into it she heard the silver-topped glass perfume bottle topple over.

'Rae, I—'

'Just . . . just give me a minute. Please just give me a minute.' She spoke quite clearly, softly, as she digested the facts, newly delivered and wrapped in shards of glass that would cut her to the core as they slid from his mouth, into her ears and down her throat, coming to rest in her heart, where they would stay lodged.

'So . . . so you . . . you met her and you had sex with her, just like that?' She was trying, with difficulty, to make the facts stick.

Howard nodded.

'And then you saw her outside of work for a couple of weeks?'

He nodded again.

Rae felt as if she were sinking into the carpet, and placed her hands flat on the floor to stop herself from falling right through and ending up in Hannah's bedroom on the floor below. Her silence encouraged him to talk. Fill the quiet with his admission. She wished he would stop talking, just for a second, to allow her to gather her thoughts and process the information, which was coming at her quicker than she could handle, as if her body and mind were out of sync.

'It was a moment of madness! I can't tell you how sorry I am. But I am, I am, Rae, truly sorry. I hated myself the very second I realised what I had done. And then I didn't know how to get out of it and I was scared of ending it because she was demanding and I suppose on some level I was quite flattered.'

As if his words could make any difference, as if there was anything he could possibly say that might be a balm for this. She was aware that new facts, apologies, reasons, excuses and regrets were coming thick and fast in so many variants, whereas all she could hear was the first sentence: *we had sex, when everyone had gone; in the restaurant.*

Howard sniffed, and she tuned in to what he was saying. 'Paul called me earlier this evening, just before we set off, to tell me that he had sacked her for something completely unrelated and she told him what had happened. He called me immediately to see if it was true.'

Paul knows! She thought about his lingering look earlier, which she had thought was a look of love. But it wasn't. She now knew it was a look of pity. *Oh my God! Paul knows, which means Sadie will know, which means everyone will know . . .* Her thoughts flew to Hannah and George, who had more than enough to cope with right now. She had done all in her power to keep a happy, stable home for all these years, only for it to be pulled from under her by one night – no, two weeks – of selfish, selfish drunken sex. She curled her fingers into her palm and dug her nails into the skin. The pain gave her something to concentrate on.

Howard was still talking. 'And Paul told me she wanted some money or she was going to contact you, and so he gave her money and told her to sod off, but he said, and I agreed, that it was best to tell you the truth and to ask for forgiveness, because I can't live with it hanging over me. I feel like shit; it was a mistake, the biggest mistake I have ever made. I love you, Rae! I really do; I love you so much, I—'

Rae held up her hand and he stopped talking. She tried to stand, but on legs made of jelly; she could only lean forward, and that's how she came to rest, on her knees with her arms straight, on all fours, staring at the floor. Her fair hair fell over her face and she concentrated on taking a breath. She wasn't sure whether she was going to vomit or faint; both felt like distinct possibilities. Her tears were hot and angry and they fell steadily as her mouth twisted and her body shook.

No! No! No! No! No! Not this, no! Not you, Howard! Not us!

Eventually, as her crying slowed, she once again sat back against the chest of drawers with her knees drawn up to her chin and her arms locked around her shins, as if this position could protect her from the sharp tips of his words that had pierced her.

'You . . . you did this to me because of booze?'

'Yes,' he mumbled. 'Initially.'

'You . . . you might think that that makes it better, but it doesn't.' She shook her head. 'It makes it worse, much worse. It's like we – me and the kids, our marriage – were incidental, unimportant . . .'

'No! No that's not true, you and the kids . . .' He cried again, loudly, between words. 'You are everything!'

'I can't believe it. I just can't believe it.' It was odd that she spoke these words out loud, because strangely she *did* believe it – why else would he be in this much of a state?

'If I could turn back time,' he began. 'If only . . .'

Rae looked at him and felt a small snort of laughter leave her nose and mouth. If only it were that simple. She wiped her eyes with the back of her hand and took a breath. 'And we both know that if Paul hadn't sacked her, for whatever reason, then you would never have told me and I would never have known.'

'I wanted to tell you. I did!'

She noticed that he didn't deny it.

'I thought about it, Rae. I practised telling you in my head, but I didn't know how. Not with our anniversary party planned and everyone looking forward to it. I didn't want to hurt you.'

At this last point she actually laughed. 'Well, thank you for that. Which girl was it? What's her name?'

He shook his head, as if unwilling to give the detail.

'Which girl, Howard?' she pressed.

Whether instinctively or not he gave a slight shrug of his shoulder, as if the girl in question were just a faceless, insignificant, bedazzled waitress who had got to sleep with the boss, the one with the flashy house, fancy car, nice watch . . . But he was wrong. She was not insignificant. She was in fact extremely significant. She was the person who had taken a sledge-hammer to twenty-five years of marriage and smashed it to smithereens.

'Karina.' He paused. 'But I don't want you to contact her; she's vicious, she is angry and—'

'Why would I contact her?' She looked at him, genuinely puzzled. 'I don't blame her.' *Karina.* An image formed in her mind of the svelte young girl she had met once when dropping off spare car keys to Vinnie. Younger than her, much younger. Nearer Hannah's age, in fact. 'No.' She held his eyeline. 'I don't blame her at all. Karina is not married to me, Howard. You are.'

His tears fell afresh. 'I am sorry, Rae. I am sorry. I love you. I do . . . Please.' She wasn't sure what he was pleading for. 'Please, I . . .' He stared her, as if trying to find the words.

She bit her lip and ignored the fresh batch of tears that now trickled down her own face. 'Two weeks.' She took a breath. 'You snuck out of here and lied to me for two weeks of what, sex? Companionship? Thrills?'

'I don't know what to say to you.'

She watched him run his fingers over his face, trying to order his thoughts. Her eyes narrowed and her nose wrinkled in disdain, as if his words were so predictable, so clichéd, they stung as much as his message.

How can you not know what to say to me? Me! Your wife!

Finally she took a breath and when she spoke, to her surprise, her voice was level.

'Were you with her a few weeks back when you said you were at that trade fair in Manchester?' She didn't know why she thought of this – call it instinct – but something about his behaviour that day . . . his manner had seemed a little off. That, and he had placed his laundry directly in the machine instead of balling it on the floor for her to retrieve; she had thought he was being helpful, considerate . . .

'Yes.' He looked down.

'I had this feeling,' she murmured. 'But I put it down to my own insecurities, stupid jealousy. I know the girl you mean. I was introduced to her briefly when I dropped off the spare keys. I didn't know her name was Karina, but I saw her across the floor in the restaurant and she looked very, very confident and she walked like . . .' She whispered, trying to find the words. 'She walked like she had a secret: cocky and untouchable.' Calmly, Rae rubbed her hand across her stomach, as if to indicate that this was where the hurt lay. 'Is she confident? Did you like to talk to her?'

'Why does that matter?'

'It matters to me!' she shot, the flash of anger reminding him that he was in no position to ask.

He gave a single nod and she was glad of his honesty.

'And it was just for two weeks?'

He looked up, looking away instantly, indicating that the sight of her distress caused a flare of shame inside him for which she felt no sympathy.

'Yes, that was all. It was nothing,' he replied, swallowing, his words sticky, issued from a mouth that was dry.

Oh, no, Howard, it was not nothing.

'Did you ever bring her here?' She hugged the tops of her arms, which shook, preparing for the wave of revulsion that might overwhelm her.

'Never here, no.' He shook his head. 'Her place and hotels . . .' His voice trailed off.

She hated the images that now formed in her mind: the two of them standing in reception to collect keys for a mid-priced room where complimentary tea, coffee and a cellophane-wrapped biscuit sat on a prepared tray . . .

'Does anyone else apart from Paul know?' She considered this possibility and her stomach dropped. It would be more than she could stand.

'No.' He briefly held her gaze. 'No one knows.'

'Correction. I know,' she reminded him.

Howard nodded.

'Did she never ask about me?' she whispered.

'No.'

'It feels strange that she could do something so divisive, so destructive to another woman, to me – her employer, technically – without there being any mention of me.'

They sat in silence for a moment or two, each adjusting to the new sensation of mistrust and alienation in which they found themselves.

'Does she love you?' she asked, quietly, fearful of the response no matter what it might be.

'No, not at all.' He shook his head without any concept of how much worse this felt, knowing that to this woman who stole her husband's time and his body it was just a game, a nasty game of sex in which the only person who seemed to be throwing any emotion into the mix was her. Rae again fought the urge to throw up.

'Do you . . . do *you* have feelings for *her*?' she squeaked, looking down, braced to hear the admission.

'No! God no!' He shook his head and she heard the slight reverb of laughter in his tone, as if to say, *Don't be ridiculous! Of course I don't!*

She swallowed loudly. 'I don't know if that's worse or better.' She looked at him. 'To throw away *us* for something that isn't even important. It's . . .' It was a second or two before she located the word she sought. 'Cheap. It makes me feel worthless. Have there been others?' She lowered her gaze and spoke again to the floor; easier somehow than looking at him. She figured if he were capable of doing this once, he had probably done it on other occasions.

'No!' He was emphatic. 'Never before and never again. I swear to you, I promise.'

She shook her head a little. 'Don't you get it, Howard? You can't promise me anything.'

'I can, I swear.'

'Just stop it! Stop it.' Her voice was surprisingly calm now as she cut him short. 'There is no such thing as degrees of trust. There is only the truth and a lie. Honest and dishonest. It's not a grey area. Not for me. We have always told the kids that.' At the mention of the kids a fresh batch of tears found their way down her cheeks. 'You made me promises, twenty-five years ago. You took my hand from my dad's . . .' She thought about her quiet dad, placing her manicured hand into Howard's, after spending all their savings on a bit of crappy cake. Her voice cracked. 'And you stood there in that church with all the people we loved around us and you made promises to me and I made promises to you and they were good, reliable vows that worked until you did this.' This realisation sent a jolt of distress through her bones. He had broken things, Howard, her husband, the man she had trusted to be the father of her children, the keeper of her heart – he'd taken the loving relationship they had shared for all those years and he'd destroyed it. 'You *broke* your promise and so now, as I said, you can't promise me anything because it means nothing.'

He cried noisily, messily, with his eyes streaming and his nose running. She hated the way he let his secretions run over his skin; disliked the display. It reminded her of when George was little and scraped himself or sustained a minor cut. He would squeeze and prod to make blood appear, thinking this was the route to more attention and a whole heap of indulgence from his mum. He was right. But her husband's tears had the opposite effect.

She thought about Dolly, hatching a plot for her to meet the brother she adored . . . *Supposing I do go out for a drink with him and he is just disappointed and things get messed up and he doesn't like me or I don't like him? Then it would make things weird between us . . . Things wouldn't be weird between us, no matter what happened* . . . Rae wasn't so sure now. She had seen the curl of dislike in her best friend's top lip more than once over the years at the mention of someone who had said or done something in opposition to the Latimers.

'Paul won't tell anyone, and if you choose not to, then that is the end of it.'

'You think so?' she fired. 'You don't think he might tell Sadie? You don't think she, Karina, might have told someone she works with? You don't think there's the remotest possibility that our staff are laughing behind our backs because they all know? You don't think they might in turn tell one of your nieces or nephews or Hannah or George?'

'No. I don't think that. She's gone and that's that.'

His words sounded a lot like a fait accompli and she was again struck by his naivety, as if that could possibly be the end of it. As her numbness began to fade and her limbs stopped trembling, she felt the oddest of sensations, as if someone had turned on a tap deep in her gut and all her hope, optimism, love and respect for the man had started to drain away, and it was happening quicker than she would ever have thought possible.

It was such a shift that she felt embarrassed to be braless in her cotton nightie in front of him, a stranger now; something she could not have imagined. She folded her arms across her chest, shielding herself from the man she had planned on having sex with only minutes ago.

Howard slipped down from the bed and crawled over to her. He reached up and held her by the shoulders; he was crying again and his limbs were shaking, his eyes bloodshot, his breathing laboured, laden with the fumes of booze drunk in celebration of their marriage.

'Rae, please, listen to me,' he began, and she felt his grip tighten as his desperate words were met with her silence. 'I know it doesn't make much sense, but it's as though this has made me realise what I stand to lose – and I can't lose you! I can't!' He looked into her eyes and she tuned out his voice, thinking instead how this felt a lot more like restraint than affection and she didn't like it one bit.

Shrugging free from his grip, she scrambled to her feet and stood looking down at her husband, who now lay in a foetal position on the carpet.

'We have lied to each other,' she began. 'You have lived with me for the last few weeks without owning up to the thing you did, probably hoping it would never come to light, and I lied to you, Howard. I told you earlier that everything was going to be okay, but that wasn't true. It won't be. It can't be. Not now.'

She grabbed her robe from the foot of the bed and made her way downstairs, where she laid her head on a cushion on the sofa and waited for dawn to break.

◆ ◆ ◆

As the days passed by, Rae looked back at the path they had trodden since that night, and in the aftermath she saw the way littered with hurt, mistrust and physical pain, barriers simply too numerous for them to clear quickly, if at all. And yet here they were, keeping up the facade, living under the same roof and chatting with jollity to anyone who called. She knew she felt differently about the man she had married and wrestled with two questions. First, would a *happy* man choose a moment of madness with a stranger to throw his marriage away? She didn't think so. And second, what on earth she was going to do now? Rae wondered in her quieter moments just what sadness or issues had been brewing away inside her husband's mind, of which she had been unaware. Not that this made what he did excusable, not even a little bit.

'Right, pizza and movie night – our place or yours?' Dolly yelled down the phone.

'Oh . . . we can't. Not tonight.'

'What do you mean, you can't?' Dolly spat.

'I mean, the kids are busy with stuff, we have a lot on and we're . . . exhausted.'

'For God's sake, Rae! Have you been taking your Make-Me-Extra-Boring pills again? Because I think you need to cut back on your dosage!'

Rae closed her eyes, in no mood for her friend's humour. 'Yep, something like that.'

In the wake of Howard's confession, she coped with the aching void of loneliness that filled her by adopting silence. It felt easier. Retreating to the furthest corners of the house, with sadness and bewilderment seeping from every pore, she contemplated the icy wind that whipped through any room when they were both in it. She wanted to be as far away from him as possible, figuring it was easier than to face him and recount in her mind the moment of confession that led to her sense of estrangement, with her feelings towards him altered. Their verbal exchanges were rare, words barbed and sharp, chosen carefully for maximum effect; a crescendo of emotion could now flare from the smallest of kindling. Rae found she couldn't look at him, she was so angered, disgusted, ashamed, hurt – and he couldn't look at her; probably, she suspected, for much the same reasons.

'Is this how it's going to be?' he would snap on occasion, his shirt collar askew, sitting in the dark of night, as he placed the glass tumbler down hard on the kitchen table, his breath laden with fumes of the brandy that oiled his conscience and skewed his memory.

'I didn't choose this,' she said once.

'I know, I know, *I know!*' he yelled. 'But how long, Rae? How long exactly is the right amount of punishment for two weeks of indiscretion?'

She stared at him, hating this statement of fact: *two weeks* . . . Fast, inadequate, lazy coupling without love, mere weeks, a thrill, so easy . . . thoughtless . . . ruinous . . . An odd amount of time for an affair to rise and fizzle. Not long enough, in her opinion, for anything meaningful to evolve and yet long enough for the sordid interaction to squash her marriage under its heel.

'I don't know, Howard – you tell me.'

The moment she found out lived in her mind, playing like a sharp-focused movie she didn't know how to erase. And it played when she left her warm bed to visit the bathroom in the middle of the night. It played while she idled in traffic. It played while she queued in the super-market, cooked supper, ran the vacuum over the carpets of their home, unplugging it four times to enable her to cover the square footage, and it played every time her husband left the house alone.

There was the occasional time when Rae would remember a moment so tender: the birth of the kids; his kindness as a dad; how he wept when she miscarried after Hannah and before George. Yes, in these moments, with her guard down and her bruised heart offered up for inspection, she thought she might be able to sweep the whole thing under the carpet, get over it and go back to normal – forget, even – but these moments were fleeting.

She was ridiculously saddened by the timing of it, coming as it did in the wake of such an important marker, a milestone, twenty-five years. She could not now think about their anniversary party without the throb of shame and embarrassment, remembering how Paul handed her a glass of champagne with a knowing look, and it made her shiver.

Cards inscribed with heartfelt messages still stood tall on the mantelpiece and on the shelves of the sitting room. She could hardly bear to look at them, thinking of how she had pulled them from the envelopes and read the messages of congratulation with a smile, before Howard's infidelity had changed their nature into something mocking.

Their simmering silence kept a tsunami of words at bay. It wasn't pleasant, but it was a rut they had fallen into: the new normal. It was also a hard, hard habit to break. Each of them, she suspected, and for very different reasons, was wary of unplugging the dam that lurked in their throats: a barrier built of so many thoughts knotted together, forming a wall behind which sat howls of sadness, recrimination and apology, growing bigger and pushing harder until sometimes she felt it was almost impossible to take a breath.

Rae felt lost, adrift and strangely like an interloper in the house she had called home since the kids were little. For the first time since her teens she felt like Rae-Valentine Pritchard, looking in with awe at the life and workings of the Latimer family. She continued to cook Howard's supper, but left it on the stove for him to collect and take to the study or the TV room, where he watched his noisy documentaries. They no longer ate together. They no longer shared a bed. She laundered his clothes, but to do this or any task without love turned each exercise into a proper chore that left her feeling quite exhausted as well as exploited. As a couple they lay low, made excuses. They missed a birthday party, and a housewarming for Paul's youngest daughter, Ella.

Rae could not face seeing Paul, who she guessed would either pretend he had no knowledge and greet her as if everything was normal, or offer some sort of sign that he was aware but was trying his best to remain neutral, supportive of them as a couple while acting as the keeper of her husband's tawdry secret. She couldn't decide which she'd find worse. The thought of meeting the family while feeling this exposed, no longer able to reach for Howard's arm on the stairs, nod to him across the crowded room when she wanted to go home or smile at his booming voice, taking comfort from the fact that he was close by, filled her with a cold, hard dread. It meant her world was now built on shaky foundations and it took all of her strength not to fall.

One of the hardest aspects was that there was no one she could talk to. Rae was wise enough to know that if she confided in her parents they would carry the anger around silently in their hearts like a grudge, fearful for and protective of their youngest daughter, something she didn't want for them or her. They were still only able to utter the name 'Tracy Moxon' with a shake of the head and a fixed sneer. Tracy Moxon: the girl who had won the County Amateur Ballroom Cup 1989, robbing Debbie-Jo of an all-expenses-paid, three-week course at the Barry Newcombe Dance Academy. She couldn't stand the idea of them doing the same to Howard, no matter that he might deserve their malice a whole lot more than Tracy Moxon had. Even if she and Debbie-Jo had been close enough for her to confide in, Rae knew she was busy with her own family. Lee hadn't worked for a while on account of his bad back; her oldest boy, Taylor, had just split up with his girlfriend; and Debbie-Jo was working long shifts at the garden centre as well as singing in the Lower Red Lion of a weekend, putting on her sequinned frock and hammering out hits while the punters played darts and laughed over warm chicken and chips.

And the one person she wanted to talk to was her best friend, who still, with very little prompting, was more than ready to extol the virtues of her beloved brother, his deification an ongoing process. Not only did Rae fear that Dolly would try to defend Howard, she also didn't want to be the person who might dull the shiny esteem in which Dolly held him. This situation only added to her feeling of loneliness. It hurt that the one person in the whole wide world who she knew would fight her corner would, she suspected, on this topic, sit on the fence. Rae needed more.

It was unspoken but curiously appeared perfectly choreographed, the way they put up the facade when the kids called or came around. Smiling politely, chatting to the children and through the children, they were wary of letting the cracks show. Protecting them as well as themselves.

People noticed; of course they did.

'Can you take Dad his coffee, love?' She placed the mug on the table in front of George, home for a weekend.

'Why don't you take it?' Her son eyed his bowl of cereal with something that looked a lot like longing. 'Oh my God, have you guys had a row?' He jumped up from the table with mock horror. 'Please don't get divorced! Don't make me choose! I don't want to live in a broken home!' he yelled comically and took the mug, disappearing out of the kitchen with a chuckle.

'You already do, George. You already do,' Rae whispered under her breath.

Dolly in particular eyed her with suspicion. 'What's up with you?' she asked as she poured wine into glasses and rummaged in the fridge for leftover apple pie. 'You have a face like a smacked arse.'

'Nothing is wrong with me,' Rae lied – not something that came easy when talking to her best friend.

'Well, there obviously is! You are doing your fake smile and talking with that little edge to your voice that means you might be saying nice things but your thoughts are murderous! I know you.'

Dolly placed the dish containing half a pie on the granite countertop in her kitchen and cut it into three slices. Lifting one with her fingers, she dangled the narrow end of the puff pastry into her mouth and bit down, scooping apple juice from her chin with her finger. This was how they were: at ease, friends for so long – and having slept top to toe most weekends of their teens in Rae's single bed – that they could now eat, talk and live as comfortably together as they did when they were alone. It also meant Dolly knew things were not good.

'I've just got a lot going on right now.'

'Oh, pull up your big-girl pants, Rae-Valentine! Life is good!' She spoke with her mouth full and Rae gave a dry laugh. It was for Dolly, that was for sure.

◆　◆　◆

Rae was stacking the dishwasher in the kitchen when she heard him walk into the room.

'I found this on my desk.'

She turned and acknowledged the black velvet box in his hand, in which nestled the teardrop necklace. He walked towards her with his hand outstretched. She smelled the whiff of brandy on his breath, probably sipped in the dining room before coming to talk to her. She knew that he now needed Dutch courage, wary of her reaction. Well, that was his fault.

'I don't want it and so I thought you might be able to take it back.'

'You don't want it?' he asked with thinly disguised dismay.

'That's right. I don't want it.' She spoke clearly, wondering in disbelief how he supposed she might be glad of the diamond.

'But—' He started off with indignation but clearly ran out of steam.

She decided to help him out. 'But what, Howard? You think I want to own that gift bought while you were in full knowledge of the situation but I was not, happy to be given such an extravagant thing? What did you think? That if you showered me with diamonds and trips to the Caribbean I might just be able to turn a blind eye to the whole thing? Laugh it off and polish my jewels?'

'No, no, I . . .'

'Good. Because if you thought that then you really don't know me at all – which is kind of funny because I now realise that I don't know you.'

'Don't say that,' he whispered. 'You do. You know me and you know us.'

Rae whipped around to face him. 'I don't, not really. I am so hurt, Howard. I'm so hurt!' She placed her hand on her heart. 'I feel empty, completely empty, and it feels crap! I would have bet my final dollar on you being the last man in the world to have an affair. Vinnie, Paul, any of them . . . I could in the right circumstances imagine a situation where they might have been tempted. But you?' She shook her head, trying her best to keep her tears at bay. 'Not you, Howard. I felt smug. I did! I thought we had cracked it. We have been together nearly all my life and I never . . .' Emotion robbed her of the thread. 'It's kind of smashed everything because you were the anchor, you were the starting point and the finish line, my compass, my everything; and now that's gone, I'm left wondering what the hell am I doing? I am lost. I am so lost.'

He let his head hang down and cried tears that matched her own.

'I don't want to take this back; I want you to keep it. Please,' he managed eventually.

'No.' She was resolute. 'I won't.'

'Antigua . . .' he began.

Rae laughed. 'Well you can forget Antigua – as if we could go on holiday and drink cocktails and sit by a pool! I don't want to be any-where with you – not here, not there; nowhere. I wish I could disappear.'

'I can't cancel it.'

'So, take the necklace back and at least you won't be too down on the deal.' She slammed the dishwasher shut.

'I didn't mean that. I was just saying.'

'What do you want, Howard? What exactly do you want me to say? What do you expect?'

He shook his head, seeming as much at a loss to answer this as she was.

'Why don't you go without me?' he suggested.

'What?'

'Go to Antigua without me. You said you want to get away. Go on our holiday – it's all paid for and it might help.'

She stared at him, wondering if anything would help, ever.

'I just want things to be right again, Rae; that's all.'

It sounded like a simple request. She could tell by his manner that he considered it possible that they might as a couple heal, as if it were as simple as finding a way to reach a compromise.

'I love you, Rae-Valentine, and I will not let two weeks of madness spoil our lifetime together. I can't. It would be such a waste.'

'It's not your decision to make. But you are right, and that is the tragedy of it; it is such a bloody waste.'

He placed the black velvet box on the granite countertop and left the room.

She watched him climb the stairs to make his way to the spare bedroom and wished it were that clear-cut for her. She left the box on the countertop and hoped that he would get rid of it, knowing she never wanted the necklace to touch her skin again.

FOUR

Rae folded two sets of pyjamas, her linen jumpsuit and a white crinkle-cotton maxi-dress, placing them in the suitcase that lay open on the bed before crossing the items from her list. She counted the pairs of knickers balled neatly into the corners: fourteen, with two spares, along with various sandals, swimming costumes, tunics, T-shirts and shorts and a couple more formal frocks, just in case. She held up the floral halterneck bikini to the mirror; placing it over her shirt, she ran the flat of her palm over the fabric, remembering the last holiday she and Howard had taken, when they had gone to Malta. She saw herself in the pool, laughing at something he had said, *happy, so happy* . . . Her tears caught in her throat and clogged her nose. It happened like this sometimes; sadness came over her in a wave, robbing her breath of rhythm and leaving her feeling weakened. It was a reminder that she was still fragile. The reason for this emotional fracture in her day was a pin-sharp memory, a glimpse of her old life, when things had been perfect, before the shine came off. She thought about a winter's day a few years ago now: the kids had been at school and she and Howard had, unusually, shared a bottle of wine over lunch and decided in the giddy aftermath that the best thing to stave off the chill of the day would be to run a big hot steaming bath. Flinging their clothes on to the cold, tiled floor, they'd laughed at the illicitness of it all. And the mere frivolity of their actions had made her feel young. She'd liked it.

The tub had brimmed with bubbles and the heat steamed up the big mirror on the bathroom wall. She'd lain back and raised her knee in the small gap at the side of the tub and pushed her hair back from her face, letting the hot water soothe her muscles. It had been sheer genius to choose a bath with the taps in the middle, meaning they could both languish in the water without the inconvenience or pain of taps in the back. It might have been winter outside, but here in the bathroom of their splendid Georgian house it was positively tropical.

'So come on – your turn.' She'd smiled at him over the rim of her mug.

'Give me a minute. Let me think.' He looked skyward.

'You shouldn't have to think! It's supposed to be spontaneous, your innermost desire: the one place that if time and money were no object and you could jump on a plane without fear, spur of the moment, just one ticket – where would you go?' She squeezed her knees together and trapped his legs, sliding against him in the foamy water.

'Your talking is not helping my thought process.'

She snorted her laughter. 'God, Howard, you'd think you'd be used to me rattling on by now.'

He winked at her and continued his ponderings. 'I'm torn.'

'Between what?' She sighed her impatience, eyes wide. 'Come on!'

'If I only have one ticket, am I allowed to go by bus on to somewhere else? Can it be a two-centre trip?'

'Two-centre trip?' She threw her head back and chuckled. 'Listen to yourself; you are being way too practical. What are you, a holiday rep?'

'You know what I mean.'

'Not really.' She laughed. 'You can go anywhere! The moon!' She splashed the surface of the water.

He pushed his fringe back over his head. 'Definitely not the moon: no good restaurants.'

'You could open one. Latimers Moon Grill has quite a nice ring to it.'

'Now you're talking!' He laughed. 'No, I'm thinking somewhere a little closer to home. New York and Las Vegas – so we could fly to one and then catch a bus to the other.'

'Howard, you don't get the bus in London; why do you think you might like to be in a bus across the States? Anyway it sounds like a long bus ride. Better to take an internal flight; we don't want to get bored.'

'Urgh.' He shuddered. 'Bored? You know I hate that word with a passion! Only boring people get bored! Bored is a mind that can't think of something fun and inventive to do!'

She laughed. 'Okay.' She put her mug on the tiled side of the bath and grabbed her phone from the Victorian washstand within reach along the back wall, dexterously jabbing at the screen. 'It says here that to get a bus from New York to Las Vegas would take two days, ten hours and twenty-five minutes.' She pointed to the squiggly blue line denoting the route across the USA.

He sat back and laughed heartily. 'Well I could definitely manage the two days and ten hours but the last twenty-five minutes might be a challenge!'

'Do you think it stops en route?' She looked up at him.

'Sometimes I question if you have the sense you were born with, Rae-Valentine. As if it would travel for two days and ten hours without stopping for fuel or a loo break!'

'Some of them have loos!' She looked at him sternly.

'It would need to have. Good Lord. I think I'll pass. You have put me off. Okay, serious thinking head on now.'

She put her phone back down and reached again for her cooling tea. 'Come on! Where?'

'Norway.' He folded his arms across his chest, as if satisfied.

'Norway? Norway! I thought you were going to go for a Caribbean island or the Great Wall of China!'

'Great Wall of China . . .' he muttered under his breath. 'I sometimes think you don't know me at all.'

'Maybe I don't. A man of mystery!' She raised her eyebrows in the most alluring way she could manage. 'How exciting.'

They both chuckled.

'Okay, why Norway?'

'Ooh, hang on, I've got a bit of cramp!'

She felt him flex his foot beneath the water.

'Mind my bottom!' she howled.

'It's hard to mind your bottom in this situation! We need a bigger bath.'

'Or I need a smaller bottom.' She grimaced.

'Okay, so Norway,' he began again. 'When I was learning the trade, my dad sent me to work at the Savoy as a pot wash for the summer.'

'Really? Why have you never mentioned this?' She winked at him; he liked to tell the story.

'Ha ha! Very funny. Yes, but what you might not know is that I worked alongside a chap from Oslo. In those days I was of course a smoker and we'd take our breaks together, standing in the London drizzle down a cold alleyway, and he'd tell me about the fjords and the skyline and the snow and the cities and it just stuck with me and I always thought that would be a lovely thing to do: take a cruise up the fjords, a spot of whale watching.'

'It does sound lovely,' she conceded. 'Okay, I am in. Norway it is.'

'We could sit under a blanket on the deck of the ship and hold hands under the stars.' He smiled at her.

'Howard, you old romantic!' She liked the flush of warmth that the picture filled her with.

'Less of the "old", if you don't mind. So what about you, Miss Rae-Valentine; where would you head?'

'Hmm. I think I'd like to go island-hopping in Greece. I remember reading about it when I was at school and in my head I saw this confident girl with a red knapsack and a ponytail, taking great big strides like a giant from one island to the other; she was tanned and she looked like she could take on the world. I thought I might like to be that girl.'

'I think she might need a bit more than a knapsack if she's going away for any length of time.'

'There you go again with your practicalities! Ooh! It's our programme tonight! We need to set the recorder. I think we should eat with the kids but I don't want to miss it.' She was looking forward to the second part of the period drama they had got into – loving the costumes and poetic language of a bygone era – and looking forward just as much to nestling on the sofa with her feet warming on her husband's thigh, as was their way.

He smiled and sank down further and she watched the water rise over her chest.

'I used to like my boobs,' she commented out of the blue.

He snickered with his eyes closed. 'Well, if it's any consolation, I *still* like your boobs.'

'It's not really, but thank you.' She cupped her small chest and lifted.

'When did you start to dislike them? Just curious.'

She took a deep breath and considered this. 'I suppose after George. I fed him until he was eight months.'

'I do remember,' he interjected, as if to remind her that he *had* been there.

'And by the time he was on solids my boobs, what little I had of them, had gone south.'

'I never noticed!'

'You bloody liar!' She flicked water at him. 'I wonder how Lisa Hopkirk's boobs have fared.' She eyed him mischievously.

'Don't be so ridiculous!'

'What's ridiculous?' She chuckled. 'I only asked the question!'

'You are being ridiculous. I have told you: she was just a friend!'

'Says you. Your sister says different!' She loved teasing him.

'I'm not discussing it any more. I was a teenager – a long, long time ago! And you should know by now that Dolly is an unreliable witness; she is the one convinced that a ghost came and stood by the side of her bed and told her to take better care of her hair.'

They both howled with laughter at the memory of that particular confession.

'I mean, come on, Rae! Of all the messages from the afterlife, they came with a shampoo recommendation? She is nuts!'

'Don't be mean about my best friend.' Their laughter settled. 'And you always do that; make me laugh to change the subject. That makes me suspicious.'

'Oh for God's sake!'

'I can't help it. I admit it: I get jealous. I love you too much.'

'Well, don't. Get jealous, that is. Loving me too much is just fine.'

'I do love you,' she confirmed, smiling at the man with a rush of love in her stomach. It was a mock jealousy that she knew flattered him. She knew she had no reason to be jealous. They had been together for all this time, shared kids, a home . . . they were all set.

'I love you too.' He smiled.

They both looked towards the bathroom door at the sound of the front doorbell.

'Shit!'

'Bugger it!'

'Shall we sit still and hope they go away?' she whispered.

'Might be an emergency,' he suggested. 'Or it might be the kids?'

'No, they've both got—'

It was as she formed the words 'keys' on her tongue that the sound of Hannah's voice floated up the stairs.

'Hello! Where is everyone? I'm starving.'

'Shit!' she mouthed again, as her husband stood, bottom in her face, grabbed a towel from the rack and made for the door. He opened it a smidge, calling down to Hannah.

'Shan't be a sec, love; Mum's just having a bath!'

Rae felt the blast of cool air rob the bathroom of its tropical fug. That was it then. Luxury bath time over . . .

'How're you doing?' Howard asked now from the bedroom doorway, his question making her jump and pulling her from the memory of that lovely day, the echo of it in her chest making her feel sad with longing for the woman who had felt as if she had the whole wide world in the palm of her hand, and longing for the man who she thought was good, honest, a man worthy of her trust, her friend. A reminder of the wonderful closeness they had lost. It felt a lot like grief. She threw the bikini into the suitcase.

'I'm just trying to figure out what I need to take.' She disliked the new clipped tone with which she addressed him; she sounded like a stranger, but it felt a lot like self-preservation, another way of armouring her already dented heart.

'I wouldn't worry too much. You can guarantee that Dolly will be taking more than you could both possibly need; she always does.'

It was Howard who had suggested that Dolly take his place on their trip. They had given the excuse of his workload and Rae was actually a little relieved, knowing she would have felt too nervous to travel that far alone.

'True.' Rae busied herself with the bottles, jars and tubes of potions, lotions and medicines on the bed, popping them into grip-seal bags and hiding them among her clothing. 'I was also thinking about that day when we took a bath in the afternoon after too much wine.'

Howard stepped forward and sat on the edge of the bed. He took a deep breath and bit his lip, as if he too might be remembering the easy laughter, the physical contact, both glorious.

'I loved that day.' He spoke with a catch to his throat. 'I miss days like that.'

'Yes. Well . . .' *It feels like a different person, someone other than me . . .*

'I am trying to make it up to you, Rae. I am and I won't stop trying. You know that, don't you?'

She turned to look at his pleading expression and it killed her, realising how little impact his hurt had on her, how far they had slipped off course. Her words when she found them were more softly delivered. 'Buying me gifts, throwing parties and sending me on trips is not the answer; you must realise that. They are all the same thing, skimming over the real issues, papering over the cracks. A distraction, a delay.'

'What are we delaying?' He sounded anguished.

'Deciding how this ends.' She paused in organising her clothes and held his gaze. The words had leaped unbidden from a place deep inside, and to hear them spoken out loud filled her with a new and sharp anxiety. *What will you do, Rae?* She still found it hard to picture herself as anything other than Mrs Howard Latimer.

'Or how it continues.' He swallowed. 'Truth is, Rae, I don't know what else to do.'

'I know.' She felt the first stir of pity for the man. 'And if it's any consolation, I don't know what to do either.'

'It's not. Not really. I kind of hoped one of us might have our hands on the wheel.'

Rae sat on the other side of the bed.

'I wish it wasn't so complicated, such a bloody mess.' She heard his snort of agreement. 'And it hurts to say this, Howard, but it's now not only about Karina, not any more.' She saw him wince as she spoke her name. 'Although that's undoubtedly when the earthquake hit. But I'm beginning to think that maybe over time we had started to tilt, tip without realising, and when you told me what had happened we tumbled over, smashed, and what is left is rubble. So no matter how much we try to build we are skating on stones and nothing can take root, because we don't have any foundations.'

'No foundations? Please don't say that. We have kids! A home! A business! Is that not enough?'

'It was for me.' She saw the slope to his shoulders. 'And I can only imagine how it feels to hear me remind you of that again – and, believe me, I don't mean to keep bringing up your infidelity; it does neither of us any good.' She again saw the movie playing in her head that night when her feet were sore from dancing and her face ached from laughing: *Rae, there is something I need to tell you. I don't know how to say it, but I know I must* . . . 'But it opened up this chasm and everything we had fell into it and the words I have aren't adequate for how I am now. Hurt, disappointed, lonely, angry – they are all valid, but none really convey how I feel.'

'How do you feel?' he asked quietly, hopefully, as if her response might give him the clue he was looking for about how to go forward.

She looked out of the window at life passing by in their beautiful street. 'I feel lost. Like I've lost my place and my purpose and at the same time I feel trapped. It's hard to describe.'

'I love you, I—'

'Please stop saying that to me, Howard! It isn't like when the kids hurt their knee and we could give it a magic kiss to make everything better! "I love you" isn't some charmed phrase that resets my emotions or erases hurt. Part of me loves you too, of course – you gave me my kids; we have shared this life – but I love you differently. Less, I suppose, and that means I am not sure I want to share the rest of my time on earth with you. "I love you" doesn't mean automatically that we can go on, doesn't mean we have a future . . .'

His expression was pained, his voice indignant, shocked. 'You don't mean that! You can't mean that, Rae.'

'What did you think?' She held his gaze. 'That we would just carry on?'

'I don't know. I wasn't thinking. I was caught up in the moment. It was alcohol, it was fun, a diversion, and it was a mistake!'

Rae hated the image in her mind of the young girl who had unwittingly wielded so much power as much as she hated his facile justification.

'Other people get through much worse.'

'Is that right?' She again felt the flare of anger. 'Do you think I could possibly care about what other people do? Because I don't. I care about you and me and Hannah and George.'

'Me too; I only care about us. I was just . . .'

She watched him flounder, again with something close to pity in her heart at the fact that he just didn't get it.

'Whether we like it or not, things have changed between us.' She thought again of the easy conversation that had been a constant in their lives, the familiar, comfortable sex, and the assumption that this was how it would always be. '*I* feel different now and I feel differently about us.'

'I don't want us to be different. I don't want things to change,' he pleaded.

She noted the tremble to his bottom lip and thought he looked a lot as George had when he was little.

'I want us to go back to how we were, all those wonderful years, Rae, you and me against the world!'

'It's not that easy, Howard. It's already happened. It's like we are this very knotty piece of string and trying to figure out where to start to unpick the mess is hard enough, let alone how we move forward. If we *can* move forward.'

Howard stood and faced her. 'We need to find a way forward, Rae, or we give up. I know those are the options. I know it, but I can't stand the thought of not having you by my side. I want to go back to how we were, completely how we were, friends, lovers, without this cloud of awkwardness hanging over us. How we live now, it's a half-life. It's draining, depressing.'

'I agree and I wish I could wave a magic wand, but I can't. Or, trust me, I would have waved it a few times in recent weeks.'

'I know. I also know that we are running out of time, not because we are over the hill but because the longer this stalemate goes on the harder it will be to come back from. I've already told you I am out of solutions.' He raised his arms and let them fall by his sides. 'I will do anything to prove to you how sorry I am – so sorry – but we can't let my wrongdoing be the filter through which we live every aspect of our lives. We can't. People make mistakes, Rae. I did: I made a mistake; I fucked up. Big time. I know it. But you can't crucify me for it each and every day for the rest of our lives. That would be a big mistake too. The biggest. We have too much good stuff going on to end up like that. And I want us to be happy, I do – happy together. But if we can't be happy together . . .'

She watched him close his mouth, rethinking whatever he had been about to say. Rae walked to the window and looked to the street below. It had rained and the London pavements were shiny like glossy stones on the seashore.

She spotted the young woman who had Fifi on the leash, walking slowly, letting her pooch sniff her way along the street. The woman looked up towards Rae and then away suddenly, head down, hands jammed into the pockets of her padded gilet. Rae smiled at her any-way, knowing what it felt like to be that shy, to wish that the rest of the world would just leave you alone. The woman looked pretty, nice, and Rae imagined inviting her into the kitchen for a cup of tea and getting to know her. She looked like the kind of woman who might be her friend. A friend who had no part in her family, who might be able to offer neutral advice on her marriage, a friend without an agenda, a good listener . . .

'Have a good think while you are away, Rae. Really think about what you want and how we can work things out.'

She looked back into the room, having almost forgotten that Howard was still standing there.

'I will try. I promise. But there's a lot to think about.' She shrugged.

'I know and I know this has been the hardest time. And my pain is also a physical thing.' He touched his fingers to his chest. 'I have hated it, all of it, every bloody day of us not talking and you being back to the quiet girl you used to be.'

The girl in the corner . . .

'I have hated it.' He swallowed his emotion. 'And I can only imagine what it has been like for you. But I feel like this trip might be a new start, a chance for you to clear your head, away from here. I really hope so.'

Rae stepped forward and closed the suitcase. 'I really hope so too.'

She had said goodbye to the kids, left food in the freezer, spoken to her parents and ordered their groceries for the coming two weeks. As Howard loaded her suitcase into the back of the car, she buckled up in the front seat, thinking of how happy she had been when she first heard they were taking a trip – never in a million years able to imagine that in just a few weeks this might be how they'd end up. There was an air of awkwardness as Howard climbed into the driver's seat beside her. Rae realised that for the first time since her childhood she felt alone, and she had quite forgotten the fear that bookended this. There was the painful twist of anxiety in her gut as she considered and rejected several things she thought she might say, topics that ranged from the minutiae to the more fundamental, swallowing them before they found their way to her tongue. Nothing felt appropriate, not any more. And all carried a sour accusatory note that she felt helped no one. It felt like every topic in her mind circled back to Howard's infidelity.

Keep an eye on the kids for me – the kids you let down; the babies you vowed to keep safe in our happy, stable family . . .

There's food in the freezer. Or will you be eating out and if so with whom?

Hope work's not too busy. Work: where you met and had sex with Karina . . .

She looked across at her husband and felt an unfamiliar pang of mistrust, questioning for the first time ever what he might get up to while she was away. It was another reminder of the new rules that now governed her emotions. When the silence reached a crescendo, Howard sighed heavily and made a noise that was part snort, part laugh, as if he figured it was better to fill the weighted pauses with something, anything. At one point he reached over and briefly took her reluctant hand. She no longer liked the way it felt, her hand inside his; once as natural to her as breathing, it now reminded her of clothing that had been badly washed and over-dried – it didn't quite fit. There were a number of clumsy seconds while they both waited for him to release her. She wondered how he might do it in the least obvious fashion. He chose to cough and wrench his fingers away to cover his mouth. Rae instantly folded her hands inside the cardigan that sat on her lap, hiding them, in case he should be tempted to try again.

Dolly stood by the car at the drop-off point at Heathrow as Vinnie unloaded her luggage. Howard had been right: Rae spied suitcases, a vanity box and various carrier bags stuffed to the gunwales. She caught her husband's eye and he smiled at her. It was a sad reminder of the telepathy that remained between them, one of the last lingering threads of their closeness, where each knew the exact thoughts of the other with no more than a slight lift to their lips or the raise of an eyebrow. This closeness, borne of years of shared experience and through being good friends, had now washed away like a dam in a flood and it had happened just as quickly.

Howard parked behind his brother-in-law and the two jumped out of the car with something akin to relief.

'Howard!' Dolly ran towards him and squashed him against her in a fierce hug. 'I feel so bad that I'm going on your holiday!'

'Don't.' He coughed. 'I have appointments with the bank and tax deadlines that I can't miss and it's just the way it is.'

Rae noted the ease with which the lies slipped from his tongue and it made her shiver.

'Right, formal thanks out of the way . . .' Dolly turned to Rae. 'I am so bloody excited!'

Rae smiled at her. 'Me too,' she offered in a manner that belied her words.

'Is that the lot?' Dolly tried to peer into the boot of Vinnie's BMW.

'No. Hang on a minute . . .' Vinnie reached into the deep recesses of the car. 'You've got the kitchen sink in here too.'

The four of them laughed. Dolly's voice boomed. 'You can laugh, Vincent, but it's you not me who's going to be needing the kitchen sink for the next two weeks! You will be stuck at home heating up beans from the tin while I sun myself on a bloody beach!'

'And I will miss you too, my sweet.' Vinnie held her gently and kissed her cheek. 'Be good. Keep in touch; stay safe.'

'I'll miss you too,' Dolly whispered with rare tenderness. 'Look after my house, my cat, my plants and my kid!' she shouted.

'In that order?' Vinnie shook his head.

Dolly considered this. 'No, you are right. Cat. Plants. House. Kid.'

As she began to walk away, Vinnie grabbed her around the waist and like a smitten teen on a park bench wheeled her towards him, kissing her again. Rae felt a spike of misplaced envy at how far she and Howard had slipped off track.

She felt awkward, knowing she would be expected to repeat the fond farewell with her own husband and wishing they could say goodbye unobserved. She stepped into his arms and stood stiffly with her head on his chest. He held her tightly. She felt the nervous quake along his limbs.

'Come back to me, Rae. Please come back to me.' He spoke into her hair.

'Come back to you? Don't be so ridiculous! She's only going for two bloody weeks!' Dolly boomed, listening in where her attentions were not wanted and robbing them of the moment. And doing what she did best: easing the tension and turning the moment into a joke.

The women walked towards the glass double doors of the departures area, turning to wave to their husbands as they pulled away. Rae looked at Howard intently. *I will try . . .*

'Okay!' Dolly shouted, studying the board. 'Check-in desk twenty-three. This way! Follow me!' She raised her arm, as if she was directing a large group and not just Rae with her measly one suitcase and her cotton cardigan over her arm in case it got chilly on the plane.

The luggage was distributed between the two of them and as they approached the desk with passports held aloft, Dolly turned to her friend and smiled.

'Good morning. Iwanttohavesexwithyourbrother,' Dolly mumbled.

The stony-faced attendant looked up from his computer and glanced from one to the other. 'Good morning, ladies, and where are we travelling to today?'

'We are off to Antigua.' Dolly did her best to control her titters. 'All alone without grown-up supervision!'

'That sounds dangerous,' he offered drily.

Rae felt her face colour and bit down on her bottom lip to stop her laughter spilling from her mouth. It was a welcome moment of joyful mischief; a reminder of her youth, when she thought that to marry a Latimer was quite possibly the greatest thing imaginable – better even than signing up to the cookery course, which had been her plan until her parents put paid to it.

Cooking? That's a dead-end, thankless job if ever there was one! Slaving away in a hot basement kitchen. No, you get your typing certificate, girl, then there'll be no hot kitchen for you – you'll get to work in an office, maybe one with a view! She had watched the way her parents smiled at each other with their eyes lit up, as if this was what *they* would have loved.

She and Dolly had their passports checked and answered the security questions accordingly.

'Here we go.' The man smiled as he handed them their relevant boarding passes. 'You will see I have taken the liberty of upgrading you to our business-class service today.'

'You are shitting me?' Dolly stared at him.

'No, I figured it was the least I could do, as I don't have a brother and my sister is taken,' he offered with a clipped voice and a brief shake of the head.

'Oh my God! No way!' Dolly screamed and banged the countertop. 'I bloody love you! I do! I actually love you!'

'The feeling is mutual. Have a nice flight. Next please!' he called to the queue behind them, and tapped the counter without breaking his stride.

Rae stared at the man. Sometimes there were no words.

On the plane, she watched the flight attendant give her colleague an exaggerated smile as Dolly squealed with delight at the width of the seat, the amount of leg room, the free bottle of water and the natty vanity kit with a mini-toothbrush, a dinky tube of toothpaste and a freshen-up towel in a sachet. Business class was not new to her friend, but Dolly was still delighted by the luxury.

'This is the life, Rae!' She eased into the seat and kicked off her shoes. 'This is going to be like a party before we even arrive! We can have a glass of wine and chat and watch a movie! Like a girls' night out but in the sky!'

Rae nodded. 'That'll be nice.' She took her seat and tried to ignore the stares from other more sedate travellers who were judging her friend for the volume of her voice and her energy. She looked at Dolly, who was making herself comfortable, loving her lack of awareness and her authenticity.

Approximately twenty minutes after the plane had taken off, Dolly reclined her seat and fell into a deep, deep sleep with the soft blanket over her shoulders and her eye mask securely fastened. Her snores were intermittent, and she pretty much stayed this way until the plane began its descent into VC Bird International airport, Antigua.

'Oh rats! Did I nod off?' Dolly asked, coming to and trying to fix her flattened hairdo, rubbing at the deep pillow crease on her cheek.

'Just for a while.'

Rae hadn't minded. It had been a rare chance for her to sit and do nothing. Much-needed peace, as her mind coasted on chaos. At home there was always a bathroom to be cleaned, beds to be made, supper to prepare, laundry, recycling, grocery shopping – and this in between being on call to the various restaurants, where the staff knew she was the person who'd fetch, carry and fix in an emergency. And with Debbie-Jo now living in Northampton, she was also the one responsible for ferrying her parents to and from the appointments that seemed to be getting more frequent and varied. It struck her that now, in her mid-forties, she made an annual trip to the dentist and maybe two or three visits a year to the GP, whereas her mum and dad had a diary that was chock-full of appointments. Almost weekly they were buttoning up their coats and heading out to see chiropodists, audiologists, chiropractors, ophthalmologists and a whole host of other professionals with a wide range of specialisations, each visited with the express hope of fixing, patching up or preventing whatever ailed them most that day.

It made her think about Hannah's dough teddy, a salt-baked lumpy thing that had been fashioned for the Christmas tree when she was in nursery school. Hannah, however, rather than hang the glittery painted trinket and let it do its job of prettifying a branch, insisted on naming it 'Sparkle Ted' and carrying it around in her pudgy hand. She played with it, danced it on the tabletop, set it on the side of her bath. Each day a chunk worked loose, eventually falling off. Each night Howard would set to with sticky tape, glue and even small elastic bands, trying to pro-long the life of this lump of misshapen dough to which their three-year-old daughter had become so attached. It was futile, of course; Sparkle Ted was not designed to last forever and eventually he was so mangled, reduced and fractured that they had no choice but to throw him in the bin with the cold chips and redundant peas of supper. Hannah had gone nuts, of course. That had not been a good day. Rae felt a rush of warmth at the memory of her husband's attention to the challenging chore others would have scoffed at. Not that she was comparing her ageing parents to Sparkle Ted – and when the time came she certainly wouldn't be putting them out for collection with the cold chips and peas – but it did make her think about the nature of life and how we, like all living things, were designed to decay. Almost instinctively she ran her hand over the soft pouch of flesh that bulged over the waistband of her jeans, aware that her decay had begun and that time was indeed running out . . .

Unbidden, the image of Howard popped into her head, placing his hand on the flat stomach of Karina the waitress.

FIVE

Stepping from the plane and giggling at the intense heat, the two popped their sunglasses on and welcomed the first feel of warmth on their skin. They gathered their bags from the carousel and made their way through the airport. It was a striking building, large, gleaming and echoey with snatches of the clear tropical sky peeking through the windows. White pillar-shaped structures held up the cathedral-like apex ceiling. Seating areas were dotted around the cool marble floor and there were occasional grand displays of ferns and tropical plants. The people Rae saw fell into two camps: agitated and trying to find their way out of the building in this new and intimidating environment, looking for their connection, lift, taxi or holiday rep; or laughing, relaxed, now on their way home, making the return journey with the island magic and a little Caribbean laissez-faire still clinging to their sun-kissed skin.

She liked to take in the sights and smells of any new place, and travel was always exciting, but this trip felt different. Lovely as it was to spend time with Dolly and to be in this glorious place, she couldn't shake the feeling that it was, like her necklace and party, something of a consolation prize designed to ease her husband's conscience. She was also very conscious of the fact that she was putting on a show, trying not to let Dolly see her hurt, which was always only a heartbeat away. But a promise was a promise and she would try to use the time away to clear her head, to try to find the path that would give them a clear way forward.

As they stepped outside, Rae was again struck by the heat, which crept under her cotton clothes, covered her skin and filled her lungs. It would take some getting used to. They were ferried to their resort by a luxury minibus with all mod-cons, the type of air-conditioned, well-sprung, comfy bus that no one would mind being sat in for two days, ten hours and twenty-five minutes. Her mouth twitched into a smile in response to a conversation that had taken place when she was someone else, in another time, when her view on the world had been very different.

She stared out at the winding lanes, where the shimmering heat of the sun distorted the surface of the tarmac, feeling the swell of antici-pation as they navigated the roads edged with lush green vegetation, palm trees and giant ferns, banana trees and steep banks, which hid the planted fields beyond. It was really beautiful.

She glanced to her left at Dolly, who was making small talk with an elderly couple from Cheshire. The man was dressed in full safari kit: khaki trousers and jacket. They were rather shouty and had been to the island many, many times. Dolly looked over and pulled a face, crossing her eyes and sticking out her tongue. Rae knew her friend would not want to be with shouty people – too much competition; and especially these two, who knew everything there was to know about Antigua. Rae and Dolly would much prefer to discover things for themselves.

With their baggage wheeled ahead, the two friends trod the marble steps and walked into the foyer of the Blue Lodge, Parakeet Bay, a boutique hotel with twenty rooms, all housed under a double-height wooden ceiling. A vast fan whirred overhead. The furniture was rich, dark rattan, topped with white overstuffed upholstery with cushions in teal and turquoise. It was stunning.

Rae gazed through the square reception room towards the pool, where a line of palm trees partly obscured the view of the curved beach and the crystal-clear waters beyond. She thought of how she and Howard would react if they were still living in that parallel universe where everything was outwardly rosy and she was unaware. Arriving at this paradise, she would squeal her delight and he would stand tall: the big man, the provider.

'This'll do, mate.' Dolly gave a satisfied smile, pulling Rae from her thoughts. 'The boy did good.' She of course referred to her brother.

With her straw hat in her hand, Rae nodded her agreement and went to look out of the window rather than engage in chat about how marvellous Howard was.

The two women made their way to their apartment, up a flight of stairs and along a corridor at the back, where the one-bedroom apartment with a spacious lounge area and decked balcony afforded them a glorious view of the sea.

'God, it's hot!' Dolly exhaled, fanning her face with the plastic travel wallet containing their welcome pack, a map and tourist leaflets of local attractions.

The well-informed couple from Cheshire called from the path below and waved at them.

'Oh my God, hide me – now they know where we live! And there is no way I am getting saddled with Nick and Nora Knowitall for my whole bloody holiday! I would actually die!'

'Are those their names, Nick and Nora?'

Dolly laughed loudly. 'I so want to say yes so that you call them that, just to make me laugh, but I love you too much. No, I think it was something like Douglas and Mary. To be honest I stopped listening after the phrase "We are like walking guidebooks!" Apparently, "Douglas once had to interrupt the captain of our cruise mid-welcome speech when he said there were twenty-two luxury cabins on board and we knew he was wrong, didn't we, Douglas? Because we had counted them. There were twenty-four . . ." I mean, kill me now!'

Rae laughed loudly, her friend's mimicry as impressive as ever. 'I do wish you had said something earlier; I told them we'd meet up for dinner.'

'Oh my God, Rae, you didn't!'

'No, I didn't, and I love you too much to pretend for more than a second that I did.'

Dolly twisted her jaw. 'I will get you back. I will.'

Rae would have quite been quite content to stay on the balcony, where she had a perfect view of the crystal-clear water, the glorious palm-lined beach and the small boats dotted along the horizon. It was a world away from her bedroom window with its view up and down the London crescent.

The apartment's bedroom was more compact than she had imagined and furnished with two single beds – a mistake that Howard would have been rectifying immediately. The beds were a mere two feet apart and the en-suite bathroom was certainly not spacious. Rae noted that the proportions here would have been perfect if she were travelling alone, but with a roommate like Dolly, who managed to fill every space with her presence and her scattered belongings, she figured that two weeks might prove to be a challenge.

'This is not a room, it's a bloody cupboard!' Dolly stated with her hands on her hips, surveying her mountain of luggage.

'You can have my wardrobe space,' Rae suggested. 'I can leave my stuff in my case and fish out what I need out every day.'

'Mate, I am going to need next door's wardrobe space as well.' Dolly sighed. 'I think we need to go and get a cocktail. This can wait.'

Rae felt a spike of happiness at the realisation that they were on holiday; it was the first crest of joy that had risen in the misery of the last few weeks.

'Let's do it!' she clapped, grabbing her bag and her straw hat before following Dolly along the narrow corridor and down a flight of stairs that led them to a warren of walkways around a garden. It was beautiful, with varieties of aloe, hibiscus, oleander and bougainvillea growing in beds dug among the spiky grass and filling the air with glorious scents that were only heightened by the midday heat. Tiny green lizards stared at them from branches and peeked out from beneath the shade of leaves.

'I think we should have tied a piece of string to the handle of our apartment and unwound it so we can follow it back again,' said Rae, laughing, as they wandered up and down walkways and along plant-lined paths that all looked remarkably similar.

'Or breadcrumbs, like Hansel and whatshername,' Dolly suggested.

'Yes, breadcrumbs are probably better; I'm sure they'd never get eaten by the birds.' Rae rolled her eyes.

'Okay, smartarse, we'll stick to string – how long do you think the string needs to be?'

Rae shrugged. 'I don't know, but we could unravel a pair of your knickers and still have spare.'

Dolly gave her friend a long, hard glare. 'I am about a second away from giving you a dead leg. And if you don't think I'm capable, just ask Howard.'

'Oh, I know you're capable.' Rae ran ahead of her friend as Dolly chased her along the path. And in that moment of happy frivolity she forgot the ache of confusion that had been fogging her thoughts – and that beautiful second of clarity felt wonderful, like a gift.

The two women found themselves in a clearing with a wide and tranquil kidney-shaped pool, where shallow steps ran along one side and sunloungers with white fluffy beach towels, rolled invitingly, were dotted around the water's edge to catch the best of the day's sunshine. Parasols were positioned to provide just the right amount of shade. Rae took a deep breath and could already feel the restorative powers of being somewhere so beautiful, so luxurious. In front of them lay a narrow path to the beach, and to the left of the pool, with a wide, dark-wood terrace littered with rattan sofas like the ones she had seen in reception, was a bar. An aged wooden sign swung on rope, inscribed with the word 'Max's'.

Dolly walked in ahead and Rae followed. Despite being open to the elements on three sides, the bar housed deep white bookshelves along the back wall, crammed with all sorts of *objets trouvés*: wide conch shells, a stack of pale coral, weathered rope and rocks shaped into near perfect spheres by the sea; a wide china bowl that was full of opaque sea glass in a variety of blue and green shades. There were books too – coffee-table volumes with glorious pictures of beach houses with the sea as their backdrop.

'Fabulous!' Dolly sighed.

Rae nodded in agreement, feeling the weight shift from her shoulders; and even though she was far, far away from the London postcode that held nearly all the people she loved, this place already felt familiar, safe.

'Oh, I am sorry, ladies, but we are not open officially. The main hotel bar is open twenty-four seven and they'd be happy to serve you. I could call a waiter?'

Rae tore herself away from the mesmeric view afforded from the vast open deck, taking in the incredible colours of the sea and sky and the particular hue of blue-green where they met on the horizon. Beyond the bar she could see the coconut trees swaying in the gentle breeze.

Beautiful. So beautiful. I think Howard and I would have had a wonderful time here together, before . . .

91

The young barman was carrying a flat box of glasses and had rolled his shirtsleeves up over his elbows.

'What about *un*officially?' Dolly asked in her blunt fashion.

He laughed and looked back towards the main hotel. 'Unofficially I could tell you that I am not allowed to serve you drinks and pour for another hour.' He reached under the bar and pulled out two mini-bottles of pink champagne, which he uncorked. 'Also unofficially, I will be leaving these two on the bar and if you and your friend unofficially take them and sit quietly on the terrace and drink them and if anyone asks you say you brought them in with you, then that might work. Officially, if anyone found out I would have to walk the pier and jump off the end.'

Rae let laughter burble from her, the most amusing thing about his statement being that he assumed Dolly might be able to sit anywhere and do anything quietly.

'You are a superstar and you are my favourite person in this whole resort, apart from her.' Dolly thumbed in Rae's direction. 'What's your name?'

'Antonio.' He flashed his white-toothed, megawatt smile.

'Nice to meet you, Antonio. I'm Dolly and this is my friend Rae-Valentine.'

'Rae-Valentine,' he repeated in a way that for no reason in particular sent a quiver of embarrassment through her core. It had been a long time since she had felt so shy – another realisation of the shift in her world.

Rae took one of the cold bottles in her palm and joined Dolly on a low, pale-blue linen sofa on the edge of the terrace with the most incredible view over the white, powder-soft sand.

'To Howard!' Dolly raised her glass of wine.

Rae didn't intend to show the falter in her face – she had meant to smile and not knit her brow for a second – but Dolly was quicker at spotting it than she was at rectifying it.

She watched her sister-in-law place her drink down on the coffee table, hard.

'Okay, Rae, enough. Now, are you going to tell me what the fuck's been going on?'

Rae ran a finger around the rim of her bottle and wondered how best to field the question. It was all well and good being evasive, but Dolly was asking her outright and this meant she would inevitably lie to her – something alien when it came to her best friend. And she hated this feeling of being pulled. Hated it.

'What do you mean?' She sipped the sweet foam, buying time.

Dolly laughed – 'What do I mean?' – shaking her head and sighing, reminding Rae so much of Mitzy, her mother-in-law, it was scary. 'I mean I am many things, but I am not stupid. I have known Howard my whole life and there is no amount of work that could keep him from a bloody holiday – no bank meeting that couldn't be attended by Paul in his absence, no tax matter that the accountant can't handle. So why didn't he want to come on holiday? There's something going on with you two and I want to know what.'

Rae looked at her, weighing how much to burden her sister-in-law with and how much she wanted to keep to herself, thinking of the old adage that had served her well in the past: *least said, soonest mended . . .* She took another slug of champagne. 'I guess you could say we've been going through a bit of a rocky patch.'

'No shit, Sherlock! What else is news? Don't tell me the *Titanic* didn't make it?' Dolly placed her hand at her throat in mock horror.

'Has it been that obvious?'

Dolly looked wide-eyed out over the beach. 'What do you think? It's been weird since your party. You have gone to ground, not answering your phone, and he is like a cat on hot bricks, nervy. You think the family doesn't notice the atmosphere in your house that you can cut with a knife? Or the way you and Howard act with this new politeness, as if you were strangers?'

We are *strangers now. I don't feel like I know him.*

'Have you had a row?' Dolly pushed.

'Kind of.'

'Kind of? That wasn't a "kind of" question – it's either a "yes" or a "no",' Dolly huffed.

'Yes,' Rae enunciated to satisfy her friend. 'We have had a row.'

'Is one of you in trouble? Gambling? Booze?' Dolly asked with typical directness.

Rae gave a wry laugh, thinking that either of these things might be easier to deal with. 'No, nothing like that. I don't want to talk about it.'

'Fun fact: I am not that person who when the shit is hitting the fan and her sister-in-law/best-friend says "I don't want to talk about it" will say "Oh, okay then" and not mention it again!'

'Fun fact: I already knew that. You are so bloody nosy,' Rae retaliated.

'Scrub out "nosy" and replace with "caring"! Jesus, I mean even Hannah said to me—'

'Hannah spoke to you about it?' Rae felt her heart race, a combination of out-and-out jealousy and the fact that she had wanted nothing more than to keep the worry from her daughter's door. Rae felt more than a little hurt that her girl had not felt able to speak to her directly.

'Don't look like that! You should be happy that Hannah has me to speak to! It's kids who don't have anyone to talk to who take drugs, streak at festivals and go trekking in some bloody godforsaken jungle and then come home with face tattoos and an STD – when all they want is someone to take them by the hand and tell them everything is going to be all right.'

Rae laughed, in spite of the topic. 'Firstly, I don't think Hannah is the type to streak or go trekking; and secondly, she knows that I will, whenever required, take her hand and tell her everything is going to be all right.' She spoke with quiet indignation, taking Dolly's comments as a slight on her parenting that she would not allow. It hurt.

'Yes, but saying it and meaning it are two different things – and she didn't speak to you, did she? She spoke to me.' Dolly tapped her bottle.

'What exactly did she say to you?' Rae bit her lip, waiting to hear second-hand what was troubling her girl.

'She said there was something going on and that you and Howard were being weird. I told her you *were* bloody weird and she said, "Weirder than usual."'

Rae felt her mouth lift in a smile despite her best efforts.

'I pushed her, of course, and she said you were spending a lot of time in your room and she thought her dad might be sleeping in the spare room, as she saw his dressing gown hanging over the door; and she said that you'd been quiet, as if you were hiding.'

'I guess she's right. Maybe I was,' Rae softly admitted.

Dolly joined her hands and took a breath. 'You haven't been yourself for a few weeks and I thought maybe it was because you were worried about the kids being away and Hannah struggling a bit.'

'That's right.'

'Are you menopausal?'

'Probably.'

Her friend stared at her across the table. 'How long have I known you?'

'A thousand years.'

'Yes, a thousand years – and it still amazes me that you think you can give me vague answers that sound rehearsed and not think I won't know it's bullshit!'

'What do you want me to say to you, Dolly?' Rae rubbed her temples, hoping this mild ache that had sprung wasn't going to develop into a headache.

Dolly shrugged. 'Er . . . I don't know. The truth?'

Rae looked out over the beach and wondered if she was destined to feel trapped no matter where she was. 'The truth is, it is complicated and all I can say is that we are trying to work things out.'

'"Trying to work things out" sounds serious.' Dolly had lost her undertone of humour. She sat up straight.

Rae's lip trembled. 'Can we please not let it spoil the first day of our trip?' She felt her tears pool, as happened with embarrassing regularity.

'Of course.' Dolly reached for her drink. 'But I want you to know that, firstly, I am only letting it drop because I don't want you to get upset in public and, secondly, I am here if and when you want to talk to me, properly talk. You might be my sister-in-law but you are also my friend, my best friend. Plus you and Howard are my favourite people on the planet, after Vinnie, my child, my parents, my cat, the man who cleans my windows, Nick and Nora who I only met earlier today and whatever the name was of the barman who gave me champagne.'

'Got it. And thank you.'

'I do love you, even though you failed your O levels and could never properly smoke a cigarette. Sogging up the filter: ugh!'

'I love you too.' Rae smiled at her friend over the rim of her champagne bottle, this time hiding the pulse of sadness in her chest at how things might be changing; trying to quell the pain she felt at not being able to speak the words and seek the solace she so desperately craved from the woman she loved.

'Ah, here we are!'

They both turned to see Nick and Nora approaching. Nick had swapped his khaki trousers for short shorts. His socks and sandals, however, remained in place.

'If you are waiting for drinks,' he boomed, 'you might be in for quite a wait; this bar is only operational in the afternoon and evening, but the one in the main hotel is open right now.'

Dolly lifted her champagne bottle. 'We're good thanks. Always carry our own.'

Nick looked at Nora with a look of distaste.

'We have to.' Dolly pointed at Rae and raised an invisible glass to her mouth a couple of times, the universal sign for 'boozer' – enough to make Rae choke on her bubbles.

◆ ◆ ◆

It was in the lull before dinner. The two women had unpacked their clothes and it was hard to believe they had only arrived at the Blue Lodge earlier that day.

Dolly was on the phone to Vinnie, sitting on her bed. 'It's lovely, Vin. Paradise! Beautiful beach and a great hotel. Bloody hot! . . . Yes, yes, phone Howard and tell him we are safe and we are settled. I can't say we are happy, as Rae still has a face like thunder – and I am only saying that because I know she is listening from the lounge.'

'I am not listening!' Rae called from the sofa.

'No, no, I already asked her and she just said they were having a rocky patch, but I'll keep digging.'

'For God's sake, do you have to be so blatant?' Rae yelled. Her anxiety flared at the fact that the couple were probing the subject she was desperate to contain. Their guessing and interfering felt a lot like ripping off a scab.

'Thought you weren't listening – now who's nosy?'

Rae buried her face in a cushion.

'Vinnie sends you his love!'

Rae signalled thumbs-up.

Dolly ended her phone call and held up the hotel brochure as she stood in her bra and pants at the open wardrobe door. 'What does "resort casual" mean?'

'I'm not sure. Do you want me to nip down to the restaurant and see what other people are wearing?'

'No, let's wing it. If we get it wrong it'll give Nick and Nora something to talk about.'

With a piano player tinkling out a tune in the centre of the intimate dining room, couples and well-dressed families swanned in. There was the excited burble of any good restaurant, but the backdrop of the Caribbean Sea made it extraordinary.

Dolly and Rae took a table by the window. Rae was relieved to see that her choice of a cotton maxi-dress and Dolly's linen tunic with white cropped trousers were indeed appropriate resort casual wear. Dolly picked up the menu card and studied it.

'Chicken, fish or vegetarian lasagne?'

'Chicken.'

Dolly beckoned the waiter.

'Good evening; welcome to the Blue Lodge restaurant. Have you made your decision?' he asked, with a fixed smile.

Dolly nodded. 'Two chicken, please. And a bottle of whatever white you've got that's cold and decent.'

'Certainly, madam.' The waiter gave a small bow of his head and walked briskly away.

'I feel like we've been here a week.' Dolly yawned.

'Me too. And I know you and Vinnie have our best interests at heart – I know you love us – but please let me sort my head out, Dolly. That's the point of me being here: to try to think straight.' Rae again rubbed at her temples where a tension headache threatened.

'Okay!' Dolly held up her palms. 'But you and Howard, you are more than any other couple. You are my family and you are a huge part of the business; our lives are interlocked. And I can only help you fix things or help sort your head if you let me in.'

Rae looked out towards the water and wished at that moment that they were not so interlocked. The idea of telling Dolly what had happened left her feeling a little overwhelmed. She had always known the two siblings were close and she had learned to navigate the waters of that closeness over the years, selective about what and how she shared regarding certain aspects of their lives. Howard had of course always put Rae first, taken her part, but there were nonetheless times when she felt unable to fully express her wrath at her husband when talking to Dolly; and she couldn't ask advice on anything of a delicate nature, like sex – not when it was Dolly's brother she was having sex with.

What a bloody mess, Howard. What a bloody mess . . .

'Two chicken.' The waiter bent forward with a plate in each hand.

'Actually, just one chicken.' Dolly patted the table in front of her and looked across at Rae. 'I think you'll find *I* am very brave and am happy to say it like it is. My friend, on the other hand, is keeping it all bottled up, a bit shady . . .'

Rae tried to laugh but bit her lip, fighting the desire to cry.

It might have been the chicken, as Dolly suggested. It might have been too much wine on top of champagne in the heat, or – as several of the guests they passed on the path back their room agreed – jet lag. Either way, Dolly was all of a wobble. Rae held her arm as her friend leaned heavily on her and they made their way back to their apartment. Dolly kicked off her slingbacks and fell face down on to the bed.

'I feel terrible. Sick and like I'm hungover. I don't want to be poorly, not on my holiday!'

'Don't worry. We have two whole weeks to enjoy all of it – one night getting settled won't hurt. I'll sit here and keep an eye on you. Go to sleep. When you wake up you'll feel better.'

'Don't sit and watch me! Not on your first night. I feel bad. Go walking, get some sea air, play whist with Nick and Nora . . .' Dolly slurred, as she closed her eyes and gave in to the slumber. Rae shook her head; the last thing she wanted to do was venture out into the labyrinth of corridors and walkways by herself.

After half an hour of sitting on the bed watching Dolly snore and listening to the whir of the air conditioning, she changed her mind. Rae walked into the bathroom and appraised the middle-aged woman looking back at her. It still surprised, how time had so altered her shape, eroding bits of her, like the sea-smoothed rocks on the shelf in the bar, yet sending unexpected bumps and pouches to spring up in other places. She tried not to think of Karina, with her skinny hips and pert bottom. She wondered how and when sex had become less important to her, to them as a couple. Was that the problem, the reason they had drifted apart? She thought of her own parents and one particular night.

She had been only five years of age when she stood with her heart beating too fast and a cold clammy feeling on her skin. With the nightmare still fresh in her mind, she loitered in the doorway, watching. As was often the case, the only thing that was going to help her get back to sleep was a drink of water and some reassurance from her mum. But there she stood, confused. It was an odd thing. Instead of her mum and dad lying side by side, as was the norm – with her mum on the right and her dad on the left, her mum in her nightie and her dad with his head tipped back on the soft pillow, snoring – she found something quite different. She couldn't figure out what was going on. The alarm clock tick-ticked by the side of the bed, as it always did, but what she saw in the middle of the bed was a large mound, like a whale under the covers, one big lumpy, shifting bump instead of two smaller still ones.

She took a tentative step forward and placed her little hand on the brass foot of the bed, about to call out or tap the lump when she heard her mum making a strange low sound. It was quite a sad noise, a bit like the sound Prince, the neighbour's dog, made when she took his ball and hid it behind her back, but then the noise got louder and sounded a bit more like a little laugh. Her dad was breathing in a funny way and she felt her fear rising. Something was going on; she didn't know what, but she knew it was nothing good. She was torn between going to call for her sister, Debbie-Jo, who hated to be woken up, or calling out. She chose the latter.

'Mummy!' she shouted.

Her mum screamed. Loudly.

Her dad said, 'Shit!' and suddenly they were back to being side by side on the mattress. With much relief she noticed that the whale-like lump had disappeared.

'Rae-Valentine! What on earth are you doing?' Her mum was still shouting; Rae wasn't sure why, as she was standing only a little way from her and she hadn't done anything wrong. Her heart beat even faster nonetheless.

'I . . . I had a bad dream.'

She felt her lip tremble, not only at the memory of her nightmare, which still lingered on the edge of her consciousness, but because her mum, usually so placid, had shrieked at her for no apparent reason.

'Oh. Oh, honey, was it the tunnel one again?' Her mum sat up in the bed, calmer now, as she ran her fingers through her hair and fastened the top two buttons at the neck of her nightie.

Rae nodded: yes, the tunnel dream again; the one where no matter where she ran, she'd face another dark corridor and she knew that however how far she went, or however many turns she took, she would always, always be stuck, underground. Like a mole.

'What's happening?' Debbie-Jo, arriving a little late to the party, jumped up and down on the spot, no doubt excited by the possible drama. 'Did you see a mouse?' she yelled.

Rae-Valentine shook her head, wondering if she should mention that she might have seen a whale.

'Are we being burgulated?' Debbie-Jo came up with the scenario and immediately started screaming. She shoved her fingers in her hair, just as she had seen those in peril do in the movies. 'Help! Help us! Save us!' she shrieked, loudly.

Maureen jumped out of the bed. 'For goodness sake, Debbie-Jo, will you calm down! We are not being burgled and there is no mouse! Rae-Valentine had a bad dream, that's all.'

'Oh.' Debbie-Jo stopped screaming and sneered at her sister with a narrowed gaze, removing her fingers from her hair and letting her shoulders slope with something close to disappointment as she headed back to bed.

Rae-Valentine stood with her back against the open door, wondering what on earth had just happened. Bad dreams, the whale, burgulations and a mouse! It was all a bit much for her five-year-old brain to cope with, especially at this hour of the night.

Her mum smiled at her. 'Tell you what, sweetheart, you go hop back into bed and I'll be right with you. I'll go and get you a glass of water and I'll sit with you until you get back to sleep, how about that?'

''Kay.' Rae had stared at her dad, who was making out he was asleep. She could tell he was only pretending by his fast breathing, the way his hands were gripped uncomfortably over the top of his off-white vest and the fact that his eyes were too tightly squished shut. Rae tiptoed barefoot across the landing and back to her little bedroom, where her teddies were lined up in order of size along the back of her chest of drawers, and the curtains, which her nan had made, were the same pink floral fabric as her duvet cover. She preferred to sleep with a slight gap in the curtains so that at the right time of year, on cloudless nights, the moonlight could find its way in and lie across her room in a cool silver slice that fascinated her. These were for her the most magical nights, when the moon, the *actual* moon, was up her wall and across her carpet. She would stare at it, making wish after wish after wish . . .

Hopping into bed, she pulled the cover up to her chin and waited for her mum, who when she arrived placed the glass of water on the night stand and sat gently on the floor by the side of her bed before smoothing the hair from her face.

'You mustn't let bad dreams scare you, sweetheart. They are just dreams, like smoke. And just like smoke, if you wave your hand they will all disappear and you can choose a different dream.'

Rae nodded, trying to remember this for next time.

Her mum coughed to clear her throat. 'How . . . how long were you standing in our room, little one?'

'Not long,' she whispered.

'Right.' Her mum bit her lip and looked up towards the corner of the room, as she did sometimes when she was thinking. 'It's just that Daddy was helping me find something I had lost down my side of the mattress.' She coughed again.

'What was it?' Rae asked in her small voice, interested in case she might be able to locate the item and win praise – and if she curried favour over Debbie-Jo in the process then that was just a bonus.

'What was what?' her mum asked, distractedly.

'What was the thing Daddy was helping you find down your side of the mattress?'

'My passport,' her mum stated with confidence. 'He was helping me find my passport.'

Rae stared at the reddening plume on her mum's neck and wondered why she might need to locate her passport in the middle of the night when to her knowledge there were no trips planned.

'Are we going to Boulogne?'

'Boulogne?' Her mum seemed to have lost the thread.

'Yes! Is that why you need your passport?' Rae felt excitement flare in her tummy.

'No. We are not going to Boulogne. I need it for another matter.'

Rae didn't know what that meant. Something in her mum's manner told her not to question it further, but it struck her as odd. She might have been only five, but she wasn't stupid . . .

Rae felt a nostalgic burst of affection for her parents and their inti-macy, still in love even now. Straightening her frock, she draped her pale-pink fringed shawl over her shoulders and over her bust, securing it with a china rose on a gold pin that had belonged to her nan. She thought of her parents, who had made a whale shape under the cov-ers and who still held hands as they watched television of an evening, side by side on the sofa in their dotage. A lump rose in her throat. Rae shuddered at the thought that, in no more than a blink of any eye, it would be her who, like her mum, sported deep wrinkles and grey hair and had a creak to her bones if she knelt for too long. The difference was she was no longer sure that Howard would be by her side. It was a strange thing, how she felt exactly the same at forty-three as she had at twenty-five; it was only mirrors like these, her increasing forgetfulness and the fact that she had grown-up kids that reminded her of just how many decades had passed.

Dolly hadn't moved and was snoring louder than ever. Rae swal-lowed her nerves and dug deep to find courage. She grabbed the room key and her book, thinking she might find a secluded spot out on the deck at Max's to read, hopefully without the presence of Nick and Nora. Quietly she closed the door on her friend, who was dead to the world, wishing she had that long piece of string to tie to the door handle after all, or a slack handful of breadcrumbs.

This was not how she had anticipated her first night on this island paradise and it made her smile, thinking of Dolly, the party animal of her youth, who with her backcombed hair and impressive bosom was always the first on the dance floor and the last to leave, dancing wildly with a cigarette held above her head.

The other residents of the Blue Lodge seemed friendly, smil-ing or offering 'Goodnight' as they passed her. She ran her thumb over the gold band on the third finger of her left hand and felt the bloom of loneliness in her chest. She had never been alone in a foreign country, not from that first day trip to Boulogne to her last holiday with Howard. She took a deep breath and ventured on, knowing this was the time to be brave.

Walking out on to the soft sand felt a lot like coming up for air. The warm breeze fanned her face and sent a shiver of joy through her bones. She slipped off her leather sandals and held them in her fingers, walking slowly along the seashore littered with shells whose iridescent beauty was picked out by the moonlight.

With the solid tread of the beach beneath her feet, the sound of the foaming waves, the smell of the salt-tinged night air all around and the most incredible canopy of stars hanging in the Yale-blue sky, Rae felt thoughtful. She liked the half-light, figuring she could blend into the background, hide in plain sight.

She found a spot and sat down on the sand, with her shawl about her shoulders and her book on her lap. It felt good to be in summer clothes and even better to be in the warm air, which even at this time of night warmed her muscles. She looked out into the vast space of the ocean and let the wind lift her hair, liking the feeling very much. It reminded her of the honeymoon she and Howard had taken: three days in Barcelona, strolling Las Ramblas to watch the street performers; stopping along the seafront to eat spiced prawn paella washed down with rich red Spanish wine. They would then rush back to their hotel room to spend the evening entwined on the crisp white linen sheets. It had been a magical time. And after three days in the city, they hired a convertible and at their leisure made their way along the coast before taking a ferry to Ibiza, where their honeymoon villa awaited on the east side of the island.

Rae remembered standing on the ferry with Howard behind her, his hands around her waist as the stars shone overhead. 'I've got a wife,' he had whispered in her ear.

'You have.' She felt him kiss her neck.

'And not just any wife; the most amazing wife in the world.'

'You know, Howard, we've only been married five days; you might want to reserve judgement.' She giggled.

He twisted her around and held her close, his fingers holding her face close to his. 'I don't need to reserve judgement. You are perfect.'

'Don't know about that.' She felt her face colour.

'Perfect for me,' he clarified.

Rae had looked up at his handsome face, his dark skin, blue eyes and confident manner, and felt a bubble of joy rising. This was what it felt like to be part of the Latimer tribe. This was what it felt like to live like a rock star – and she liked it. She liked it very much.

'When did I stop being perfect for you, Howard?' she whispered now into the night air, as the wind whipped her words from her mouth and carried them far out to sea. She didn't want to feel this melancholy. It felt like a disservice to this most magical of settings. Her sob came without warning; her nose ran and tears seeped down her throat and sprang from her eyes. She hid her face in her hands and cried quietly, trying to catch her breath and wishing the pain in her heart would ease. With the end of her shawl she wiped her eyes and mopped her tears and carried on crying until her breath stuttered into a normal rhythm and her nose and throat cleared.

'I don't know what's happening to me,' she mouthed. 'I don't know what's happened. I liked it before. I liked being half of us. I miss it. I miss you.'

Rae pulled up her legs and tucked her skirt beneath them, resting her arms and head on her knees, alone on the beach. She screwed her eyes shut and rocked gently on the sandy incline. 'I don't know what I am supposed to do. I don't know how I am supposed to be,' she whispered.

Rae had over the years played out various scenarios in her mind, wondering how they would cope with illness or, God forbid, if anything happened to the kids, but even in her most maudlin of imaginings she could not have foreseen an event that saw her and Howard so fractured, separated, lost to each other with no obvious way back.

It needed so much more than a long piece of string or a trail of breadcrumbs.

'Ah! My unofficial first customer of the day! Where is your shy friend?'

The man's voice cut through her thoughts. She whipped around, swiping at her tears, embarrassed. It took a second or two for her to place the young guy who had been behind the bar earlier.

'Oh, she's not feeling too well. I think it's just a bit of jet lag and possibly too much wine; I don't know.' She swallowed, feeling her confidence evaporate as it often did when she spoke to a stranger, doubt lingering with a sour aftertaste coating every word, as if what she had to say would be of no interest.

'Well, you can't sit here all on your own! Come and have a drink at Max's.' He held her gaze. 'I've just been collecting glasses; you'd be amazed how far they travel.' He held up a tray laden with plastic cocktail glasses.

'I'm amazed at how far I've travelled. It feels like one minute I was in dreary London and the next I am here!' She felt a little giddy; maybe that too was jet lag.

'London, eh?'

'Yep.'

'Well, I mix a mean pina colada if you like?'

Rae wrinkled her nose. 'I don't drink pina colada. Bit too sweet.'

'There are plenty of other drinks. Come on, I'm heading there now.' He pointed over his shoulder.

She looked at him standing there with his tray full of glasses, watching her and waiting. Slowly she stood and brushed the sand from her dress.

'Forgive me. I can't remember your name?'

'Antonio.' He smiled.

'Antonio,' she repeated. 'Where do you come from?' She couldn't quite place his accent.

'Lisboa, Portugal. Do you know it?'

Rae shook her head. 'No. I've never been.'

'It's a beautiful city. But this is a good life for me for here.'

She looked out over the beach. 'I can see why; it's beautiful.' She fell into step. 'By the way . . .' She swallowed. 'My name is—'

'Rae-Valentine.' He finished the sentence. 'I know. I have remembered you all day.'

She opened her mouth to respond but instead let out a loud burst of laughter.

'You are kidding me! That's funny!' She closed her eyes and shook her head at the young man, who was of course playing a part – but no matter: it still sent a flush of unexpected joy into her forty-three-year-old gut.

'I am not kidding you.' He sounded almost hurt.

Rae looked down and made sure her shawl was securely fastened over her chest, fiddling with the dainty china rose on the gold pin. What she experienced felt a lot like being shoved or shaken. This single compliment, flattery in its purest form and no doubt much rehearsed, filled her with excitement and also a flutter of nerves at the idea that she might be doing something that was not quite above board, illicit. Which was of course ridiculous; she was going to have a drink in a public bar – being shown the way by a young barman who had remembered her all day . . .

What a line!

As soon as she stepped into the softly lit Max's bar, Antonio looked at her face, which she knew bore the residue of tears.

'You are crying.'

'I'm not now, but I was.' She looked down, trying to wrestle with the blush that bloomed on her face.

'Why are you crying? Has something bad happened or are you just sad?'

'Both, actually.' She took a stool at the bar and looked around, happy to see the place was quite empty. She wiped her face and took a deep breath.

'Are you missing your family?'

'My kids, yes, always.'

'I think people can feel a little lost when they first arrive here and have time to think. I know lots of people who at home look after everyone else – it's their purpose; it validates their place in the family – and they think coming here will be a wonderful break, but actually they feel a little anxious, like having time off from a demanding job. They are worried that if everyone at home or at work copes without them, what does that say about how much they are needed? I get it. It takes a few days of Caribbean living for you to get into it.'

Rae wondered if this could be true of her.

Antonio deposited his tray and rushed around to stand in front of the array of jewel-coloured bottles, behind the white distressed bar top with blue uplighters that seemed to lift it from the floor.

'What would you like to drink?'

'I don't know.' She stared at the shiny bottles lined up on a glass shelf and struggled with what might be appropriate for a woman alone on the first night of her holiday.

'You like sweet, bitter, sharp, fruity?'

She shrugged and looked at her book, wondering when it would be polite to grab it and make her exit.

'Ah ha!' He clicked his fingers. 'I know what to make you.' He worked at speed, grabbing glass bottles and small vials of syrup, sloshing measures into a shaker, along with crushed ice and a generous squeeze of lime, which he mixed and poured with flair into a tall glass, finished off with a paper straw and a sliver of apple perched on the side of the pale-green concoction.

'Taste.' He pushed it towards her.

Rae tucked her hair behind her ears and sipped the cocktail. It was lovely – sharp, fruity, cold and slightly metallic with citrus and the soft warmth of rum against the back of her throat.

'That's actually very nice, thank you. What's it called?'

'It's called a "Cheer Up, Rae-Valentine".'

'Wow!' She shook her head and giggled; this guy was good.

SIX

Rae woke with a start. Not only did she not in the very first instance know where she was, but Dolly was standing over her, peering inches from her face.

'Jesus, Dolly! What are you doing?' She pushed her friend away and sat up, trying to slow her racing heartbeat.

'I am trying to make you wake up because I have been awake since six and I am bored and hungry. And I've tried humming, slamming my phone on the table; I even flushed the loo, twice. Nothing, nada. You were sparko.'

Rae watched as her friend huffed and puffed, agitated, in the small space between the beds, as if caged.

'You are honestly worse than a child.'

'You are honestly worse than a *chi-ald*!' Dolly mimicked in an affected childlike voice, which only proved the point.

Rae laughed loudly. 'God! I can see I am not going to get any peace until I give in and get up.' She flung back the coverlet and rubbed her face. 'Give me five minutes to shower and I'll be good to go.' She yawned. 'Are you feeling better? You certainly look it. I think I preferred you dazed and unconscious.'

'Oh, I'm fine; think the tiredness just caught up with me.'

'Tiredness? Dolly, you slept for the entire plane journey!'

'What time did you get in last night?' Dolly asked casually, changing the subject.

'Oh, not late. Eleven – something like that.' She felt the bloom of colour on her cheeks as she rummaged for her washbag.

'What did you get up to?'

'I didn't get up to anything. Just a bit of a stroll on the beach and then I sat with my book in Max's, the bar we found.' She was aware of the half-truth that left a taste on her lips. She had definitely had her book with her at the bar, but she hadn't actually opened it.

'Was cutie there?'

'Cutie?'

'Yes! How could you not remember him? The young Oliver Reed lookalike – the Spanish guy with the eyes and the secret stash of champagne mini-bottles that he gave us, unofficially?'

He's not Spanish; he's Portuguese. The youngest of four and he is the only one unmarried. His mother, a widow, is a teacher. Her name is Liliana. He has strayed from his faith and studied architecture at university before feeling the pull of wanderlust and jumping on a ship that brought him here to the Caribbean . . .

'Oh, yes, I did see him.' *And then I thought about him, in the way you do when someone has been kind; a diversion, as I followed the heart-string that ties me to my life in London and my family, all the way back to this room . . .*

'I think he fancied me,' Dolly announced, sitting on the bed and using floss on her front teeth. 'In fact I'm sure of it.' She ran her tongue around her gum. 'Do you think he gives away champagne out of hours to any old person? Uh-uh.'

'I am sure you are right.' Rae laughed and slipped into the shower.

◆ ◆ ◆

The two took up their now-favourite spot at the table by the window and spent a minute or two looking out at the early morning sun on the water. It was a glorious day. The sky was like a painting; barely a cloud spoiled the brilliant clear blue.

'Paradise, eh?' Dolly speared a piece of sausage and dipped it in ketchup before devouring it. 'Imagine waking up in a place like this every day. Do you think people get used to it or bored of it, or do you think they still look at it with wonder, like us?'

'I don't know.' Rae considered. 'I hope they are still in awe of it, but I guess you get used to anything, don't you? I know people come into our street, tourists mainly, and they take pictures of the Georgian crescent and the lampposts. I don't take photos or marvel at it in the same way, but I do appreciate it. Maybe it's like that?'

'Maybe. I guess the main difference is no one in your street is walking around in a bikini and sarong with a palm tree within grabbing distance.'

'No, but Mrs Williams does do her recycling in her nightie with a London plane tree within reach.'

'Good for her.' Dolly cut another chunk of sausage and dipped.

Rae selected a large chunk of melon from her bowl. 'So, what's the plan today?'

'We pack our beach bag, find a spot, sit on the sand, soak up the sun, have a break for lunch – I quite fancy the salad buffet with something barbecued.'

'God, I love how we are discussing lunch while we eat our breakfast. We are turning into our parents.'

'Please don't say that! Mum literally pulls back the cover as she wakes, turns to Dad and says, "I thought I'd do a nice piece of haddock, Arturo, with some chips and peas. For tea." And he is like, "Lovely." I have heard her, Rae, planning supper before they have so much as ingested a cornflake.'

Rae laughed, not only at the truth of this, but at her friend's marvellous mimicry of her in-laws.

It only encouraged Dolly. "'Oh, remind me to get the mince out of the freezer, Arturo; I'm going to make a shepherd's pie. Or do you fancy roast chicken? No, forget that: I need to use up the sausages in the fridge. Bangers and mash with onion gravy? Or how about omelette and salad with chips to share?'"

Rae wheezed her laughter. 'Stop it!'

'But it's true!' Dolly laughed.

'I know it's true, but I don't want to laugh this much this early on – we need to pace ourselves; save some for later.'

Their laughter subsided and the two ate their breakfast, always nicer when prepared by someone else and without the morning rush.

'I can't stand the idea of becoming like that, where my life is reduced to menus and doctors' appointments and aches and pains,' said Dolly with a wry smile.

Rae chuckled. 'I know what you are thinking – that we are already on that path.'

'I was thinking that.' Dolly reached over and gave her friend a gentle squeeze on the arm. 'But it's not true. Mid-forties is now the equivalent of mid-twenties when we were young.'

'I don't believe that; I think we just hope it's true because we are in our mid-forties.'

'Possibly.' Dolly took a large swig of her coffee. 'I know I want to put off becoming that old person for as long as possible. I think we all feel like it to a degree and it's something you only really think about as you hurtle towards your fifties, when you suddenly realise that you have more years behind you than ahead. It's a bit scary. I'm thinking of overhauling my diet,' she announced, as she loaded up her fork with bacon and fried bread.

Rae laughed again. Dolly had been promising this since they were teenagers.

'I don't think it's the actual getting old, Dolly, that bothers me so much as what being old will be like. I don't want to reach old age and wonder what the hell I did with my life.'

'You have a very full life, an important life!'

Rae smiled at her, suppressing her desire to scream, *I thought so too! I have always put everyone else first and look where that has got me!* Instead, she kept her tone calm, remembering that her friend was operating without full sight of the facts. 'Bless you for saying that. I think if I knew I was going to be eighty and sprightly then I'd be fine. That's what I fear the most. My mum and dad are, you know, like yours. My dad used to be so busy and when he worked at BT he had a kind of purpose. He ran his life like clockwork and as soon as he retired he switched his purpose and his attention to tablet reminders and bin day . . .'

She heard her dad's voice, thinking about their phone call right before she left. *Have a lovely time, sweetheart. Be careful. Don't let that Dolly get you into trouble. Don't drink water that isn't bottled and don't worry about souvenirs for everyone; a nice postcard will suffice.* It amused her that he still pictured Dolly as the overconfident teen who might lead her astray. Which on occasion, she did.

'Howard has as much energy now as he did when he was a kid – that'll keep you young.'

'Yep.' She turned her attention to her fruit salad.

'He is a good man, Rae.'

Rae looked at her friend and saw Howard sitting on the end of their bed with tears dripping on to the carpet. 'Christ, I don't need you to keep recommending him to me! It's not like our first date, when you more or less sold him to me right up until I met him.' *Oh, my brother is so great with kids! He cooks a mean steak! He is loyal . . .* 'We've been married for twenty-five long years – hence this holiday!' She spoke with uncharacteristic sharpness.

Clearly startled, Dolly laid her fork on her plate. 'Where the bloody hell did that come from?'

'I don't know! I don't know!' Rae took a sip of her orange juice. It seemed she wasn't as good as suppressing her anger as she thought. 'I'm sorry, Dolly. I shouldn't snap at you.'

'Oh, I don't give a shit. Snap away. But I am worried about you. I want to know what's going on inside your head.' Dolly rapped her knuckles on the tabletop.

'I don't think it's one thing. I think it's lots of things.'

'Well, that's a good start,' Dolly offered sincerely. 'And luckily we have lots of time.'

There was a pause while Rae considered how and what to say that might satisfy her friend. 'I guess, if I—'

'Hello there, you two!'

Rae turned towards the high-pitched voice that had interrupted her and smiled at Nora and Nick, who approached with heavily laden breakfast trays. Nick was still wearing his very short shorts.

'Mind if we join you?' he asked, as he edged the chair from the table with his sandalled foot, making their response quite redundant.

'Oh! Yes, of course.' Rae could feel the burn of Dolly's hot stare.

'So, how are we settling in?' Nick asked, as he placed his gargantuan feast on the tabletop and took a seat next to Dolly.

'Very well, thank you,' Rae offered politely, watching as Dolly pushed her plate away, indicating that for her, breakfast was over.

'There was a wonderful singer in the bar down the beach last night, sounded just like a young Michael Bolton.' Nora beamed.

'Oh, I'm sorry we missed that.' Rae downed her juice. 'Dolly had a bit of an early night and I went wandering alone, then read my book in the bar.' She felt the brush of guilt against her skin as she gave more detail that wasn't strictly true. What bothered her more than the untruth was the fact she felt the need to lie at all – all because of the slick-tongued, well-practised chat-up lines of the kid behind the bar. It really was as ridiculous as she made it sound. 'We were just leaving, actually.' She patted her mouth with the linen napkin and placed it on her plate. 'We wanted to stand on the pier and watch the big boat, a cruise going past; apparently it's quite a sight. I've never been on one but my sister has. She used to work on one. A dancer.'

Both she and her sister-in-law heard the symphonic gasp from the knowledgeable duo.

'What's wrong?' Dolly asked.

Nick leaned forward with a theatrical, conspiratorial twist and spoke in low tones. 'Don't let any cruise-goer ever hear you call such a vessel a "boat". She's not a boat. She's a *ship*.' He nodded and took up a teaspoon, with which he then chopped the top off his boiled egg.

Dolly linked her arm through Rae's and the two giggled their way back to the cabin. 'Ship? Boat?' Dolly squealed. 'I'd rather be on a bloody pedalo or a lilo alone in the ocean than have to do anything with that couple. God, Rae, kill me now! Please don't ever tell them again that they can join us!'

'I'm sorry. I was on the spot and I didn't know what else to say! I didn't want to offend them. And might I remind you that it was you who made friends with them on the bus.'

Dolly turned to her sharply with her hand to her mouth. 'Bus? Bus? Do not ever let any coach-goer hear you say "bus"! She was a coach of fine proportions, with air conditioning and drinks holders. Bus? What were you thinking?'

Rae, as ever the perfect audience, laughed loudly.

Dolly fished for their room key in her pocket. 'You are too nice. Leave it to me. I have no problem in offending them at all.'

Dolly was in the bathroom when the call came in to Rae's mobile. She saw the display and remembered when the sight of his name popping up on her screen would give a lift to the most ordinary of moments throughout the day. But not now. Now it elicited something quite different. She thought it had been hard to speak to him face to face, but this disconnection across the miles made it even harder somehow; she didn't know how to start. It was alien for her to feel nervous at the prospect of talking to her husband.

'Howard.' She spoke softly, cradling the phone to her face and walking to the far end of the terrace, in the hope that Dolly would not or could not hear their conversation. She wanted to capture any potentially harmful or revealing words like a collector with a butterfly net and keep them hidden.

'Vinnie said you'd . . . you'd arrived okay,' he began, clearly a little nervous.

'Yes, and the place is lovely.'

'Good, good.'

There was a pause for a second longer than was comfortable.

'Have you heard from the kids?' She pictured Hannah and George and hoped they were doing okay. No matter that they were young adults; she felt the same level of anxiety as when they were no more than toddlers and away from her at nursery.

'George is at Ruby's mum's and Hannah called to see if you'd got away okay. She's fine; said she was going out with a girl on her course for supper – Niamh, I think her name was.'

'Good! That's good.' Rae smiled; she wanted her child to be sociable. 'Hope she has a nice time.'

'She did ask why I didn't go on holiday with you.'

'I already told her it was because of your work commitments.'

'I know, but she's a clever girl . . .' He let this trail.

'Let's hope not too clever, eh?' She regretted the jibe the moment the words had left her mouth, wishing the butterfly net had captured this phrase and kept it from escaping. 'I just meant—'

'I know what you meant and trust me, it's one of the things that keeps me awake in the early hours: what you suggested – that maybe someone knows, someone who might tell people, who might tell my kids.'

Rae felt torn, part of her wanting him to have this worry, thinking it would be no bad thing for him to feel the full force of the damage he had caused, to lose face; but the other part of her, a bigger part, wanting nothing to reach her kids that might cause them a moment of unrest. They were what mattered the most.

'Well, all we can do is deal with whatever crops up.'

'I'm glad you said "we".' He swallowed.

'Because no matter what happens, they are our kids and always will be.'

'Yes.' She heard the unmistakable crackle of emotion in his voice. 'Feels like you have been gone for an age,' he managed.

'I know. It does for me too.'

'So.' He coughed. 'So, where are your thoughts at?'

Rae sighed, and suddenly her words flowed and telling him how she felt seemed easier. 'All over the place. I feel just as hurt, just as angry. I can't stop the showreel playing in my head of the night you told me – and then, straight after, I have the most terrible images of you and Karina.'

'Please stop saying her name.'

Rae gave a dry laugh. 'Okay.' Again the pause while she recalibrated. 'The ridiculous thing is that I know it happened but I can't believe it did, if that makes any sense. And everything I want to say is just a repeat, a cliché – How could you? Why did you? Where did you? – and so I don't see the point in going around in circles.'

'It might be that we need to; like being stuck in a maze, where all we can do is keep walking around and around until we find a way out.'

'Maybe.' She gave this a little credence. 'I keep thinking about the fact that you are my husband, Howard, and I am your wife and my body has been yours since the day I met you and yours was mine and that was one of the most important things, possibly the most important, and now that's gone.'

'It's not gone! It's not.'

'It is.' She silenced him. 'You gave your body to someone else, *put* your body in someone else, someone you didn't even love . . .' Rae shook her head and let her tears fall, tiny waterfalls of sadness that were the accompaniment to this unpalatable truth. 'And that is the crux of it right there. It doesn't matter how sorry you are.'

'I am. I am so sorry!' He was crying openly now.

She was disturbed by his distress, but more occupied in trying to contain her own. 'And it doesn't matter what we suggest or how we plan. If I can't get past that one fact, if I can't figure out how to move forward, then I truly think we are done.' As much as it hurt, it felt strangely empowering to utter these words, take control.

'Please don't say that, Rae; please don't even think it! It's early days and it's still so raw and we need to give it time.'

'Where the bloody hell are you?' Dolly yelled from the bathroom, making her way out to the terrace.

'Dolly's here,' Rae explained to Howard, indicating that their conversation would now have to return to the more general.

'Is that my lovely brother?'

Rae gave a single nod.

'Tell him we are running up huge bills on his credit card and I've got me a toy boy, young Spanish Antonio who gives me champagne!'

'I am guessing you heard most of that?' Rae swallowed her sadness, speaking a little louder now.

'I did.' He took a deep breath. 'I know you can't talk right now, but can I call you tomorrow or in a couple of days?'

'Of course.' She watched Dolly make her way in her towel towards the bedroom.

'I love you, Rae.'

'Bye, Howard.'

She sat with the phone in her palm, watching the waves break out at sea, as fishermen steered their boats into the water, tourists walked the shoreline and parasols were put up on the sand. The bay was coming to life, as she and Dolly prepared for the day ahead. It was the first time in her whole life that her husband had ended a call by saying 'I love you' and she had not replied in kind.

It felt like a marker in the sand.

◆　◆　◆

Rae sat with a full tummy.

'Fancy a drink?' she asked casually, pushing her plate away after supper, which they had eaten with one eye on the door in case Nick and Nora Knowitall spotted them. She wanted to go to Max's bar, to take in the view and sink into the soft sofas.

'Yes,' Dolly yawned. 'But no late night for me. I am exhausted.'

'You are always exhausted. It's like being on holiday with Rip Van Winkle. You even slept on the beach today!'

'I can't help it. I think it's because I just keep going at home. I never sit down; there's always something that needs doing. If I'm not running around for Vinnie I've got Lyall on the phone in search of food, money or clean laundry – you know what it's like.'

Rae nodded; she did.

'And I've come here and it's like someone has pulled my plug out! I have to be on high alert at home, waiting for the next job, but here I can really unwind and it's as if my body is on catch-up. At least yours are away at uni.'

'I wish they weren't.' Rae tapped the table. 'Well, that's not true. I mean, of course I want them to live their lives, make their dreams come true, yada yada, but I hate how quiet the house is sometimes without them.'

She thought about when Hannah and George were younger and she and Howard used to relish every second they were out at a birthday party or off on an adventure with their grandparents. Often, she would pull her husband on to the sofa and they would reconnect, doze, chat or kiss, enjoying each precious moment of grown-up time. The sound of the kids at the door would be met with a combination of joy and the smallest flicker of disappointment that she was back on duty. Not that she would ever admit this. Not to anyone. And yet now, even though she had a full life, a busy life, she missed their noise, their presence, even their mess. She had always thought that when they left home, the time together would be a reward for Howard and her, but now everything felt pointless.

'This is when you and Howard get your privacy back, though, right?'

'Yes, in theory.'

Dolly shifted in her chair and rested her elbows on the table. Her expression was sober and Rae knew that whatever was coming next was not without prior planning. She felt discomfort gripping her.

'Are you happy, Rae?'

The question caught her a little off-guard and she took a moment to respond. 'I'm having a lovely time—'

'Not here.' Dolly cut her off with a shake of her head. 'That's not what I mean and I think you know it. Generally. At home, with your everyday life, are you happy?'

'Happy?' Rae tried to recall the characteristics that made her happy and saw huge holes that used to be filled with joy.

'Yes! It's not a trick question. Are you happy?' Dolly pushed.

Rae was embarrassed by the sudden swell of tears at the back of her throat. 'Sometimes. I don't believe everyone is happy all of the time.'

'That's probably true; but which are you the most, happier or sadder?'

'I don't know.' *Numb. Hurt. Confused. I am all of these things right now.*

'Well, I have this theory that if you were happier, that would be the thing that popped out of your mouth fairly easily. And I also think that my question would not make you cry.'

'I guess.' She kept her head low and her voice was soft, embarrassed.

'It was something you said earlier about getting old and wondering what the hell you did with your life. That must mean you are thinking about it now.'

Rae took her time in responding, wiping her eyes. 'I just sometimes think about the ideas I had. You know, I always wanted to be a chef, to properly learn to cook. But then I had the kids . . .'

'You are a wonderful cook! You don't need lessons!'

Rae smiled; that wasn't quite what she'd meant.

Dolly spoke warmly. 'You have a lot to be happy about. You have a lovely life and you have great kids and Howard adores you.'

'Does he?' Rae looked up through lashes still dotted with tears.

'Of course he does! Look at us here in this beautiful place, all because he wanted to make you happy!'

Or wanted to ease his guilt . . . Rae swallowed the thought as she reached for a tissue from her pocket and blew her nose. 'I feel like everything is falling apart, Dolly.'

'Look, I love you and I am here for you, but this wishy-washy making me guess what the fuck is going on is wearing a bit thin. I can't help you if I don't know what's happened and I'm not stupid: if it's not addiction and it's not illness . . . ?'

'No.' Rae shook her head.

'Then it must be that one of you has discovered something about the other that has put a crack in your relationship.'

'Bit more than a crack. It's ripped us in half, broken us.' With the words came a small feeling of relief, as if her stomach had untwisted a little.

'Okay.' Dolly ran her hand over her face. 'So it's either something illegal or it's sex.'

Rae let her head hang down again. 'I don't know how to talk to you about it, Dolly. I want to and at the same time I really don't.' She felt as she had when she was sixteen: nervous of saying the wrong thing to the girl she wanted so much to like her.

'Come on.' Dolly spoke softly. 'Let's go and sit on the beach where it's a little darker and we don't have to look at each other and we can talk.'

Rae stood with a tremble to her limbs, knowing she was about to break Howard's confidence, but also that it was inevitable.

The two women walked arm in arm along the walkways, heading towards the beach. The pink-tinged dusk pulled its pretty shade on the day. Rae looked at the lights strung between the trees and around the garden, which gave the place a magical quality.

'Do you remember when we first met and I was trying to get us to go to Majorca so I could sleep with Vinnie?'

'Of course I do,' Rae laughed. 'Poor bloke never stood a chance.'

'He was lucky I chose him!' Dolly countered.

Rae could only admire, as she always had, her friend's level of self-confidence.

'Let's go to Max's and get wine to take to the beach,' Dolly suggested.

'Sure.'

They headed in the direction of the bar and were soon stepping up on to the deck.

'Good evening, Antonio!' Dolly called out. Several patrons looked up from the sofas and tables where they sat quietly. 'We are in need of wine.'

'Coming right up.' He smiled at Rae, who looked away as he reached into the fridge for a cooled bottle.

Dolly winked at her. 'Told you, he fancies me.'

The two took their plastic wine glasses of chilled plonk and walked out into the semi-darkness, stepping barefoot on the powder-soft sand that was now cool underfoot.

Rae sat down and felt Dolly settle by her side.

'I feel like I breathe differently here.' Dolly took a sip. 'It's like I can take great big lungfuls of air and it blows out the cobwebs. Do you know what I mean?'

'I absolutely do.' Rae closed her eyes and breathed in through her nose, knowing she would never tire of the salt-tinged air that felt like imbibing health; her breaths were bigger and filled her with what she could only describe as a lightness to her being. It felt a lot like freedom.

'So,' Dolly began, with an air of practicality usually reserved for work situations and problem solving, 'the way I see it, we have always managed to keep our friendship and the fact that we are related separate, right?'

'Yes, to a degree.'

'I mean, you can't come and tell me what arseholes your in-laws are, because they are my mum and dad, and I can't tell you that my nephew is a shit, because he's your son.'

'You think George is a shit?' Rae's voice went up an octave and her heart thudded as she extended her tiger-mummy claws.

'No! Of course I don't. I am speaking hypothetically – although there was one Christmas when he was about seven when he ate all the jelly beans from Lyall's jelly-bean dispenser. Ruined the whole bloody thing.'

'Really?'

'Look, we are getting sidetracked. I love your kids, and you know this.'

Appeased, Rae settled back in the sand. She did know this, thinking of Lyall, George and Hannah in their matching jerseys hand-knitted by Mitzy and the cute photos of the three of them throughout the years. *Family . . .*

'The thing is, Rae, we need to preserve each part of how we are connected. Our friendship is as important to me as the fact that you are my sister-in-law. And believe it or not I don't want to pry, but I do want to help.'

'I know.' Rae leaned over and briefly rested her head on Dolly's shoulder. Dolly kissed her forehead.

'Rather than try to make you give me the details, which I under-stand might be painful, how about I ask you questions and you can answer "yes" or "no" and then after we have established the facts, if – and I mean only if – you want, we can talk about it some more?'

'Okay.' Rae sat up straight and took a slug of wine, hoping it might ease what came next.

'I am guessing that what is upsetting you is something Howard has done?'

'Yes.' Her voice was steady.

'And it's something you have found out about quite recently?'

'Yes.' She again saw him sitting on the end of the bed and immedi-ately pictured him kissing Karina, whose name now apparently offended him. She heard Dolly sigh.

'And . . .' Her friend paused. 'Would I be right in guessing it's some-thing to do with someone who used to work for the Latimer chain?'

Rae twisted in the sand to face her friend. Her mouth went dry and she felt her breath quicken. 'You . . . you *know*?' She couldn't disguise her shock; her heart seemed to boom in her chest.

'Oh, mate, oh my God!' Dolly sighed and ran her palm over her face. 'Oh no! No, no, no!'

'Dolly! I can't believe you would know and not tell me! What the hell is going on? Does everyone know? Is everyone laughing at me? Jesus Christ! You must have found it amusing, me skirting around the issue, not wanting to say anything negative about your brother, and all the bloody time you *knew*?' She felt as if her body were sinking into the sand under the weight of betrayal; it physically hurt. 'I feel sick! I actually feel bloody sick!' Her chest heaved.

'It wasn't like that! It wasn't. I heard something from Vinnie who heard it from Paul and I dismissed it and said it was gossip and I went nuts, as you can imagine – I didn't want it getting back to you. I refused to believe it. I was bloody furious! And I was upset.'

'You were upset?' Rae laughed but felt hurt, her lip trembling at the thought that her best friend knew, and that she had been the topic of conversation. 'I knew it couldn't be kept a secret,' she admitted. 'Shit!'

'Don't think it was traded as something salacious. It wasn't like that, not at all. I didn't believe it! I laughed, Rae; I laughed out loud and I told them it was nuts! Vinnie said Paul had had to make the girl a cash payment and that's how he found out. He was in bits, the poor love; he came home in a state and I had to force it out of him. He said he didn't know what to do or whether to tell me, and I swear when he did I laughed it off, because . . .' Dolly's voice broke away. 'Because I didn't want to think that Howard had done that to you and I didn't want to think of the hurt it would cause you. And I have put it out of my head, literally not thought about it, because it was too crazy, too ludicrous! You two are so solid, strong . . . but then as soon as I noticed the way you were behaving I suspected you knew. I couldn't say anything in case you didn't, plus I hoped – prayed – that it would all blow over without us having to have this conversation.'

'It's gone too far for that.' Rae again felt the familiar slide of tears over her cheeks.

'Oh my darling.' Dolly reached out and held Rae's hand. 'Is it true? Are you absolutely sure?'

Rae admired the note of hope in her friend's tone that her brother's immaculate status might yet be confirmed. She nodded. 'Howard told me himself. He told me everything.'

Dolly started to cry, rubbing at her eyes and nose and making a loud, wailing noise. 'I can't believe it, Rae! And I am sorry. I was in the shittiest position. I am in the shittiest position.'

'I can imagine,' Rae offered conciliatorily, feeling a mixture of anger that her best friend had not raised it, but also, fairly, trying to imagine what she'd have done if the boot had been on the other foot. Would she have brought it to Dolly's door? Probably not. *Least said, soonest mended . . .*

For a brief moment the reality of her broken heart and fractured marriage sat squarely in her mind. She could feel the enormity of their conversation wrap itself around her and Dolly like a tie that bound. It was constricting. And she knew that if it was this tough discussing what had happened, it would be nigh on impossible to end her marriage without causing tremors through the world in which they all lived; it would open up ravines into which some relationships would fall. She glanced at her best friend, who sat on the sand, crying noisily, and wondered if theirs would be one of them. The thought was more than she could stand.

'I hate it, Rae. I bloody hate it!'

'I hate it too. I don't know what to do.' It felt good to admit this; she hoped doing so was the route to getting the guidance and advice she so desperately craved.

Dolly removed her hand from Rae's and wiped her eyes.

'I feel so ashamed, Dolly,' Rae whispered, looking out towards the horizon, where a thin line of ink joined the ocean to the sky.

'Ashamed? Why should you feel ashamed?' Her friend twisted in the sand to face her.

Rae continued to gaze out over the sea. 'I feel ashamed that I was not enough for him and I feel ashamed that things have got so broken. I just wanted us to make it through to the end like my mum and dad, like your parents and you and Vinnie . . .'

'Christ, Rae, none of us knows what's around the corner; and you and Howard can make it – of course you can! Don't you dare feel ashamed, not when it's down to some dozy tart coming along and working her magic with an agenda.'

'I don't think like that. Not really,' Rae answered truthfully. 'As I said to Howard, I didn't make my vows with some girl at the restaurant. I made them with him. He owed me more; she owed me nothing.'

'But I have seen them, Rae. These girls can be so devious.'

'No, Dolly, I really don't blame her, no matter what her intentions. I dislike her, and I wouldn't want to see her. I'm angry at her and at the thought of how dismissive she has been of all I hold dear; I know I could never do that to another woman. But blame? I blame him. I blame Howard.'

I am never going to get married, Mum . . . Marriage is outdated, restrictive and pointless . . .

'You need to figure out how to get over this, Rae. You need to look ahead and not dwell on that one bump in the road.'

'It's not a bump; it's a bloody boulder, a mountain! And I wish I *could* just forget it. I wish it was as simple as booking a holiday, but I see them together all the time and I hear him telling me about it all the time! I don't think I will ever forget it. I was kneeling on the floor, concerned for his welfare, worried that he might be poorly because he looked so pale, and then when he spoke he launched daggers that have struck my heart! And I don't know why you think it's me that needs to try to get things back on track – how does *that* work? Why is *that* the case? *He* broke things, *he* messed up and yet *I* have to try to fix them?' She shook her head. 'And the thing is, Dolly, I don't know if I can and I don't know if I want to.'

'Of course you do! Of course you do!' Dolly's tone was proof that her loyalties were split and her advice skewed. 'I can't stand it, Rae! I can't stand the thought of you two not making it through; it kills me!' Dolly placed her hand on her heart.

'I can't talk about it any more. Not tonight.' In truth Rae thought this safer than risking expanding the conversation, which might reveal her utter disappointment that her friend's concern appeared to be how the situation might affect Dolly, and not its impact on Rae – that, seemingly, her wants and needs were again being sidelined.

The two sat quietly in the moonlight with the sound of waves breaking on the shore. Rae looked across and felt a quiver of dismay that Dolly had been in receipt of this knowledge all along, her big secret. She felt the stays of trust being severed under the weight of this fact. She did understand Dolly's dilemma, but ultimately she had put the interests of the family, of her brother, first and not the welfare of her best friend. It left Rae feeling conflicted. As she looked out to sea she realised that the course of their friendship had changed tonight; maybe only by a few degrees, but changed nonetheless. And it might just be that those few degrees were enough to send them wildly off course over time.

Dolly stood. 'I'm going to bed. I want to call Vinnie and I just want to shut down and go to sleep.'

Rae nodded; she understood. In the past when something had upset her, all she'd wanted was to hear reassurance from the one source that could calm her thoughts and ease her worries: Howard.

'Are you coming?' Dolly asked.

'No, I think I'll just sit here for a bit longer, if that's okay?'

Dolly nodded. 'Sure. I'll take the glasses back.' She held their empty wine glasses in her hand. 'You know, Rae, this has been the worst conversation we have ever had, one of the hardest.' She sniffed at the tears that just kept on coming.

Rae pictured Dolly and Vinnie pitching up at the hospital when she lost the baby, remembered her friend sitting in the chair crying and holding her hand. She shook her head, unable to handle that memory tonight.

'What I need to do, Rae, is lie in bed and replay it all and think about what I say to you next and how I can help you, how I can help both of you. I love you both, I really do.'

Rae stood and took her best friend in her arms. 'I know you do and I love you too.'

Twenty minutes later, with the shiver of cool night air around her, Rae stood and made her way along the beach to Max's. She took a stool at the bar and noticed Nick and Nora sitting on the sofa in the corner and gave a small wave.

Antonio was busy, mixing a drink with his long dark curly hair tucked behind his ears, concentrating. She felt a flicker of awkwardness that he hadn't noticed her. He stood with his broad back turned.

Rae decided to give it a minute or two and then leave; she silently cursed herself for not having brought her book with her, the one time she truly needed the prop.

Suddenly Antonio spun around and placed a tall glass on the counter with the obligatory paper straw and slice of apple. 'Here we go, madam: one Cheer Up, Rae-Valentine.'

'Thank you.' She smiled weakly as she pulled the pale green drink towards her. 'And tonight I need it more than ever.'

She realised that at some level, she wanted to be in the company of this young charmer with the well-rehearsed lines whose flattery had hovered at the back of her mind all day. It was a cheap balm of sorts that made her feel a little less bruised.

'You are sad again?'

She gave a dry laugh. 'Not again, no. I am still sad; it hasn't gone away, not really – not for a while now – and now my sadness is getting complicated and I am getting more and more confused.' She pictured Dolly's reaction. 'And I really don't know why I am telling you this.' She shook her head at the absurdity and sighed, wondering if being here and chatting to this stranger was really better than being alone with her thoughts.

'This your first time in Antigua?'

'Yes.' She nodded, grateful for the change in topic as the sharp, icy-cold drink slipped down her throat. 'We have a family business, restaurants, and it's hard work for everyone; the hours are long – but I don't need to tell you that.' She looked up to see him nodding. 'Holidays tend to be short and in Europe, a couple of days here and there. Not that I am moaning. We have a lovely life. A lovely life.' *Or at least I thought we did . . .*

Antonio laughed out loud.

'Why are you laughing?'

He bit his lip, hesitant. 'It always amazes me how many people sit here and tell me they are not lonely, how they *like* being alone, that they wouldn't change a thing! Or how very happy they are; and I find it odd that the ones who say they are happiest – the ones who skip and laugh the loudest, who play at being happy – they are usually the people who cry alone on the beach.'

'People like me,' she whispered.

'Just like you.'

'I suppose you have a point. The happiest among us probably don't spend time sitting alone at your bar.'

'That's often the case. Sometimes they are happiest when they are with me, of course.' He grinned.

'Oh my word.' She rolled her eyes at his nerve.

'So what does make you happy?' he asked, wiping glasses fresh out of the dishwasher and placing them on the shelf at the back of the bar.

Rae laughed out loud; he was the second person to ask that question this evening. 'Being with my kids, or not even being with them; it makes me happy to know they are happy.'

'So not being with your husband?' He avoided eye contact.

'Well, he used to make me happy, and who knows?' She took a sip. 'We have had a lot of happy years, but we seem to have hit a bump in the road, a boulder . . . a mountain, in fact, and again, I have no idea why I am telling you this.' She shook her head and closed her mouth.

'So you have said, but it's the job of the barman – did you not know that? People mistakenly think we are here to give you drinks but that's only part of the job; the other part is being a listening ear and giving good advice.'

Rae laughed.

'So what would you do or where would you go if you could go anywhere? Do anything?'

Rae thought of the conversation she and Howard had had in the bath so long ago, and felt the familiar pang of loss. 'I would go put on my little red knapsack and I would go island-hopping.' She pictured the confident girl with the red knapsack, taking great big strides like a giant from one island to the other, tanned, her ponytail swinging and looking like she could take on the world . . .

'Here in the Caribbean?' he asked.

'No.' She shook her head. 'Greece, actually. I would like to see all the Greek islands. And then, when I had hopped enough, I would enrol on a course and train to be a chef.' She smiled at the idea of fulfilling the dream she had harboured for so long, picturing herself in chef whites, busy as part of a brigade in a hot basement kitchen – the kind her parents warned her about.

'So why don't you?'

'Life is not that straightforward, I'm afraid. There are things I need to do and places I need to be . . .' She let this hang, picturing the street on which she lived, where she put out the rubbish and swept the pavement, nodded to her neighbours and tried to befriend the lonely lady who had a dog called Fifi. A small life, really, but one that was comfortable no doubt, if a little . . . unfulfilling. A life lived without the confidence to seek out change. Rae pictured herself on a hamster wheel, running continually without looking up or stepping off.

'What about you, Antonio? What would you like to do?'

'I'm genuinely happy now, here. Free. But I guess this life might wear thin one day and when that happens I will go back to Portugal, the Douro valley to be precise. It's beautiful. I will buy a plot of land and build a house and grow vines, make wine, get married, make babies. Simple.'

'I used to think it was simple.'

'But now?' Antonio coaxed.

'I am a bit lost. I thought I had a steady life, a stable life. I was satisfied, pretty much like you describe, with wine and babies and our lovely home, but now I don't know. I can't see a clear way ahead, and that's a scary thought at my age – and not the adventure it might feel like at yours.'

'Maybe. But you are far from old.'

She huffed. 'I feel it. I thought I filled my husband's head and heart the way he did mine.' She stopped talking; this was more information than she should be giving.

'Well,' Antonio stared at her. 'I do not know him, but if he has let you slip from his mind he must be a crazy man!' He tapped his temple.

'I think maybe we got complacent. I don't know.' Again she hushed up and looked around the bar.

'In case you were wondering, you did not slip from my mind. I remembered you all day today as well,' he whispered.

'That's very sweet of you to say, but a little embarrassing too!' Rae shook her head, hoping her joviality might help make light of the words that danced in her mind.

'Please don't dismiss it, Rae-Valentine. I *want* you to think about it.' He held her eye.

'Goodness me, Antonio, I am old enough to be your mother.' She tutted, but still looked up at him through her eyelashes in the coquettish manner she used to practise in the mirror when courting Howard, back when she was seventeen and Antonio would have been . . . one. Urgh! That was too revolting to think about.

'Not old enough to be my mother, not at all, and attraction is not about age or numbers. It's about two souls who, for whatever reason, become stitched together in time, even if only for a brief while.'

She laughed loudly. 'How brief a while? Like, two weeks? Ten days?' she asked with mock sincerity.

'You can laugh, Rae-Valentine, but there is something going on.' He pointed to his chest and then hers and back to his. 'A connection.'

She instinctively placed her hand on her chest and felt her skin shiver at the prospect of a beautiful young man like Antonio seeing her in her bra and panties with all her lumps, bumps, stretch marks, scars and pouches. She could never do it. Never. Not only would she be far too embarrassed even if she were single, but also the thought of doing something to Howard that might cause him a tenth of the pain he had caused her was absolutely inconceivable. This was followed instantly by a jolt of remorse that she was even thinking these things.

'You are very slick, Antonio. Do women actually fall for the things you say?'

'I only speak the truth.' He held her gaze for a fraction of a second longer than was comfortable.

'So, I have to ask, how often do you find your soul stitched together in time with another? I should imagine it happens quite frequently while working here in paradise, with potent Cheer Up cocktails flying around.' She took another sip.

'Yes.' He nodded, his mouth twitching into the semblance of a smile. 'Quite frequently.'

'Weekly?' she pushed.

'No! Not weekly!' he answered sternly, his smile fading. 'Occasionally.'

'And what happens at the end of the vacation – do you miraculously become unstitched and go about your normal business?'

'Sometimes, yes.' He grinned. 'Sometimes the end of the vacation can't come fast enough. But sometimes . . .' He placed the cloth on the bar top and braced his arms on the surface; his words when they came were softly delivered. 'Sometimes I feel a new emptiness and a kind of deeper loneliness because she has gone and I know she will think of me from time to time, but I cannot have her. She will be back to her office, back to her home, and I am still here.'

'Poor you, stuck here in paradise waiting for the next soul to get stitched to . . .' Rae blinked at him. 'I suspect – and correct me if I am speaking out of turn, as I don't know you at all, and this is largely the cocktail and wine talking – but I suspect that one of the reasons you want those women is because you can't have them.'

'Maybe.' He opened two beers and pushed the cold bottles across the bar towards a man in linen shorts and shirt, who took them to his companion sitting on the steps that led down to the beach. 'Maybe not. Sometimes, but not always.' He held her gaze again and she felt more than a little self-conscious, as if this confident eye contact was crossing a line.

'I do hope you know that I am not one of those women, Antonio.'

'None of the women I meet are "those women".' Again he managed to make it sound sincere.

'No, I am being serious; you need to listen to me.' She banged her palm flat on the surface of the bar. 'I have already told you: I am someone's wife and I am someone's mum and I don't go around letting my soul get stitched to anyone else's. Even if he makes the best cocktails this side of Watford and knows how to make me feel ten years younger.'

He laughed. 'You think I am a trickster? I am not. I will never ever tell you a lie. And you think you have a choice? You think you can control when fate is going to deal you a hand that you have to play? Of course not; you can't control it.'

'Okay.' She looked up towards the heavens. 'Maybe I can't control it, but I don't have to listen to it and I certainly don't have to act on it.' It was the closest she could come to admitting to the frisson of excitement that ran though her veins, a lovely, lovely diversion for a woman feeling so very low.

Antonio leaned forward and spoke so quietly that she had to bend her head to hear him. 'But you *are* listening to it, Rae-Valentine, and you *are* acting on it because we are talking about it.'

She stood and grabbed her bag and shawl. 'Goodnight, Antonio.'

'Goodnight, Rae-Valentine.' He smiled at her.

Treading quietly with caution she let herself into the apartment, peeking in on Dolly, who lay still and silent, the absence of her snore suggesting she wasn't yet asleep. Rae made her way across the floor and slid open the glass door to the terrace, where the cicadas and the hum of tropical life greeted her on this slice of island paradise. She walked outside and sat on the lounger, where she could lie back looking up at the canopy of stars under the clear Caribbean sky.

'Stitched together in time!' she chuckled, covering her face with her shawl. Her laughter almost instantly turned to tears. It was a combination of too much alcohol and the memory again, crisp and uncensored, of Howard and Karina. Leaning forward, she cried quietly until, for the time being, she ran out of tears.

SEVEN

She and Dolly woke, showered and dressed with a new formality between them – nothing marked, nothing obvious; but knowing each other the way they did, even the smallest variation in behaviour was noticeable. They made their way along the corridor and across the main reception, their sandalled feet clip-clopping out a loud rhythm on the tiled floors that was usually muffled by their noisy chatter, laughter and observation. Their heart-to-heart the previous evening sat between like them an object made of glass, with both scared not only of its fragility but also of the consequences should they push it.

Rae had to admit that the wine-and-cocktail combination of the previous evening had washed away a little of the detail of their conversation, and the way Dolly burbled away quietly the moment they took their seats – talking about the weather and the gifts she wanted to buy Lyall and Vinnie, wondering whether they should take a bus or a taxi to Heritage Quay for shopping – suggested she was using chit-chat as a diversion to hide her own discomfort.

Breakfast was pleasant enough. It was day three of their holiday and they had fallen into a comfortable routine, choosing the same table to sit at and selecting the same items from the buffet.

'I could do with a day out of the sun today.' Dolly patted her rather crimson shoulders and chest where she had been a little neglectful with her sun cream.

'I think Heritage Quay is a good idea, spot of shopping. I want to pick up something for Hannah, George and Ruby. Lovely Ruby . . .' Rae smiled. 'She's a great girl. Good for George, I think; keeps him grounded.'

'Do you think they might go the distance? George seems keen.'

'I hope so.'

Dolly's question jogged her mind and seemingly sparked something in Dolly too. That's right, she remembered now. *You and Howard can make it – of course you can . . . You need to figure out how to get over this, Rae; you need to look ahead and not dwell on that one bump in the road . . .*

Dolly looked at her over the top of her coffee cup. 'I keep thinking of how upset you were last night and it feels awful.'

'Because it is awful.'

'Can I ask you a very strange question?' Dolly placed her cup in its saucer.

'Of course you can.' Rae laid her forearms on the table and sat forward.

'Would it be easier, better, do you think, if you didn't know about Howard? About what happened?'

Rae took a moment to steady her breathing and formulate her response. 'But I do know.'

'Yes.' Dolly paused. 'But the point I'm making is, for however long you didn't know . . .'

Weeks, mere weeks . . .

'Life carried on as normal; you and Howard were the same as you always were—'

'But we weren't – it was just that I was operating with half the facts, half the picture, and that makes me feel like such a mug, as if I don't count. I only thought everything was as it had always been.'

'I understand, but I have been awake half the night thinking and I was wondering whether maybe, just to get through it, to move on, you could pretend at some level, just until you heal properly?'

'It's not that simple, Dolly.' Rae felt an uncomfortable wave of dislike towards her friend. This request was so telling, placing Dolly firmly in her brother's corner, the suggestion made to allow him to save face – better they all pretend . . . 'He lied to me and he was unfaithful to me and it has changed things, changed the way I feel about him.'

'You thought he was perfect?' Dolly challenged.

Rae halted the first response in her mind: *pretty much* . . . 'Not perfect, no, but perfect for me. And straightforward. I thought he was honest.'

'God, one slip-up, Rae; one blot on a beautiful landscape. As I say, can't you just pretend? I think it might make it easier to heal.'

'One slip-up? Really? We are not talking about someone who forgot my birthday or picked up the wrong cheese! He has broken my trust. It's not a case of whether I can pretend things are okay, or how long I didn't know, or anything like that!' She took a breath. 'It's a case of whether I can carry on at all knowing what I do now, knowing he isn't the person I thought he was.'

'He is! He is, though, Rae. He adores you and he adores his kids! You can't give up on him! He loves you!' Dolly's passion sounded a lot like coercion.

'And as I said to him, saying that doesn't magically erase the mistake. It's indelible – it's stamped on my skin and on my heart.'

Dolly shielded her eyes and looked down, as if in prayer.

'Do you know how long it lasted?' she asked eventually.

'Two weeks, he says.'

'And you believe him?'

Rae considered this. 'I have no reason not to. Unless you know different?'

'No, not at all.' Dolly shook her head emphatically.

This assurance Rae met with no small sense of relief. 'I don't know why he would lie about it being two weeks or ten; it's irrelevant, really, in the grand scheme of things.'

'You can't throw a lifetime together away for a two-week mistake. I can't imagine what life would be like if you guys weren't a couple. And I am saying that as your friend and not just your sister-in-law. I would be saying the same to him if it was you who had done it.'

'But it wasn't me, was it?' Rae took a glug of her orange juice, frustration lacing her words. 'Can you imagine how you would feel if it was Vinnie?' She watched the twitch of an uncomfortable smile form on her friend's mouth. 'God, Dolly!' She leaned forward. 'That little smile; that thought that just went through your head – which I am guessing was something close to "Don't be so ridiculous! Vinnie would never do that to me! Vinnie and I are solid, unbreakable!" – that is *exactly* how I felt, word for word. That is the same thing I would have thought about Howard and I would have smiled in the same way. And I am so shocked, as you would be; it's unbelievable to me. No matter how many times I chase it around my brain.'

Dolly nodded and folded her arms across her chest. The silence felt like an impasse.

'When you said you wanted me to meet your brother, I said I was worried in case things didn't work out and it would make things weird between us.'

'Yes, you did.' Dolly held her gaze.

'I meant it then and I mean it now. And things do feel a little weird right now. I don't like it.'

'I can't help it.' Dolly spoke quietly.

'I know.'

'And I don't like it either, Rae.'

Rae tried to find the verbal balm that might help shake off the awkwardness. 'I guess we have to accept that inevitably we are both going to feel a little thrown, a little bruised, but it will pass, okay?'

Dolly threw her napkin on to her breakfast plate, her smile wide but a little askew, forced. 'Okay. Come on! Let's go out and start the day again; let's go shopping and enjoy the sun and try not to let things get weird or weirder. What do you say?'

'Let's do it.' Rae spoke gaily, wishing she could adjust her feelings, alter her mood, as easily as she could speak the words.

◆ ◆ ◆

Heritage Quay was busy. A vast cruise ship had docked and disgorged some of its seven thousand passengers on to the dock. They scattered like ants into the souvenir shops, cafes and the marketplace where artisan stalls sold their wares.

'Look, Rae, it's one of them big boats!'

They both laughed, shielding their eyes as they looked up at the ship that filled the immediate horizon. Its proportions were breathtaking, impressive and a little frightening. It sat like a sideways skyscraper, a huge building-like structure.

'I don't understand how it floats.' Dolly spoke for them both. 'I mean, it's the same principle as the little plastic tugs George and Lyall used to push around in the pool, but so vast, so heavy! I wouldn't trust it.'

'It's science, Dolly. And we don't know much about science.' Rae stared at the acres of shiny metal handrails that reflected the sun, and the immaculate white paintwork that shone.

'I don't think science was an option for us at our college, was it? Certainly not in our department; we were there for the typing.'

'Fucking nirvana,' Rae reminded her, remembering how easily she had capitulated when her parents told her cookery was not for her, wanting so badly to please them and heartily believing that they knew best. This followed by the usual pang of regret.

'Fucking nirvana,' Dolly confirmed, smiling at her mate.

Rae linked her arm through Dolly's and they strolled the quay with their closeness restored a little and some of the weirdness diluted. It felt good, and the relief was a reminder of how important their friendship was.

After sauntering from shop to shop and buying the kids T-shirts, leather bangles for Hannah and Ruby and a crocheted tablemat for each set of parents, the two, as recommended by their taxi driver, took a table on the first-floor terrace of Hemingways Caribbean Cafe. With relief they stepped out of the glare of the midday sun, stowing their shopping bags by the table under the green and white striped awning. A welcome breeze lifted the checked tablecloths and they had a perfect view of the comings and goings on Thames Street below.

'Phew! It's hot!' Dolly pushed her sunglasses on to her head and fanned herself with a menu.

'I gotta tell you, Dolly, it's not going to get any less hot in the next ten days or so. So feel free to stop telling me about the temperature. And in case you hadn't noticed, I am here with you, right in front of you – experiencing the same weather. I *know* it's hot!'

Dolly hit her friend on the arm with the menu. 'I see you are still taking those sarcasm pills the doctor prescribed. Have you upped your dosage?'

'I thought I was taking Make-Me-Extra-Boring pills?'

'You, my friend, are on a veritable cocktail of drugs!'

'What can I get for you today?' The young smiley waitress stood with pen and pad poised.

'I'll take the crab cakes and a fresh orange juice, and nothing for my friend – she is nil by mouth at the moment.'

'Please ignore her.' Rae laughed. 'I'll have the same.'

The food when it arrived was plentiful and tasty. Rae forked the salad into her mouth. 'It's weird, isn't it, how things can taste so different depending on where you eat them? Like, a bit of salad in the kitchen at home, grabbed on the run, can be nothing short of dull, but the same leaves and a bit of tomato, eaten here under this warm sun with all the time in the world to enjoy it . . .' She closed her eyes and savoured the flavour. 'I want to know more about ingredients. I mean, I can whip up a meal with very little, but I would love to really understand food.'

'You should write for the Latimers website; you are such a foodie!'

'I wouldn't know where to start.' Even the idea frightened her.

'You could start with a blog: "Tomatoes and lettuce and all the places I have eaten them . . ."'

'You're taking the mick.' Rae sighed and continued her lunch in silence. Dolly's comedic dismissal of something she held dear left her feeling more than a little deflated. It was another blow to the equilibrium they were trying to achieve in the wake of the previous evening's discussion.

Having devoured the delicious fare and now sipping iced coffee, Rae rotated her neck and enjoyed the warmth in her bones. There was something quite wonderful about the unhurried pace of this holiday life; it was seductive, and it had taken until now, her third day, to truly slip into the rhythm of it. She barely looked at her phone, just responding politely to the texts that came in from Howard and sending the kids messages of love with the odd amusing picture of her and their aunt holding a cocktail or standing in front of pale sugar-almond-coloured buildings that gave the island a fairy-tale quality.

'I was thinking about what you said earlier, about how I would feel if it was Vinnie.'

Rae looked at her friend. She had her attention.

Dolly took a while to form her words, the topic still prickly, distasteful, and Rae wasn't sure whether she was delighted or distraught that they were going back to it.

'And I have to admit I would be devastated, absolutely devastated, I can't deny it. But I like to think that I would forgive him, because I wouldn't want to put my kids through a break-up and wouldn't want the whole family to suffer, or to put everyone through something so hard. And I can't imagine that I would throw away all the years we have had together and all the lovely years ahead. I would try to move on.'

Rae listened to her words and felt a surge of disappointment. She had hoped that Dolly might provide a sounding board, or at least offer insight that might help Rae process what had happened. Instead her suggestion was a missive, wrapped around a rock and hurled at her. She felt the full force in her gut. 'But supposing the years ahead weren't lovely? Supposing they were years of living a half-life with the fallout from his actions clouding each day like a swirl of dust after something has collapsed? Choking you? What then?'

Rae felt a little breathless from the heartfelt verbal torrent that had rushed from deep inside her, and Dolly looked taken aback.

'I'd open the windows.'

'I can't even joke about it, Dolly.' It was a new sensation for Rae to find her sister-in-law's humour an irritating attempt at diversion and not in the least bit funny.

Dolly shook her head. 'I just don't know what to suggest. But I think you need to find a way to make it good for all of our sakes – the kids, my parents, everyone . . .'

'Really? So you think I need to turn a blind eye to make things more comfortable for you and for Arturo and Mitzy?' Rae was aware that her voice had once again gone up an octave, in anger that her needs appeared to be one of Dolly's last concerns. She expected more.

'No!' Dolly fired. 'That's not what I am saying. I think you should make it good for you and Howard – and as a consequence life carries on, unharmed, for everyone.' She sighed and rubbed her eyes. 'I can't imagine what it would be like if you guys split! Christmas, for example, birthdays, gatherings or, God forbid, if anything bad should happen, like a bereavement – that's when we need to stick together, family!'

'So you think to leave or ask him to leave would be selfish?' Rae asked steadily, feeling aggrieved that the onus was once again on her.

'No, I don't, but I think to stay or ask him to stay would be selfless.' Science-aware or not, her friend was clever.

'It sounds so easy, doesn't it, just kiss and make up. Throw a party, take a holiday. But it's not that simple. And the crazy thing is, Dolly, I was happy.' She leaned forward and banged the table with tears of anger and frustration pooling. 'I was happy! I thought I had it all. I didn't question anything; every day I went to bed feeling blessed. Like I had won a prize. Now I climb into bed feeling duped, foolish and bloody angry. And it was Howard who ripped the lid off, not me.'

'That will pass. It will fade.' Dolly swallowed and looked into her lap. Rae supposed she was unused to having to deal with outbursts like this from her friend, and felt the balance of power shift a little more.

'Will it? I don't know. The irony is that Howard is now unhappy and asking for forgiveness and saying the same things as you – that we need to make it work for the family, that it was a small slip-up and however else he justifies it – but the genie is out of the bottle and it's not going back in.' She took a breath and a mouthful of her iced coffee. Dolly blinked furiously, clearly uncomfortable. 'I am being made to feel like the baddie, the one who holds the key to future happiness; me, who hasn't done anything wrong except run around at everyone's beck and call! And let's forget the family for a minute – this is my marriage, my life; what about me? What about me, Dolly? What about making me happy again?'

'I think fixating on blame doesn't help anyone. It doesn't help you move on.' Dolly spoke with a tight mouth and Rae could feel the judgement coming off her in waves.

'I'm not fixating on it, but it's important. It's a fact. He messed up! And now if he doesn't like the consequences that's just too bad.'

'You don't mean that.'

Rae looked at her sister-in-law, whose expression was torn. She felt a jolt of sympathy for this woman whose very loyalty was being pulled in this terrible emotional tug of war. 'I guess one of the consequences is that it has made me stop and look back at my life. I felt like everything was moving so fast and it has since the day we married. We were always planning for and working towards the next thing, the next big Latimer project, and I was so happy to be a part of it, swept along, but it was all I could do to just hang on! Trying to keep up, as my life rushed by like I was watching out of a window of a train, and each scene, each event whizzed past so quickly that I could only feel the rush of it on my face but not truly *feel* the event, if that makes any sense.'

Dolly stared at her. Rae took this as her cue to continue. 'I have put the Latimers first, always.' She thought about Debbie-Jo, who she knew had struggled since giving up her dreams of the limelight, and of her parents, who were so glad to see her when she popped in on the odd occasion and who deserved more than a rushed cup of tea and to have their groceries delivered by the Tesco man. 'I have put Howard first, and I did so willingly, but this is how he has rewarded me.'

'But you *are* a Latimer.' Dolly spoke now with confidence. 'And you have had a good life. Howard has always taken care of his family—'

'You think that's a good trade-off?' She cut Dolly short, her tone a little pricklier than she had intended, drawn from a place that felt the sharp tip of disappointment that this woman, her best friend for all these years, thought she could be so easily satisfied. Did she not know her? 'The fact that he provided me with a spare bedroom and the odd bit of sparkly jewellery? Do you think that makes it okay for him to do what the hell he wants? You think that's my price? A Georgian house in Lawns Crescent? A pretty place to clean and wander in? It's a cage, a gilded cage, and no cage is big enough to contain all that I gave up on to become his wife!' Rae raised her voice and several patrons of Hemingways Cafe turned to gawp. She felt her insides cave with shame.

'What did you give up on exactly?'

Rae gasped. The question and its delivery felt like a punch. Dolly jutted her chin in defiance, challenging: Dolly, whom she had idolised since she was sixteen years of age. Rae thought she above anyone else would understand because she knew what made Rae tick, knew that she had always put herself second, third . . . This apparent dismissal, the questioning, was more than just a woman defending her beloved brother; they were the words of a woman who did not have Rae's back. It was unsupportive and it hurt. Rae felt a naked flicker of fear at the first stirring of awareness that it might not only be Howard that she stood to lose in the wake of the whole horrible episode.

She composed herself. 'Okay. Maybe it doesn't seem like much, but . . .' She struggled to find the words. 'I gave up on discovering myself. I used to think I might achieve great things, do stuff; become a chef! But instead I morphed into Howard's wife at eighteen and I got stuck. I am still stuck! And I only realised it when he held the mirror up, when he pulled the veil away from my eyes.'

Dolly rubbed her eyes. 'I think you need to be a bit less dramatic.'

'Is that what you think, really?' Rae appraised the woman sitting opposite her and realised with an ache in her chest that she had assumed the two of them would always be tight, joined by the moments that defined them – laughing as teens until they nearly peed on a bus, and holding each other's newborns with tears in their eyes. 'You think that having my marriage and my whole existence exposed as a sham is a bit dramatic?' She cursed the catch in her throat.

'That's not what I am saying, Rae, not at all.'

'Well, it sure sounds like it!' She grabbed her hat, sunglasses and bag and made her way down to the roadside, her cheeks aflame with embarrassment and something that felt very close to rage.

Dolly caught up and hailed a cab to take them back to the Blue Lodge. The two women sat as far apart as the narrow back seat would allow, comical in any other situation, each staring out the window in silence. This in no way matched the cacophony of words and reasoning flying around inside Rae's head as the row continued in her mind. It reminded her of the journey to the airport with Howard, the tense atmosphere and the passive-aggressive stance. It did nothing to help allay the thought that she might have exchanged vows with Howard but had in fact married the whole bloody family. They paid the driver and stood by the grand reception.

'I don't want to argue with you, Rae.'

'Well, sometimes that's how things get resolved,' she snapped.

'This doesn't feel like things getting resolved; it feels like you are too angry.'

'God, Dolly, I *am* angry! I am so bloody angry!' Her fingers balled into fists. 'I want you to get where I am coming from!' *Because you – you were supposed to be on my side. You are my best friend and I didn't truly believe that you might let me down, keep secrets, like your brother . . .*

'I do get where you are coming from, but I need to put both sides of the—'

'No, you don't, you don't! Sometimes you just need to forget you know Howard and be my friend. You say you can do that but you can't. And I'm not blaming you – it's just how it is, I get it.' Rae took a deep breath, not wanting to cover the same points here in the grounds of their hotel, where Nick and Nora were no doubt hiding behind a pot plant with their ear trumpets cocked ready to listen in. 'But in a funny way, considering I have been married to your brother for twenty-five years, I am only just now understanding that our friendship has boundaries. And this is all new because it's the first time these boundaries have been crossed.' *I feel hurt. I feel like an outsider. I feel like the girl in the corner . . .*

The two stood enveloped in an awkward silence until Dolly spoke. 'Are you coming up to the apartment?' she asked, pointing ahead.

'No. I'm going for a walk. I'll see you later.' Rae looked at the floor, keen to put distance between herself and her friend.

'I'll take your bags.' Dolly reached out and took the paper bags filled with gifts.

Rae put her hat on and walked steadily in the direction of the sea.

The beach was busier than she had seen it – hardly packed, but most of the sunloungers, positioned in neat twos under the raffia parasols, were either already taken by sun worshippers who lay prostrate with a slick of oil on their skin or festooned with the detritus of the experienced beachgoer: towels, books, sunglasses, beach bags; markers for those who had gone for a dip in the sea or to the restaurant to ensure no one encroached on what they considered to be their turf for the day.

With her head whirring at the latest instalment of the great Dolly showdown, Rae decided to walk along the shore, and with her wide-brimmed straw hat secured, she rolled up her linen trousers and popped her sandals in her large bag.

She had a feeling of sadness that was hard to shake and it was tinged with loneliness, because Rae knew that if she lost Howard and she lost Dolly, it would feel like the end of the world.

The sand was hot and a little painful underfoot, and with relief she reached the darker, damp sand where little holes fizzed with bubbles as the water retreated. She let the cool Caribbean Sea wash over her feet and lap her ankles, foaming as tiny waves broke, leaving a jagged reminder on the shore of their presence.

'Hey! Rae-Valentine!'

She looked up to see Antonio with an orange bucket in his hand, walking towards her. He strode with confidence through the shallow water, at ease in the sea and without the hesitancy that made her walk slowly, a city girl, wary of what her sole might encounter on the seabed and catching her breath when it came into contact with anything too sharp or too soft.

'Hi! What's in the bucket?' The interaction made her feel less conspicuous on this busy beach, and to talk to someone other than Dolly was just the distraction she needed.

'How do you feel about octopus?' He stopped a few feet short of her on the shore, waiting for her reaction.

'To eat?' She laughed.

'Well, possibly, but in this case they are my bait. And I've just hauled two up off the rocks under the dock.'

'Let me see!' She watched him stroll towards her in his shorts, his chest bare. He was extremely tanned and the tautness to his skin was the biggest indicator of youth. He was quite beautiful and she wished she was wearing a looser shirt to better disguise the slack tops of her arms and the slight bulge to her stomach, unsure why it mattered.

He held the bucket at an angle and showed her the bulbous, slimy-looking creatures that were curiously intertwined. Their skin was a mottled brown, white and purple, an almost marbled effect, with tentacles lying languidly up the sides of the pail, displaying perfect round white suckers that looked so uniformly spaced it was a miracle of nature.

'They are ugly little creatures.' She wrinkled her nose.

'You think? I find them beautiful, but then I have funny taste.' He grinned at her and she felt her blush spread.

'What do you catch with them – you said they were bait?' She took a step back and fixed her sunglasses on her nose, glad that they hid her eyes, still puffy no doubt from crying quietly in the taxi earlier as she tried desperately to hide her distress from Dolly.

'Black-fin tuna or whatever else takes a fancy. My friend JJ who works up at Sandals has a boat and we go out, take a few beers and try our luck. It reminds me of summers in Portugal when I was young.'

Younger . . . she silently corrected.

'Portugal is famous for its sardines. My brothers and my sister and I would go out with my grandfather in the summer and come back with boxes full, pulled straight from the sea, and we'd grill them on charcoal right there on the beach and eat them on fresh bread with blackened red peppers or my *mãe* would make caldeirada, kind of a fish stew and it's the best, the absolute best! Oh! Even talking about it now I can taste it! It tasted of the sea and of sunshine!' He laughed. His description was enough to make her mouth water as she imagined the blackened flesh of the fish, thinking she would pair it with a chilled white wine and a fat squeeze of lemon. 'Do you have things like that, foods that take you to a certain place and time, so that all you have to do is taste it or smell it and you are right there?' His enthusiasm was charming.

Rae thought about this. 'Not really. I mean I love cooking, I love food and I have had nice meals in nice places, but not in the way you describe. My childhood was lived in the suburbs and my mum used to sometimes make spaghetti Bolognese and serve it with a big smile on her face, as if it were an occasion. Perhaps it was; I don't really remember.' She felt a tightening in her throat as she thought about her parents and, wanting to hear their voices, planned to call them later.

'It's those little things in life that make life. That's what I think.'

Rae nodded. 'I think you are right, but sometimes you are so busy living life that you forget to take time for the little things. You forget to go fishing.'

'Not me.' He grinned and lifted the bucket.

'Well, you are lucky. You are confident and you are travelling, living the dream! God, I spent my childhood hiding, scared a stranger was going to talk to me, and then I spent my teens wishing I was like my big sister, who was really outgoing and fun. Everyone remembered Debbie-Jo, but me . . .' She swallowed the emotion that threatened. 'I married into a loud, glamorous family and that made me happy. It was wonderful.' She pictured herself on Howard's arm, strolling Las Ramblas and unable to wipe the smile from her face, feeling like she had the whole world in her hands. 'Before that I was just the girl in the corner, faded into the background, and it wasn't nice; no one wants to be like that, like furniture!'

He stared at her and spoke softly, with a sincerity to his words that moved her. 'You are not like that, not at all. There are fifty women staying here and I can't tell you the name or the slightest detail about any of them, but you . . .' For the briefest second she could see how easy it would be to allow her soul to be stitched to his, even if it were only for a fortnight. 'You stand out, you shine brightly. Yes, you are quietly spoken, but you have energy and kindness; you are many things, but you are not furniture.'

Rae hated the tears that came on cue. It was wearying. 'Well . . .' She swallowed. 'I thank you for saying that to me, Antonio.' She drew breath and sniffed, wiping her tears that slipped beneath the frame of her sunglasses. 'But I think people must regard you as a girl like that to lie to you, to betray you, because if you mattered to them that much – if you shone brightly, stood out, if you were the most important thing to them – they wouldn't do that, would they?'

'I guess not.' He held her eye and took a step towards her and lifted his hand, as if he was about to wipe away her tears. Suddenly he leaped backwards and shouted, 'Shit!'

Rae looked down and screamed as an octopus climbed out of the bucket and made its break for freedom.

'Shit!' he called again.

Rae shouted and ran back up the beach a little way, where she stood to watch the drama unfold. It was one thing to see the creature ensconced in a bucket, but quite another to have it slither near her feet. Antonio leaped forward into the water and tried to grab the wily cephalopod but it was too quick and seemed almost rocket propelled as it fired through the water. Antonio stumbled, misjudged his footing as he tried to balance the bucket in one hand and catch his escapee bait with the other. There was an almighty splash as he fell forward into the sea. The second octopus, sensing its opportunity, moved with alarming speed to join his mate. Two escapees on the run together. Antonio sat in the water laughing, his bucket empty, his shorts soaked through and his pride in tatters.

'Oh no!' Rae bent double, laughing hard. 'I wish I'd recorded that!'

'You think this is funny?' he called back to her before scrambling to his feet and filling the bucket with seawater. He lumbered out of the water with his wet hair clinging to his face and began chasing her along the shoreline.

Rae gripped her bag tightly and screamed at the prospect of a cold public soaking. She ran as quickly as she could, with her heart thudding in her chest, coming to an abrupt halt along the beach when she saw Dolly standing with her sunglasses in her hand and her mouth open, watching.

Antonio took his lead from Rae and stopped to catch his breath. Dolly glared at him. Rae watched as he emptied the bucket of seawater on to the hot sand and slowly made his way back along the beach, walking towards the wooden dock where octopus lurked.

'He . . . he lost his octopus,' Rae tried to explain.

'Is that right?' Dolly's tone was clipped, her mouth tight.

Rae looked around and could see several sun worshippers watching her from their vantage points. She felt embarrassment colour her neck and chest. 'Do you want to get a drink?'

Dolly gave a single nod in response and turned on her heel; Rae followed her up the beach and past the pool. She walked a few paces behind until they found themselves on a terrace in the main hotel, which was thankfully quiet except for a couple taking tea at a table in the corner. Rae sat on the wicker chair and pulled off her hat and glasses, raking her hair with her fingers.

'I spoke to Vinnie.' Dolly looked at the view rather than Rae's face.

'How is he?'

'Fine, said Howard was going over later and they were going on a jaunt together.'

Rae nodded. 'Good. That'll be nice.' She watched her friend's jaw muscles tense as she bit down, grinding her teeth. It reminded Rae of when she was young and had smashed her mum's vase with a ping-pong bat after being told not to use it inside the house, and was waiting for her dad to come home so they could both tell her off. This felt similar. It was agonising, waiting for the words that she knew had been formed and rehearsed in the last few minutes: weapons that Dolly would launch hoping they found their way to their intended target. Her.

Rae felt awash with shame, as if she had been caught out, exposed, and this gave her another unwelcome insight into the hierarchy of their relationship. How was Dolly in such a position of power?

She didn't have to wait too long for her dressing down. They ordered a pot of tea and a bottle of water, and as soon as the waiter had returned, placed their beverages on the table and left, Dolly leaned forward. With her eyes narrowed she spoke, firing a tiny glob of spittle that landed on the sugar bowl in the centre of the table.

'What the hell do you think you are playing at, Rae?'

'What do you mean?' Rae knew exactly what her sister-in-law meant, but wanted more time to think, compose herself. She disliked Dolly's accusatory tone, especially as she was not the one who had been unfaithful.

'You know what I mean. Jesus Christ! Flirting with Antonio, making a dick of yourself. Running up the beach and squealing like a banshee.'

Rae knew this was not the moment to point out the irony: that it was Dolly who spent her life speaking and screeching at a volume that would put any banshee to shame. She also disliked being told she was behaving inappropriately; always wary of how she was perceived, she found the thought of making a show of herself in public mortifying. She felt undermined. Small. And it didn't feel nice at all, especially as the accusation came from Dolly.

'Seriously, Rae, I am worried about you – it's like you are going off the rails! You wander about half the night, you hang out in that bloody bar. It's dangerous!'

'God, you make me sound like a ticking time bomb! I don't wander about half the night. I come up at eleven, rather than sit and watch you sleep. And I don't hang out in the bar. I, like everyone else in the resort, go for a drink. One drink!'

'Yes, but not everyone else in the resort is being chased up the beach by the Spanish cutie playing wet T-shirt competitions!'

'He's Portuguese actually.'

Dolly bit the inside of her cheek. 'The way you are acting, it's like you've lost your head, hanging out with the bloody barman, Portuguese, Spanish, whichever, who is only ten years older than George! You *are* a ticking time bomb that could blow my brother's world sky high and I won't sit back and watch it. I can't.' She pursed her lips.

'Oh, yes, poor Howard! God forbid I might do anything that might pull the rug from under him, shock him, hurt him! Well luckily for him and for you I am not like him; I am not selfish. I am not weak and I am not bloody stupid.'

'Oh, is this what it's all about? Getting him back. Is it revenge?' Dolly asked with a slight laugh to her question, even though there was nothing about their exchange that was remotely funny.

'How could you say that to me? How could you? You know me, Dolly, you have known me since I was sixteen and you think that's how my mind works?' Rae hated the wobble of emotion in her tone, wanting to sound strong, commanding.

'Seeing the way you behaved earlier made me wonder just how much of you I do know.' Dolly sat back and folded her arms across her chest.

'Well, join the bloody club!' Rae shook her head and pulled the napkin from the table, using it to wipe her eyes. 'Because I don't know who I am! I don't know who I am . . . And it's the worst feeling in the whole world!' She stopped and tried to breathe, her words robbed by the sob that built in her throat. 'I am so fucking lonely! So empty, sad. I am trying to figure everything out and I am alone and it's shit!' she sobbed. 'My world has been turned upside down!'

The couple taking tea at the end of the terrace stood quietly and sidled from the floor, making their way back into the hotel.

'Now we've scared them off.' Rae tried to laugh, but it was hard through her tears.

Dolly took a deep breath and it was some seconds later that she spoke – and when she did, her tone was calmer. 'You do know who you are.' She paused again, waiting for Rae to stop crying. 'You do. You are my best friend, you are Howard's wife, you are Hannah and George's mum, Lyall's auntie, Sadie and Paul's sister-in-law, Maureen and Len's daughter and Debbie-Jo's much less talented sister.'

Rae couldn't help but smile a little. 'Please don't make me laugh, not now.' But Dolly's words, meant to console, left her feeling bereft. She knew this was how she was viewed, defined by her relationships with everyone else, diluted. No one was ever going to look at her and say, 'Oh, that's Rae, the traveller, the chef . . .' She craved a title that was just hers, something she could claim regardless of who she was related to.

'I can't help it. Fun fact: making you laugh is the only skill I have. But it's true, we all love you, all of us.'

'Thank you.' Rae calmed a little. 'But that's not what I am talking about, Dolly.' She dug deep to find the confidence to speak her mind. 'I don't mean those labels that you each stick on me, the labels you stuck on me decades ago, owning me, marking me, making me part of the circus that is life with the Latimers!'

'What are you talking about now?' Dolly's chest heaved and she looked genuinely perplexed.

Rae stared at her and gathered the strength to explain. 'I mean I was quiet but happy – and the day I met you, all I wanted was to be part of the glamorous world you lived in.'

'It was hardly glamorous!' Dolly snorted.

'It was to me! There was my mum and dad counting yoghurts in the fridge to make sure we had one each, and if we didn't my dad would go out with the shopping basket and pick up one yoghurt – one bloody yoghurt! And in contrast there was your family . . .' She shook her head and swiped at her tears that persisted. 'Flinging around smoked salmon and laughing and drinking wine and sitting by the pool and it felt like . . .'

'Like what?' Dolly's voice was softer now.

'It felt like a permanent celebration. It felt like the life I was craving and it felt like escape. Exciting escape.'

'God . . .' Dolly shook her head. 'You are kidding me! I used to love being at your house. Your mum quiet and your dad sober and all eating together; supper around the table and no rows, no shouting, no hiding final demands for payment under the cushion on the sofa, no living off credit, overstretched; no drama. It was peaceful and lovely.'

Rae remembered with guilt the simmering shame she had felt at the mundaneness of the meals taken at the Formica-topped table under the clock, while her dad shared highlights of his day driving a BT van. Her lovely, reliable dad, who would rather go without than live off credit, the man who paid for everything in their peaceful, cosy home with its cement frogs and woodchip wallpaper.

Dolly stared at her. 'It was more than just escape, though, Rae – right? We got close very quickly, you and me; we clicked, didn't we?'

'Yes, yes, we did and I know and you are my best friend.' The admission was strained, reed thin; coasting out on an exhalation of emotion, a manifestation of her hurt at how Dolly had spoken to her. 'And it was you who invited me in. And you couldn't have possibly engineered how Howard and I felt about each other, of course not. I met him and I loved him – I love him, I do! I thought your family, the life you all led was chaotic, exhausting, but oh-so exciting! And I remember saying to my mum, just after we had got married and things had calmed down a bit, "They are noisy and busy and it's draining." And she said . . .' Her tears came again as she recalled her lovely mum's soft voice. '"Well, it's the life you have chosen and it's a lovely life, darling. Everyone's family is strange compared to your own; and when you get used to it, it will be less exhausting."'

Dolly stared at her with nothing to add, it seemed, though her expression suggested she was a little perplexed by her friend's high emotion.

'But I'm still exhausted, Dolly! I am still tired; and learning about Howard has made me realise just how much. It's made me step off the conveyor belt and take a good hard look at my life. I have got lost – lost in the phone calls, demands, dramas, births, divorces, engagements, parties, birthdays, launches, restaurants, feast or famine, the ups and downs, highs and lows.'

'But that's every family!'

'Possibly.' Rae nodded. 'Possibly. But what is not every family is how I was given my junior role in it. Good old Rae – she'll run the cake up to Barnet; good old Rae – she can get the cleaner organised; Rae can take Mum in the car and the rest of us will jump in a cab; Rae will babysit – she won't mind; Rae can make cupcakes for bloody Halloween or Easter or Christmas! And all the while we all bow to what Dolly wants! Better turn up or Dolly will get mad! Better let Dolly know if the plans change – you know what she's like! God! No one wants to upset Dolly!' She saw her friend bristle and raised her voice a little. 'Jesus Christ, you picked my husband, you chose my wedding dress and Hannah comes and talks to you about me! Even for my anniversary, Howard gave me a necklace but of course you knew all about that – he told me you had a hand in it!' Rae felt her breath stutter in her throat; her words had flowed and had even taken her a little by surprise.

Dolly stared at her. 'Are you losing your mind? Are you actually mental right now? Can you hear yourself? You are having a go at me for coming with you to choose the wedding dress that my parents paid for and for helping my brother choose you a beautiful necklace for your anniversary?'

'You are not getting it!' Rae knew she wasn't making herself understood and the lack of clarity frustrated her. 'The way you idolise Howard, the way you still think he's the blue-eyed boy. So funny! So handsome! And I can't properly talk to you, my best friend, about what goes on because he's your sodding brother! But you can't keep defending him, Dolly! You can't ask me to pretend nothing has happened, act like I don't know – because I do know. Howard's not ten any more! He doesn't make me laugh by breaking a window like he did you, and I couldn't give a shit that he caught you smoking and didn't tell your nan.' She paused and took a breath, glancing at her friend, who sat wide-eyed, her mouth slack. 'He has made me feel less than a woman, Dolly, by choosing another over me. He has pushed me into the background. And Antonio has made me feel glorious! Yes, the Portuguese barman we have only known for a few days! And for the record I am not stupid or in denial; he's a barman who flirts for tips, I know it! He has the chat, all the lines, but I tell you something: he has made me feel a bit happier. He has lifted the gloom – and of course the moment I leave this place there will be another Rae-Valentine with her specially named bloody cocktail sitting at the bar, but I don't care! I don't! And I could be here trying to clear my head for a week – two weeks, two months – and it would not be enough to wipe out what has happened to Howard and me. We have crumbled, we are unstuck, and I am . . .' She let her head hang down to her chest. 'I am sad, Dolly. I am so sad. Because I love him! I love him so much! And he was perfect in my eyes! The Latimer life was perfect. And you and I were perfect and he has spoiled it! He spoiled it all!'

Her friend jumped up from the table and raced around to where she sat, taking Rae in her arms. 'Shhhh,' she cooed, holding her gently, as Rae did nothing to calm her sobs. 'It's okay, Rae-Valentine. It's all going to be okay, just breathe . . . I promise you it's all going to be okay. I've got you.'

EIGHT

Rae slept well after eventually falling asleep in the early hours. She had forgotten how exhausting distress could be. When she woke with a slight headache and swollen eyes, Dolly was already up, dressed in her hot-pink linen trousers and tunic – which clashed gloriously with her red hair – and sitting on the terrace.

Rae took a deep breath and approached with a feeling of trepidation, alien to her when thinking of her friend.

'Morning.' Rae stretched and stood on the edge of the balcony, looking out over the garden to the beach beyond, letting the sun's rays on her face help restore her wellbeing. Their heated words, fired like arrows, sat in her breast. She could feel the puncture wounds through everything she held dear. She waited to hear Dolly speak, knowing her words and manner would set the tone for the day. She didn't have long to wait, and her relief was instant.

'You have had a good old sleep, snoring and farting like a trooper.'

'That, Dolly Latimer, is rich coming from you. Give me a mo to jump in the shower and we can go and get some breakfast.'

'I'm not hungry.'

'Are you sick?' Rae asked, only half-joking.

'No, just got no appetite.'

'Oh my God – you are pregnant!'

'Very funny. No, I just feel a bit . . .' She shrugged.

'Because of all the things I said?' Rae sat on the lounger next to her friend.

'Yes. But particularly one thing. Did you mean it: am I that pushy?' It was a rare flash of self-consciousness from her extrovert friend.

Rae nodded. 'You are, but neither I nor any one of us would change a single thing about you. You are the glue, Dolly. The energy. And, to steal your words, we love you, all of us.' She reached out and took her friend's hand into her own, knowing that, despite their frank exchange, they were still mates and needed the close contact to bring healing. In truth she hadn't planned what she wanted to say; but now her words were out in the open, Rae hoped they would help them find a way forward on a more open footing. 'I know some of what I said yesterday didn't make sense – it doesn't to me – but it was just the best way I could describe how completely overwhelmed I feel by everything. And how I don't know which way to turn. I don't want to forgive and forget if it means I am a pushover or that he might do it again. And I meant it: the only reason it hurts is because I love him.' She bit her lip and looked out over the sea as this admission sank in. 'I love him so much, I always have, and I am only just able to admit that now that my anger is fading a little. And I can see how being in the company of someone who flatters you makes you feel nice.'

'You are talking about Spanish-octopus-cocktail guy.'

'Yes.' Rae smiled. 'Not that it means anything and not that I would ever do anything, but it has made me think about where I am heading, and where Howard was at if he was tempted, susceptible – and why. Like I said, it's confusing.'

'I get it. I do. And only you and Howard can figure it all out.' Dolly paused. 'I want you to know that you play so much more than a junior role in this family. You do.'

Rae wasn't so sure, still smarting from the sharp reminder from her friend that the Latimers had paid for her life – and the underlying, unpleasant suggestion that she therefore owed them.

Dolly looked up at the clear blue sky. 'You are magnificent; you always were. I saw you across the hall on that day at college and you weren't like the rest of the sheep, rushing to shake a stranger's hand; that wasn't your way. You were cool and thinking of doing a runner, I could tell, and you were sweet and lovely, kind and generous, and so were your mum and dad when they welcomed me into their home, and I hoped that if I had a friend like you I might learn to be a bit like you.'

'That's funny. I wanted to be like you – you were so fearless!'

'Not really. Just better at hiding the fear,' Dolly admitted. 'It's true, Rae: you are the best person I know and you always have been. Everything I do, interfering old bag that I am, I do because I believe I am helping to make your life better. I love you so much, I guess I just want to be a part of everything.'

'I know that and I am sorry, Dolly. I wouldn't hurt you for the world.' Rae spoke the truth but failed to mention that she would from now on, at some level, approach Dolly with a certain caution when it came to being open about her feelings. And this alien concept of censorship saddened her more than she could say.

'I'm sorry too.' Dolly squeezed her hand. 'And in this new spirit of openness, there is something I need to tell you.' She coughed to clear her throat. 'I wasn't sure whether to or not, but I think I should. I only found out myself yesterday evening and with so much going on it didn't feel like the right time to mention it, so all I would say is don't shout at me – don't shoot the messenger! It's partly the reason I am up so early . . .'

'Okay, go on.' Rae folded her arms across her pyjamas and readied herself to hear whatever it was her sister-in-law had to say.

'The thing is, Rae—'

The doorbell of their apartment rang.

'Hang on a sec. Stay right there.' Rae jumped up and skipped across the tiled floor in her bare feet. She looked down and made sure her pyjama top was fastened before opening the door. Her hand flew over her mouth, partly to stifle a scream of surprise, and partly to stop any inappropriate response that threatened.

Her stomach sank. Into the apartment with suitcases in tow stepped Vinnie and Howard. Rae felt rooted to the spot. She turned to the balcony as Dolly walked in.

'Vinnie and Howard are coming out to Antigua.' Dolly finished her sentence before running towards her husband and throwing herself into his arms.

Rae closed the door of the apartment with a nervous stutter to her heart as Dolly and Vinnie, clearly so happy to be reunited, waltzed giggling down the corridor to the apartment Vinnie had taken. She watched her husband walk around the room, opening the cupboards and checking out the view from the terrace, as he did whenever they arrived at a holiday destination. She found his presence a little invasive and was reminded of the new awkwardness that existed between them. Her mood, she knew, was slightly deflated; this had, after all, been her chance to come away and clear her head and yet here he was. And while it was a hard thing to admit, the fact that he was here was the mental equivalent of a tiny stone in her shoe. Rae knew that if he started pressuring her here, too, it would make her feel railroaded yet again – the only difference being that he would be doing it in a warmer climate.

'This is a surprise.' She managed, trying to keep the negativity from her tone, flopping down on to the sofa in her nightwear.

'You look well, Rae, even after just a few days; you have caught the sun. It suits you.'

She nodded.

'I didn't know whether to come or not. Vinnie suggested it when we dropped you guys off at the airport, kind of as a joke at first, wondering if there was a quicker flight we could get so we'd be here when you arrived. But then it got me thinking. If being away in a new place without the distraction of work and the kids is what it takes to get your head straight, then it must be a good place for the two of us to figure things out.'

Rae felt torn, wishing he were far away to give her the space she desperately needed, and yet reminded by the echo of Dolly's words that he had paid for the trip and had every right . . .

Howard sat down hard at the other end of the sofa. 'I've missed you. I mean, I was missing you before you left, but at least you were close, even if we weren't really talking. The last few days, though, the house has felt empty and I have *really* missed you, and for me it just confirms that I need you by my side.'

She stared at him, unable to offer the words of reciprocation he sought.

He sat forward and held her gaze. 'I wanted to say to you that I realise I don't know what it feels like for you. And I understand that I will never fully get exactly what I put you through, and I regret that as much as what I did.' He nodded, his mouth a thin set line. 'I wish you could get inside my head and see how sorry I am. I wish you could see how it happened.'

'I'd rather not,' she huffed.

He held out his hands. 'That's not what I mean, not the detail. I mean if there's any way I could show you how sorry I am . . .' He let this hang. 'What I really want to say is that I have made a couple of decisions.' His foot jumped on the floor: one of the giveaway signs that he was nervous. 'And I promise I am not going to push you or harass you towards making a choice about our future. I realise that kind of pressure is unfair. Especially when it was me who fucked up. And after everything I have put you through.'

She concentrated on his words, wanting to hear his grand plan and wondering if anything he might say could ever be enough to restore her faith, to patch up the holes – and even if it were, what about her relationship with Dolly, and what about her? *Oh, that's Rae, the chef . . .*

She heard him swallow.

'I have thought long and hard about things and I know that I have no right to expect anything from you – forgiveness or anything else. I hurt you. I get it. But I want you to know that I am going to keep trying to win you back. I'm going to keep trying to convince you that I love you and that I need you by my side to be happy. I can't imagine my life without you, Rae – I don't want to – and I will do anything, *anything* to get my girl back; my girl, who has been my friend and my love since we were no more than kids. My girl, who made coming home a pleasure on the darkest, rainiest London day. My girl, the mother of my kids, my bath buddy.'

She gave a small laugh. 'Thank you for saying that, Howard.' It was all she could give him, but his words had permeated her shell, dissolved some of the numbness. It was, she supposed, a start.

Dolly radiated happiness, and positively shone to be back in the presence of the man she loved. And it might have been Rae's imagination, but she was certain that Vinnie was giving off a vibe she hadn't sensed before, hinted at with odd sideways looks and a faster blink rate when addressing her. She was in no doubt that Dolly would have filled him in – not only on all that Rae had said and done, but also on the Antonio situation. It created a new layer of anxiety, lovely Vinnie judging her – the man she had known as long as she'd known Howard, and who was always kind, happy to live in Dolly's shadow, propping her up, loving her unconditionally.

That evening, the four sat in the restaurant at Rae and Dolly's regular table by the window, and the conversation flowed. The men were giddy with 'first day of holiday' excitement, which had by now settled a little for herself and Dolly. Rae enjoyed the chat and the jokes that flew between them all; it felt a lot like old times, and she knew that anyone looking in would not guess at the hurt and turmoil and anxiety that swirled in her gut.

When dinner was finished and the four were deciding where to go next, Nick and Nora Knowitall stopped by their table with no less than four desserts nestling in their greedy mitts.

'Good evening, ladies.' Nick might have been speaking to her and Dolly, but his gaze swept over Vinnie and Howard. 'I see your party has grown!'

'Yes, we just met these two fellas earlier today, but I fancy my chances.' Dolly winked, as if she was whispering, but her volume was at best loud. 'I would introduce you, but I can't for the life of me remember their names!' She spoke from behind her hand, as if the rest of them weren't present.

'Oh! Well! Have a . . . have a lovely evening,' Nick managed. Nora meanwhile had let her mouth shrink in disapproval until it was no more than a tight little O.

'You are a terrible person!' Rae laughed as the four made their way from the restaurant.

'You want to try living with her!' Vinnie chimed.

'I really don't. A few days in that little room with her snoring and I have had enough – and she took all the wardrobe space.'

'Not my fault you only brought a bloody toothbrush and a thong!' Dolly chuckled and linked her arm through Vinnie's. 'How about we go to Max's and get a cocktail? We can sit and look at the beach; it's beautiful.'

'Sure.'

'Sounds good,' Howard agreed.

Rae felt her stomach flip over. She took in the smiles of reassurance Dolly offered to her brother and a small part of her wanted to shriek from the rooftops that just because they had managed to eat dinner as a foursome did not mean things were back to normal. She now knew that she wanted things to change, and she wanted to be heard. But, as ever, she didn't want to be the one to smash the harmony that pervaded.

The prospect of waltzing into Max's bar with her husband was not a comfortable one. She struggled to remember exactly how much she had told Antonio about her situation; the liberal consumption of wine and cocktails meant her recollection wasn't pin-sharp. She felt instantly fearful that the barman might let something slip in front of Howard or say something wildly inappropriate in the way he had since she arrived. There was a vast difference between wildly inappropriate when she was alone, laughing and sipping cocktails, and wildly inappropriate in front of Howard. As they stepped up on to the dark teak flooring of Max's and the men admired this new, sleek surrounding, she felt the shame of disingenuousness, her husband's presence a reminder that she was not free to flirt and give in to flattery, no matter what her current situation.

'Wow! This place is incredible!' Howard stood with his hands on his hips inside his white linen shirt and looked around the terrace, taking in the low lighting and soft sofas.

She instantly noticed Antonio behind the bar. He looked at her husband and then Dolly and Vinnie and finally her. He let his mouth lift in a small smile of recognition, but his expression to anyone who had studied his face for a number of hours carried a look of regret, and this alone was enough to make her feel a little sad.

As was his way, Howard marched to the bar, confident, interested and making whoever he spoke to feel like a million dollars. 'Hello! This is some place. Just beautiful.'

'Thank you. Welcome to Max's.' Antonio spoke with the fixed smile of a professional.

'We run some bars and restaurants in the UK,' Howard began, and Antonio lifted his eyebrows in surprise, as if this was news. 'It's a tricky job to make them appealing, on-trend and yet family friendly. I think of all the hours of consultation we spend trying to get it right and yet here we are . . .' He threw his arm around in an arc. 'Effectively in a fancy gazebo – no gimmicks, no art, no theme, just this incredible view – and you can't beat it. Maybe that's the answer: we need to move lock, stock and barrel to Antigua! What do you think, Rae? Can you imagine waking up every day to this view?'

She gave a nod and a short smile, wishing they could go and sit down on the sofas where Vinnie and Dolly had made themselves comfortable, away from the bar. She had no desire to prolong this interaction.

'So, what do you recommend?' Howard rubbed his palms together as he eagerly browsed the fancy row of shiny bottles on the glass shelf.

'I have just the thing.' Antonio pointed at Howard and clicked his fingers. Working at speed, he grabbed glass bottles and small vials of syrup, sloshing measures into a shaker, along with crushed ice and a generous squeeze of lime, which he mixed and poured with flair into a tall glass, finishing with a paper straw and a sliver of apple perched on the side of the pale-green concoction.

'Fantastic! You've done that before!' Howard chuckled, impressed.

'Once or twice,' Antonio acknowledged with a wink, and Rae felt her stomach sink.

Howard took a sip. 'Oh, this is good! Do you want to try it, Rae?' He held the glass towards her.

'No. I'm fine.' She turned away.

'What's it called?' Howard asked.

Rae looked at Antonio, silently imploring him.

'It's called "The Idiot Returns".' He spoke while she was still for-mulating her thought.

Her heart jumped and her tongue stuck to the dry roof of her mouth.

'Why's it called that?' Howard asked jovially, sipping again.

'Because it's potent and once you have finished it, you'll be stumbling back up here for another and another – time and again, The Idiot Returns . . .' Antonio finished with a small flourish of his hand and a bow.

Howard laughed loudly. 'I like it! Vinnie!' he called across the bar. 'You want one of these?'

'Sure.' Vinnie nodded and turned back to Dolly, who had kicked off her sandals and now rested her feet on his lap, as if they were on the couch at home. 'You sure you don't want one, Rae?' Howard pushed.

'Positive,' she answered, not enjoying the fact that Antonio was making a fool of her husband, no matter how well intentioned or disguised. Howard, this man, this flawed man, the father of her children, was not an object for Antonio's ridicule.

It was nearing midnight when they decided to call it a night, and Rae was grateful. She had spent an uncomfortable hour or so perched on the edge of the sofa, listening to Dolly, Vinnie and Howard wittering and reminiscing, from which she felt curiously remote, while watching Antonio out of the corner of her eye, afraid that at any given moment he might come over. Not that there was much to reveal; but the thought that he might in some way suggest that all between the two of them was less than above board would mean that Rae had lost the high ground. Her anger and mistrust in Howard would then be seen as misplaced, and she would be deemed no better than him. And that was not how she could effect change.

It was therefore with no small measure of relief that Rae, burdened with a new and growing anxiety, walked back to the apartment behind Dolly and Vinnie, who linked hands like magnets and walked hip to hip along the narrow path. She looked at Howard, preoccupied with his phone and with his jacket slung over his shoulder. She wondered what it would be like to be alone with him at night in the small apartment and felt a flicker of apprehension, wary of his expectations but holding on to her resolution to stand firm.

She took her time showering and cleaning her teeth before slipping into her pyjamas ready to climb into her single bed. Howard waited to use the bathroom, sitting on the sofa, scrolling through his phone.

'I just told the kids we are all good. Hannah sent a kiss emoji and George a thumbs-up sign.'

'I remember the days when everyone used more words, but I think that's just how young people are now, pushed for time to communicate. They live their lives in a hurry.' She pictured her kids and smiled.

'We all do.'

'Yep.' She acknowledged this truth, thinking of how even putting the rubbish out had a sense of urgency about it and recognising the tragedy in that.

Rae went about her bedtime rituals, plumping her pillow and smoothing the top sheet, nervous around Howard in a way that was familiar of late, but no less strange for that. It was an odd feeling, regardless of the event that had blown them apart; now in the twilight of their marriage they were past the passionate days of nightly sex that in the early years had happened without thought or preplanning. This had waned over the years, falling into a steady state where holding hands, a peck on the cheek or falling asleep with a book on each other's chests was just as likely; so why she felt this acute awareness tonight of their physical separation, she wasn't sure. Maybe because they were on holiday, and in the past, that had always been a time to revamp intimacy that might have been flagging due to busy lives and tired bodies. She got into bed and pulled the sheet and blanket up to her chin, a protective shield of sorts.

The last time the two of them had slept in adjoining beds without moving furniture out of the way and pushing them together was in a cosy B&B after Paul and Sadie's daughter married somewhere in the

Cotswolds. The beds would stay where they were tonight too. It was a gap of only a couple of feet, but it might as well have been the Grand Canyon.

Howard chuckled to himself. 'Do you know, I think the last time I slept in Dolly's bed was when I came home drunk as a teenager and took a right at the top of the stairs instead of a left, and my mum left me there. Dolly ended up in with them.'

'It has fresh sheets.'

'Well, I'm glad to hear it.' He pulled back the covers and she heard the creak of the mattress springs as her husband lay in the bed previously occupied by the snoring Dolly. It was some relief to know that he snored marginally less than his sister.

'I've had a nice day. It's felt good, Rae, like old times, and the first time I have felt like this in a long while. I feel a little bit happy.'

'That'll be the cocktails.' She felt the flash of anger that he could be so easily seduced by a slosh of rum and a blue, sun-filled sky, knowing it would take a whole lot more than that for them to resolve what ailed them.

'The Idiot Returns!' Howard boomed and she closed her eyes in the darkness, cringing at the sly antics of Antonio. She hadn't spoken up and her silence made her feel complicit. Rae felt the beginnings of a headache, still trying to process that her husband was actually here.

'Single beds.' He spoke into the darkness, and she heard him pat the mattress. 'I told them we were an anniversary couple when I booked the holiday. I definitely did not request two singles.'

'Well, you know, Howard, you don't get everything you want in life. You might have an expectation, but often things don't turn out the way you want. You expect roses, you get dandelions.' *At least, that's my life, Howard; but not yours. For you, if you want roses you bloody take roses and be damned with the consequences!*

There were one or two seconds of silence until Rae became aware of a stifled wheezing sound. 'Howard?' She turned her head towards the noise. 'Howard, speak to me. Are you okay?' She wondered if he was ill or distressed; it was hard to fathom.

The wheezing sound grew louder until she realised that he was giggling.

'Are you laughing?' She sat up a little, resting on her elbows.

'I'm . . . sorry!' he managed.

'In God's name, what is so funny?'

'You! You are so funny! I'm sorry, I know we don't laugh like this any more, but honestly, Rae, I am lying here listening to you offering teacup wisdom – "Things don't turn out the way you want . . . you expect roses, you get dandelions . . ." You sound like Yoda!' He laughed again.

She felt her face break into a reluctant smile. His jollity was quite infectious. 'I think you'll find that if I sounded like Yoda it would be "Roses you expect, dandelions you get . . ."' she offered in her best Yoda voice, and this time laughter exploded from them both. She had forgotten that they could find each other this funny. It was definitely the cocktails.

That Antonio . . . She pictured him. *Terrible he is . . .*

'This is good, Rae, this is good.'

She turned on to her side and lay facing him. Her husband did the same and gradually she was able to decipher his outline as her eyes grew accustomed to the semi-darkness.

'Can I ask you something, Howard?'

'Of course,' he whispered.

'Have you always loved me? I mean, from the day that we met?'

'I tell you every day. But if you don't know it then it's my fault.'

'It's not about saying it, as you know – it's all about the actions.' She stopped talking; this was not where she wanted the conversation to head. 'You did tell me every day, Howard, you do, but that's not what I am driving at. I suppose what I mean is, in all the years we have been together, have you ever hated me or gone off me and then gone back on me?'

She heard him shift on the mattress and saw him pull the sheet up over his bare shoulder.

'This sounds suspiciously like you are looking for clues as to how to go back to liking me. Trying to figure out how to stop hating me.'

'Hate is too strong, but that's about right. I need to know how people do it because I am really struggling.' She spoke the truth tenderly.

'I have never, ever hated you. Not once, not for a single second.' He swallowed. 'I love you and I always have, but there have been times when I have found being with you difficult.'

Rae shifted her head on the pillow and listened hard. 'Like when?' She heard his sigh.

'Tell me, Howard,' she whispered.

'I guess after George was born. It was a difficult pregnancy for you, I know, and I spent all of it waiting for the worst to happen.'

She knew he was referring to the late miscarriage they had suffered. She had been twenty-three weeks pregnant. It was never mentioned. And Rae had always felt that if he didn't mention it then neither should she. *Least said, soonest mended . . .* Not that her silence had meant she hadn't grieved – quite the opposite; she just did so alone and in secret, presenting her smiling face to the world and crumbling when she was alone. A sham.

'I could only be there for you through the pregnancy and tried to hide all the anxiety I felt, but it was hard for me not knowing how best to help you. I was trying to look after the business and help with Hannah and I guess I felt quite overwhelmed and I felt a bit like . . .' He swallowed again. 'I felt a bit like you shut me out. I know your mum was around, and Dolly, but I was lonely, I think. I never stopped loving you, of course not. But when I look back, it was a hard time. I was so worried and didn't know how best to support you and I had no one to talk to.'

Rae remembered the anxiety that gripped her for the first few months of that pregnancy; the tiredness of looking after a toddler while pregnant was almost too much. He was right: overwhelming.

'You never said anything to me.' She felt that their words came easier, cutting through the darkness in this half-light.

'No. We haven't been very good at talking about the hard stuff, have we?'

'I guess not,' she admitted. 'Maybe we needed to use more words too.'

'Or we could be like the kids and communicate solely in emoji?'

'That would certainly be easy. We only need one to sum up the last few months – that nasty poo one. Just hold your finger on that until it fills the screen.'

'I won't do that. I can't stand to dwell on it.'

Easy for you, buster . . .

'I'd send lots of the little flower bouquets,' Howard suggested.

Rae thought this summed them up quite well. Thinking of the good things, the funny things, the celebrations – that was what they focused on. But miscarriage, George's dyslexia, Hannah's anger and tendency towards depression? No, they didn't really talk about anything like that. Not in detail.

'After I had George,' Rae began, 'I remember feeling quite trapped and I thought it was your fault, because I had these two kids to look after and I was tied to the house and exhausted, yet you were still free to go out of the front door or take a shower, things that often felt impossible for me. Looking back, I think I was suffering from post-natal depression, but we called it "baby blues" and waited for everything to improve – and it did, eventually.'

'I remember you used to cry a lot and I didn't know what to do. I asked your mother and she said it was best not to make a fuss or make you feel guilty, or worry you that you might not be coping, and that I was probably best off not mentioning it.'

'And you took advice from her?' It felt incredible that he had been able to speak to her mum rather than her. Yet another secret, lurking with the rest of the skeletons in the back of their emotional cupboard. Rae thought of how much easier things would have been if they had been able to discuss the situation openly. She might have felt less lonely, Howard a little less isolated . . . It might have set them on a very different path; one where he didn't seek a thrill and flattery from a skinny waitress called Karina.

He gave a wry laugh. 'Yes, and I don't know why I did; I wouldn't take her advice on anything else, not really. I don't think she has ever really forgiven me for marrying you so young. It was like I had taken her little girl away.'

'You did.' She smiled, thinking about that day. 'Our wedding day, Howard – I was so excited.'

'I remember, but you know . . .' He paused. 'For me, the day I proposed and you said yes was better than our wedding day. At least, I think so.'

'What? No! Really?' It was the first time she had heard this. She pictured him lying nonchalantly on her wedding dress with his head on her lap while she opened their many gifts.

He nodded at her, sharing the confidence. 'Yes, our wedding day was lovely. Perfect, and you looked . . . oh my God, you looked so beautiful.' The gasp to his tone warmed her. 'But all those people, Rae, and all the planning and frills – it was a bit too much. And that cake with those bloody things stuck on top!'

'They were a bride and groom; little models from Selfridges, no less.' *And my mum and dad bought that cake with their last pennies . . .*

'They didn't even look like us.' He sighed.

'Are they supposed to?' she asked, in all innocence.

'How should I know?'

They both gave a single laugh.

'Rae?'

'Yes?'

'Can I . . . can I hold your hand?'

Here in the dark and under the cosy blanket of reminiscence, it felt like a reasonable request. Slowly, with a measure of reluctance, she reached out and their hands met across the gap; his fingers gently gripped hers and their palms slid together. Turned out it was a journey of twelve inches that her hand had to travel, not the Grand Canyon after all. It felt nice, comforting and familiar, with an underlying sadness to it. Rae felt confident that no matter what had occurred, this kind of intimacy was one he shared with no other, because it was built on shared history, and that alone made her heart glad.

'No, the day I asked you to marry me, it was . . .'

'It was what?' she whispered into the dark.

He shook his head as if urging her not to rush him, to let him find the right words. 'When you said yes, it was like there was a beam of light shining ahead of me, showing me the way. For the first time ever I could see this wonderful, bright future because I knew that no matter what, you were going to be in it. And all the things that had felt so important – like where I lived and making the restaurants a success, growing the business – all of it fell into insignificance because I could only see me joined to you forever, no matter what, and it felt . . .' He paused again. 'It felt like I had arrived at a place that I didn't know I was travelling to, and regardless of how fast the march of time, it held no fear for me because it was the end of my loneliness.'

'Had you been lonely then, up until that point?'

'No,' he answered, softly, 'but I had a fear of loneliness and that disappeared the moment you said you would be my wife.'

She looked at him in the dim light and saw the bright-eyed young thing down on one knee on the path that circled the lake in the park, while joggers skirted around them, paying them no more heed than if they were rocks littering the way. It was raining. Her wool coat had smelled of wet dog and she'd hoped he didn't notice, far more concerned about this than she was about her hair being stuck flat to her head or her soggy shoe leather.

'I want you to marry me . . .' He'd looked up at her.

'Really?' Her heart felt like it was going to jump out of her chest.

'Yes, really!'

'I'd love to marry you, Howard! I would!'

They had hugged closely, keenly, with a new understanding, and she had kissed him goodbye and practically run home, bursting into the lounge where her Mum and Dad sat on the sofa watching the news, with empty supper plates on their laps, still fresh with the licks of gravy and stray peas, and cups of tea in their hands. They'd looked up and she'd jumped in front of the television; her dad cocked his head to look around her as she spoke with tears falling down her face. 'I never expected this! But Mum, Dad . . . my boyfriend – Howard, my amazing boyfriend – he wants to marry me!' And she'd stood there in that room with joy filling her right up and she knew what it felt like to be someone special, someone *so* special that a man as incredible as Howard Latimer, who had met Simply Red, Bryan Adams and the woman who cut Annie Lennox's hair, wanted to marry her! Quiet, dull, flat-chested Rae-Valentine Pritchard. And in that moment she'd felt memorable, like a rock star, like a Latimer and not in the least bit like something forgettable, in the background . . .

'I could only picture us happy,' Howard whispered, squeezing her hand. 'Happy together. I assumed we'd be lucky and have kids and that was it. I really didn't want anything more. The way it felt, just you and me on that path . . .' He took a breath. 'I know this is going to sound ridiculous, but it was at that moment, when you said yes, and the way you looked at me – *that* was when I felt married, connected to you. The actual wedding and that whole circus, it was a great party, but the soul-to-soul, body-to-body thing, that for me had already happened.'

Rae felt moved by his words. 'You sounded pretty certain that we'd stay together.'

'I was. I am,' he corrected. 'Because if I think of anything different, that loneliness looms large on my horizon and I can't stand to think of it. I just can't stand it.'

She felt the pull of his hand against hers, and just like that she pictured him hand in hand checking into a hotel; Karina hovering in her heels, wearing a smug grin and walking in her cocky way towards the lift . . . Rae pulled her hand away and turned towards the wall.

'Night, Howard.'

'Goodnight, Rae. I am talking too much, I know. Go to sleep. I don't know what's in The Idiot Returns, but I definitely want another one tomorrow.'

And just this one line was enough to send them back to the verge of laughter, quickly followed by her silent tears that seeped into the pillowslip.

NINE

Dolly and Vinnie were at the breakfast table by the time Rae and Howard made their way to the restaurant.

'Here they are!' Dolly shouted across the room and waved.

Rae tried to ignore the turning heads of all the other residents, who had no doubt been informed by Nick and Nora, now tutting in the corner, of how the two women had picked up these nameless fellas. Rae was treading a fine line. She didn't want to ruin this time away for everyone, but was damned if she was going to be bulldozed into a show of forgive and forget just to keep the status quo. She did feel better this morning, a little calmer, and this was due in no small part to her and Howard's whispered exchange in the dim light; but with images of him and Karina still fresh in her mind, she was miles away from playing happy families.

Howard went straight to the buffet table in search of bacon and eggs. Vinnie went to join his mate and Rae slotted into a chair.

'Well?' Dolly stared at her, chewing on toast and marmalade.

'What do you mean, *well*?' Rae reached for the coffee pot, irritated that her friend sounded like a teen wanting an update on romantic progress rather than a grown woman who was aware that her friend's marriage hung in the balance. Dolly had made it quite clear that she thought it possible, if not prudent, for Rae to sweep the whole thing under the carpet and pop the kettle on for tea.

'I mean how did it go last night – any progress? Did you guys talk?'

'We talked.'

Dolly beamed and stamped her feet, again reminding Rae of when they were excitable teens, with the associated level of hysteria. 'Tell me! Tell me everything! If you don't I might literally die!'

'Yes, we talked, Dolly, but we are a long way from sorted. As I might have mentioned, it's going to take a bit more than a cocktail or two and holding hands in the moonlight to wipe the slate clean.'

'So you held hands in the moonlight?' Dolly leaned forward.

Rae sipped her coffee. 'Not exactly. Kind of.'

'This is good, this is good, Rae.' Dolly unwittingly mimicked the words of her brother. 'Vinnie wants to take a boat out. What do you think?'

Rae could tell by her friend's wide smile that she was keen. 'I am not a fan of boats, as you know, but I really don't mind.' Her heart didn't exactly leap with joy at the prospect, but she knew it was all about getting through the day.

'It'll be lovely! Out on the water, catching the sun!'

'Whatever everyone else wants to do.' Rae realised that her days of mental healing on the beach with a cool drink under a parasol were probably gone.

'So, a boat trip. I think we should hire a beautiful yacht and go out a bit, and we can sit back on the deck with a gin and tonic and make a day of it.' Vinnie rubbed his hands together excitedly as the men took their seats at the table.

'Sound great!' Howard enthused, tucking in to his bacon and eggs with gusto, as Vinnie pulled out a map and began to trace the coastline with his finger, planning their route.

'Better get my fancy hat!' Dolly beamed and gave an excited clap.

And just like that, with the other three plotting and planning with enthusiasm for the jaunt ahead, Rae realised that she was a passenger, in the background, in the corner.

She reluctantly followed the three of them along the dock, but looked back towards Max's bar and felt a ridiculous yearning to sit at the bar alone and talk to the young barman who had made her feel happy, even just for a moment or two. Her husband had spoiled that too. Rae felt unjustifiably robbed.

Twenty minutes into their trip, the two couples bobbed silently on the ocean in their small catamaran with the single sail of the Hobie Cat flopping dejectedly for the want of wind. They each perched on the mesh between the two narrow fibreglass hulls. Rae sat next to Dolly, who was wearing her fancy hat, and they both sat opposite their husbands with their hands in their laps, their legs outstretched. Huddled together, they reminded Rae of sardines in a tin, which apparently when cooked over a fire on the beach were the best thing to eat, tasting of sea and sunshine . . .

It was eerily quiet, the only sound the waves hitting the bottom of the catamaran and the squeak of the large life jackets, which rubbed against their skin or under their chins whenever they moved.

'Remind me again why we couldn't hire a boat with an engine and more than a few square inches of space to move in?' Howard asked Vinnie.

'I told you, they said the reefs and the water around here were dangerous for non-yachtsmen and this was all we were allowed.' Vinnie sighed.

'You should have told them we have taken pedalos out every year in Majorca since we were kids! And you were very good on that inflatable banana, Vin!' Dolly enthused.

Rae smiled at Howard from behind her sunglasses. 'I don't think that's what they mean when they use the term "yachting", Doll.'

'Well, what are we supposed to do now?' Dolly sighed. 'I wish I'd brought snacks.'

'You've only just had your breakfast!' Howard reminded her. 'Plus, snacks are a bad idea: they attract the sharks.'

'Sharks?' Dolly screamed. 'Oh, please don't say that, Howard! I don't like it! I want to go back!' She grabbed Rae's arm.

'He's only joking, Dolly; not that it's funny. But you don't need to worry – there are no sharks here.' Rae glared at the men, who laughed. 'And be under no illusion: we *all* want to go back. But therein lies the problem. No bloody wind.'

Dolly seemed to relax a bit. 'I need the loo.'

'Oh, Dolly!'

'For God's sake!'

'Why am I not surprised?'

All three laughed and made their views known.

'Don't all shout at me! I can't help it!' she shrieked. 'I was cursed with a bladder meant for a shrew!'

'Well, I wish you'd learn to tame it,' Vinnie chortled. 'See what I did there? Shakespeare!'

'We got it, Vinnie,' Howard snapped, 'but it's hard to find you amusing right now when you have taken us out on this floating postage stamp, which we don't know how to make move without wind – and thus the lack of the aforementioned breeze means we face the prospect of being out here for bloody hours. And anyway, if we were linking Dolly with Shakespeare, I think *Macbeth* would be more up her street.'

'Because of Lady Macbeth being mad?'

All three looked at Vinnie, who essentially bought fruit and veg for a living, and tried to hide their surprise at his literary knowledge.

'Nice one, but no, I was thinking of the witches.'

'I am here, you two!' Dolly shouted. 'And I am not a witch, although I do admit to having more than a passing interest in the spirit world.' She adjusted her bosom inside her floral swimming costume, which had got rucked up inside the life vest.

'Oh, please! Not the bloody ghost visit again!' Vinnie wailed.

'I for one would really like to hear the story.' Howard spoke calmly.

'I've told you it before!'

'I know, Dolly, but I think at this time of quiet reflection, here in the middle of the ocean, it would be good to hear it again.' He smiled at Rae, and she knew her friend wouldn't need too much persuading.

'Well, if you insist.' Dolly adjusted her position, making the whole catamaran list slightly and causing a gasp of concern until it settled again. Rae tried not to consider that the only thing sitting between her and the vast, dark ocean was the thin stretch of webbing and the two narrow hulls of this inadequate craft. 'I was in my late teens and I was asleep in my bedroom when something woke me up in the early hours – and I know I was awake and not dreaming because I remember seeing my glass of water on the bedside table, which was actually there, not a dream at all. I sat up in bed and a white, shadowy figure walked into the room.' She pre-empted the question: 'The door was open, and he stood by the side of my bed. Yes, a ghost.'

'How do you know it was a male ghost?' Howard asked, feigning interest.

Rae pulled a face at him, the rotter.

'He had a man's face and a penis.'

They all roared their laughter. It was in these moments of improvised humour that Dolly was at her funniest.

'Okay, I am joking about the penis – I couldn't see inside his night-dress/cloak thing – but it was definitely a male; he looked like a man and he had a man's voice.'

'Ah, yes.' Howard nodded his encouragement. 'I forgot he spoke to you. And what did he say?'

'I was coming to that.' Dolly took a deep breath. 'He said, "Don't scrimp on conditioner and always get your ends trimmed; your hair is very important."'

Rae laughed softly until her tears sprang. Vinnie, Howard too, all three were tittering, trying to hold in the loud laughter that was on the verge of bursting from them.

'Oh, sod off, all of you! I know what I saw!' Dolly tried and failed to fold her arms across her generous bust, encased inside the rather unwieldy life jacket.

'Why? Why, Dolly?' Howard gasped through his laughter. 'Why would a ghost bother making contact – coming all the way from wherever and selecting you out of all the people on the earth – only to tell you to take good care of your hair?'

'I don't know, Howard; I am not a ghost expert.' Dolly seemed to be considering this. 'Maybe it was the ghost of a hairdresser?'

This suggestion served only to make the three of them laugh harder. Dolly sat, mock stony-faced.

'Was it Vidal Saswhooooooo-hooooon?' Vinnie was in fine form.

The laughter eventually subsided and Rae felt the inner glow of happy embers that had been cold for some time. These people . . . She had forgotten just how easy it was to be in their company. Days like this reminded her of how and why she loved them all. The recognition was tinged with sadness. She liked the life before, when she was untroubled by the image of Howard and the waitress, before she'd starting thinking deeper about her life and asking the question that was new: are *you* happy, Rae-Valentine?

After a minute or two of silence a strange noise reached her ears. She sat still and noted that Howard and Vinnie were similarly concentrating, heads turned, trying to locate the source of the deep trickle that sounded like water running, bizarrely right there, out in the ocean.

Dolly looked skyward and at that very moment Rae, Vinnie and Howard realised that Dolly was peeing through her swimming costume and out through the webbing of the boat.

'Jesus Christ, Dolly!' Howard shouted. 'You have got to be kidding me!'

Vinnie removed his glasses to wipe his eyes; his hysterics rendered speech impossible. Rae looked at her friend and shook her head.

'What?' Dolly asked, laughing. 'A girl's gotta do what a girl's gotta do!'

It was a day Rae knew she would never forget: getting stranded out at sea, only to be rescued by a rather indifferent waterski-boat driver, who hitched the small catamaran to the back of his sleek vessel and hauled them to shore – that, and the fact that her sister-in-law had peed publicly in front of them all. She laughed to herself as she slipped into her nightdress, feeling the sting of cotton on her shoulders: her skin, a little taut, had not fared too well bobbing about in the midday Caribbean sun on that bloody boat.

There was a newly relaxed air between her and Howard, something she could feel – a softening in their demeanour, and recognition that each interaction was kinder, slower, without the rasp of anger, the chill of regret or the harsh tone of blame. It wasn't that she'd forgiven him; nor had she forgotten – her emotional wounds were still raw. But there was certainly a thawing in her ice-cold rejection of him and in truth she felt better for it, less preoccupied and not so ill. Their friendlier exchanges made her think about what it might feel like to put his infidelity behind them and move on, made her consider a life where that was actually possible. And if it were not, then at least being friends would make everything easier, especially for the kids, for the family.

◆　◆　◆

Howard and Vinnie had been in Antigua for a few days now; for Rae and Dolly, it was the end of day nine. It had been a long, sunny day spent on the beach and playing cards over a lazy lunch on the terrace. Dolly behaved as if their altercation before the men arrived had never happened and Rae envied her the ability to move on, knowing she would be in less turmoil if she could do likewise. But still the nagging thought remained: did Dolly know her at all? And how could she expect Dolly – or anyone else, for that matter – to know her if she felt like a shadow of the person she had always hoped she might become?

That night she climbed between the sheets and Howard cleaned his teeth while she rubbed in her hand cream. He switched off the main light and got into bed, lying back with a loud, satisfied exhalation.

'I keep remembering how Dolly peed off that boat!' he tittered.

This was still the highlight of the last few days and the thing they kept going back to when there was a lull in the conversation; the kind of happening that they would, she figured, talk about for years to come. She pictured them as octogenarians sitting around the table, recalling Dolly's lack of bladder control, and Rae noted that it wasn't only the idea of being that age, when the issue might be common to them all, that plunged her into dark thoughts – but the idea that she might be there at all, plodding on in her half-life, keeping her thoughts to herself, playing along.

'Nothing surprises me about her any more.' She spoke the truth. 'To think, I used to be completely shocked by the things Dolly said and did – but now I just shrug it off and add it to the list.'

'Yes, but here's the thing, Rae.' Howard turned on to his side to face her across the Grand Canyon. 'I have no choice about knowing Dolly – nature hitched my wagon to hers on the day she was born. But you? You chose to be her friend!'

'Yes, and I chose to marry her brother. I guess that was when my wagon was properly hitched.'

'I guess it was.' He paused. 'Can I hold your hand?'

'No.' She spoke bluntly, irritated by his cockiness.

It didn't feel right, a little forced maybe. This conversation and the atmosphere were very different from a few nights ago, when holding hands had felt like the most natural thing in the world. The last couple of nights she had gone to bed first and, having fallen into a deep sleep, hadn't heard him come to bed. It had taken the pressure off a little.

The two lay quietly for some moments until Howard whispered into the darkness, 'Are you awake?'

She hesitated before responding. 'Yes.' Turning on to her side, she faced him and pulled the blanket up to her chin.

'I want to tell you something.' He spoke softly.

'Okay.'

'I've been thinking about this for a long, long time, but I want to tell you now.'

There were seconds of silence before he spoke again, and she lay waiting for him to begin.

'I . . . I saw him.'

'You saw who?' She wondered if in her sleepy state she had lost the thread.

'Our baby. Our little boy.'

Rae felt her body freeze on the mattress. She saw a flash in her mind of the moment she finished giving birth, without contractions and with only a midwife present, tears falling, hands gripping the sheet and a prayer on her lips: *Please, please, Lord, please let them have made a horrible mistake; let there be a chance, just give him a chance . . . let him live, please, please . . .*

'You . . . you saw him?' The words caught in her throat.

'Yes.' He swallowed.

'When?' Rae felt torn; she both did and did not want the detail.

'Before they took him out of the room.'

She could hear he was crying.

'Was . . .' She struggled to find the right words for what she wanted to know. 'Did he . . .' She paused again. 'How did he look?' Her own tears now fell like hot glass slipping over her cheek.

'Perfect, Rae. He was perfect.'

'He was?'

'Yes, he was.'

'Small, though?' she managed, her voice no more than a squeak.

'Yes, yes, small – his head was about the size of a tennis ball – but he was . . . he was perfect,' he stuttered through his tears.

'Just asleep?' She smiled, superimposing this image with those of Hannah and George snoozing as newborns, and it helped.

'Yes,' he wept. 'Just asleep.'

The two lay for a second or two, until Howard, without asking permission, climbed from his bed and pulled back her covers. Rae pressed herself against the wall and made space. He gently lay down by her side and took her in his arms and this was how they stayed for quite a while, her head resting on his chest, both weeping for the loss of their baby: joined in a powerful grief that swept away all recent hurt, because it was stronger, unifying and long, long overdue.

Rae liked the feel of her cheek against his warm chest. She felt safe. 'I still feel him.'

'You do?' he asked gently, kissing her forehead.

She nodded against him. 'I never got to hold him, never saw him and yet I feel him where I always felt him, right here.' She placed the flat of her hand on the pouch of her stomach. 'I am glad you saw him, Howard. I sometimes thought . . .'

'What?'

'I sometimes thought that maybe he looked bad or something was very wrong and it has haunted me. Frightened me, even.' She was ashamed to admit this.

'No, no,' he soothed, 'nothing like that at all. He was perfect, he really was.'

'I try to imagine what it would be like if he had lived and we had three, Hannah and George and one in between.'

'Toby.' He spoke the name they had settled on: the name she had not mentioned since leaving the hospital that day because that made him real. And losing him, Toby, was, she knew, possibly more than she could cope with.

'Toby.' She cried.

And this was how they stayed until the early hours, locked together in sadness, crying for the loss of their boy.

Toby.

Rae woke early and looked across at Howard, unsure when he had crept back to his own bed, but grateful that he had, knowing neither of them would have got much sleep squashed together in such a narrow space. She picked up her bottle of water and went to sit on the terrace, listening to the calls and chatter of hummingbirds and warblers who, like her, watched the coral-pink sunrise behind the coconut trees, which sat in shadow against the magnificent backdrop. The air, already warm, was heady with the floral and woody scents of the lush gardens, damp with dew. She felt lighter, as if a dark rock that had been weighing her down had been lifted.

Howard disturbed her thoughts as he came out on to the balcony in his pyjama bottoms with bare chest and feet. 'This is beautiful.' He looked towards the horizon.

'It really is.'

'That was quite some night, Rae.'

'It was, and I was just thinking that I feel better, lighter. Just talking about it was good, Howard.'

He nodded.

'But . . .' She paused and he held her gaze. 'You know that this doesn't make everything okay? It doesn't mean we laugh and skip off into the sunset. We are still pretty broken, you and I. Closer, I admit; healed a little, even. But being able to move closer over our loss and being estranged because of Karina – they are two very different things.

You do know that, don't you?' It felt important for her to lay down the distinction.

'I do.' He swallowed and looked down. 'But the fact you let me hold you in my arms and comfort you has given me hope, Rae. And I will cling to that hope, and pray that it's a beginning, the beginning of forgiveness. Is that too much to ask?'

'No, not too much to ask.' She looked away. 'But it might be too much for me to give.'

She stood slowly and, with sadness flowing in her veins that they might never be able to go back to that time of love and happiness, took one last look at the glorious sunrise before slipping inside for her shower.

TEN

After lunch, Howard and Vinnie took a taxi into St John's to go shopping. Rae and Dolly chose two sunloungers by the edge of the pool and sat down.

'Nice to be back to just of the two of us, isn't it?' Dolly asked.

'It is, and only three days left of our holiday.'

'Don't even say that!' Dolly huffed, as she unpacked from her beach bag books, water, straw hat, sun oil, earphones, phone, magazine, sunglasses, a packet of boiled sweets and a spare towel.

Rae laughed. 'You do know that your apartment is only a ten-minute walk away?'

'Of course. Why?' Dolly smoothed the creases from her towel and kicked off her sandals.

'Because it looks like you are either moving here or preparing for an emergency, I'm not sure which.'

'I do like to be prepared.' Dolly took up position and the two women lay back. Rae closed her eyes and thought that she was really going to miss the warmth of the sun.

'And yes, and I mean it. It *is* nice to be just the two of us, Dolly – but I know you have loved seeing your man.' It was the first time the two had been alone since the men's arrival and Rae knew it was good to break the ice. The feelings of wariness when in her friend's company still felt strange; the changes were almost imperceptible, but to her – and, she was certain, for Dolly too – they seemed huge.

'I can't help it. I love him.'

'I had noticed. It's gone quick, this holiday, hasn't it?'

'It has, but that's the way with any vacation, isn't it? At the beginning you are so excited because you have this long period of time stretching ahead of you that feels like forever, and then one day you look up and realise you are halfway through and then the last few days pass in the blink of an eye; and when you have been back home for two days in the rain, it's like you were never away and it's hard to believe that "this time last week . . ."'

Rae smiled at this truth, no matter how depressing. 'Please don't talk about rainy old London. Not yet.'

'You and Howard seem to be getting on well – and I am not prying.'

Rae sat up and stared at her friend. 'You are not prying? Who are you and what have you done with Dolly?'

'Okay, so I might be prying a bit. But you do seem to be getting on well.' There was an unmistakable note of hope in Dolly's voice. It might have been toned down – perhaps there'd even been some coaching from Vinnie – but it was still prying.

'Better, yes, I think so. But, as I reminded him, it's a slow process and there are no guarantees.'

'True, but this sounds very different to the angry "ain't never going to happen" tone that you had only a week ago.'

'I guess so.' Rae considered this. 'It's funny, I feel better for letting go of some of the anger; almost like I don't have the energy to carry on a fight like that.'

'I hear ya!' Dolly fanned her face with her hand. 'I mean, I don't even have the energy to go and get a drink even though I really want one!'

'Do you want me to go and get you a drink?' Rae shielded her eyes and looked at her friend, who stuck her tongue out to one side as if parched.

'Oh, Rae, well . . . only if you are going anyway – that'd be lovely!'

Dolly picked up her magazine. Rae tied her long kimono over her swimming costume and made her way along the path to Max's. Her stomach flipped at the sight of Antonio behind the bar. She had been avoiding the place for the last few days – or avoiding him, to put it more accurately.

'Rae-Valentine!' he called loudly, and she was glad the place was empty but for a young couple sitting on the step by the beach, far more interested in each other than what was going on behind them.

'Good afternoon, Antonio.' The sight of him brought a flutter of joy, no matter how misplaced.

'Oh, good afternoon! I see how it is: we are all formal now!'

She felt the sharp barb in his tone, an undercurrent that lurked behind his wide smile. Her joy turned into something closer to embarrassment.

'Can I get two Cokes, please?'

'Of course, of course.' He reached into the fridge. 'So where is your gang?'

'Hardly a gang! My husband, brother-in-law and Dolly.'

Antonio placed the bottles on the bar.

'Thank you.' She smiled, trying for friendly while attempting to reset the over-familiar tone she had used before Howard and Vinnie turned up. She felt instantly guilty at this acknowledgement.

'I miss the real Rae-Valentine.' He spoke softly.

'I am the real Rae-Valentine,' she answered with a slight tremor to her voice.

Antonio shook his head. 'I don't think so. I think the real Rae-Valentine is the girl who laughed on the beach, the girl who I think I might have persuaded to come octopus fishing with me, the girl who blushed if I complimented her, the girl who was considering letting her soul get stitched to mine . . . I was so close!' He held her eye and thumped the bar top.

Rae reached for the cold bottles and spoke levelly. 'You were not so close. Not at all. I liked talking to you, Antonio, I did. But, as I told you before, I am someone's wife and I am someone's mum. And there is very little space for anything else.'

'Barmen are the best medicine.' He smiled. 'And I know I made you feel better.'

She stared at him.

'It's a great shame.' He kept his eyes trained on her face.

'Oh, please don't start with that.' She looked around the bar with an embarrassed shake of her head. 'There will be another lonely heart along in a few—'

'No! No!' He knitted his brows. 'You misunderstand me. I don't mean it's a shame I could not get closer to you – although, yes, for me that is true.'

'What did you mean?' She was curious, knowing she should probably leave and head back to Dolly, yet wanting at some level to know that she might be missed. Her fragile ego was drawn to the practised words of this man, who was quite beautiful.

'I mean it's a shame you stay with the man with the loud voice and the fancy watch who stops you hopping from island to island with your red knapsack. He's not for you.'

She glared at the barman, who had gone a step too far, not only in his judgement of Howard, but also for taking her innermost desire and expressing it so freely when she had done her best to tamp down the longing to pack up and go. Her plan to travel was a mental escape hatch, nothing more, and to hear him spout it now felt like mockery. 'You don't know anything about him or us, nothing.'

'I know that you think to betray someone, you have to think they shine less than brightly, that they are not worthy of consideration, because if they mattered to you that much – if they stood out, if they were the most important thing to you – you wouldn't betray them, would you? Remember?'

'Yes, I do remember. I also know that I shouldn't have told you that and I wish I hadn't and I also wish you hadn't been mean to my husband over the whole cocktail thing. I know you thought that was funny, but it wasn't. Not at all. It wasn't very kind.'

'I see things, Rae-Valentine,' he countered, his stare unwavering.

Rae stood tall and dug deep to find a confident voice that might help her stop the quake in her gut. 'You might think you see things, Antonio, but what you are actually getting is a snapshot of a life, a glimpse of a marriage while people are here for this short window of time on vacation. You don't see the whole picture, and that skews everything.'

'Maybe.' He smiled at her.

Rae put her sunglasses on, picked up the cold Cokes and left without looking back, stomping along the path to find Dolly.

'Flipping 'eck, I thought you'd forgotten and jumped in the sea! I was just about to send a catamaran out to find you, but then I realised there is no wind and we fly in three days.'

Rae laughed.

Dolly reached out and took her drink. 'Thank you, Rae.'

'My pleasure.'

'Did you see whatshisname?'

'Yes.' Rae looked down at her friend and wondered if she knew Antonio was behind the bar.

'And we're all good?' Dolly asked knowingly.

'Yes, Dolly, we are all good.'

The two sat quietly, each with their own thoughts. Rae hated the ball of confusion that bounced inside her, a potent mixture of anger and foolishness. She placed her palm on her stomach and took a deep breath. *How dare he!*

Lying back in the sun, alone with her thoughts, she must have fallen into a doze, because when she awoke she found Howard and Vinnie standing at the end of the lounger. The sun had dropped a little and the heat had been drawn from the day. She felt her skin goosebump and pulled her kimono around her body.

'Did you have a nice time in town?' she asked, rubbing the sleep from her eyes.

'We did!' Vinnie smiled.

'We did indeed!' Howard clapped and spoke loudly, and she saw the glint of sunshine on his fancy watch.

'All set?' Dolly asked.

The men nodded conspiratorially and Rae noted that they avoided eye contact with her.

'All set for what?' she asked, a little confused.

'I'll tell you all about it later.' Howard smiled at her.

'Okay . . . Sounds mysterious.' She laughed nervously.

'I need a wee.' Dolly sat round on the sunlounger.

'Are you going to go and use the bathroom or just stick your butt over the edge of the swimming pool?' Howard asked his sister.

And just like that, the four of them were laughing.

'Are you lot ever going to let me forget that?'

'No!'

'Definitely not!'

'As if!'

Rae looked at the three of them, people she cared about, people who shared her history, and she realised that this – *this* – was actually the best medicine.

◆ ◆ ◆

With Howard in the shower, she put a call in to Hannah.

'Mum! Oh my God, Mum! It wasn't my fault!'

Her daughter's panicked tone caused Rae's heart to miss a beat. 'Hannah? What a very odd way to answer the phone – is everything okay?'

'Yes! Kind of. I just thought you might have spoken to George or Uncle Paul.'

'Okay, why would I have spoken to Uncle Paul? And now I am worried – what's going on?' Rae sat down on the sofa and her mind raced with all the terrible possibilities, ranging from Hannah having totalled the car to being injured or something having happened to George and a million scenarios in between, all equally unpleasant.

'Nothing!'

Then there was silence, and Rae felt she could hear her daughter's cogs whirring.

'How long have you known me, Hannah Bee Banana?'

'My whole life. Obvs.'

'Right, and do you think there is any chance that I am joking when I say that I am sorely tempted right now to jump on a plane and get home as soon as is humanly possible because you are scaring the living daylights out of me?'

'No, Mother, no chance at all.'

'Right, so what has happened?' Rae swallowed, her breath coming in short bursts.

'Okay, well, don't freak out!'

'For the love of God, Hannah!' Her patience was waning fast. 'The one phrase to guarantee that I actually freak out is "Don't freak out"!'

'Okay, Mum, I get it!' She heard Hannah take a deep breath. 'Niamh and I were staying at the house.'

'Niamh your friend from college?' Rae recalled Howard mentioning her.

'Yes.'

'At our house, in London?' She wondered if Hannah meant her student place in Liverpool.

'Yes, Mum, we're at home right now. And we decided to put a pizza in the oven.'

'So far so good,' Rae encouraged.

'Anyway, we jumped in the bath and forgot about the pizza and . . .' Hannah paused. 'Cutting a long story short, the oven caught fire and the kitchen got a little bit burned and the fireman came with these massive foamy fire-extinguisher things that they keep on the fire engine, and it was all sorted very quickly – all much more dramatic than it needed to be, in my opinion, and the house smells a bit, well, smoky, but it's all okay. I called George but he was out with Ruby so he called Uncle Paul, who came over with Sadie. And Paul says it's all covered on the insurance and Sadie cleaned up a bit and I spoke to Nana Mitzy and she said you needed a new kitchen anyway because your cupboards were a bit dated, and I called George back and told him exactly what had happened and he and Ruby went crazy, and George said—'

'Hannah!' Rae raised her voice. 'Darling, hold it right there. Stop talking! Just for a minute.' There was a moment of silence while she digested the facts and her heart rate slowed. 'You are not hurt?'

'No.'

'No one is hurt?'

'No, Mum, no one is hurt.'

Rae nodded and took a deep breath. 'Did you say you were in the bath with Niamh?'

'Uh-huh.' She heard the tremble to her daughter's voice and the loud swallow that followed.

'Is . . . is she nice?' Rae asked.

'Mu . . .' Hannah took a while to answer, as if keeping her emotion at bay and struggling a little. 'She's really nice. She is in fact wonderful.'

Rae let her head drop to her chest and closed her eyes. 'Does she make you happy?' she whispered, clutching the phone to her face.

'Happier than I ever thought was possible. In fact, just happy for the first time ever, properly happy. I love her and I hope you like her, Mum.'

Rae nodded and her heart swelled at the sound of her daughter's voice, edged with that slightly dazed, delirious quality that was present in the first throes of love. She remembered it well. 'My darling girl, if she truly loves you then I will truly love her. It really is that simple.'

She and Hannah sat in silence on the phone. No words were needed as their love flowed across the ocean, straight down the telephone and into the heart of the other.

Howard came out of the bathroom after she'd hung up, towel-drying his hair. He stopped in front of her as she sat very still on the sofa, staring into space.

'Were you on the phone?' he asked casually, reaching into his open suitcase on the floor.

'Yes.' Rae nodded.

'Who was it?' he asked. He stepped into clean pants and sprayed aftershave over his chest.

'It was Hannah, actually.'

He smiled. 'Oh! Is she okay?'

'Yes, more than okay. She is at home. And she's gay. She's in love with Niamh and they burned the kitchen down.'

Howard's mouth dropped open. Then his lips moved, but no words came out.

'I know, Howard. I know. Take your time. We'll talk about it later.'

With that, Rae headed into the shower.

By the time she and Howard arrived at the table in the restaurant, Dolly and Vinnie had devoured the bread rolls.

'Thank the Lord! We are starving! I am actually dying here!' Dolly reached for her wine.

'Sorry, bit of a crisis at home.' Howard grimaced and sat down.

'Glass of wine, Rae?' Vinnie offered.

'Not for me, thanks. Think I'll stick to the water tonight.'

'So . . .' Dolly coughed. 'Is the crisis about the fact that your daughter has burned your house to the ground or is it something else?'

'You spoke to Sadie?' Rae asked.

'Of course I spoke to Sadie!' Dolly banged the table. 'Everyone has spoken to Sadie! Jesus, that woman is more efficient than *The Times* at spreading news – and a hell of a lot cheaper.'

Rae knew her other sister-in-law would have been keen to fill everyone in on the details and probably add a few of her own observations for good measure. An image of Karina flashed into her mind and she wondered how many people Sadie had filled in with *those* details and which of her own observations she might have added for good measure. She swallowed, still surprised by the feeling of vulnerability that coated her skin. Things felt different now she was not entirely sure of Dolly's unwavering support in all matters; it was as if she had lost one of the pillars that kept her upright. It was all she could do not to hold the table and cling on for dear life.

'So what do you think?' Rae took a sip of water and asked Dolly, knowing this was the best way to move forward: with everything laid out in plain sight.

'About the kitchen? I think go to Ikea; they have some great units and if you don't spend a fortune you won't feel bad about replacing it in a few years' time if you get fed up with it.'

'And the lesbian thing?'

Dolly took a slug of wine. 'I don't know if they have those in Ikea.'

Howard laughed.

Dolly placed her glass on the table and sat forward. 'I think . . .' she began, 'that I love Hannah and I think I always have and I know I always will.' She spoke sincerely. 'And if she is happy, we are happy. That's it, isn't it? I mean, for the love of God, it's the twenty-first century – love is love!'

Rae smiled at her best friend, warmed by her words, so lovingly spoken. 'My thoughts exactly.'

Howard reached for her hand across the tabletop to give it a squeeze and she let him. She saw the way Dolly dug Vinnie in the ribs with her elbow and she looked around for the waiter, feeling cornered. Actually, now would be a very good time for a glass of wine.

The four ate dinner in good humour, once they had established that Hannah wasn't hurt and the damage had been limited to the kitchen. Rae decided to suppress any concern over how her favourite room in the house might now look; Hannah's revelation was the big news, not a scorched countertop. There was, however, a flicker of sadness at the thought that the square room at the heart of her home, where she indulged in her favourite activity, might be changed. The kitchen might have been 'dated', to coin Mitzy's phrase, but it was Rae's place of escape; where, with her hands in pastry, kneading dough or stirring a sauce, she felt her heart soar with gladness and a sense of wellbeing as she prepared food for her loved ones.

'Who's in the mood for a nightcap?' Vinnie suggested.

'Not for me.' Howard sat back in the chair. 'I was going to ask you if you fancied a walk, Rae?'

'Oh, sure.' She looked over at Dolly. 'Are you guys coming?'

'No, love. Think we'll have a quick snifter on the terrace and call it a night.'

'Well, night night. Sweet dreams. See you in the morning.' Rae blew a kiss to Dolly and followed Howard out of the restaurant towards the beach.

As they trod the path through the garden, Howard called ahead, 'Ah, good evening, Nick and Nora!'

He was too loud and too quick for Rae to intervene, and she felt her heart race with embarrassment. Nick – or rather Douglas – held his wife's hand and stared at them.

'Are you talking to us?' Nick asked, defensively.

'Yes, of course!'

'Why are you calling us Nick and Nora?' he asked, with a look of utter confusion.

'I'm sorry?' Howard looked at Rae, who felt her face turn puce. 'Dolly said those were your names.'

'No!' Nick shook his head. 'My name is Douglas and my wife is Mary.'

Not for the first time that evening, Howard looked at a loss for words. 'Well, h . . . have a lovely evening, Douglas and Mary.' Rae watched her husband as he affected a kind of bow, and her face flamed with the kind of high-level awkwardness usually reserved for his sister. 'And sorry about the mix-up!'

He walked on briskly and she followed him. It wasn't until they reached the beach that she bent forward and closed her eyes, laughing with relief. 'Oh my God, Howard! She calls them Nick and Nora Knowitall – but that's not their real names! And not to their face!'

'Well, obviously I know that now!' Howard laughed. 'That bloody Dolly!'

'I can't believe you just did that. I am so embarrassed!' Rae covered her mouth with her hand.

'Good news is you are not likely to see them again once we leave here.' Howard reached up and took her wrist and pulled her hand into his. 'That thing you do, when you cover your mouth. You used to do it all the time when I first met you.'

'I did?'

He nodded. 'It was like you were hiding, covering up what you might want to say or your smile, and it used to make me sad because I know you better than anyone and you only have good things to say and funny comments and your smile is beautiful. It is so beautiful and you had stopped doing it, a long time ago. This is the first time I've seen it in years.'

Rae nodded. Her heart still fluttered a little when he called her beautiful. 'I guess my confidence has taken a bit of a beating.'

'I know.' He looked down at the sand. 'I know. And I know it's my fault.'

She didn't correct him.

Howard started to walk towards the shoreline and she fell in beside him. 'You said Hannah sounded happy?'

Rae felt gladness swell inside as she looked out towards the horizon, where the moonlight danced on the calm sea and the flip and twist of fins and tails broke the surface, sending ripples along the water. 'She did. Happier than I have ever heard her. That angry base note was gone, you know? She was always wound up; and as much as I loved talking to her, seeing her, I was always wary because she could be on the verge of losing her temper. But tonight, despite the drama, she sounded calm – nervous, but calm.'

'It took a lot of guts to tell you so plainly.'

'It did, Howard. I'm not so happy about the potential state of the kitchen . . .' She grimaced. 'But I'm trying not to think about it until I get home.'

Home . . . She glanced briefly at her husband and wondered if he, like her, was thinking that it hadn't felt like home for a while.

'We can get another kitchen and no one was hurt.' He kicked at the sand.

'That's true.'

'There is something I want to say to you.' He stopped walking, and faced her. 'Firstly, I want to give you this.' He reached into his pocket and pulled out the flat black velvet box.

'Oh, Howard.' She ran her fingertips over her forehead. She felt conflicted: conscious of this gesture of apology but still hating the beautiful bauble, which for her would always carry the connotation of being a consolation prize, a sweetener her husband hoped might help her forgive his horrible misdemeanour. 'I don't really know what to say.'

She shook her head as he stepped behind her and placed the necklace around her neck. The weight of the teardrop against her chest was heavy, heavier than was comfortable for her.

Still standing there, Howard pulled her close to him, breathing against the nape of her neck. 'What I want to say, Rae-Valentine, is this: I want us to renew our vows.'

She spun around to face him and couldn't stop her sharp burst of laughter. 'What?'

'I want to renew our marriage vows, retake the promises that I made to you twenty-five years ago.' His eyes were misty. 'It's what Vinnie and I were sorting out in town today. This was always the purpose of coming here. It was always my plan: to stand together, just you and me, and for me to recommit myself to you.'

Rae tried to sort the jumble of phrases that jostled on her tongue – of which *Are you fucking crazy?* was the loudest. She toned it down. 'Are you kidding me? There's absolutely no way we can do that, Howard!'

She stepped away from him, embarrassed and irritated by his lack of awareness. The fact that he even thought this was possible showed how mentally wide of the mark he was. She considered that maybe he, like Dolly, thought it was possible to pretend . . .

'Of course there is!' he enthused, undeterred. 'And it's nothing to do with frocks or cakes or even guests. It's just something between you and me – the two of us, making promises.'

'Promises you found hard to keep.' This as much a reminder to herself as to her husband.

'Promises that I want to say out loud again. Promises that will be the new glue, spoken from the heart to reconnect us and make us feel how we did on the path of that lake; I had never felt so connected to anyone or anything before in my whole life and I haven't since: soul to soul, body to body. Please, Rae.'

'But don't you see? Don't you get it?' She spoke softly, hiding the anguish that blossomed in her chest. 'It would be fake, trying to fast-track something that can't be rushed – a sticking plaster! Another way to mask the hurt. But I am not ready and I am not sure. I'm sorry, Howard.' She reached around to the back of her neck and unclipped the necklace, then placed it in his palm.

'Can you at least think about it?'

She looked at him and felt the stirring of sympathy for her husband, who was trying and failing. She recognised that it was now not only about his infidelity, but the direction in which she wanted to head, wondering not for the first time if paving her own way might actually be possible. She pictured a red knapsack.

'I don't need to think about it, Howard. It's not something I feel comfortable doing. And I won't do it. I can't.'

'Maybe in the future?' He looked at her wide-eyed with hope.

She reached out and took his hand into her own, where it sat, warm and familiar. 'Maybe. Or maybe we will always be like china that got smashed and no matter how meticulously we glue ourselves back together things will never be quite the same again; there will always be small fragments of us missing, hairline cracks, if you look hard enough. It means we would always be fragile. Do you want to live like that?'

'If it means I have you, then yes.'

'Oh, Howard.' She sighed and rubbed her eyes. 'Don't look so dejected.'

'I can't help it. I feel dejected.' He sniffed.

'You were right, you know.' She took a deep breath.

'About what?'

'This holiday. Being in a new place without the distraction of work and the kids, away from our routine – it's been good to help get our heads straight, to figure things out.'

'But we are not there yet, are we?'

'No, Howard, we are not there yet.'

'I told you I would do whatever it takes and that I would wait for as long as it takes – and I will, Rae. I will.'

'Well, that's got to be a good start.' She smiled at him.

'Do you fancy going to Max's for an Idiot Returns?'

Rae looked skyward and remembered her chat with Antonio: *I see things . . .*

'I would like nothing less. How about we go and find Dolly and Vinnie on the terrace and join them for that nightcap?' She let go of his hand and started to walk up the beach.

'Sounds like a plan.' He followed her. 'So, Niamh, eh?'

'Yep, Niamh.' She glanced at him over her shoulder.

'It's ironic really.'

'What is, Howard?'

'We own a restaurant business. Cooking simple food is our livelihood; and between the two of them they couldn't manage to heat up a bloody pizza without burning down the house!'

'I know, right? As Dolly would say, kill me now!'

They laughed together. Rae looked to her right and spied Antonio gathering glasses at the back of Max's bar. She slipped her hand through Howard's arm and leaned in close. *Yes, Antonio, all you get is a snapshot, a glimpse; and we, as a couple, as a family, are so much more than this . . .*

ELEVEN

'Don't make me stay here! Please take me back to the sunshine! I promise I'll be good!' Dolly banged on the inside window of the taxi that had just dropped Rae and Howard in front of the house in Lawns Crescent. Rae laughed, mainly at the bewildered look on the taxi driver's face.

'Don't forget: if you can't cope without a kitchen, come and stay with us!' Dolly called out.

'Dolly, I have been with you for the last ten days, Rae even longer – we want to be far away from you for a while. At the very least to let our hearing recover.' Howard laughed.

Rae placed her single suitcase on the pavement and looked at her sister-in-law with her shock of red hair. As the cab drove past, Dolly was looking straight ahead, but flipping the bird at them in an almost regal manner.

She laughed. 'That sister of yours.'

'Tell me about it.' Howard dug around in his travel bag for the house keys.

Rae stood at the bend in the street and felt the autumnal chill against her skin. Looking up and down the crescent, she wondered what she had missed while she had been away, besides the near burning down of their house by Hannah and her new girlfriend. She pictured the twitch of net curtains as the fire brigade rolled up.

Mrs Williams's light was on and Mr Jeffries had put his plastic recycling out in good time for tomorrow, which was good: all was as it was meant to be in the world of Lawns Crescent. Rae found some small sense of peace in the ordinariness of being home with life slowly ticking by, but noticed for the first time the chipped paint on the windowsills, the weeds growing between the cracks on the uneven pavement and the broken shade on the street lamp opposite. She wondered how she had not acknowledged these imperfections before. She recognised that she felt a little different, less adrift than she had before she left for Antigua. And strangely it was no longer the thought of Howard and Karina that filled her mind, but Dolly's words: *What did you give up on exactly?* – spoken with a slight edge of disbelief to her tone. It was as if the verbal bomb from Howard had blown up the path ahead, and with some of Dolly's patina stripped away Rae was now forced to reconsider her route, her motivation and her destination, almost as if the event had put something in motion, woken her from a stupor. And one thing Rae-Valentine knew for sure: she didn't feel like going back into hibernation anytime soon.

Howard opened the front door and the acrid smell of smoke was strong, surprising and quite overpowering.

'Oh my God! It smells terrible!' Rae placed her fingers over her nostrils and breathed through her mouth. 'That's not good!'

It was an odd thing; with the familiar scent of her home gone, the place didn't really feel like home at all. The bitter stench was vaguely reminiscent of melted plastic, and she could tell by the way her lungs reacted that it was also probably noxious.

She coughed and followed Howard along the narrow hallway, where the tell-tale marks from dirty, sooty firefighter jackets now sat in skids along the pale cream paintwork, incongruous with the gilt-framed pictures of hayricks and the idyllic country scenes that neatly lined the wall above, undisturbed. There were one or two rubber scuffmarks on the parquet flooring, probably from heavy-soled fireproof boots.

'Jesus H. Christ!' Howard walked into the kitchen first.

They both stood and silently surveyed the damage. Rae hadn't known what to expect. Mentally she had tried to strike a balance between Hannah telling her everything was 'fine' with the fact that the situation had warranted calling the fire brigade. The level of destruction was beyond what she had imagined; the smell and the way the room felt – in fact, the way the whole house felt – was worse, much worse. Her heart sank at the loss of her refuge, the one room where her skills came alive and she could practise her love of cookery.

A large black smudge now licked up the cupboards on either side of the oven. It looked like a grim carbon portal to another world. The doors were misshapen, melted at the edges, and the countertop surrounding the area was blackened, bubbled and peeling. It was odd – at the back of the counter sat her ceramic lidded jars of coffee, tea and sugar, lined up and facing the right way, like a prop that had been added. She felt a flex in her heart at the memory of the thousands of cosy warm drinks she had prepared for a thousand visitors in this very room, with her hands on the surface, now ruined. The oven itself was missing a door and the linoleum floor was scuffed and dirty. Howard opened the window and the breeze that whipped around the room gave almost instant relief.

Rae stood with a sinking feeling as her husband made his way around the house, opening more windows – though this definitely helped; either that or she was becoming accustomed to the smell. He thundered back down the stairs to the kitchen and she could tell by his footfall that he was not in the best of moods.

'It bloody stinks! We are going to have to strip down all the curtains and blinds and get them washed, and all the bed linen, clothes – anything fabric. The carpets too; they need professional cleaning. The smell is in the air up there.'

'Oh God.' Her stomach bunched at the news.

'Yep, "Oh God" is right. You know, Rae, I felt a lot better-humoured about the whole thing when I was in the sunshine with a cocktail in my hand. Here, on this rainy day, facing the gloomy destruction in what used to be our kitchen and the way the whole place smells, I feel a lot less jolly about it. The only place that doesn't really stink is the top floor; we might have to confine ourselves to the bedrooms. At least we have a TV up there, and we can get takeaway delivered.'

Rae gave a dry laugh. As if, with these two elements covered, nothing else mattered. She stared at the sorry sight of her once-pristine kitchen; and, at Howard's mention of bedrooms, wondered for the first time about their sleeping arrangements tonight. With this disaster and the new level of cordiality between them, would Howard assume it was okay to climb back into their marital bed? And did she mind? It had felt different in Antigua; they'd had no choice but to share a room and the Grand Canyon between them provided her with a comfortable barrier. She also hadn't minded the odd night when they had chatted in the darkness, keeping to topics like the kids and Toby . . . it still jarred her to use his name. She now felt conflicted and decided to discuss it that evening at bedtime, rather than have the conversation now and add to the growing tension of the day; that would feel like throwing fuel on the fire, so to speak.

She nodded. 'Cup of tea?'

'Yes, I would love a cup of tea. Thank you. At least we have a working kettle.'

'Yep, every cloud and all that.' Rae filled the kettle and placed it on the slightly gritty surface. 'The whole kitchen is going to need replacing. In my mind I thought we might be able to paint it and fix the oven, but there's no chance of that, is there?' She ran her hands over the greasy fridge door. Everything was covered in the residue of smoke, fire or whatever it was they had used to extinguish it.

'Nope.' Howard stood by the window.

Rae looked up at the blackened scorch marks that fanned out on the ceiling like the shadow branches of a tree.

'I need to talk to our daughter. This is really not good enough.' Howard sighed, taking out his phone and muttering to himself as he dialled. 'Hannah, it's Dad.' He spoke sternly with a set expression and one hand on his hip. Rae couldn't make out the words, but could hear the energised, enthused tone of her daughter down the line. When Howard spoke again, he sounded softer; his mouth twitched into a smile and his shoulders dropped. 'Yes, yes, we are home and yes, we have seen the kitchen.' He looked at Rae and rolled his eyes. 'No, there is no need for you or Niamh to feel concerned. We can sort it all out and the main thing is that you guys are okay – it could have been a lot worse, by the look of things.' There was a pause while he listened. 'Yes, I don't see why not. That sounds great. Let me just check with Mum.' He placed his cupped palm over the receiver. 'She wants to come down with Niamh next weekend. We don't have any plans, do we?'

We . . . we . . . is this it? Back to coupledom so quickly? So neatly? Rae pictured an escape hatch closing and took a deep breath, as if she were being plunged into something airless.

'Other than choosing, buying and installing a new kitchen, no.' She smiled and reached for the mugs, which she scrubbed with washing-up liquid under the hot tap.

'Mum said that's great. We shall look forward to seeing you then, Hannah Bee Banana.' He ended the call and looked at her.

'Gee, Howard, you really told her! I bet she was quaking for forgiveness.'

He folded his arms across his chest, leaning back against the sink. 'You know, you are right. She sounds different, happy, and I couldn't do it. I didn't want to burst that bubble, plus she was with Niamh and I thought it would be a little off to shout at her with her, her . . .'

'Girlfriend?'

'Yes, her girlfriend present. And what I said was true: it could have been a lot worse – just look at it, Rae!' His eyes swept the room. 'It doesn't bear thinking about. If the fire had taken hold, or they'd fallen asleep, or a million other scenarios that have gone through my mind – all ones that end with Hannah getting hurt. I can't stand the thought of it.'

'I know.' Rae felt sick at the prospect.

'I'm looking forward to seeing her next week and to meeting Niamh,' he added.

'I'm looking forward to seeing her too. How are you feeling about the whole thing? I mean, I know you're happy that she's happy, of course, but I guess it's different from what you envisaged for her.'

He looked out of the kitchen window and seemed to consider this. 'It is. And I guess at some level I always hoped that the guy she settled with might be like George, another son, and then I would picture all the things we could do together – bloke stuff, like fishing and smoking cigars.'

Rae couldn't contain her burst of offended laughter. 'First, I think you'll find there are some girls who like to smoke cigars and go fishing too, and second, neither you nor George has to my knowledge ever done either of those things!'

'I was just saying.' He stood with his palms open and upturned, all innocence.

'You amaze me, Howard. You are the best dad – loving, considerate, open – and so for me this makes your casual, everyday sexism even harder to fathom.' She wasn't sure if he had always been this way or whether with the loss of his superstar status in her mind she was now more aware of the negative aspects of Howard Latimer.

'I was only saying!'

'I know, I know, but just think before you speak next weekend. We don't want to burst Hannah's bubble, as you say, or worse, scare off Niamh. And I don't want Hannah to fly into one of her rants over something you have said or done – it won't show her at her best.'

'I think if Niamh has spent any time with our daughter, she will already know of her rants.'

'Probably,' Rae conceded.

'But you know, when you love someone, Rae, you love all of them, faults and all.'

She smirked to herself, half-admiring his constant attempt to coerce her. 'Is that right?'

She let this hang, and poured water into the mugs.

'So next week I can't say, keep those girls away from the kitchen!'

'Oh no, Howard, you can say that! I'm not letting either of them within feet of my kitchen. Sweet Jesus!' She looked again at the mess and wondered where she should begin.

Rae languished in the bath, soaking her muscles, which were tired from the day of travelling, three laundry loads, the taking down of curtains and the scrubbing of the paintwork in the hallway. It had been a busy few hours and already the feeling of lying under hot sun on warm sand was a distant memory.

She had written a long and daunting list of chores that included:

Empty kitchen cupboards

Run down freezer

Organise new kitchen

Remove old one

Find out Niamh's favourite food

Figure out a plan, Rae – how you go forward

MAKE DECISIONS!!

BE BRAVE!!

Eventually she hauled herself reluctantly from the bubbles and headed for the bedroom. She rubbed body lotion into her skin, which for the last two weeks had grown used to the kiss of warm sunshine and was already missing it. The phone on the bedside table rang.

'I don't want to be here! I want to live on holiday where someone else makes my bed and my breakfast. Plus I miss you.'

'You can't miss me, Dolly – we only said goodbye a few hours ago.'

'Well, I do! I got used to you being around and now you are not. How's the house?'

Rae took a deep breath. 'Worse than I imagined, actually. It smells. Really stinks. The smoke has got everywhere apart from the top floor. I have just had a bath, but I can still smell it on my hair. Or it might be that it's up my nose and so I can smell it everywhere.'

'Yuck. If it's any consolation, my house smells too. Lyall has been staying here with his mates and it reeks of fried food and spilled beer. I have all the windows open; it's bloody freezing. I have a jumper on over my pyjamas.'

'Well, I have all the windows open trying to get rid of the smell of the fire, and I too am bloody freezing.'

'What kind of pizza was it?' Dolly asked.

Rae guffawed. 'How should I know, and why does that matter?'

'Just wondered.'

'Way too involved.' Rae smiled.

Dolly laughed. 'I am proud of you, Rae-Valentine.'

'What are you proud of me for?' She sat back against her soft pillows and pulled up her knees, knotting the curly phone wire around her fingers.

'For a million things, but right now because of the way you are treating Howard and the way you are kind and the way you are keeping all the doors open for the future.'

'Doors *and* windows; no wonder I'm so cold.'

'You know what I mean.'

'Yep.' Rae bit her bottom lip, feeling a flash of guilt and knowing that this was not the time or place to share the fact that equally, she thought about a life beyond those doors and windows . . . Dolly's blindness to the situation and her assumption that everything was fine irritated her. Just because Howard had schlepped out to the Caribbean and they had enjoyed one or two cocktail-fuelled tête-à-têtes was not enough to guarantee happy ever after. She needed more: more time and more discussion. The fact was, her wound was still fresh, even if padded with promises.

'And I wanted to say I am sorry. I am, really sorry,' Dolly gushed.

'Dolly . . .' Rae took a breath. 'There are so many terrible things you have done in our lives that I am literally sitting here trying to figure out which one you are apologising for right now.'

'I don't know what you mean!'

'God, too many to choose from – you photocopied my work at college and passed it off as your own; you told the registrar at the town hall when we went to register her birth that Hannah's name was Chlamydia and it was only because I shouted for her to stop writing and she managed to scrub out the *c*, *h* and *l* that we managed to get it changed!'

'Okay, that was bad. But it was funny!' Dolly wheezed.

'You say inappropriate things to bus drivers and check-in attendants.'

'Hey, I will stop you right there, missy. It got us upgraded!'

'Okay, I'll let you have that one. So what exactly is it you are apologising for this evening?' Rae pulled her shawl around her shoulders.

Dolly's response, when it came, was sober. 'I was rude to you about Antonio and your intentions. I panicked. And I'm sorry because I never told you about what I'd heard.'

It felt odd to hear the barman's name, now, back at home, when the idea of him was already diluted, faded into no more than one thread of the tapestry that formed their time away.

'I doubted you, Rae, and I said hurtful things about your behaviour. I was mean and I should have known you better than that. I could only think that I needed to shout Howard's corner. And when I did hear the rumour from Vinnie, I remember laughing! Laughing loudly because it was so completely unbelievable!'

To me too . . . Rae felt a swell of affection for her friend; these words meant the world. 'I get it, Dolly. I can't say I would have done differently. And I don't know, maybe you were right about the barman. I think I was a bit bowled over at first. I'd been feeling so rubbish, so low, and it felt good to have someone make a fuss over me.'

'It doesn't matter now, Rae. It's done.'

'It is.' She swallowed. 'It's all done.' She said this wishing it were true, and knowing in her heart that things were far from done. In fact, she suspected they might just be getting started. The thought of choosing a new kitchen felt a little overwhelming, as if she did not want to make the emotional investment; and earlier, as she'd scrubbed the rubber marks from the parquet flooring, she'd wondered if it might not be easier to pick up her suitcase and waltz right back out of the door, leaving the mess, the smell and the whole debacle with Howard for someone else to clear up. Ridiculously, she closed her eyes and thought about jumping on a plane and sauntering into Max's with her hair up and her shorts on: *Come on then! Take me fishing! I am making the time!*

'Anyway, it's getting late and I am tired.' Dolly's voice drew her from her daydream. 'I guess I just wanted to call and say I love you.'

'I love you too.' Rae felt the comforting spread of warmth through her bones at the familiar closeness with her best friend. But, hard though it was for her to admit, this did little to fill the gully of disappointment that lined her stomach. She could still hear Dolly's words, her tone, and could see her expression – almost one of dislike – as she leaped to her brother's defence. Rae knew that she would not be unseeing it any time soon.

'I'm looking forward to the party next weekend,' Dolly added.

'What party?' Rae wondered what she had forgotten about.

'Hannah and Niamh! At your house!'

'Is it a party?' She was confused.

'Yes, according to the WhatsApp group! Hannah said we should all come over. She promised champagne and finger food, so . . .'

'Bloody finger food!' Rae shook her head. 'The state of the kitchen, anyone will be lucky to get cheese and crackers.'

'Don't worry about it!' Dolly yawned. 'We'll get one of the restaurants to whip up a buffet. Night, Rae.'

There she goes, thought Rae – straight into solution mode, without allowing for Rae's love of planning and preparing food for any gathering, which gave her a moment to shine. Maybe she was being ridiculous. It had been a long day.

'Goodnight, Dolly.'

She replaced the receiver just as Howard padded into the room, walked confidently to the window and shut the curtains, closing out her view to the top and bottom of the crescent but leaving the creep of light through the gap where the fabric failed to meet. He unbuttoned his shirt and pulled it over his head, balling it in his hands and throwing it to land next to the dirty laundry hamper. He walked into the bathroom and the sound of him peeing filtered back into the room, followed by the sound of him cleaning him teeth, spitting into the sink and gargling mouthwash. Intimate sounds of a life lived together. Ordinarily she paid no heed, but tonight they seemed deafening.

She looked at the end of the bed and pictured him bent over crying and she saw herself on all fours with her hair falling over her face, fighting for breath on the night her world changed.

He flicked the main light switch, made his way over to the bed and, without any discussion or hesitation, drew back the duvet cover and hopped in, throwing the soft top pillow on to the floor and tucking the duvet across his chest with his arms on top, holding it in place.

Just like he always did.

'God, I am exhausted.' He let out a deep, long breath and it felt like mere seconds before his breathing found its slumbering rhythm and he emitted a gentle snore, accompanied by the slackening of his muscles and the murmur of dreamlike oblivion.

Rae watched him in the half-light as shards of moonlight fell across their bed and lit the way over the biscuit-coloured carpet to the door. It reminded her of a landing strip, like markers to help something find its way home in the darkness. It was her favourite thing, magical, when the moon found a way into the bedroom. She looked at her husband; there he was, back in their bed, sleeping the sleep of those who closed their eyes with an easy conscience and a short memory, safe in the knowledge that they would wake happy.

She turned on to her side with an ache in her gut that felt a lot like longing, watching the leaves on the plane trees outside the window dance like shadow puppets in front of the moonlight, reflected on the duvet. She laid her fingers on them, tried to grab them and smiled at the illusion of beauty that for a second had fooled her.

Rae was happy to be out of the house. They had only been back in the UK for a couple of days and just like Dolly the witch had foreseen, it was as if they had never been away. The summer clothes were packed away in hampers that lived under the bed in the spare bedroom; other items were placed in the cherrywood chest of drawers. Her sun-kissed bronze skin had all but lost its sheen, and a team of builders who usually worked on shop fits and remodelling for the restaurants were busy ripping out the frazzled carcass of her kitchen and prepping the walls. All this for the new shiny kitchen she had yet to decide on. She had reluctantly agreed with Howard that it was vital to get the smelly burned units out to give the house a chance to breathe. He didn't seem remotely as fussed as she was that they would be without a kitchen at all during the whole process. She had, this morning, stepped gingerly around the large bins ready to be loaded on to the flat-bed truck full of plasterboard, MDF, strips of wood and the odd appliance as she jumped into her little car. And now she pulled up in front of her childhood home in Purbeck Avenue, looking at the redbrick house with the curved path where a whole family of cement frogs had once lived and she had kissed a boy goodbye at the gate.

The boy who had cheated.

Rae grabbed the paper bags with the gifts for her parents and knocked on the front door.

'She's here! She's here, Maureen!' she heard her dad call out, and it made her heart sing. She knew there were no other people in the whole wide world who would greet her arrival with such excitement. It made her feel like . . . like a rock star.

Her dad opened the door and she walked into the hallway, where he wrapped her briefly in his arms. 'Goodness me, you look very well. Did you have a lovely time?'

'I did, Dad.' She followed him into the sitting room and took a chair next to the sofa.

'Hello, sweetie!' her mum called, bounding in from the kitchen. Her joviality amid the normality of her daily routine made Rae catch her breath. She wondered how it could be that, while things for her were so changed, life in her childhood home in Purbeck Avenue carried on as it always had. She felt the urge to fall into her mum's arms and be held, or to sneak upstairs, kick off her shoes and slip into the single bed of her old room, listening as her parents pottered below with the hum of the television and the occasional whistle of the kettle, safe and sound under her bedspread without too much to trouble her.

'Are you okay, darling? You look miles away.' Her mum touched her arm, gently.

'I'm fine! I am absolutely fine, Mum!' she lied. 'Got you this – just a little something.'

Her mum peered into the bag and pulled out the crocheted tablemat.

'Oh, will you look at that, Len? Thank you, Rae, it's beautiful. I'll put it on the sideboard, under Nan's vase.'

Rae smiled at her mum, knowing that putting it on display meant approval; otherwise it would have been popped into the drawer along with the terracotta coasters she had brought them from Spain last year, clearly not to their taste, and the rather crudely painted, small plaster figurine George had made them of Dumbledore.

'It's so nice to see you. How about a cup of tea?'

'Yes, please, Mum. We have no kitchen and so even making a hot drink is a nightmare. We have put a kettle on a tray on top of an old fridge in the dining room, but it's not exactly convenient. And builders are swarming all over the place.'

'Yes, we heard! George rang while you were away and he said Hannah and her friend were mucking about and the kitchen caught fire, is that right?' Her mum shook her head, as if unable to imagine such a carry-on.

'I don't know that they were mucking about. Apparently they were heating up a pizza and forgot about it. The irony is she didn't order one in, as they were economising! If only they hadn't economised and had spent the extra money on a big pizza to be delivered, it would have saved us a few thousand pounds forking out for a new kitchen!' Rae gave a wry laugh.

'Goodness me. Well, at least no one was hurt. I couldn't sleep, could I, Len? Worrying about what might have happened. I once had an oven glove catch fire on the stove when you kids were little and that scared me half to death. I thought I had turned the gas off and I hadn't, not fully. No actual fire, mind you, but a horrible smouldering mess and we did have to get a new oven glove. I'll go and get that tea.'

'You look tired.' Her dad sat forward in his chair and folded his newspaper in half, placing it on the side table. Of her parents, her dad was the one she was more likely to confide in, for no other reason than that he was less likely to react emotionally and fret: a practical man who she knew could offer practical advice.

'I don't know why. I've done the best part of nothing for two weeks; I have no reason to be tired.'

'Maybe it's the travelling. Travelling can take it out of you.'

'It can,' she agreed.

'And worry – worry can be exhausting.' He spoke knowingly and she got the impression he wanted to say more. Her heart leaped at the thought that their situation might have got back to her dad. How would it be if he knew Howard had let her down, let him down . . . ? This dilemma made her realise that if she was worried about how her parents viewed Howard, then she must at some level believe it possible that they, as a couple, had a future. *Is that it, Rae? A couple of dissenting thoughts and a daydream about a barman – is that the extent of your rebellion?* She felt her cheeks flame with embarrassment.

'It can,' she agreed, again.

The two sat wrapped in an awkward silence for a moment or two, he seemingly waiting for her to divulge more and her waging an internal battle, wondering whether it was best to speak up or shut up. Her dad verbally steered them back into safe waters.

'I have an appointment next week at the hospital, just a blood test thing and a check-up; waste of time probably.' He tutted, but the sparkle in his eye told her that he was actually looking forward to it.

'Oh, well, I'll take you, Dad; just let me know when.'

'Are you sure, love? I know you are busy.'

'Of course!'

Her mum came in with a tray laden with three floral china cups in matching saucers and it made her a little sad – seeing how she had brought out the best tea set, knowing she would have had to stand on her tiptoes and stretch to reach the top shelf for the precious china. The stuff was usually reserved for strangers on whom she wanted to make a good impression, or the infrequent visits of VIPs. Rae was aware that, of late, she was considered both. She pictured coming home from school and sitting in this very spot with her bare feet tucked under her legs, watching television with a chipped mug in her palms, and swallowed the wave of nostalgia.

'Thank you for our grocery deliveries, Rae – it is quite amazing.' Her mum took up the space next to her dad. And there they sat, like they had throughout her life, with him on the left and her on the right. This was how they sat on the sofa, or in the car, and how they lay on their mattress. Rae thought briefly of the lumpy whale and took a sip of her tea. 'The van pulls right up outside and he knocks on the door and gives me a list of all the things he is about to bring in.'

'Yes, I do the list on my computer and so I get a repeat order for you with any extras you might need,' Rae explained.

'It's absolutely marvellous,' her mum continued, as if Rae hadn't spoken. 'He puts the bags right in the kitchen and it always feels like Christmas! So many lovely things. And it's all the brands we like – Dad's favourite yoghurts, our biscuits, everything; just as we like it. Quite amazing!'

'Yes, I do the list on my computer and I *tell* them what to bring.'

'And all the groceries are sorted into different bags: things for the freezer and some things for the cupboard. It's wonderful, all that brought to our door without us having to leave the house.'

'Like magic!' Rae smiled.

'It is, Rae!' her mum agreed, nodding. 'Just like magic.'

'So didn't you have a lovely time at your party!' her dad stated.

It felt like a lifetime ago when she considered how much she had learned since then, remembering the carefree dancing with Hannah and Debbie-Jo, drinking champagne and chatting to George and Ruby – and only hours later being on all fours on the floor as her husband wept his way through his confession.

'I did.' She clattered her teacup on the saucer. *It was a sham! The whole bloody thing was a sham! A distraction!* the voice shouted in her head. 'Did you . . . did you enjoy it, Dad?'

'Oh, yes, it was lovely to see George and his young lady, Ruby – she's a poppet – and of course Hannah. I do wish she'd meet someone nice too and settle down.'

'Well . . .' Rae began, only to be cut short by her mum.

'Debbie-Jo and Lee stayed here afterwards and there were a few sore heads floating around the next morning, I can tell you.'

'I think we kept the bottle bank busy that week – lots of empties. But it was lovely; a nice surprise.' Rae smiled. 'I appreciated everyone coming such a long way.'

'And what about your caravan gift from Debbie-Jo? Wasn't that something?' her dad beamed.

Rae nodded. *Shit!* She had in the midst of her life upheaval quite forgotten about the caravan gift.

'That reminds me: Debbie-Jo needs the dates from you for Lee's parents. Can you let her know?' her mum cut in.

'I will.' Rae mentally added the job to her list.

'It's so lovely down there.' Her dad spoke fondly. 'Your mum and I went for a long weekend last Easter. It's a smashing little place. We used to stroll to the fish and chip shop and ate tea every night on a little deck overlooking the play area. Kids were laughing, sun was out. As I said: smashing. I suggested to your mum we could go back but she's not too keen, are you, love?'

'It's not that I'm not keen, Len. I thought it was a lovely place and we had a nice break, but it's this damn heartburn.' She swallowed with the heel of her hand on her chest. 'It drives me round the twist and I'd rather be in my own bed feeling poorly than anywhere else.'

'You've still got heartburn?' Rae remembered it being mentioned a few months ago; but unlike most of her mum's ailments – which got forgotten or faded, knocked off the top spot by a new illness with its own range of symptoms – this one seemed to be lingering.

'Yes, nearly all the time. I take antacids like sweeties, but they don't seem to do any good.'

'You need to go and see your doctor.' Rae spoke sternly in the way she did when she was trying to get the kids to do her bidding. Not that she had much control over them. She pictured her burned-out kitchen, mostly now lying in a bin.

'I've been, but I might go again.'

Her dad reached across and patted his wife's leg.

'You *need* to,' said Rae. 'Go again, tell them it's getting worse and that you want tests; and if they don't do anything about it, tell me and I will take you see a specialist. I mean it. Don't let them fob you off.'

'Rae, you sound proper bossy!' Her mum laughed, like this was a revelation.

'That's me! Bossy! I think you might be confusing me with Debbie-Jo or Dolly!'

'Did Dolly have a nice holiday? Did she keep out of trouble? I know the lads came out – Howard called us. He couldn't keep away from you.' They smiled at each other; the lads, now nearing fifty, whom her parents still pictured as the teenagers who used to park outside and beep the car horn before whisking their daughter off for a night out, returning her before 10 p.m.

'Are you crying, Rae?'

Rae touched her fingers to her cheek. 'Oh, I'm sorry, Dad. I didn't know I was. I don't know why!' She beamed to prove the ridiculous nature of her tears. 'I just feel a bit—'

'A bit what, love?' Her mum looked concerned.

'I don't know, Mum. I guess I was just thinking how surprising it is to everyone when I sound bossy or assertive. Me!' She sniffed. 'And I wish that wasn't the case. I wish I was more like Dolly or Debbie-Jo. Do you remember when we were little and she would always be singing and performing . . . and I'd be . . . I'd be clinging to the wall.'

'She was a proper little show-off.'

'I think you encouraged her!' Rae laughed now, genuinely, blowing her nose into her tissue and wiping her eyes.

'Oh, we did! We did!' Her mum smiled. 'We had to. I mean, you were always clever, smart, reading books and stuff. You had something about you, but Debbie-Jo, she only had her singing and dancing and I thought we needed to encourage her, give her confidence. You were a different kettle of fish, Rae-Valentine.' Her mum looked at her, holding her gaze.

'I remember telling you I wanted to be a chef, to learn how to cook . . .' she reminded them with more than a whiff of admonishment.

'Yes, but we wanted a special life for you,' her mum insisted. 'An office job. You had the potential, Rae.'

'You did, love. I had spent my working life on the road in a van, getting my hands dirty, grime under my fingernails, but you?' Her dad shook his head. 'We saw you behind a desk.'

Rae looked at her sweet parents and recognised that for her blue-collar dad it was quite some aspiration. To sit behind a desk was seen as an accolade. She felt words stutter in her throat.

Her mum fixed her with a stare. 'You were special and I was just waiting for the day you roared – and I knew that when you did the world would listen. Isn't that right, Len?'

'It's true.' Her dad nodded. 'Your mum used to say, "When that girl finds her voice, she will also find her feet and there'll be no stopping her!"'

'I didn't know that.' Rae swallowed the news like it was sugar and let it flow through her, sweet and restoring. 'I always felt . . .'

'Felt what, love?' Her mum leaned towards her.

'I always felt my life was about to start. I have spent years waiting for it to start.' *And I am still waiting! Still a little lost, but more aware now than I ever have been that what I have and who I have become is not enough!*

Her mum laughed and her expression was one of confusion. 'But you have a wonderful life! Two fantastic kids, a good marriage, you've just come back from Antigua! And you are getting a new kitchen. So much to look forward to.'

Rae opened her mouth and tried to summon the words that might adequately explain how she felt – that she was on the outside looking in, being all things to all people but not the person she needed to be for herself . . .

'So Hannah is home this weekend? She said to come to yours for a party. How are you going to manage with no kitchen?' Her dad changed the tone and the topic and it was probably for the best. Stick to the good topics. The easy stuff.

'Oh, we'll get the restaurant to cater it.'

'Of course. But I do stand by what I said: I wish she'd find someone nice and settle down.'

'I think she is seeing someone, actually, Dad.'

'Oh?' They both sat forward, faces eager for detail, excited and happy all at once.

'Who is it?' her mum asked.

'Well, she is bringing her home this weekend, I think, so we can all meet her. And her name is Niamh, which I think is Irish. A pretty name.' Rae placed her empty cup and saucer on the tray and sat back in the chair, waiting . . .

'So when you say she is seeing someone . . .' Her dad was trying to get the facts straight.

'Yes, she is seeing Niamh. I mean, it's her story to tell and her news. But it's ironic that Hannah, who found her feet and her voice when she was very small, hasn't been that happy, not really. Until now, that is – and she sounds *really* happy. Possibly for the first time. And that's all we want, isn't it? For our kids to be happy? It doesn't matter how or why or who they are with; it's all about being happy – that's the goal! That's everything!'

She saw the look that passed between her parents before they nodded at her with an expression on their faces that was almost sad, and she wondered how much they knew of her situation. Her mum reached out and placed a hand on her knee.

'It is, Rae-Valentine. It really is.'

TWELVE

Rae folded the clean bed linen and placed it in piles on the bed before standing and looking out of the window down at the street below. She gazed up and down the crescent, watching the lights pop on behind drapes and windows closing as the nip of dusk bit on a day of bright autumn sunshine. She saw Mr Jeffries through his kitchen window. He appeared to be singing loudly; not that she could hear a thing, but by the look of his stance – one hand raised at his chest and the other in the air – along with the taut oval of his mouth and his closed eyes, she would guess opera. It was fascinating to watch and yet it felt like an intrusion, staring at this man in his moment of abandon. She looked away. It made her think of Debbie-Jo, whose talent for performing had been encouraged, and she wondered how different things might have been for her, Rae-Valentine, if she had been pushed in the same way. At least now she understood why. It wasn't that her parents had been holding her back. They were in their clumsy way trying to redress the balance in their daughters' lives: she had apparently had the choice of several futures . . . She just hadn't known it. Maybe she could have been smart like Hannah and gone to university, or become a chef, or she could have been a confident world traveller like red-knapsack girl.

Too late now . . . all too late . . . How could I make it happen? Where would I start? She wished the path ahead were not so mired in fog; she wished there were clear pointers helping her find her way.

Out of the corner of her eye she saw darling little Fifi trotting daintily along the kerb with her mum in tow. Rae saw the woman look back over her shoulder. She smiled down at her, wishing they lived in a world where it wouldn't be weird to invite her in and introduce her to the family. She hated to think of her being lonely, too shy to mix when she lived on this busy street of this amazing city.

'What are you up to?'

Howard's arrival made her jump – and there was that familiar air of mock accusation he never ceased to find amusing; as if it were unthinkable that his quiet and reliable wife would ever do anything surprising.

'Just looking out the window.'

'So I see. Are you nervous?'

'About my little girl coming home? Of course not.' She shot him a look. 'I can't wait. And it will be lovely to have George and Ruby here.'

'You know what I mean.' He sat on the edge of the bed.

'I guess the only thing I am a little nervous about is other people's reactions – maybe unnecessarily so, but I'm worried that everyone asking questions about Hannah and her life, as if it *is* a big deal, might just turn it into one.' She turned to fully face him. 'I want everyone to be comfortable, relaxed. All of our guests, of course, but mainly Hannah and Niamh. It's important.'

'I know. And it means the world to me, Rae, that we can show this united front, show Niamh that we are the family Hannah will have described us as.'

An involuntary laugh left her mouth. 'Honestly, Howard? I think it's more important that we work on actually *becoming* united rather than worrying about showing a united front.'

'Well, of course!'

'You say "of course", but since we've been back you have just jumped into bed as if everything is rosy, and you seem . . .'

'I seem what?'

She noticed the pulse of tension on his temple. 'You seem to think that everything is forgiven, forgotten . . . and it's not. The reason we got on better, were able to chat more openly in Antigua, was that you were not only giving me a bit of space, but showing contrition. It was quite seductive; I loved our openness, talking about the baby.'

'About Toby,' he corrected.

She nodded, closing her eyes briefly, the words and image still painful. 'Yes, talking about Toby. It meant the world; and I was interested to see where greater remorse and explanation from you and greater exploration from me might lead us. But instead it's like we were running a race. We got halfway around the track and you saw a shortcut and ran off – leaving me to plod on, alone again.'

He stared at her. 'Just so I understand, you were happiest when I was on my knees, begging for forgiveness?'

'No, not happiest, far from it. But I was willing to listen. And you don't have to be on your knees – that's not what I am saying – but I did like the sincerity of it and we do need to talk about it more. I still have so many questions. I feel—'

'Oh God, Rae!' he interrupted. 'I am trying, you know I am, but you seem to think there is some mystery to it, some deep-rooted reason that needs exploring, and there isn't! There really isn't!' He raised his palms and looked skyward, and this she understood, as she too recently had been hoping for some divine inspiration to shed light on the whole sordid episode. 'It was sex, drunk sex, nothing more, and I let it go to my head and it turned into a flattering two-week thing that I regret. I bitterly, bitterly regret it and I wish . . .' He now balled his fingers into fists and spoke through gritted teeth. 'I wish I could erase it and I wish you knew just how sorry I am. Because I am.'

She looked at her husband standing before her, his expression one of frustration. And she felt a spike of guilt, no matter how misplaced, because it was her who had raised the topic – and also her who was thinking about the possibility of a future that might not include him at all. It felt mean, making him work for forgiveness and the promise of a future when there was even the smallest chance she was going to walk anyway.

'I love you, Rae. I love you so much and I love my kids and I can't, *we* can't, let this one thing sour everything. That would be such a waste. Please. Especially not tonight. Please.'

'Okay.' She nodded, knowing she too did not have the energy for the fight, looking back down through the window as Fifi sniffed around the lamppost outside their house. 'Okay.'

◆ ◆ ◆

She and Dolly stared at the walls of the stripped-out space that only a few weeks ago had been the cosy heart of the home. With just this one room so cold and bare, the whole house had been thrown out of kilter.

'All this because of a pizza?'

'I know, right.' Rae sighed and pressed her hand to the newly plastered wall, which had a kind of earthy smell that was a little unpleasant but miles better than the smoke-infused cupboards that used to be there. 'I am trying to look on the bright side: a new kitchen – yay! – but my heart sinks at the thought of it.'

'Did you ever find out what kind of pizza it was?'

'No! I did not.' Rae laughed. 'But as Hannah and Niamh are due any minute, you can ask them yourself.'

Dolly folded her arms over her scarlet cold-shoulder blouse and chewed her gum. 'So how do you feel about it all?'

'The kitchen?'

'No, the lesbians.'

'God, I wish everyone would stop asking me about it!' Rae rubbed her forehead.

'Well, what did you expect?' Dolly raised an eyebrow.

'Not this, actually.' She sighed. 'I feel it's a shame that when George brought Ruby home for the first time we were just all looking forward to meeting her and it felt exciting. Good nerves, you know? We all wanted to make the right impression.'

'Have you met our family? Good luck with that!' Dolly yelled.

'Seriously, Dolly, it was a good feeling. But this is different and it shouldn't be. I feel like people are being more judgemental or keen to be part of the spectacle, but it's just Hannah bringing back someone she loves. Nothing more. Nothing less.'

'I think you might be a little oversensitive. People, me included, are just happy that Hannah has found someone worthy of her, someone she likes enough to want to introduce to us all. Could you be project-ing your unease?'

Rae considered this. 'I don't think so! God, I hope not! I just want Niamh to feel welcome. I want to help her like Hannah and that means liking us, I think. I remember the first time I met Mitzy and Arturo and they were so nice to me – it kind of drew me in.'

'That was their cunning plan, to hide how nuts they were!'

'Put on a united front?' Rae suggested, recalling her exchange with Howard.

'Exactly!' Dolly boomed. 'We could put rainbow flags up and set my Joan Armatrading CD on repeat.'

'You are not funny, Dolly.' Rae fired her friend a look as the front doorbell rang. She swept from the room and along the hallway, opening the door with a smile.

'George! Ruby! Hello, darlings!' She gathered first Ruby and then George into wide hugs. 'It's so good to see you!'

'How was Antigua?' George asked, as he placed a hand on Ruby's lower back and followed her inside.

'It was lovely. I got you these.' Rae reached for the two little wrapped parcels from the hall table and handed them out.

Ruby pulled her leather bangles from the wrappings first.

'Thank you, Rae!' Ruby kissed her cheek. 'They are gorgeous.'

Rae liked the way the girl admired them on her arm, her delight genuine. Then George opened his own gift, and stared at the T-shirt that in the sunshine had seemed like a good bet. Now, however, in the grey gloom of a London evening, even she could see that a bright yellow sunshine rising over the water with the word 'Cool' written on it was in fact anything but.

'Is that an epic fail, George?' she asked sheepishly.

'No! It's great, Mum. I'm always looking for T-shirts to wear under my football top.'

She laughed, and Ruby, George and Dolly joined in.

'Hey, kids!' Howard came up the lower stairs with Vinnie, the two no doubt having been colluding in front of the TV.

'Mum bought me this!' George held up the T-shirt with a fixed grin.

'Wow!' Howard sucked air through his teeth. 'I would like you to know that I was not present when that particular beauty was purchased.'

'It's one of her best!' George shook his head in disdain. 'I shall put it with the dreamcatcher you got me from Malta and the ice cream clock, which I seem to remember was from Santa last year.'

'But you like ice cream!' Rae pointed out. 'And that's what I told Santa.'

'Mum, I do like ice cream. I also like scratching my feet at the end of the day, sunbathing naked and hummus, but I don't want a clock featuring any of those things either.'

'Don't be so mean to your mum – she was only doing something lovely for you!'

'Thank you, Ruby.' Rae smiled at the girl's defence.

'Have you seen the kitchen all stripped out?' Dolly grimaced.

'No! Hannah called us in a panic on the day of the Great Fire of Lawns Crescent. I wasn't around, so I called Sadie and Paul.' George followed his aunt, before turning back. 'Oh, Mum, can you get my dinner jacket dry-cleaned? We have a formal dinner thing at college next Friday and it's at the back of my wardrobe.'

'Of course I can.' She made a note to pop it on her list, her ever-growing list . . .

The doorbell rang again. Rae glanced at Howard and pulled her shoulders back, digging deep to find a smile.

This time, her parents stood there. 'Mum! Dad! Hello! Thought you were Hannah.'

'Is she not here yet?' her mum asked, shrugging her arms from her coat and handing it to her daughter. Rae took it and kissed her dad on the cheek.

'Not yet, no. Any minute!'

'Good Lord, public transport gets worse!' Her dad removed his hat and placed it on top of his wife's coat.

Rae stood with her arms out, feeling like the cloakroom attendant. 'Did you not get the taxi I organised to pick you up from the station?' She felt her gut bunch at the thought that all the pre-planning had been pointless.

'We did, we did, but the train was dirty. Wasn't it, Maureen?'

'It was, very dirty.' Her mum pulled a face of disapproval.

'Ah, well, taxis from the station I can organise. The cleaning of a whole train carriage? That's a bit harder.'

'Any chance of a cup of tea, love? I am gasping.' Her mum stuck out her tongue as if to prove how very parched she was.

'Of course. You guys go sit in the lounge and I'll go and make tea.' She ran up the stairs and laid her parents' coats and hat on the bed in the spare bedroom before running back down to the dining room, grabbing the kettle from the top of the small fridge they'd placed in the corner of the room and running back up the stairs to fill it in the bathroom. The basin in the downstairs cloakroom was narrow, way too small to accommodate the kettle. She looked out of the window at the encroaching drizzle and pondered how easily she had slipped back into her old life, her familiar role, running and fetching at everyone's beck and call, and it left her a little cold. She wondered at what point over the last twenty-five years it had happened – when was it, exactly, that she had become the person who did while everyone else sat? She pictured the train heading in a new direction, sitting at the platform; the engine was being stoked and she could hear the whistle signalling that it was ready to leave the station, and she felt a rising sense of panic at the thought that there was very little chance of her actually being on board.

Where does that train go, Rae? And how do you buy a ticket?

'Any chance of a beer, Mum?' George headed her off in the hallway and rubbed his hands eagerly. 'Not sure where to find them now we have no kitchen!'

'Oh, George, I know, it's a nightmare. I have things stacked in boxes and a fridge in the dining room . . . Yes, beer! Where's Dad? I thought he was on drinks?' She had rather banked on some help from him.

'With Vinnie in the garden.'

'Right, let me just get Nan and Grandad a cup of tea and I'll go find you one.'

'And can Ruby get a Coke?'

'Yes, darling, of course. Where's Dolly?'

'She's showing Ruby holiday photos on her phone. Apparently you got right into your cocktails!' he laughed.

'I did!' . . . *especially one that was rather delicious, a little green one called* Why-The-Fuck-Do-I-Have-To-Do-Everything-Around-Here-Do-You-People-Actually-Think-I-Am-Staff?

'Have you said hello to your grandparents?'

'Not yet.'

'Do me a favour, George, go and sit with them, make sure they are okay. They love to see you. I'll be back in a sec.'

Rae hurried to the dining room and made tea in the corner, looking around for somewhere to place the used tea bags and leaving them piled on the spoon, resting on top of the fridge. She carried the teas through to her parents in the sitting room who sat side by side on the sofa, her dad on the left, her mum on the right, chatting to George, who was making them chuckle with tales from college. Her heart felt gladdened by the interaction.

'Yes! Honest, Nan – fourteen of us sharing one tiny bathroom! Can you imagine how grim it gets? And the girls' bathrooms are worse!'

'Have you spoken to your sister, Rae?' her mum asked with pursed lips, as she held her teacup.

'I haven't. Is she okay?'

'She is.' Her mum sipped her tea. 'Well, I say that, but Taylor has had a tummy bug and she was worried about him giving it to Luke. I shall give her a ring later – good to keep in touch.'

Rae caught the barbed nudge that she needed to make more effort with her sister, despite her sister making none with her.

'She said to remind you she needs your dates for the caravan,' her mum continued. 'Lee's mum and dad want to know when it's available and when it's not. They rent it out, you know, and so it might seem pushy, but it's a reasonable request.'

Shit! Shit! Shit!

'Yes, of course, very reasonable – and to be honest, Mum, I forgot! It's been a bit bonkers since we got back.'

Rae pictured her list and mentally underlined *Check dates and send to Debbie-Jo.* She wondered what might be best, whether she wanted to go at all and how it might look if she asked to go alone. A trial run, maybe, of spending time without Howard; seeing how everyone coped without her and how she coped without them.

'Well, shall we tell her you will get back to her by the end of the weekend? And she can pass that on to Lee's parents? So they know when they can rent it out? It's very kind of them to let you have the caravan, without inconveniencing them as well.'

'Erm . . .' While Rae considered this, the front doorbell rang. George walked to the window and pulled the lace curtain so he could see the front door. 'It's not Hannah. Looks like a food delivery.'

'Ah, yes, thank you, George.' Rae ran to the front door and opened it wide to the three young girls in Latimers Kitchen uniforms of white T-shirts, black jeans and rust and leather aprons. Her stomach flipped at the thought that these girls might know Karina; she had looked just like them, young and sassy. She felt the cloak of inadequacy rest heavily on her middle-aged shoulders.

'Oh, hello! Thank you so much! You are absolute lifesavers.'

She stood back to let the three enter with arms full of hefty trays of pasta salad, breads and dips, a platter of various cold meats, one of cheese and a sumptuous selection of mini-puddings – profiteroles, dinky strawberry tarts, lemon panna cotta, the whole plate dotted with sugar-dusted berries. It looked beautiful. Rae was happy, knowing that in lieu of one of her homemade buffets this would do Hannah proud.

'This way!' She walked ahead and the girls followed her to the dining room, where the table was set with a white linen cloth. The girls placed the trays down and helped arrange the food. 'We have had a kitchen disaster and I am so grateful.'

'No worries. We heard.' One of the girls smiled shyly and Rae felt a flash of heat on her cheeks at the thought that these girls might know more about her life than just the fact that her kitchen had burned down – *Karina, Karina, Karina, here you are again, the thought of you making you present in my home.*

'Well, don't let me keep you.' She swallowed. 'I'm sure you want to get back to the restaurant, but thank you once again!' she offered brightly. 'I really do appreciate it.'

As she ushered them to the front door, Howard appeared with Vinnie in tow.

'The food came. I didn't know whether to tip the girls who delivered it?' Her tone was clipped, her anger swelling again.

'All taken care of; they're getting an extra coupla hours' pay on their shift later.'

'Good, great – and the food looks lovely. Thank you.' She smiled curtly, wanting, above all else tonight, to keep the peace.

'Of course!' Vinnie laughed. 'Only the best ingredients!'

'Howard, George was after a beer—?'

He pointed: 'Everything's in the dining room.'

'Righto!' She nodded.

'I am just getting some ideas from Vinnie about kitchen wholesalers who might be able to do us a deal. He's got some good ideas.' He slapped his brother-in-law on the back.

'Sure.' Rae balled her fingers into fists to try to stop them from shaking. Scooting back through to the dining room, she pulled a lukewarm beer from the cupboard along with a Coke for Ruby. She found Ruby and Dolly ensconced in the back hallway and handed Ruby the drink before heading to the lounge to give George his.

'Any chance of another cup of tea, darling?' her mum asked sweetly, holding out her now-empty teacup.

'Yes! What about you, Dad? Another cuppa?' She drummed her fingers on her thigh and fought the urge to scream.

'Oh, well, as you're making!'

Rae waited while he slurped the last of his brew and handed her his cup. She marched up the stairs to rinse the cups and made her way back to the dining room to collect the kettle for filling. As she opened the bathroom door on the second floor she heard the front doorbell. Dumping the kettle on the floor she trotted down the stairs, wanting to be the one who greeted Hannah and Niamh before all mayhem broke.

'Mitzy! Arturo! Hello! Come in, come in!' She kissed her in-laws on the cheek, trying not to stare at Mitzy's make-up: her blue eyeshadow sat in a wide block beneath her painted eyebrows and her bright orange lipstick sat on and around her lips. She hoped that she was still as glamour-conscious when she was Mitzy's age, but also that her aim with the brush might be a little better.

Mitzy grabbed her arm. 'Someone needs to tell him he can't drive any more.' She jerked her head towards her husband. 'He is going to kill himself, he goes so slowly. People were overtaking and he kept bumping the kerb – and if that's how he wants to go that is up to him, but I don't want to be in the car when it happens. He is not taking me with him! I still have a life to lead! I want to dance!'

'Ignore her, Rae-Valentine, she is senile!' Arturo shook his head. Both took off their coats and handed them to Rae, who again stood with her arms held out.

'I am not senile! But he'd like it if I was – then he'd be free to get up to God-knows-what with God-knows-who!'

'I am eighty-six, woman! What do you think I can get up to? For the love of God!' He threw his hands in the air.

'My mum and dad are in the lounge; George is there too. Let me go and dump your coats and I'll come and grab you both a drink.' Rae smiled tightly.

'Red for me.' Arturo called out.

'I'll take white.' Mitzy followed her husband into the lounge.

Rae placed her in-laws' coats on top of those already in the spare bedroom and walked back to the bathroom. She filled the kettle but instead of racing back down the stairs, she rested her head on the cold mirror and closed her eyes for a second.

Just breathe, Rae-Valentine . . . just breathe . . .

'Here they are! Hello, baby girl!' she heard Dolly shout, followed by the squeals of greetings and welcomes and the unmistakable sound of her daughter's voice.

Hannah was home on this important evening and there Rae was, hiding in the bathroom.

She walked slowly down the stairs and stared at the throng of people all clustered in the hallway. Hannah was surrounded by both sets of grandparents, her brother, Ruby, Howard, Dolly, Vinnie – they were crowding her, kissing her cheek and squeezing her to them, all so happy for her. There were mere seconds before Rae was seen. And in these seconds of undiscovery she was happy to be the girl in the corner, standing in the background, peeking out over her family, who from this angle looked like a mass of outstretched arms and smiling mouths. She briefly pictured the many-tentacled octopus, sitting cooped up in its orange bucket before making its break for freedom, remembering that loud, unfiltered laugh that had left her mouth.

She stared particularly at the pretty girl with the shiny, mahogany-coloured hair scraped into a ballerina bun and the dark-rimmed glasses framing her big, brown eyes. A petite, stylish girl who looked briefly at Hannah as Dolly crushed her to her bosom. It was only a second, no more than a glance, but it was a look that made Rae's heart flex. It was a powerful look – that of a person seeking reassurance, knowing that no matter what, the person they were seeking out had the power to make everything okay. It was a look she recognised as one she had given to Howard on more occasions than she was able to recount. The sadness that punched a hole in her chest was quite unexpected. It was a stark realisation that this was how two people very much in love behaved, something that had been missing between her and her husband for quite a while.

'Mum! There you are!' Hannah spotted her and called, breaking free from the crowd. She climbed the step and came to rest in her mother's arms.

'Welcome home, darling. I've missed you.' Rae ran her eyes over her daughter's beautiful face, newly lit from within.

'I've missed you too.' Hannah looked up at her. 'Come and meet Niamh.'

Rae let her daughter take her by the hand and drag her down the hallway, where the noise was growing along with the air of excitement.

'Niamh, this is my mum.'

'Hello, darling. Welcome!'

'Hi. I've heard so much about you and I am so, so sorry about your kitchen.' The girl placed her hand over her heart.

Rae saw the blush of mortification on her face and appreciated that it was important enough to be the first thing she said.

'Please don't worry about it; come and see what we have done.' She walked along the hall and looked into the dining room as she passed, just in time to see Mitzy and Arturo digging into the trays of food like they hadn't eaten for a week. Rae led Niamh into the kitchen with Hannah following. 'I only partly wanted to show you the kitchen, all prepped for the new one, to show you we are way ahead of schedule. But mainly, I wanted to get you away from the crowd!'

'I don't mind. I come from a tiny family and this feels like Christmas! It's exciting!'

Rae smiled at her, wary of bursting her bubble with her own deflated view on life as a Latimer. 'It is exciting sometimes, but most of the time it's just exhausting.'

'What the hell? Are you kidding me right now?' Hannah stared at the walls, where only a week or so ago cupboards had stood. 'Really? The whole kitchen gone? Because of one lousy pizza?'

'Did you see it, Hannah? Did you smell it?' Rae asked with her hands on her hips.

'I did, actually, but I kind of thought it might just all come good with a bit of a scrub. Who told you it needed to be gutted? Is it someone ripping you off? Did Dad check it out?'

Rae felt the stir of a headache as Hannah started with the tone that usually led to a rant.

Niamh walked forward and placed her hand on Hannah's arm. She spoke softly. 'Hannah, you need to calm down. You need to not think the worst of everyone. I've told you, when you get wound up like this it affects everyone around you. It sends out ripples. This is a family party, remember?'

Rae gaped at the girl who was so easily able to voice the words she had shied away from for longer than she could remember.

'You're right.' Hannah took a deep breath. 'Sorry, Mum. I guess I just feel bad. I didn't realise how badly damaged it was.'

Rae found herself a little lost for words.

Dolly came bustling in. 'So, I have two questions.'

'Fire away!' Hannah smiled.

'Ooh, bad choice of phrase.' Niamh squirmed.

'So . . .' Dolly began.

Rae watched Hannah briefly raise her eyebrows at Niamh, suggesting she might have pre-warned her about her rather forward Aunt Dolly.

'First, how did you two meet?'

'At a hockey social at uni. We both play, but for different teams,' Niamh clarified.

'Ah, lovely! Was it eyes meeting across a crowded room, that kind of thing?' Dolly probed, as she popped the last of a slice of cured ham in to her mouth.

'Not really. I was horribly drunk and being sick outside and Niamh came out and held my hair back for me. And that was it.'

'And who says romance is dead?' Dolly offered soberly.

'What was the second question?' Hannah seemed to ready herself.

'What kind of pizza was it?'

'Ham and pineapple.' Niamh tutted.

Rae laughed as her mum came into the kitchen, walking slowly and looking around for something to hold on to in this bare space.

Hannah took her arm. 'You can lean on me, Nan.'

Her mum patted Hannah's hand. 'You're a lovely girl – and Rae, darling, you did mention a cup of tea? And Mitzy and Arturo need some wine.'

Rae gazed at the woman who had told her she had potential, the woman who believed she could have worked behind a desk and yet who apparently still saw her as the bloody waitress!

'Yes, well, I tell you what, Mum, I'll stop chatting to Niamh, shall I, and jump straight to it?'

Maureen ignored her and clung to Hannah's arm.

'I think we *all* need wine.' Hannah looked at Niamh before her eyes danced over her mother's face with a smile of something that looked a lot like pride. She seemed to like this new sassy side to her mum.

Hannah walked out with her Nan to go in search of plonk and Dolly agreed to make the tea.

'I can't tell you how bad I feel about your kitchen, Rae. Honestly, I feel terrible,' Niamh confided.

Rae liked the ease with which Niamh could chat to her, and was thankful she'd ignored her outburst. 'It doesn't matter, not really, not in the scheme of things.' She sighed. 'What matters is that you and Hannah weren't hurt. We can replace kitchen cupboards . . .'

'Thank you, Rae. And if you need a hand choosing a new kitchen, I'm studying architecture and design and I'd love to come with you.'

'Oh, wonderful, that sounds like a date.' Rae looked at the girl. 'I mean, not a date, but an event, a get-together, a trip.'

'It's okay, Rae, I knew what you meant.'

It was gone midnight before everyone finally left. Hannah and Niamh, George and Ruby had all called it a night and were tucked up on the floor below, and Rae fell into bed exhausted but happy. It was nice to know that her family was sleeping under one roof; it gave her a sense of peace that was missing at other times, particularly since Howard's revelation. Again she pictured the train at the platform and wondered how far it had now travelled without her. She rubbed in her hand cream and recapped the lovely evening in her mind. With or without a kitchen, it had been a success. She laughed, picturing how Mitzy and Arturo had bagged up the leftover food and popped it into Mitzy's handbag for tomorrow. She wasn't sure how well cold salami, cheese and strawberry tarts would travel wrapped only in cling film, especially with Arturo's driving.

Howard walked slowly into the room.

'Well, that was a great evening.' He breathed what sounded like a sigh of relief, as if the more family events they managed to get under their belts, the closer they might creep back to normality – almost the exact opposite of how she felt. She wished it were that simple, his version where everything just clunked neatly back into place. Happiness restored.

'It was. I really like Niamh. I think she's good for Hannah; she can keep her in check as well as making her happy.'

'Good job someone can, Rae.'

'Yes. Your mum and dad make me laugh. They were bickering as ever.'

'They drive me crazy.' Howard unbuttoned his shirt.

'I think your parents are supposed to drive you crazy,' she surmised.

'Maybe. Do you think our kids talk about us like that?'

'Oh, undoubtedly. Right now at least one couple is under a duvet laughing at my choice of T-shirt and the other is discussing the way I got a little overwhelmed when I suggested I take Niamh on a date.'

'You did?'

'Not intentionally.' She smiled ironically.

Howard stood at the foot of the bed and spoke softly. 'I feel awkward, after our talk earlier. You are right; I did just assume that I could come back to our bed and climb in next to you. It's always been that way, for so much of our lives. And I am cringing to think that you watched me do that, wishing I was somewhere else. It feels horrible.'

'Well, I don't want to make you feel horrible.' She didn't. 'And it's not so much that I wished you were somewhere else; it's more about your assumption that you could just dive in. It's how everyone treats me, Howard: good old Rae, she just takes it.'

'So . . .' He paused, his expression one of confusion. 'Do you want me to go and sleep in the spare room? Because I can . . .' He pointed towards the door.

'No.' She looked out the window, wondering how he could still be missing the point. It was obviously her fault; maybe she needed to be more direct – but not tonight, when tiredness rendered them both fragile. That and the fact that the kids were only a few feet below them.

'Because you want to present a united front to the kids?' He eased off his shoes and slowly unbuttoned his trousers.

'I would have to admit that that's partly true, but also, Howard, because not only am I too tired, but banning you from the bedroom and having that row now feels like shutting the stable door after the horse has bolted. We should have had the discussion before that first night back home, but we didn't. Just like we should have spoken about tensions, issues, unhappiness, sex and everything else before the Karina incident, but we didn't. And I accept that that is down to me too, running around like a blind mouse, scampering to get things done and not looking up. So I am not blaming you solely; it's just how it is, how it evolved.' She yawned. 'So just come to bed. It's late. I'm tired and I don't want to start overthinking.' She was sleepy and knew that if the discussion deepened, she'd soon be wide awake and chasing the hands of the clock around until the early hours. She needed to think about her future, properly think, but now was not the time. Tomorrow she'd go for a long walk and try to give order to the muddle of her thoughts.

Howard sat down on the bed. 'Every time you say her name it makes me feel physically sick.'

Karina! Karina! Karina! It echoed in her head. 'What a coincidence, because every time I think about that name, it makes me feel physically sick too,' she responded sharply.

'How often do you think about it?' he asked quietly.

'Less than I used to: only about five hundred times a day. And when something reminds me, like the young waitresses sauntering into my home this evening.' She ran her hand over the pouch of her stomach.

He pulled back the duvet. 'I want to hold you, Rae. I want to hold you and tell you everything is going to be okay.'

She lay back on the pillows and faced the window. 'One step at a time, Howard. One step at a time.'

THIRTEEN

Dolly called first thing. It used to be their routine, this catch-up chat each morning, but since returning from Antigua the regularity had slipped a little. It was an example of how things had altered between them.

'Now that was a good evening! I love Niamh, she's great!'

'She is.'

'And George and Ruby seem happy. Looks like you have cracked it, mate. When was the last time you didn't have to worry about one of them?'

'Quite a while ago, actually.' Rae thought about the sleepless nights fretting and praying for their happiness.

'I know – maybe you swanning off to the Caribbean is the answer! So with that in mind, let's just book a flight and go back to the sunshine. I have seen the family, work is good, Vinnie's happy, laundry all done and I am so over this cold weather! Come on, Rae, let's go back to the land of sea and cocktails . . .'

'I wish. I daren't go away again – I'm not sure what room they might burn down next. It's hard enough without the kitchen; I couldn't cope if we lost the sitting room and bathroom as well.'

And I'm not sure I want to go on holiday with you, Dolly. Can't you feel the shift in the nature of us? Can't you see that things have changed, no matter how hard we try to pretend they haven't?

'Good point. So what are you doing for breakfast without a stove? Poor kids will have to go without bacon and eggs!'

'I know, right! "Deprived" is the word you are looking for. Well, luckily they are fully grown adults and able to forage on the High Street for themselves.'

Dolly chuckled loudly. 'That's made me laugh! As if you would ever send your babies out to forage for their own breakfast! You have ruined them!'

'God, you are right.' *It's because it's what I do: I look after everyone. It's my purpose, it validates my place – or at least it used to . . .* 'I am, as we speak, slipping on my trainers and heading out for croissants and pastries: no cooking and no mess. Easy.'

'I was chatting to your mum outside the house while they waited for the cab. She was making me laugh, telling me what she was cooking for lunch today. I swear they are all getting worse, Rae! There's your mum taking food planning to a whole other level. And my mum and dad arguing, constantly rowing about anything and everything and they seem to enjoy it more if they can involve the whole room. It made me think about our chat in Antigua, about turning into them.'

'Oh God, Dolly, talk of the devil. I'll have to call you back – that's my mum on the other line.'

'Ciao, ciao! Speak later.'

'Hello, Mum? I was just talking about you – were your ears burning?'

'No, Rae. Sorry, love. It's not Mum . . . it's me.' Her father's hesitant tone and croaky voice sent a bolt of alarm right through her.

'Hey, Dad, everything okay?' But she could tell by the way he spoke and the fact that he never called this early in the day that everything was not.

'Rae, I need you to come home. I . . . I need you to . . .'

'It's okay, Dad, just take your time. Sit down and take a breath. Is Mum okay? What's happened? What do you need?'

'I have just called the ambulance,' he gasped sharply. 'It's not good, Rae.' His tears came then. 'She's . . . I can't wake her up . . .'

'Oh, Dad!' She struggled to get the words out. 'I will be there as soon as I can. Don't worry. I will be there as soon as I can.' Her thoughts raced to finding car keys, waking Howard and getting to her mum's side as soon as possible . . .

'I . . . I don't know what to do, Rae.' He sounded afraid and it killed her.

'Just hang in there, Dad. Go and get Mrs Dwight from next door and if you have to leave the house, to go to the hospital or whatever, then just go and I promise I will find you. I am coming now, Dad, just hang on. Are you sure the ambulance is on its way?'

'Yes. I've left the front door open for them like they told me to.'

'Okay, Dad, take deep breaths and take your time. I'll be there as soon as I can.'

She ended the call and walked on wobbly legs to the bottom of the stairs. 'Howard!' she shouted loudly up the stairs. 'Howard! Please!'

'God, Mum! Keep it down!' came the shout from George, and she heard the door of Hannah's room slam shut. Her children's reaction to her calling out left her a little cold. She tried to imagine hearing them shout and not going running.

Her husband came to the landing, tying his dressing gown. 'What's going on?' he asked, his hair sticking up, his eyes still puffy from sleep.

'My . . . my mum. She's not well; Dad's called an ambulance. He can't wake her up,' she managed. Suddenly light-headed, she gripped the newel post with both hands so she wouldn't fall.

◆ ◆ ◆

'Did you call your sister?' Howard looked across at her in the car. It seemed they had caught every single red light en route. Now, at a pedestrian crossing, Rae's stomach twisted with tension as a woman with a pushchair and a toddler took an age to amble across the road. She chewed her thumbnail.

'Dad did. I called Mrs Dwight and she was already round at Mum and Dad's. I said we'd meet them at North Middlesex Hospital.'

'Did your dad say what had happened?'

'No, he was in shock, I could tell, and he was upset. He sounded awful. I thought I should just reassure him and get there without keeping him on the phone.'

'Of course. Did he say if she'd had a fall or—'

'He said nothing, Howard!' she snapped, because she literally had no more information and was as frustrated by her inability to answer his questions as he was. She took a calming breath. 'I'm sorry, I shouldn't shout at you. I just want to get there! Dad said nothing other than he couldn't wake her up. Oh God!'

She started crying.

'Don't cry, Rae. We'll be there in no time. The hospital will look after them both. Try not to worry. Remember: this is awful for us, but for the hospital team it's routine – they will know exactly what to do.'

His words helped a little. 'I can't believe I let them travel on public transport when my mum wasn't feeling well. She said last week she'd had ongoing heartburn – I said she needed to see the doctor again, although I still thought it was probably nothing to worry about. But she said she'd had it for months. I should have paid more attention.'

'They had a taxi from both houses to the station and an hour or so sitting on the train. It's the quickest, easiest way for them to get from door to door. You can't blame yourself. And it might be nothing to do with her heartburn; let's just wait and see. No point in worrying until we know there is something to worry about.'

Rae ignored him. Her dad was distressed in a way she had not heard before and an ambulance was on its way to pick up her mum and that felt like reason enough to worry.

'I can't stop thinking how I was a bit fed up with making them cups of tea last night – it felt like a pain, having to traipse up and down the stairs – and now I feel terrible. I snapped at my mum a bit and I wish I hadn't. I hope they know I don't mind making them tea. I really don't.'

'They do know that, love.' Howard reached over and took her hand and she let him, taking comfort from the contact and willing him to drive a bit faster.

He dropped her at the front of the hospital and went to park the car. She ran, blindly searching for signs that might help her find her way to A&E.

A smiling lady with a large sticker on her chest that said 'Volunteer' approached her. 'Can I help you?'

'I need to get to A&E – my mum's being brought here by ambulance. My dad is older and a bit flustered.'

'Follow me.' The woman walked briskly and Rae had to jog to keep up.

'Thanks.' She queued at a wide desk and was about to give her mum's name and address when she spied her dad, sitting on a chair in a corridor. He was bent over with his elbows resting on his knees. Wearing his pyjama top underneath his jacket, he hadn't brushed his hair or shaved, and he looked old and grey. It was rare for her to see him this unkempt and it tore at her heart.

'Oh, Dad!' She ran over and sat in the chair next to him, taking him in her arms. He reached up and gripped her forearms with his trembling fingers. His eyes looked close to tears and the creases on his brow seemed fixed.

'I called your sister.' He spoke softly, a little breathless.

'Yes, she'll be on her way, don't worry. What's happening?' Rae asked gently, when he seemed to have calmed a little.

'I couldn't wake her up, Rae. I thought she was dozing so I left her for a bit and went to the loo and cleaned my teeth and I was going in to see if she was ready for a cup of tea when I noticed that she looked odd. She is always up with the lark, as you know; says it's the best bit of the day . . .' He gave her a brief, lopsided smile. 'And as soon as I start moving around that usually disturbs her. I put my hand on her shoulder and she didn't move and her mouth looked a little bit open and she was breathing in a funny way; she sounded like she was struggling.' He paused and looked along the corridor. 'I want to be in there with her right now. They told me to wait here, but I would rather be by her side,' he whimpered.

'Of course you would, Dad.' *You on the left, her on the right.* 'But I expect they need to be alone with her to do their job and they don't want to be worrying about you too. So we'll just sit here and wait. It'll all be okay.'

Howard jogged in through the doorway. He knelt in front of her dad and placed his hand on his shoulder. 'Len, we'll be right here no matter what. We won't leave you.' Rae felt her heart flex with love for her husband, who knew the right thing to say. 'Can I get you a cup of tea, something to eat, anything? We need to look after you; can't have you taking up the bed next to Maureen.'

Her dad shook his head. 'No thanks, son. I just want to be in there with her.'

'They'll be calling for you any minute, I am sure.' Howard winked at her over her dad's head.

'I called your sister.' Her dad sat up straight and looked now towards the double swing door.

'Yes, don't worry, Dad, she'll be on her way.' She knew his repetition must be down to shock, but it also showed how badly he wanted his family around him.

'I expect she and Lee will stay at the house and we are a bit low on bread and milk.'

'We can sort that out, Dad; I'll pick some up. Don't worry about a thing.'

He nodded and looked down at the stone-coloured linoleum.

'Mr Pritchard?'

Rae sat up and gave the young doctor a small wave. Howard pointed at his father-in-law.

'Would you like to come through? Are you family?' he asked Howard.

'Yes, I am his son-in-law and it's my wife's mother you are treating.'

'Okay, well, why don't you all come through.'

Rae could tell from the man's straight-mouthed smile, considered expression and thoughtful tone that the news was not good. She felt her bowel spasm and her blood run cold as she walked by her dad's side. Howard followed, and all four entered a small waiting room with low squeaky orange vinyl chairs and a crude faux-oil painting of a large bowl of fruit screwed to the wall.

She and Howard sat either side of her dad and the doctor stood in front of them with his iPad raised to his chest. He looked at the painting and took a deep breath, as if about to give a speech to a much bigger audience.

'It is not good news, I am afraid.' He paused, as if giving them a chance to fill in the blanks. 'Mrs Pritchard has suffered a severe stroke, caused by a blood clot. We have given her all the medication we can and carried out a brain scan. I am sorry to say that I feel any further intervention would make little difference. She is unconscious and it is highly unlikely that she will regain consciousness.' The doctor paused again to let the facts permeate. Rae felt her blood run sluggishly in her veins and the doctor's voice echoed.

'Do you mean . . . do you mean she won't regain consciousness today?' Her dad's words cut the air with a naivety that was as desperate as it was sad.

The doctor finally made eye contact with Rae, as if seeking her assistance to help deliver the blow. She wished she wasn't so numb.

'I am so very sorry, Mr Pritchard, but I do not think your wife will regain consciousness at all. It is in my experience usually the case that patients with this level of damage to the brain do not survive. It is highly likely she will slip away any time now.'

'Slip away,' Len repeated quietly. 'Is she in any pain?'

'No. Not at all. No pain.' The doctor was adamant and Rae felt her dad's body sag with some small measure of relief. She felt strangely removed from the situation, as if it was happening to someone else and she was an observer.

Howard coughed and sat forward. 'Is there any surgery that can be done, anywhere, by anyone? We can pay. Not that I doubt she is being looked after here,' he added, 'but is there anything at all that can be done, anywhere we can take her, any experts who can maybe give a second opinion?'

Rae looked at her husband and was happy that he was able to reach through the fog of what was happening and fight her mum's corner, ask the questions that would probably only occur to her later.

'I appreciate your position, I do – if it was my mum I would be asking the same things. You can of course get a second opinion if that is what you wish, but I can say with absolute confidence that the brain scan shows there is nothing to be done. I have had my diagnosis confirmed by my senior registrar.'

Rae saw the lingering look that passed between the doctor and her husband. It was like a secret code, an affirmation from the young man to Howard, who stood out as the leader of the trio, the one whose brain was least clouded by shock and emotion.

'I see.' She heard Howard acquiesce and saw him sit back a little in the chair.

Her dad stood. 'Can I go and sit with her, please?'

'Yes, of course. I will take you through.' The doctor let out a big breath that sounded a lot like relief.

'Do you want us to come with you, Dad?' Rae stood.

He shook his head. 'No. I just want to have a chat with her and then I'll come back, okay?'

'Okay, Dad,' she managed. 'We'll be right here.'

'Keep an eye out for your sister,' he offered over his shoulder.

'Will do.' She nodded and watched as the doctor led him out of the small room. Howard almost swooped forward from his chair and wrapped his arms around her. He rocked her, as if she were sobbing and not sitting dry-eyed with a million thoughts whirring in her mind.

'It's okay, Rae.'

'It's not, though, is it? My mum is going to die and I don't know what to say and I don't know what to do or even how to feel. I don't think I will see her alive again, Howard. And that just doesn't seem possible.'

'I know. I know.'

The two leaned back in their chairs and that was where they sat. Time was skewed for Rae. Her mind was running through her to-do list – *I must put George's dinner jacket in for dry cleaning and pick up croissants for their breakfast* – when suddenly a bolt of realisation lanced her thoughts: *None of that matters! Your mum is dying! She is going to die, Rae! And no chore will matter! Nothing matters, not anything Howard has done and not your wanting to be something more than a handy number in a family phone, the person to call to get things done. Your mum is going to die!*

She wasn't sure how much time had passed, but a while later there was a gentle knock on the door. The doctor walked in and nodded at Rae and she knew.

'How is she?' She sat forward in the chair, her hand gripping Howard's.

'I am so sorry . . .' He paused. 'But your mum passed away a few minutes ago.'

'Right.' She was aware of the cold tone to her response and would have been hard pushed to explain why. Shock was a sneaky thing – it had crept up on her without her realising.

'Your dad is asking for you both.'

Rae stood and leaned against her husband. The two walked along the corridor and she heard the sounds of everyday life all around her, the beep of machines, the shutting of doors, chatter, even laughter and it felt surreal, ridiculous even that at this time, on this, a normal working day for the people in this building, her mum had died.

My mum died! She died!

It didn't matter how many times she said this inside her head or how she tried to make it seem real, the facts just wouldn't stick, and it took all of her strength not to laugh out loud at the utter absurdity of the suggestion.

'Are you sure you want to go in, Rae?' Howard asked softly. 'Because if you don't, I can go and sit with Len.'

'I'm okay,' she lied, and followed the doctor in to the narrow room, no more than a cubicle really. Her mum lay on a trolley in her night-dress with a blanket pulled up to her chin. Her dad sat by her side with his head resting on the edge of the trolley and his hands clasped at his chest, possibly in prayer.

He looked up, his cheeks wet with tears. 'She's gone.' He shook his head. 'She's gone.'

'She looks very peaceful.' Rae spoke the truth as she looked at her mum's pale face, which she found hard to accept would not laugh with joy or sigh in disapproval ever again. Nothing. Gone.

I am sorry I snapped at you last night. I didn't mean it! I love you and I need to talk to you, Mum. There are so many things I want to say to you! I am not ready. Not remotely ready . . .

Rae felt small, young and pitifully alone, even though she was only a few feet from her dad and her husband, who gripped her hand tightly.

'I can't believe it!' her dad cried again, loudly, and it frightened her, made her jump. 'I can't believe it!' he called out.

Rae kissed her mum's cheek, which was cool but not cold, soft still but already without the substance of a living thing, and it alarmed her.

'Goodbye, Mum.' She trailed her fingertips over her shoulder and turned to her dad. 'Do you want us to leave you alone for a bit, Dad, or do you want us to stay here with you?'

'Alone, please,' he managed through his sobs. 'Alone.'

His distress was hard to witness, and Rae thought she might be sick. She placed her hand over her mouth.

Howard squeezed his father-in-law's shoulder before reaching for her hand once again. This time they sat in the bigger waiting room with those waiting to head into A&E and the walking wounded. Two young lads, one with a swollen ankle inside a striped football sock, were laughing, nudging each other, eating snacks and chatting at such a volume that she felt their very presence there was misplaced. Rae leaned over and placed her head on Howard's arm. He encircled her in a hug and held her close. She felt completely numb and wished for tears, thinking that this might in some way help, might make it real. She closed her eyes briefly and, though sleep was impossible, felt herself drift to a place beyond alertness, where voices were a little muffled and the light a little hazy and she was glad of the escape. It was a relief not to have to try to think about what was happening: the truth too painful, too shocking for her to absorb.

My mum . . . not my mum! It can't be true.

Howard sat up straight and she stirred in time to see Debbie-Jo and Lee running across the linoleum. They came to a stop by their chairs.

'Where is she?' Debbie-Jo stood with her breath coming fast, and wasted no time on a greeting as she looked up towards the ward and the other way towards the corridor as if she might be able to glimpse her.

They both stood, and Rae shook her head.

'I am so sorry. She's gone.' She spoke softly with no clue how best to phrase it.

'What?' her sister spat. 'Where?'

'She's gone, Debbie-Jo. She died.' The words were foul on her tongue and caused her heart physical pain.

'Why? No! What happened?'

'She had a massive stroke,' Howard explained.

Debbie-Jo bobbed as her legs bent beneath her. She felt her way into the free chair behind her. Instantly her tears fell from red-ringed eyes and Rae could only view her sister's distress with something close to envy.

'Oh my God! Oh no!' Debbie-Jo bent forward with her forehead on her knees, while Lee sighed and palmed circles on her back.

The four stood in a cluster, as if all wondering what might happen next, all poorly rehearsed in the etiquette.

Eventually the doctor appeared. 'Your dad is in the waiting room. I said I would come and get you.'

'Thank you. This is my sister.' Rae looked at Debbie-Jo, who still sobbed, and wondered when her own tears might find their way to the surface.

The sad troupe made their way along the corridor to the waiting room, where her dad sat on the same chair as earlier. Debbie-Jo hurled herself at him and Rae watched as he clambered to his feet and the two stood locked together in a desolate embrace.

'Oh Dad!' Debbie-Jo called, as if she were a child again and he were on hand to make everything feel a little bit better. Her dad clung to her sister's jacket. It felt like an intrusion to watch. Rae felt a little surplus to requirements now her big sister had arrived.

'I would like to see her if possible.' Debbie-Jo broke away.

'They've moved her.' Her dad spoke with a croaky, remote voice that was quite alien.

There was a hush while Rae tried not to process nor imagine where they might have moved her to and why.

'I just want to see her! Please!' Debbie-Jo spoke through a mouth contorted with tears.

Rae stepped forward and faced her sister, trying to find the small aspects of comfort that she had found from standing by her mum. 'She didn't really wake up, Debbie-Jo, but I can promise you she looked peaceful. She really did, she looked peaceful and she wasn't in any pain.'

'You saw her?' Debbie-Jo fired.

'Yes,' Howard answered, also stepping forward, as if trying to form a physical barrier between her and his wife.

'You saw her too?'

'Yes. We were there for her and for your dad.' He looked sharply at his father-in-law. Rae knew he was trying to remind Debbie-Jo that Len was present and had just lost his wife.

'Well, good for you two! Of course you got your goodbyes!' Debbie-Jo shook her head. 'Of course you did.'

'It wasn't a goodbye.' Rae swallowed. 'She had already gone.'

'Well, I want to see her now,' Debbie-Jo asserted. 'I don't mind that it's not the experience you had, that I am too late. I still want to see my mum!'

'You shall.' Lee stepped towards her and rubbed his wife's back. 'You'll get your goodbye.'

'What do we need to do, Dad? Do we have to fill in some paperwork or see someone or can we take you home?' Rae asked, thinking now about getting her dad out of here and back to the house, where she could make him a cup of tea.

'I don't know. I don't know what to do.' He sat back down on the chair and looked at the door, and Rae wondered if, like her, he half-expected someone to walk in and tell them that the whole thing had been a terrible mistake and her mum was coming home.

◆ ◆ ◆

Debbie-Jo had insisted she drive their dad home. Rae and Howard followed behind in their car.

'I can't believe it.' Rae pictured her mum sipping tea on the sofa the night before and then saw her lying on the gurney, pale, gone, and she wondered how her life could be so altered in just a couple of hours. This seemed to be a habit of late: one minute she was happy, secure, and the next, wham! The rug was pulled from under her and she was sent spiralling.

She looked over at her husband, who drove silently, slowly, through the traffic. Gone was the urgency of earlier.

'Thank you, Howard.' Her voice had the gravelly undertone of exhaustion and yet she was curiously energised, wired, as if her mind couldn't settle.

'What for?'

'For . . . handling that, for asking the right questions and for not shouting at Debbie-Jo even though I know you probably wanted to.'

'Today is not the day for shouting; everyone is finding their way. And of course I will handle it. I am your husband and I have known Maureen since I was a young man and she was always very kind to me.'

'Do you think I should give the kids a call?' Rae changed the topic, quite unable to cope with his kindness.

'Probably best, and maybe call Dolly too and get her to go and sit with them so they're not on their own until we get back later. I know they are with Niamh and Ruby, but I think it might be good to have Dolly with them.'

Rae nodded and dialled Dolly's number. It was a strange thing, but as she did so she realised that her mum had been one of the only people who truly had her best interests at heart. Unlike with Dolly, there was no split loyalty, no doubt in her mum's mind about Rae's potential. And now she was gone . . . *gone* . . .

'Don't tell me? You are sick of camping in your own home and are going to come and stay with us! Hallebloodylujah! I'll shove a leg of lamb in the oven.'

'No, it's not that. Actually, Dolly, we've had some bad news—'

'Oh no! Is Howard okay?' She paused. 'The kids?'

'Howard and the kids are fine, but . . .' She paused, recognising that saying the words out loud would not get any easier, no matter how many times she rehearsed them. 'My mum died.'

'No! No she didn't!'

Rae held the phone silently while her friend gasped her denial.

'Oh Rae, darling! I am so sorry. I can't believe it – I was just chatting to her last night. She was great, she had such a good evening, she was talking about the kids . . . Oh God, Rae, I don't know what to say. What can I do? How can I help? Tell me what I can do!'

'Do you think you might go and sit with the kids? I am going to call them now, but I don't really want them there alone until we get back.'

'I am leaving now. Right now.'

Rae was grateful for her friend's instant response and it made her think how important family was, regardless of what had passed between them. This was what mattered, being there in times of need. Dolly's words came to her now and Rae considered that maybe she was right. *I can't imagine what it would be like if you guys split! Christmas, for example, birthdays, gatherings or, God forbid, if anything bad should happen, like a bereavement – that's when we need to stick together, family!*

Howard indicated and parked at the front of her dad's house. 'Whenever I pull up here I think about coming to knock for you all those years ago, knowing I loved you and wondering what your mum and dad would make of it all. Feels like yesterday.'

Rae unclipped her seat belt, unable to process what was happening; shock made her limbs tremble. 'Time goes fast,' she whispered. She stared at the front door and pictured coming home from school, her mum opening it in a pinny with floury hands, and the smell of baking wafting from the little kitchen at the back.

'Shoes off!' she'd shout, before kissing her cheek.

Lee's car was already there.

Rae took a deep breath. 'I don't know if I want to go inside. I feel like it's going to be crazy and I don't want to be there.'

'It won't be crazy. It will be fine – and if at any point it is not fine, you know the rule: you look at me and I will pick up the car keys, take your hand and drive you home, just like that. But it's not about what we want, or even what Debbie-Jo and Lee want; it's about all working together to get your dad through this. This is the day that Len has had nightmares about, the day we have all dreaded, and that day has arrived for him, sooner than any of us hoped or planned for, and so we are going to go inside and do what needs to be done. Okay?'

'Okay.' She nodded, liking the way her husband was giving her this verbal crutch as she stepped from the car.

Lee let her in and stood back.

'How's Dad?' she asked quietly.

'Shocked, quiet, upset, just as you'd expect really.'

'Have you told Luke and Taylor?' She pictured her nephews and hoped they had someone like Dolly they could call upon.

'We spoke to Luke. Couldn't get hold of Taylor but left him a message to call.'

Howard walked in and shook Lee's hand as if this was the first time they had met that day, erasing the uncomfortable moments from the hospital.

The quiet atmosphere in the house was strange. To Rae it felt very much like she was there alone, despite it being busier with people than usual. Her dad was sitting on the sofa with his left hand flat on the sofa next to him. She wondered whether he was trying, like her, to understand how someone as central to his life, as vital as her mum, could have gone, disappeared, leaving this gap in their lives and this space on the couch. She wondered what she could possibly say to take away his hurt, to make things better.

Kneeling in front of him, Rae reached for his hand. It was an odd thing, but she and her dad had never been that physical, and yet today it felt like the most natural and necessary thing in the world to hold his hand, wrap him in a hug, smooth his hair. Rae wondered if this was the true beginning of the role reversal, when she would start to parent him. Not that it felt like much of an option with Debbie-Jo around, busying in the kitchen, after claiming him for her car. She remembered Howard's words and dismissed her meanness. Right now it was all about her lovely dad, the man who had lost his wife.

'Just making him a cup of tea – do you want one?' Debbie-Jo asked from the doorway.

'Yes, please.' Rae nodded. She sat back against the coffee table and watched her dad. She could hear Howard and Lee mumbling in the hallway, deliberately talking quietly, which was irritating, especially when the odd word – funeral . . . catering . . . eulogy . . . cremation – floated back to her, alien words that were almost comical until she considered their connotation.

'How are you doing, Dad?'

He looked up and blinked, seemingly noticing her for the first time.

'I don't know, love.' He looked out towards the window, as if trying to fathom the time of day.

'You don't have to think, Dad. You just sit here and we will sit with you. There's nothing you need to think about and nothing you need to worry about. We are all right here.'

He scratched his stubble and Rae realised it was a long, long time since she had seen him unshaven. 'Your mum's got some heartburn medication that needs picking up from the chemist. I got a call about it yesterday and I said I'd go in today.'

'Don't worry about that now, Dad.' She felt her words navigate the boulder in her throat.

'But I told them, Rae, I said we'd be in to collect it – they phoned.' He looked and sounded a little agitated.

'I'll take care of it.' Rae smiled at him, and pictured adding *Mum's medicine* to her list.

◆ ◆ ◆

It had been a very long day.

Rae had found it difficult to say goodbye to her dad, although in fairness Debbie-Jo seemed to have everything under control. She found it equally heartbreaking to come home to the kids all squashed on the sofas in the sitting room, with legs tucked up on the cushions, discarded mugs on the floor and damp tissues balled in their fists. Ruby and Niamh, who didn't really know Maureen, seemed to be feeling sadness by association and sat slumped-shouldered next to the ones they loved.

Dolly had been crying. She opened the door to Rae and Howard and held Rae fast in a tight hug. It was some small comfort to know that Maureen had meant something to Dolly, and Rae was grateful.

'You know, Rae, the only thing you need to ask yourself when your parents pass away is "Was I a good daughter?" – and you were, you were the absolute best. I mean, you were no Debbie-Jo, but . . .'

Rae couldn't believe she actually laughed, though this moment was immediately replaced by a feeling of disbelief, almost confusion.

Dolly held her hands. 'I mean it. You loved your mum and you did what you could to help out and you made her proud and that means you only have to think about all the good things. You can get on with missing her, but don't let the sadness overwhelm you because, as hard as it is, it's the natural order of things, if we are very, very lucky.'

Rae nodded: this she knew. 'Thank you, Dolly.'

Her friend stepped forward and again wrapped her in a warm, tight hug. 'I love you, Rae, my best friend in the whole wide world.'

Rae closed her eyes and rested her head on her friend's shoulder, feeling the glass barrier that had stood between them since Antigua slide away. This was everything, family and being loved, comforted at a time when she needed it the most. 'I love you too. My best friend in the whole wide world.'

Having waved Dolly off, it was George and Hannah's turn to hug her. She felt like a sponge, absorbing everyone else's grief, and it was exhausting.

'I am going to miss her,' Hannah mumbled.

'I know, darling, I know.' Rae kissed her girl.

With pizza delivered for everyone and the odd quip about how delivery saved on firefighter visits, Rae realised she had zero appetite. She slowly made her way upstairs, removed her make-up and brushed her teeth, then slipped her nightdress over her head and climbed into bed. Her ritual was the same as every night, but it felt odd. She gazed over at the lace curtain shielding her from the world outside, where Mr Jeffries put out his milk bottles, Mrs Williams called her cat in for the night and Fifi's mum walked up and down the crescent with her hands in her pockets, casting a furtive look over her shoulder. And yet it was a very different world this evening. It was a world without her mum in it. A world where her mum would never call her again or leave her a rambling message about bread or thank her for a food delivery that came like magic with all their favourite things. She would never sit at the Christmas table and pass judgement on the gravy or lament the lack of bread sauce. She would not demand a cup of tea at the single most inconvenient moment, and she would not be ready with a list of ailments that was long and ever changing – ailments she was worried might rob her of her life in her sleep.

It was a very different world because the worst thing had happened: her mum had died, and for the first time that day Rae felt the full weight of this knowledge. It sat in her stomach like a rock, it hung on her shoulders and it stifled the breath in her throat.

She looked up as Howard came into the room, treading softly across the carpet and throwing his watch on to the cherrywood chest of drawers. She felt something strange, like a rumble, a quake in her very soul. And it frightened her.

'Howard?' she whispered.

'Yes, love?' He stared at her as the quake grew until it was thunderous in her ears.

'Can you . . . can you hold me?'

He walked to the bed, and as if sensing her urgency, did not stop to remove his trousers or shirt. Instead he pulled back the duvet and slid across the mattress, taking her swiftly and firmly into his arms with one hand cupping her face to him, anchoring her as he slipped down the bed, taking her with him, holding her fast against his chest. Shielding her, a safe harbour, waiting for the danger to pass. And with the moonlight streaking the duvet and a hush throughout the house, Rae-Valentine gave in to the tears that finally found their way to the surface. Tears that shook her body and clogged her nose and throat, hot spiky tears that burned her skin with the injustice of their cause.

'My . . . mum!' she stuttered. 'Mum . . . oh no! No! No! No! Not my mum . . .'

As her tears subsided and her breath found its natural rhythm, Rae closed her eyes and, with her cheek pressed against his skin, she spoke the words that were a rope, cast out in her moment of need, pulling her and her husband together, where in unity she knew they would find strength to weather the storm.

'I think we should try to carry on, Howard. I don't have the energy for anything else, not now. I want us to put everything behind us. I want us to focus on the good and I want us to move forward. Together.'

'Oh, Rae! Rae!' He placed her hand on his heart. 'You have no idea how much this means to me! I love you and I am thankful and I will not let you down. I love you. I love you!'

And, right there in the moonlight, the magic spell worked, those three words that fixed just about everything.

FOURTEEN

In the ten days since her mum had died, Rae had fluctuated between bouts of sobbing and extreme cleaning, both of which left her feeling exhausted. The lack of kitchen had worn very thin, and she was now at the point where she couldn't care less about the intricacies of design; she just wanted the situation fixed. In the end she simply pointed to a glossy page in the catalogue that had been popped through the door by a contact of Vinnie's and said, 'That one. That's fine. These cabinets, this oven, marvellous! And I will have it designed exactly like the one that was taken out. Thank you.' She had closed the catalogue and handed it to Howard, who had nodded and made a phone call to organise delivery and labour.

Easy.

In the sitting room of the house in Lawns Crescent on this grey afternoon, however, her best friend took exception to the news.

'But this is a chance to remodel. It should be fun! You can have a walk-in larder, a new range or one of those fancy-pants coffee machines that you need an engineering degree to operate!'

'I don't need all that. I'll just be glad to have a working stove and a countertop to make pastry on. And to not have to wander up and down the stairs with a washing-up bowl full of dirty mugs, which I then have to clean in the bathroom, will be wonderful.'

'Most people would like the opportunity to have a new kitchen,' Dolly asserted. 'They would give it a lot more thought than pointing at a random kitchen and going, "That one!"' She mimicked her friend.

'That might be true.' Rae spat on the iron to check it was hot enough and proceeded to iron the first of Howard's shirts that lay crumpled in the ironing basket. She had the ironing board set up in the lounge and Dolly lay on the sofa. 'But most people are not trying to organise a new kitchen as well as their mother's funeral and to deal with their grief, and forgive me if it all feels like a bit much right now.'

'I get it, but I don't want you so suffer from Post-Kitchen-Order Regret Syndrome.' Dolly flicked through her magazine and flexed her toes. 'You know how you do when we go out to lunch and you don't order the same as me and the waiter brings the food and you look longingly at mine and I know you are suffering Post-Lunch-Order Regret Syndrome. This might be the same and it's a lot harder to fix. You won't be able to just click your fingers and have the man bring you a whole new set of floor tiles!'

Rae smiled at her friend. 'I won't. It will be fine. And the reason I covet your food is because you always order the bad stuff, the stuff accompanied by fries, covered in cheese and deep-fried and stuffed with things and rolled in things and dripping with fat and calories, the stuff I deny myself! Which, I have to confess, often looks better than my Caesar salad without dressing.'

'I can assure you it doesn't only look better . . .' Dolly paused. 'It tastes better too.'

'Probably,' Rae conceded, gliding the hot iron up and down the fabric.

Dolly gave her a quizzical expression and grabbed the roll of fat that sat over the waistband of her jeans. 'Do you think that's why I am fat?'

Rae shook her head as she finished the flat back panel of the shirt. 'No. I *know* it's why you are fat.'

Dolly laughed loudly.

'I know you mean well, and thank you for caring about my kitchen. But the one I've chosen is soft wood, painted cream with a dark countertop – it matches all the bits and bobs I had previously and is very similar to the old one. Don't forget that I am only getting a new kitchen because I have to and not because I want to.'

'Okay, well, as long as you are happy.'

'I think "happy" is a bit of a stretch.' Rae felt her face crumple with sadness.

'Oh, honey.' Dolly waited until her tears abated. 'Are things all set for the funeral?' Her tone was now a little more reserved.

'Yes.' Rae nodded and turned the shirt to start on the sleeves. 'I am dreading it.'

'Which bit?'

'All of it. I hate seeing my dad so upset and he can't seem to get it together. Not that I am saying he should – of course not; he is completely floored by the whole thing – but to see him so sad, vacant, when there is nothing I can do to fix it is one of the hardest things. I spend half my time wishing we could wind the clock back for him so he doesn't have to go through it, and the other half wishing I could wind it forward to a time when hopefully he will have healed a bit.'

'I bet. And how's Debbie-Jo?'

Rae shook her head and looked out of the window before resuming her chore. 'It's weird, Dolly. We have never been that close, as you know, but I think at the back of my mind I always assumed that when something terrible like this happened we would come together and work as a team, set any petty differences aside and ease each other's pain, like they do in the movies. But it is nothing like that.'

'Honey, if life was like the movies, I would click my heels and we'd be back in Antigua.'

'I think if life was like the movies, you'd click your heels and we'd be back in Kansas.'

'Is it sunny in Kansas? Do they have cocktails?'

'I don't know, Dolly. Probably. The point is, Debbie-Jo is an odd fish. Every time I sit down to chat to Dad, just to get five minutes with him, she bursts into the room and joins in or asks questions. I know it sounds odd, but it's like she thinks we are conspiring. And I don't mind her joining in – it would be nice to all have a meaningful chat – but she assumes this stance that makes me feel . . . like a guest. It's horrible.'

'That's so unfair on your dad. Poor Len.'

Rae bit her lip. 'I got to my mum and dad's the other morning . . .' She stopped ironing and closed her eyes briefly, finding it hard to mentally amend the phrase that had been leaving her mouth for her whole life, impossible to think of the house in Purbeck Avenue as anything other than where her mum and dad lived.

'You okay?'

Rae nodded and took a breath. 'I got to the house and she had started sorting Mum's jewellery out. She had laid it in piles on the dressing table and insisted on dragging me upstairs right away. I followed her because I thought she wanted to say something to me out of earshot about the funeral or whatever. Dad was sat at the dining table and it was like it was Debbie-Jo's house and not his. It felt really invasive and she had clearly been through all of my mum's drawers and jewellery boxes, whereas I'd feel terrible about touching her stuff, and she started saying, "This pile is for Taylor; he did love his Nan . . ." – kind of implying that Hannah and George did not. And, "This pile is for me; she always wanted me to have her engagement ring, she told me . . ." And I stood there and I thought, *I don't want any of it! Nothing! I don't care; I just want my mum back.* But I knew I couldn't say that and so I just nodded and left her to it. But I didn't like her very much for it.'

'Maybe that's her way of dealing with it. Grief is a very personal thing and I think different people handle it in different ways.'

'Gee, thanks for that, Dr Phil.' Rae tutted.

Dolly pulled a face and Rae felt an instant flash of guilt. Her friend was an angel, sitting with her during the day and doing whatever she could to get her through this horrible time.

'I'm sorry, Dolly. I am a cranky cow and I know you are right, but it's like my sister is taking over at the house and my dad is so low and sad that he's letting her do it. I also think he's worried that if he says anything negative or contrary to what she is planning, she'll hotfoot it back up the motorway to Northampton – and the one thing he doesn't want, and I completely get it, is to be by himself right now.'

'Have you told him to come and stay here?'

'Of course! And I would love that! I have even suggested the kids go and stay, but he says he's fine and he wants to be with all his stuff and wants to get into the bed he shared with Mum, and I understand, I do. And I think not having a kitchen here is a bit off-putting for him. We can rethink things in time; I just want to get the funeral out of the way.'

'How are things with you and Howard? I noticed you seem very . . .' Dolly raised her eyebrows.

'We are very . . .' Rae pictured the night of reconciliation after losing her mum, when he had held her close and they had taken the first emotional steps towards healing.

'So tell me more!' Dolly probed.

Rae set down the iron and spoke thoughtfully. 'It's almost like Mum dying was this big tsunami that came and washed all other worries away. Howard has been brilliant, absolutely brilliant.' She smiled at her sister-in-law. 'I mean, amazing. I don't think I would be coping without him. From that very first morning when the call came in, and at the hospital, until now . . . He just takes care of stuff and has been so kind. He knows what to say to make it better. He asks the right questions, has helped us organise the funeral, paid for everything . . . I couldn't ask for anything more. And on top of that he's scheduled the new kitchen to be fitted and he's keeping tabs on the kids. I feel thankful for him and I realise that he is right, and that you are right: I can't let one stupid,

273

shitty fortnight ruin what is essentially a good marriage. We are so much more than that.' Rae knew that this was the best way forward, the right thing to do for all their sakes. It was the easiest path ahead, for everyone, and to have made the decision felt like a burden lifted.

She heard her mum's words loud and clear and her throat tightened. *It's the life you have chosen and it's a lovely life and you will get used to it, darling. Everyone's family is strange compared to your own; and when you get used to it, it will be less exhausting . . .*

Dolly threw the magazine on to the table and jumped up. She pulled Rae into a big hug and kissed her face, hard. 'You have no idea how very, very happy I am to hear this, Rae. No idea! I was so worried. But you two are good together. I told you he was a good guy.'

'You did. And you were right. I love him.' Rae felt a spike of joy at this truth and welcomed it when there was so much to feel sad about right now. She pictured saying goodbye to her mum as she lay on the gurney, and saw her dad with his hands clasped.

And just like that, it hit her again. The freight train of loss hijacked the moment and hurtled through the wall, knocking her backwards. The force of it left her struggling for air, as she staggered back against the fireplace and fell forward, crying with such force it left her winded.

Dolly grabbed her and kept her upright.

'It's okay, Rae-Valentine, I've got you. I've got you.'

'My mum!' she managed. 'I want my mum, Dolly . . . I miss her! I just want to see her, one more time . . .'

On the day of the funeral, the day she had dreaded, Rae woke early and climbed from the bed, taking care not to disturb her husband, who slept soundly. She peeked through the curtains at the street still bathed in darkness and noted the drizzle. Most appropriate for what lay ahead. She took her shower and cleaned the bathroom then went downstairs, treading carefully so as not to wake up George, Ruby and Hannah, who all slept soundly. Niamh was still in Liverpool, busy with lectures. She walked into her half-finished kitchen and in her slippers trod the sawdust and curls of wood that littered the floor. Having reached for the kettle, which thankfully she could now plug in, she ran her fingertips over the new countertop, crowned with a thin layer of dust, and felt a little indifferent to her choice. A kitchen was a kitchen in the grand scheme of things.

'Hey, Mum.'

'Morning, darling, did I wake you? I forget your room is directly below ours.'

'I was awake anyway.' Hannah yawned and leaned against the wall, scrolling through her phone before she was even fully awake.

Rae walked over to her daughter and kissed her forehead. 'Do you know, I think you are beautiful all the time, Hannah, but there is something about the way you look when you first wake up, all sleepy-eyed and muzzy-headed, that makes my heart swell. You might be in your twenties, but you have that same look about you as you did when you were a baby.'

Hannah looked at her screen, embarrassed. 'I am feeling really nervous about today.'

'I can understand that, but remember Dad and I will be by your side; and George and Dolly – everyone will be keeping an eye out for you. I have been to many funerals, more than I care to remember, and it is never as bad as you think it's going to be. Cup of tea?'

'Please.' Hannah looked up. 'I don't want to see her coffin.'

Rae nodded. 'I get that. But, you know, losing Nan feels like a tragedy for us because we love her and we will miss her . . .' She made no attempt to mop her tears that fell. 'But it's not a tragedy, not really, even if we can't see it like that right now. She lived well, she got old, she was loved, she had a great family, a happy marriage and she simply didn't wake up one day; that's a pretty perfect life. We should all be so lucky. The fact that we are all so sad about losing her, missing her . . . well, that really should be celebrated, not mourned.' Rae hoped that when her time came, someone might be able to say something similar.

'I guess so. But it's made me think about—'

'Think about what, love?' Rae poured the hot water into the two mugs, tossed out the tea bags and handed the drink to her daughter.

'It's made me think about losing you.'

'It's bound to, but I will do my very best to stick around until I am old enough to be a proper pain in the backside.'

'Promise?'

'I promise.' Rae cradled her mug. 'And I expect you'd fare a bit better if Niamh was here today?'

'I would.' Hannah smiled at the thought – almost involuntarily, it seemed.

'You really love her.'

'I do, Mum.'

'Is she your first girlfriend?' Rae felt now was the time to ask the many questions that swirled in her head.

'Yes. I mean I've hooked up with people, but I've never felt like this.'

Rae nodded, not one hundred per cent sure on the definition of 'hooked up', but able to guess. 'I can see why, Hannah. She's great.'

'I know, right?' There it was again, that smile. 'I can't believe she feels the same way about me – I mean, have you seen her?'

'Don't ever think like that. She is very lucky to have you.' Rae felt the tap on the shoulder from her own ghost of inadequacy, still lurking. 'You are a smart, beautiful girl and I am so proud of you, always.'

'Dad was your first boyfriend, right?' Hannah gulped her tea.

'Yes. I was only a baby really. Sixteen!'

'And did you know instantly that he was the one?'

'Not instantly, no. I liked the idea of him – Dolly had of course painted a picture of him – but our first date was a bit of a disaster.' She laughed and wiped her eyes on the sleeve of her dressing gown.

'Why?'

'Why do you think? Who is the architect of all my life's disastrous days?'

'Dolly!' They spoke in unison.

'Yep, Dolly. She was trying to impress Vinnie and was boisterous, shouty and getting sloshed.'

'Really? When did she change?' Hannah quipped.

Rae chuckled. 'Dad and I kind of sat like spectators at the Dolly show and I couldn't wait to get home. I remember Nan had bought me a new floral blouse and I was fed up, thinking that it had been a waste of money. I figured he'd think I was the most boring date ever and that would be that! But no: he walked me to the gate and we laughed at how terrible the evening had been, and he asked to see me again. And then we had our second date, just the two of us, in the park of all places, and it was lovely and I knew then, I think.'

'Are you and Dad okay?'

The question caught Rae a little off guard and she concentrated on keeping a neutral face, relieved that she was finally able to answer the question truthfully: a decision had been made. 'Yes! We are good.' She took a sip of her tea. 'Why do you ask, darling?' Her hand shook. It was still her greatest dread that her kids would get wind of what had happened.

Hannah gave a half-shrug. 'It was just something that Lyall said a while ago.'

Rae felt her heart bang in fear.

'Something that he had heard – and I know it's rubbish; Lyall is a total idiot – but I just wanted to ask you. It's been bothering me.'

She noted Hannah's lack of eye contact and it tore at her heart that her little girl had been harbouring these thoughts, these worries. It shouldn't have been a shock – Lyall, Hannah's cousin, lived in the house where Dolly shouted constantly and spoke uncensored with Vinnie – but still, she knew the revelation was more than Hannah, or she herself for that matter, could really handle today. But however uncomfortable, the truth could not be avoided. She reached for her daughter's hand.

'I've never lied to you, Hannah, and I won't start today. I will give you the outline, but I don't want to go into detail, not right now. But if you want to talk about it some more when things have settled, you know where I am, okay?'

'Okay.' Hannah smiled at her mum and placed her phone on the counter.

Rae took a deep breath. 'I don't know what you heard from Lyall and I am not asking you to tell me. But Dad and I did hit a bump in the road, that's true. He let me down – let *us* down – and it's been hard for me to understand and to accept and it made me look at all aspects of my life in a way that I haven't really done before.'

'In what way, Mum?'

'I guess the way I am seen by everyone. It made me think about who I am, Hannah.' She rubbed the tops of her arms, overcome by a sudden chill, as the words flew from her mouth. 'And I know I don't want to die like my mum and never find out. I wanted to do so many things in my life – not that having you and George hasn't been my greatest thing; it has, never doubt that! But I wanted to learn to cook, really learn to cook; I wanted to travel; I wanted to do lots of things. But it feels like other people always felt they knew best and I stood back and let them tell me what to do – hiding, in the background, going with the flow.'

She looked at her daughter, who stared at her with the same expression of concern she had worn since she was three years of age, and it killed Rae.

'But Nan dying . . .' Rae sighed. 'It's put things in perspective and I can see that no bump in the road is worth giving up on a marriage. And it's made me realise something that she knew all along: that family is the most important thing. It's everything. And maybe that is my greatest achievement and that's okay. And maybe I want too much, maybe I need to simply be grateful for all the wonderful things I do have.' She hoped her positivity might be infectious. She didn't want to give Hannah any more to worry about.

'Did you think you might give up on your marriage?' Hannah asked, wide-eyed. She looked like a small child who was afraid.

'I don't know. I considered it. I didn't know what to do. I was hurt and that felt like an option. But I do know that your dad loves you, loves us all more than anything; he's the same dad he always was and you can count on him. You can. And I also know that today is the day we think about Nan and we think about how we can help Grandad and we stick together and we look out for each other. That's what's important, not something Lyall might have mentioned or overheard.'

'Yep, you are right. I do love you, Mum. I want you both to be happy. I want that more than anything because I am happy now and I can see how brilliant it is! I want everyone to feel this way. And I do want you to know who you are, because I finally know who *I* am and it feels like the weight of the world has been lifted from my shoulders.'

Rae pulled her girl into a hug and kissed the top of her head. 'I love you Hannah Bee Banana.'

The crematorium was busy. One of the concerns that had kept Rae awake was a fear that the place might be empty, as if the measure of her mum's life would be in some way represented by the number of people who turned up to mourn her. It was a relief to see the whole family there and their kids, her parents' neighbours, her mum's cousins and their children and a couple of her dad's old work colleagues. Howard stood close by, holding her hand and asking softly and regularly, 'How're we doing?' and she was grateful for his concern. In response, she nodded at him and greeted the next relative with a grateful smile or a shake of their hand. When the time came, her dad sat quietly at the front with

Debbie-Jo on one side and Rae on the other. Howard was to the left of her with his hand resting on her leg. She stared at his splayed fingers and pictured them like an anchor, keeping her steady on this day when she needed his guidance more than ever. It occurred to her that to lose a spouse through death was, of course, hard, wreaking life-changing devastation, but she hoped her dad would take some small comfort from that fact that his wife had left him only when the last breath escaped her body; the decision to go was taken by a force much greater than her. The same could not be said of someone who left you for another, someone who cheated, committed infidelity, broke their vows; those people left you just as much alone, but also with a sense of failure and the uncomfortable cloak of inadequacy that wrapped you tight. She was grateful that she and Howard had found their way back to each other, especially today.

All of her mum's grandchildren sat in the pew behind. Rae felt waves of pride at the way they conducted themselves, supporting each other in every sense and all with one eye on the man who had lost his wife. Debbie-Jo kept turning around and grabbing her boys' hands, which in turn made them cry. It was a difficult day for them all and one without a blueprint. Rae felt lost and guilty at the fact that she just wanted it to be over.

It was an odd thing that, having thought about her mum every second of every day since she had passed away, she found her mind wandering during the funeral – almost as if this was how she was going to get through it. She looked at the architecture, admired the floral display and sang 'All Things Bright and Beautiful' with gusto, and even mentally pictured the wake and how she might distribute the food, etc. – anything other than give in to the howl of distress that hovered in her chest when she looked at the pale wood coffin sitting inside the red velvet curtains only feet away.

And it seemed that as quickly as the service had begun, it was over. She would have been hard pushed to remember the exact words of the eulogy, read eloquently by her nephew Luke, who did them all proud – but she would forever recall the tone of it, heartfelt and given in thanks for a life well lived. She hugged him closely outside the church.

'You did brilliantly.'

'Thank you, Auntie Rae.'

It felt odd to see the little house in Purbeck Avenue so full of people. The rooms were crowded and she busied around with a tray of canapés, walking among the mourners and not chatting for too long, using her role as waitress as a neat excuse for flitting from person to person before her sadness had a chance to reveal itself publicly. George sat next to his grandad and Ruby sat at his feet; Rae ruffled her hair as she walked past and smiled at her son, mouthing, 'Thank you.'

Hannah cosied up in the corner with her cousins and Rae felt a flicker of unease at what the topic under discussion might be, instantly chastising herself for being so narcissistic as to assume it would be about her and Howard, today of all days.

Debbie-Jo filled the kettle for the umpteenth time and rinsed and prepped their mum's floral china teacups for the next round of tea.

'Can I help with that?' Rae placed the empty sausage roll plate in the sink.

'No.'

'Okay, so give me a new job – or shall I carry another tray around?' She eyed the mushroom vol-au-vents, which had started to look a little deflated. She knew how they felt.

'It must be nice being you.' Debbie-Jo turned and spoke to her sister with her arms folded across her bust and a tremble to her mouth. 'I have always thought so.'

'I'm sorry?' Rae had caught the tone but not the exact words; her mind had been on other things, staring at the tray of food next to her mum's burned oven glove and wondering how many cakes baked for those she loved she had pulled from the oven with that very mitt.

'I said it must be nice being you, swanning in and swanning out when it suits you. Leaving me to do all the hard stuff, like getting up for Dad when he's distressed in the middle of the night and sorting through Mum's clothes, bagging them up and taking them to the charity shop. Then you get to come here with the whole of the Latimer clan, crowding the rooms, taking over, eating the spread – and that Dolly, always so bloody loud!' Debbie-Jo placed her hands briefly over her ears.

Rae felt her mouth go dry and her stomach bunch. She looked towards the hall for Howard, her default if she ever found herself in an uncomfortable situation, but he wasn't there. She looked back at her sister, not wanting this conversation to happen, not today and not in this house, but she was trapped.

She took a breath and spoke calmly. 'There's no need to talk to me like that, Debbie-Jo. Especially not today.' She went to reach for the tray.

'You are only part of this family when it suits you. Dropping in with your flash car parked outside like Lady Never-Shit.'

'Where is this coming from? I live close by; I come here all the time! It's not me who used to practically drive past the front door to go to a concert or catch a flight – how much would mum and dad have loved a visit on those days?'

'I don't know who you think you are and I don't know why all those people are here!' Debbie-Jo repeated.

Rae faced her sister. 'The Latimers are here because I am a Latimer and they are my family. Plus they loved Mum, always made a fuss of her, invited her to their homes and their celebrations; they have known her for decades – it's absolutely right they've come. And Dolly is loud, that's true, but she is my best friend, my family too, and she is kind and she loved Mum, very much.'

'Mum didn't like her. She told me that once.'

Rae felt the punch of her sister's words and didn't know how to back down. What she wanted more than anything was for her mum to come into the kitchen and separate them and to make them hot chocolate and sit them down on the sofa and to tell them it was all going to be all right.

'Well, she once told me she thought Lee was lazy and work-shy and she doubted he had a bad back at all – you really want to do this?'

As if on cue, the sound of Dolly's very loud laugh filled the air.

While Debbie-Jo floundered for words Rae again adopted a conciliatory tone, wanting to pour water on this verbal fire. 'I don't believe our mum would say point-blank that she didn't like someone, because she was kind and she liked everyone and that's a nice trait to have. We should try to be like her. And I have offered to take Dad to my house but he wants to stay here; and I've figured that if you are here then it's best that I'm not. You don't exactly make me feel welcome and that makes me sad. I always feel like I have done something wrong. You have always made me feel that way. And why you felt the need to go through Mum's clothes so soon, before we had even . . .' She paused. 'I just don't know.'

'That's right, you don't know! You haven't got a bloody clue! You think because you married a bit of money you know life, but you don't.'

'Debbie-Jo, I don't know where this is coming from, but I am going to assume it's because you are hurting and I understand that, so I am going to leave this room and avoid you for the rest of the day – and then, when you are ready, call me and we can talk properly.'

'Would it have killed you to give me the dates for the caravan?'

Rae's mouth dropped open. 'Are you serious right now? Is this what this is all about? The caravan?' she asked with disbelief.

'No, but that just about sums you up. We got you that as a gift and it meant we didn't get a holiday, as they only give us one free week, but I didn't want to turn up to one of your big flash dos at your very own restaurant and give you a bottle of cheap wine that would get lost alongside the bloody champagne! I wanted to do something nice, extravagant; I thought you'd like it and I thought it might make Mum and Dad happy that we were going to so much trouble. But you didn't mention it, not really.'

'I did! I said thank you! I thought it was great!'

'So great you buggered off to the Caribbean, no doubt sitting on a beach laughing at the thought of a week in a caravan in Devon.'

'Not at all – and Mum only reminded me about the dates the night before . . .' The sob caught in her throat. 'The night before she died; and here we are!' She looked at her sister hiding away in the kitchen, making tea and with this torrent of feelings that must have been swirling inside her for God knows how long. Rae realised that Debbie-Jo reminded her a bit of herself, battling with the feeling of not being quite good enough.

'Well, you can forget about it. Lee's mum and dad thought you were taking the piss and said we can't have it any week now; they've freed up all the dates on the booking calendar online.'

Rae stared at her sister. 'I don't know what you want me to say to you, Debbie-Jo, I really don't.'

'I want you to not treat me like a second-class citizen! Everything I have ever tried to do, you have had to trump.'

'Like what?' Rae was mystified.

'Like I go to the high seas and I am a dancer on a five-star cruise line but when I come home, all Mum and Dad can talk about is your bloody wedding and the bloody wedding cake! I get pregnant and so do you! I buy a flat in Northampton; you buy a fucking mansion in London!'

Rae found herself reeling. It took a while for her response to form. 'I have never intentionally done anything to make you feel that way. You are my sister! Not that you were ever really that kind to me. Do you know you made me feel like shit my whole childhood? You were always angry, crying, sulking – or dancing and performing. Never any happy medium. Everything had to revolve around Debbie-Jo – her classes, her hobbies, her moods and her glittering future career! You told me I was the girl in the corner! And I believed you!'

'What are you talking about?' Debbie-Jo fired.

Rae ran her fingers through her hair. 'I knew I could never live up to you with your many, many talents, and so when Howard wanted to marry me I grabbed that chance! Because someone as wonderful as him wanted to marry a plain Jane like me. I couldn't believe it! You made me feel like shit and you are still making me feel like shit. Right now, today, having a go at me on the day of Mum's funeral. It's disgraceful!'

There was a moment of realignment while her words permeated. Debbie-Jo raised her shaking hand to her mouth and slowly began crying into her palm. 'I . . . I'm sorry,' she managed, through a mouth contorted with sadness.

'Yes, well, I am sorry too! The way you treated me shaped the person I became. I believed I was the girl destined to stay in the corner and that was it! But not any more, Debbie-Jo. I am more than that. I always was. I just didn't know it.'

Debbie-Jo stared at her with a pained look that suggested she had not fully considered things from her sister's perspective. Her tears fell harder. 'I am sorry, Rae.' She looked at the floor, almost in shame.

Quite overwhelmed not only by her sister's apology but also by her own ballsy performance, Rae matched her tear for tear. 'I'm sorry too.' She took a step forward and took her big sister into her arms. And that was how they stood, the two of them, locked in an embrace in front of the kitchen sink where their mum had toiled her whole life.

'I never got to say my goodbye to her, Rae. By the time I got to the hospital she had been packed off to the morgue. I miss her. I miss her so much it hurts and I never got to say goodbye and I never got to tell her how much I loved her,' whimpered Debbie-Jo.

'She knew, Debbie-Jo! Never, ever doubt that she knew how much you loved her. You made her so proud. She used to keep the photographs of you in your costumes on that little shelf over the toaster, remember?'

Rae tried to stifle her sob. Her sister did the same.

Rae whispered softly into Debbie-Jo's ear. 'She knew how much we loved her and we know how much she loved us and that really is something. A gift.'

◆ ◆ ◆

A fire crackled in the grate of the sitting room of Lawns Crescent. Howard poured generous slugs of brandy into the tumblers and handed them around the room. George and Ruby were as ever sitting hip to hip on the sofa, with Hannah at the other end; Rae and Howard took the other sofa. Rae eased off her pumps and curled her aching feet under her legs.

'To Maureen!' Howard raised his glass and took a sip.

They all did the same and sipped the warm, honey-coloured liquid.

Howard loosened his tie and undid the top button of his shirt. 'I think that, as terrible days go, today was the best terrible day. It went well, a proper send-off; it was good to hear so many people speaking so fondly about your mum and it was great company for your dad.'

'It was. I am absolutely exhausted.' Rae threw her head back on the cushions.

'I think you've probably been running on adrenaline for a week or so and now you will crash and we will pick you up if you fall,' Howard reassured her.

'Thank you all. I love you all so much,' she cried, swiping at her tears with her fingertips, unsure of exactly why she was crying now, as a multitude of emotions swirled inside her. 'I was so proud of you guys today.'

'We were proud of you, Mum.' Hannah smiled at her. 'And for the record, Debbie-Jo is a bit of a nutcase!'

George and Ruby snickered into their glasses: evidently their alter-cation had been heard.

Rae shook her head. 'No, she's not, Hannah. She's grieving and sad and a bit confused and angry, but not a nutcase. We all have our issues, right?'

'Suppose so,' Hannah offered reluctantly. 'Niamh sends you all her love.'

They all smiled, sharing the joy of this new relationship.

Rae yawned loudly. 'I think I need to go to bed. I can hardly stay awake.' She swung her legs from the sofa and stood.

'I'll come up now too. Night, kids.' Howard downed his brandy and the two trod the stairs slowly. She felt his fingers reach for her hand, stroking her palm in a way that was familiar, if somewhat forgotten. She felt electricity flow through them. This was the first time he had touched her with something that felt a lot like promise and her heart raced.

Still holding her hand in his, Howard closed the bedroom door behind him and without switching on the light pulled her sharply to him, kissing her on the lips and working his way with his mouth along her jaw to her neck. He paused and whispered in her ear, 'Hannah is right, though: Debbie-Jo is a bit of a nutcase!'

Rae laughed and pressed her body up against him, kissing him hungrily with energy and a longing that had lain dormant for a long time. There was a need for the union, not only for the sweet escape it offered but also to erase the memory of his infidelity and to pave the way forward, a recalibration of this new and changed relationship in which she found herself slipping back into the role of Howard Latimer's wife. Gripping each other, the two waltzed clumsily to the bed and fell on to it. As he pulled at her sombre black frock, the feel of his hand on her skin was new and glorious, sending shards of desire from the point of contact to her very core. She placed her face against his chest and inhaled the scent, revelling in the feel of him, the weight of him.

Theirs was an urgent need that was so much more than sex; it was about reconnecting, renewal and a promise for the future.

It was, at a physical level, forgiveness.

'I love you, Rae. I love you completely.'

'I love you too. I do. I love you.' She wept, crying for so many reasons that all fought for space in her mind. Closing her eyes, she tried to remember how sex had felt before, when he was hers and hers alone and no dark thoughts threatened to suck the joy from the moment.

FIFTEEN

With the whiff of summer in the air, Rae waved Howard off to work, rather liking the lingering kiss he planted on her cheek before jumping into his car. Like waking one day and looking out of the window and realising that this was where you belonged, she realised that she had returned to the beginnings of happy and it was a comforting place to live. Safe.

She placed the recycling on the pavement, sorted into separate boxes for cardboard, plastic and glass, and wiped her hands on her apron before running to the kitchen, where the phone was ringing on the wall. The kitchen might have been only a few months old, but the sharp edges had already softened and the new paint and shiny appliances had settled, becoming part of the home. It felt lovely to have the beating heart of the building back in use, and she was happy with her choice, no matter that it wasn't radical or exciting and there was no fancy-pants built-in coffee machine. She enjoyed the fact that there was no need for her to click her fingers and ask the waiter to bring new tiles.

'Hi, Rae, it's John here from Barnet.'

'Hello, John from Barnet!' She smiled at how the young manager of the Latimer Kitchen gave his name and location. 'How are you?'

'Good, great – actually, no, not good and great at all, and a little bit stuck!'

'Ah, now we get to it.' She looked along the countertop until she had located her handbag and car keys.

'We are running really low on foil trays with lids, both large and small, and I can't get up to the wholesalers and don't have any spare staff with access to a car. They can only deliver tomorrow and I need them, like, now! We are batch cooking today for the freezer.'

'No worries; I'm on it, John. I'll scoot by, pick some up and have them with you as soon as traffic allows.'

'Rae, thank you. You are a godsend!'

'So I've been told.' She hung up and grabbed her car keys. Out of the window went her plan for planting the tubs in the back yard.

She sat in the traffic with the radio on, tapping her steering wheel in time to Black's 'Wonderful Life', thinking of how she and Dolly used to have the song on repeat on a Walkman. She knew the words by heart. She recalled walking along the pavement to her house and pictured her mum opening the door to greet them.

Oh dear . . . Has someone been smoking?

Someone probably has, yes . . .

Rae felt the familiar wave of sadness. 'I miss you, Mum, so much,' she whispered. This was as true now as it had been on the day she died, and she wondered if the longing for contact with her would ever diminish. Her dad had, over the last couple of weeks, perked up a little. He could now talk about his wife without the onset of tears and this was progress in itself. He had also started to get out and about a bit more. He had asked that Rae stop their grocery delivery, preferring to walk each day to the shops for the bits and pieces he needed, and she and Debbie-Jo had agreed that it was probably for the best, killing two birds with one stone. It gave him much-needed social interaction as well as a bit of exercise.

Things between her and Debbie-Jo were better: much better. The frost that had set in had all but thawed and Rae was almost glad of their crappy, selfish row on the day of her mum's funeral. It meant that her big sister had got to say all the things that had sat on her chest, she suspected, for a number of years. She had phoned Debbie-Jo when she eventually went back to Northampton.

'You know, my life is not and never has been perfect. I often feel a bit lost and a bit surplus to requirements. I kind of fill my day with chores and work for the restaurant where I can get it, because I think without it I might go a bit crazy. My family is all I have; I live for the kids, for Howard.'

'I shouldn't have gone on about the caravan! I don't know why it felt so important. But it did.' Her sister spoke openly.

'I think losing Mum messed with our heads – and of course it was always going to; she was our mum.'

'I think you are right. And you know I always wanted to be like you, Rae-Valentine, always.'

'And I always wanted to be like you, Barbara Gordon.'

Debbie-Jo's laugh was loud and instant. 'Oh my God! Barbara Gordon! I had forgotten about that; I wanted to change my name.'

'Yes, and you were furious when Mum and Dad wouldn't let you!'

The two giggled into the phone.

Rae sniffed. 'And you know what this means, don't you?'

'What?'

'It means that our parents did such a good job of raising two phenomenal girls that we were the envy of each other – we are bloody brilliant!'

'We are!' Debbie-Jo chuckled. 'We are bloody brilliant!'

'I caught them having sex once,' Rae revealed.

'Oh my God, you did not! That's gross!'

'I did! Not that I realised it at the time.'

'Eeuuuw, that's horrific! How old were you?'

'About five.' Rae laughed, settling back on the sofa. 'I had had a bad dream . . .'

◆ ◆ ◆

Rae scoured the shelves of the wholesaler and spent far too long running her fingers over the myriad herbs and spices, wondering how she might incorporate them into rubs, marinades and seasonings. It was a knack: she could look at and smell a herb or spice, and picture the finished dish it would enhance. Not that she had time for this today . . . She went off in search of the foil dishes, grabbed them in bulk and loaded them into her trolley, then waited for the rather slow cashier to deal with the man in front of her and his hundred-plus bottles of ketchup.

Her mobile rang.

'Guess what? I am in Latimers Barnet and John has just told me you are on your way!'

'Yes, just waiting to pay at the cash and carry.'

'Good, I'll grab a table and we can have lunch.'

'Do you know, Dolly, you never ask me if I have plans or if I am able to make lunch; you always tell me what I am going to do. It's annoying.'

Dolly laughed loudly, and Rae had to pull the phone away from her ear. 'As if anything you have to do or were planning to do could be nearly as important or so much fun as seeing me!'

Rae gave a wry smile and ended the call. She glanced at ketchup man, who she knew had been earwigging. She realised as she loaded her wares on to the counter that Dolly was right: nothing Rae was planning was as important or fun as seeing her friend, not now she had given up on her thoughts of a life outside her family. Helping out in the restaurants, seeing Dolly, being there for Howard and the kids and keeping house – this was, for her, as good as it got.

Rae waited until she'd slipped into the driver's seat of the car before giving way to the tears that had built up. It got her like this sometimes, caught her by surprise – the thought that a change had been within reach but that the train had firmly left the station. It could be a little overwhelming. Not that she wasn't happy. She was, but she also recognised that, along with the pain and devastation of the last few months, there had been an awakening – a door opening that she now realised might actually have been an escape hatch in disguise. A door that led to the infinite possibilities that came with independence. Not that it mattered now. It was all too late.

At the restaurant, Dolly placed a cup of coffee in front of her as Rae slid into the booth.

'How's tricks?' Dolly asked.

'Tricks are good. I am not sure what that means exactly, but I am just trying to keep up and it sounds about right.'

'So, big news: Lyall has a new girlfriend.'

'Oh great!' Rae beamed.

'No, no, no!' Dolly shook her head and waggled her finger, as if scolding a child. 'Not great. We don't like her.'

'We don't?' Rae wiped her smile.

'No.'

'Why don't we like her?' Rae was nervous to ask.

'She is very forward, a bit bossy, loud, and she's just, just . . .' Dolly stumbled, trying to find the right words. 'She says, "Jump!" and Lyall says, "How high?" She's no good for him. I should know. I am his mother. But he's besotted. She is all boobs and bouffant and has him under her spell.'

Rae stared at her friend, thinking of how to delicately phrase all the words that leaped to her tongue.

'I mean, you know, Rae, of all the girls I thought he might end up with, this one is . . .' Dolly shook her head with a look of disdain. 'She is not right for him.'

'You'd think, looking at how happy you and Vinnie are, Lyall might try to find someone like you.' Rae sipped her coffee and hid her smiling mouth behind the rim.

'Exactly!' Dolly banged the table. 'Someone like me. What are you laughing at?'

'Nothing, Dolly. Nothing.'

'So, now your turn: what's your news?'

Rae placed her cup in its saucer. 'I don't really have anything exciting to tell.' She thought about it. 'Dad has gone to stay in Northampton for a couple of weeks, but I thought it was a good sign that he was a little reluctant to go, happy to be at home alone – that's progress.'

'It really is.' Dolly nodded.

'George and Ruby have booked to go to Cyprus for a fortnight in August and are already excited. Hannah and Niamh are coming home today, just for a couple of days; Niamh has an interview with a firm of architects in town for an internship over the summer. I'm looking forward to seeing them. That's about it.' She shrugged.

'Don't let them near the new kitchen – and definitely no pizza, especially not ham and pineapple.'

'That's a given.' Rae laughed. 'Come over if you like, you and Vinnie. I am cooking a chicken and I know Hannah would love to see you.'

'Of course she would. I am her favourite auntie.'

'You are.'

'Mind you, the competition is not that stiff. I mean, the best thing about Debbie-Jo is her name!'

'Don't be mean! That's my sister you are talking about.'

'Yes, but not really. *I* am your sister really.'

'Well, if you are my sister it's no wonder Mum gave you to the Latimers and disowned you. You are a nightmare!'

The waiter approached the table cautiously. He looked at the two plates in his hand, one piled high with a burger, fries, onion rings, coleslaw and a large pickle. On the other was a small pile of green leaves and a beautifully sliced avocado.

'Who is having what?' he asked.

'The salad is for me.' Dolly smiled sweetly as the boy put the plates in front of them and walked away.

'You are so not funny.' Rae laughed, reaching out and swapping the plates. By the time she had finished speaking Dolly had picked up the burger and taken a bite so big she could barely close her mouth.

'You are also disgusting.' She laughed again and picked up her fork. 'You can't intervene – you know that, don't you? Where Lyall is concerned you need to let him make his own mistakes and figure things out.'

'I do know that.' Dolly chewed her burger. 'But I can still shout and influence from the wings. Like I do.'

'Yep.' Rae took a sip of water. 'Like you do.'

◆ ◆ ◆

'Only me!'

Rae heard Howard close the front door.

'In the kitchen!'

He came in and placed his arm around her waist. 'How was your day? I heard you bailed John out and then met Dolly for lunch?'

'Ah, you are having me watched!' She smiled up at him. This was how things were now; they no longer argued and the atmosphere was pleasant, softer. They were undoubtedly healing, and it felt good.

'Dolly and Vinnie are coming for supper too.'

'This I already know. I was going over the accounts with Vinnie and Paul when Dolly called to say bring wine.'

'Paul okay?'

'Yep. He's good.'

It was sad but inevitable that, since the whole Karina incident and Paul's part in it – no matter how small or unwanted – relations between him and Rae had been strained. Nothing was said, but it was as if neither could get past the unspoken awkwardness that their shared knowledge made impossible to ignore. Her heart rate increased when they chatted and she became clumsy, overly conscious of her actions. Sadie too, she noticed, called less.

'What time are Hannah and Niamh due in?'

She looked at the clock on the wall. 'Any time now. Supper is nearly ready so I can whisk them straight into the dining room. Can't wait to see them!'

'And George called me earlier. He's excited about Cyprus.'

'Oh God, Howard, it's only June. I truly can't feign enthusiasm for a bloody holiday that's taking place in August, bless him!'

Howard laughed and opened the fridge, reaching for yesterday's bottle of wine. He emptied the remains into a wine glass and set it to rest on the draining board. Rae sidled past and grabbed the bottle; the two moved in a well-choreographed dance in the square space of the kitchen, a routine perfected over the last twenty-five years. She carried it down the hallway and out of the front door, placing it in the recycling bin just as Fifi came along, sniffing her way as usual.

'Ah, hello, Fifi!' She crouched down and ran her palm over the cute pup's flank. 'She is so beautiful. How old is she?'

Fifi's owner stared at her. Rae looked up and smiled, trying to encourage the shy woman to talk.

'Erm . . .' The woman coughed. 'She's . . . she's nearly three, but just as inquisitive as a pup.' Her voice was soft but not quiet, and she was well spoken.

'Well, she's an absolute beauty! I always think so.' Rae straightened.

'Come on, Fifi!' The woman spoke a little more sharply than Rae deemed necessary. Rae cursed that she had clearly made her feel uncomfortable, as if she had undone all the good work of smiling and waving. She stood and watched the pair walk briskly along the crescent; before she turned the corner, the woman gave Rae her customary look over her shoulder.

Howard had been watching from the hallway. 'All okay?' he asked, draining his glass as she walked in.

Rae headed for the kitchen. 'Yes, the darnedest thing: I just spoke to the woman from down the road – you know, Fifi's mum . . .'

'I'm not sure,' he mumbled behind her.

The front doorbell rang.

'I'll go.' She scooted past him back down the hallway.

'Hello! Hello!'

In marched Dolly and Vinnie, armed with two bottles of chilled white and, for some reason, a wheel of Brie.

'It was going off.' Dolly pointed at the cheese and kissed her sister-in-law on the cheek.

'Nice.' Rae smiled.

'Well, Howard, old son! Haven't seen you for an age!' Vinnie laughed. 'Are you okay, mate? You look a bit pale.'

Rae turned to see Vinnie with his hand on her husband's back. He was right; Howard did look a bit pale.

'I'm fine!' Howard spoke in the way he did when he didn't want to make a fuss.

Rae led the way to the sitting room and watched as Dolly and Vinnie sat close to each other on the sofa, he on the left, she on the right; it made her think of her mum and dad and her heart flexed with the memory of her loss.

'You look thoughtful,' Howard commented.

'Just thinking.' She looked at the floor, still holding the cheese. The doorbell rang again. Rae rushed out to answer the door and beamed at the sight of her girl. 'Hello, darling! You've had your hair done – you look gorgeous. Welcome home! And Niamh, welcome home!'

She kissed them both and then watched as Dolly came from the right and hijacked them with hugs.

'If you don't mind me asking, why are you opening the door with a great big lump of cheese in your hand?' Niamh laughed.

'It's a gift from Dolly.'

'Are flowers out of fashion now? No one told me!' Niamh quipped.

'I'll go grab supper – Dad's on drinks!' Rae said as she skipped to the kitchen and deposited the cheese in the fridge with a bubble of happiness in her stomach. The chicken was golden, crispy-skinned and perfect. She set it proudly on the platter, surrounded by crunchy, salt-flecked roast potatoes, and in a separate tureen she piled Brussels sprouts with chestnuts and pancetta and honey-glazed carrots and parsnips.

'Dinner is served!' she hollered and smiled at the sound of the scrambling feet making their way into the dining room.

Howard walked into the kitchen.

'Are you feeling okay?' she asked, as she dug in the cupboard for the cranberry sauce.

'Yup, fine.'

'Good. In that case can you do wine, please?' she said and whisked past him to ferry the food to the table, where it was greeted with robust applause.

Vinnie began to carve and all sat back. Rae took pleasure in watching everyone heap their plates with the food she had prepared. It was still her favourite thing, to produce fine food and watch the people she loved devour it. She looked across at Howard and noticed his appetite seemed a little lacking as he picked at the slice of chicken on his plate.

She thought it might be a good idea if he laid off the wine, but wasn't about to suggest that and embarrass him. She realised he was looking at her and gave him a smile.

After clearing the plates, Rae walked back into the dining room with a large and impressive shop-bought strawberry gateau and Hannah tapped her wine glass with her fork. 'Ladies and gentlemen, may I have your attention please!'

Everyone laughed at her theatricality as the five people she addressed settled into their seats.

Hannah reached across the tabletop and took Niamh's hand into her own. 'Okay, I am not very good with the whole public-speaking thing and so I am just going to cut straight to it. I have asked Niamh to marry me and she has said yes! We are engaged!' she yelled.

'Oh, darling! Oh my goodness!' Rae jumped up and ran around the table as her tears sprang. 'That's wonderful news! Wonderful!' She felt the warmth of pride spread through her chest that her little girl was following her heart, grabbing life and running with it!

Hannah stood and embraced her mum, as Niamh and Howard hugged. Dolly whooped and cheered and Vinnie poured wine for them all. Niamh then turned to Hannah and held her close.

'Congratulations, Niamh,' Rae said. 'Welcome to this crazy family! I am so happy!'

'Me too!' Niamh grinned.

'I wish George was here.' Rae felt his absence on this historic evening.

'Don't feel bad, Mum. I've already told him. I was so nervous about asking her that I called him for advice. So technically he was the first to know.'

Rae felt thrilled, quite overwhelmed by the fact that her kids shared this wonderful closeness. She knew that, as a family, they would steady each other when and if things came along to throw them off balance. This thought brought her peace. She wished the closeness she now shared with Debbie-Jo had been there throughout her life, knowing it would have made all the difference.

'I think this calls for something more than wine!' Dolly banged the table. 'Is there any champagne in the house?'

'Yes!' Rae clapped. 'Good idea! There are a couple of bottles under the sink.'

'Lead on, Macduff!' Vinnie pointed towards the kitchen and they hustled out to get the bottles. As soon as they had left the room Rae fell against Dolly laughing. Quite suddenly, everything was hilare!

Dolly jumped up and down on the spot and Rae joined in. The two were like giddy schoolgirls, quite overcome by the situation. 'Your little girl is getting married! We can plan a perfect wedding!'

'I know!' Rae squealed. 'Oh my God, I am so happy for them both. I remember her not so long ago telling me that marriage was outdated, restrictive and pointless.'

'And it can certainly look that way if you do with it with the wrong person.'

'Yep,' Rae agreed and reached under the sink for the bottles of champagne, which she popped on the countertop.

Dolly handed her a champagne flute, then stood on tiptoe and grabbed the rest of the flutes from the top cupboard as she went on, 'And you know, Rae, I look at us all around that table tonight, look at how happy we all are, and I thank God above – because if you hadn't managed to look past the whole bloody Diane thing, this would be a different story. *This* was what I was talking about, the healing, making it good for the family.'

Her voice echoed in Rae's ears and she felt her blood flow like cold treacle through her limbs. The glass tumbled to the floor from her hand and shattered into tiny pieces as Rae watched, as if in slow motion, unable to react.

'Oh, look at you, butterfingers.' Dolly bent down and grabbed the dustpan and brush and began doing what Rae usually did best, sweeping up the mess, hiding the destruction, *least said, soonest mended . . .*

Rae felt herself starting to swoon with giddiness and leaned on the sink. It was as if her brain was racing to catch up. *Diane, Karina . . . Diane . . . Karina . . .* The payoff and infidelity Dolly knew about was Diane. *Diane. Diane!*

Clarity bloomed in her mind and rang out like a note, clear and pure.

Enough was enough. For too long she had been a passenger. It was time she took control of her own destiny, time she followed her own advice and listened to that little voice of instinct. Her mum's words came to her now, offering the best advice across worlds: *You were special and I was just waiting for the day you roared – and I knew that when you did the world would listen. Isn't that right, Len?*

'Actually . . .' Rae coughed to try to clear the ricochet of the name in her ears. 'I meant to ask you, Dolly, but it never felt like the right time: how much did Paul pay Diane?'

Dolly stopped sweeping and looked up at her, clearly taken aback. 'I don't know.' She seemed to be thinking about it. 'A few hundred, I think. It can't have been much more, because it came out of the Chiswick petty cash.'

Chiswick petty cash . . . not Shepherd's Bush . . . A different girl, a different restaurant . . . a different affair . . .

'Why do you ask, mate?'

'I don't know. Just . . . just curious, really. It was a long time ago.' Rae realised that her first instinct was to keep her newfound knowledge from Dolly.

'God, yes, nearly two years now, and this is a new age! A new dawn!' Dolly beamed.

With a trembling hand Rae gathered the champagne flutes and carried them into the dining room. She could not look at Howard, who laughed loudly as he and Vinnie shared a joke. Hannah and Niamh were scrolling through Hannah's phone looking at wedding dresses with expressions of pure joy.

Rae placed her hand on her stomach. 'Oh, gosh, does everyone else feel okay?' She managed a small smile; thankfully, the colour had drained from her face, helping to endorse her feigned illness. 'You guys go ahead without me. Shan't be a mo.'

She walked briskly from the dining room and trod the stairs on legs that felt like jelly, holding the banister rail for support until she made it to the bedroom. She walked into the en-suite bathroom and slid down the back of the door. Grabbing the hand towel from the ring by the sink, she shoved it into her mouth to stifle the scream that leaped from her throat.

Two years ago. Diane.

Last year, Karina.

How many more?

How many waitresses?

How many pay-offs?

No wonder Paul and Sadie found it hard to be natural with her.

She pictured Howard sitting on the end of the bed crying, and realised that Karina must have meant business if he had been forced to tell her, especially on the night of their party. She thought about him wanting to renew their vows! Without warning she felt her gut spasm and she vomited, only just turning to the toilet bowl in time.

Rae cleaned her teeth and stepped out of her dress, pulling on her jeans and sweatshirt before tying her trainers. She opened a drawer in the cherrywood chest and began to pull out items of clothing, speaking to herself in her mind as she did so, her thoughts and ideas so bright and clear they felt like ripe fruit waiting to be picked.

There was a gentle knock on the bedroom door.

'Mum? Are you okay?'

'Oh, Hannah.' Rae felt a flush of anger at the fact that her husband's web of lies was about to become part of the fabric of her daughter's special night. She felt awash with the feeling that she had let Hannah down, going back to the man who had betrayed her. A liar! It was no example. No example at all.

'Oh God, Mum, you look awful! I am really worried about you. Can I get you anything?'

Rae placed her hands on her hips. 'No, thank you. And don't worry about me, darling. I am fine. More concerned about spoiling your night.'

'You couldn't spoil my night, Mum – I'm getting married!'

'I know, I know, sweet girl, and I am so, so happy for you.'

'She's the best thing to ever happen to me and it feels right.'

Rae placed her hands around either side of her daughter's face. 'You are a wonderful person, Hannah. Fearless and kind. I feel blessed to be your mum. Truly.' She kissed her gently on the forehead.

'Shall I tell everyone you are going to go straight to bed? Don't worry about coming down. You look like death.'

'No, that's okay, darling. I am not going to bed.' She walked past her daughter and opened the wardrobe door. Bending low, she pulled out a brand new, bright red knapsack and ripped the labels from it with her teeth before shoving her belongings into it.

'Why are you packing that bag? What are you doing, Mum?'

Rae flashed her daughter a smile, a genuine smile. 'I am going island-hopping. I'm going to Greece, to start with. I might have told you about it once: something I read about when I was at school. In my head I saw this girl with a red knapsack, taking great big strides like a giant from one island to the other; she was tanned and she looked like she could take on the world. It was me, Hannah. It was me I saw. I just didn't know it until now.'

'Greece? How long will you be gone for?'

'I don't know!' she answered with something close to excitement.

'You will keep in touch?' Hannah asked, her voice rising in concern.

'Of course I will! I'm your mum.'

'How are you doing, Rae? Do you need anything?'

Rae hadn't heard her husband come up the stairs. His question was asked with saccharine sweetness that made her tremble; as she fought to contain the ball of rage in her gut, she bit down on her bottom lip to stop herself from yelling out, *Yes! I need you to fuck off! Fuck off and leave me alone!*

'Hannah, darling, could you give us a mo?' Rae spoke calmly and her daughter left, closing the door quietly behind her.

She stared at him and he at her. The air crackled around them, as if the very building waited in anticipation for what might come next.

'I was worried about you.' He licked his dry lips nervously. 'Wasn't sure where you had got to.'

'Here I am,' she answered steadily.

'Are you . . . are you feeling any better?' He swallowed.

'Much.'

'It's wonderful news about Hannah.' He drummed his fingers lightly on his thighs.

'It is,' she agreed, holding his gaze.

He exhaled deeply, as if he had been holding his breath. 'I . . .' He swallowed. 'I get the feeling you want to say something to me.'

'You do?' she asked with relative calm.

He nodded.

She felt her limbs begin to shake and so folded her arms, tucking her hands inside her armpits. 'I know, Howard.'

'You know what?' His voice was barely more than a whisper. He rubbed his finger over his top lip.

There was a beat or two of silence before she spoke.

'I know it wasn't just Karina.' She saw his pupils dilate and she took her time. 'Not that it matters, not really. She might have been the name that broke the story for me, but the end result is just the same. It's time I listened to that little voice of instinct, Howard, the one that sits on my shoulder and shouts in my ear.'

She remembered how all those months ago he had sobbed, begged, but this was different. He had played that card and at least knew her well enough to understand that it would cut no ice now. The little colour left in his cheeks faded and he looked a little green. *The idiot returns . . .*

He gripped the bedpost and when he spoke his voice was thin, weak and actually distasteful to her. 'You are talking about Lou-Lou.'

She tried to keep the shock from her face and her stance neutral, knowing that he would only further incriminate himself, preferring to fill the silence than succumb to the sound of his own thoughts. She held his gaze and let him speak.

'I knew when you spoke to her earlier on the pavement that she had told you. I fucking knew it! I could tell.' He balled a fist – his anger, she knew, not about his actions but the assumed discovery of them.

Rae's heart beat loudly in her ears. *Lou-Lou! Fifi's mum! Surely not! Surely not here, on the street where she lived. Lou-Lou – the woman she had been trying to befriend* . . .

Howard continued to babble. 'I can't tell you what it has been like for me every time you spoke to her over the last year or so, telling me how sweet Fifi was and how you felt sorry for her because she was so shy! God, Rae, I half-expected to come home one day and find you had invited her in for a bloody coffee.' He snorted a kind of laugh that was wholly inappropriate. 'I couldn't help it,' he began.

'You couldn't help it?' It was her turn to snort.

'I know I should have told you. I knew that with her being our neighbour you would find out someday. But I prayed that either she would move or that by the time you did find out, we'd be so solid, so bound, that we could find a way around it. And we can, Rae; we can find a way around this. It wasn't my fault, not really. She came on to me and I felt sorry for her and it just happened. I need help, I know I do, but I need you too. I love you. I love you so much!'

For some reason she thought of Antonio, the sweet, good-looking bartender in Antigua. *I see things, Rae-Valentine.* And for the first time she wondered just what he might have seen.

Rae took a deep breath and stared at the man standing opposite her. 'You know, it might be too late for you, but it's not for me. I want to be the best example to my kids that I can be. And when they find out how you have lived your life they will need that role model more than ever. Because, like me, they will be shocked that you are not the man they believed you to be. I thought you were a rock star, Howard, the real deal, but you weren't. You aren't. You are a fraud and I am mad at myself for wasting all these years – but not as mad as I am at myself for giving you a second chance.'

'I need you to help me, Rae, please!'

She worked quickly, now, gathering her toothbrush, passport and underwear, stuffing everything into the red knapsack.

'We need to talk, Rae; we need to sit down and figure out a plan, work out how we go forward.'

She turned to him and waved her hands to dispel his request, as if it was no more than smoke. 'Do you know the difference between the expressions of someone who is shy and someone who is guilty, Howard?'

'No.' He looked at her, *his* expression one of bewilderment.

'No, neither did I, but I do now . . . Bloody Lou-Lou! You must have both found the whole charade most amusing.' She shook her head.

'No! It wasn't like that!'

'It doesn't matter, none of it. Not now. I will keep in touch with the kids, of course.'

'I don't know what you are talking about! Where are you going? You can't just leave! It's getting dark! Hannah is getting married and I need you, we all do! I love you, Rae! Please!'

'I will talk to the kids, Howard, don't you worry. I know they just want me to be happy. And I will tell them that I am going in search of foods to eat that will take me to a certain place and time whenever I taste them again in the future. I am going out into the world so that in my twilight years I can sit on a sofa and recount all my wonderful adventures. So that my grandchildren can pore over the yellowed pages of the photograph albums that contain snapshots of my life and they will see that I was remarkable. That I travelled, that I did something! Nana Rae the explorer – that'll do for starters.'

'I am asking you not to go, Rae. Please, please!' Howard gripped his joined hands at his chest as if in prayer and she saw the image of her dad, sitting by the side of her mum's body. Her dad: a man who lived in a small house with a small life. A man who had loved and who was loyal, a man of truth and goodness who had, she now realised, lived a life of riches.

'I have already gone. And while I am away I will learn to cook; I will follow my passion and, when the time is ready, I will follow a trail of breadcrumbs all the way home, wherever that might be, and I will continue to learn. I will be a chef. Rae-Valentine the chef! Now that'd be a nice label.'

She took in the man she was married to: the man she had once considered her husband, his breath coming fast as his tears pooled.

'These girls, Howard, these women you have slept with and whose names I bet you can't even remember – Diane, Lou-Lou, Karina and the others of which I am sure there are many – they are not memorable to you, are they? They are background girls; they won't shine brightly to you. And rightly or wrongly I do take a small amount of pleasure from the fact that you will, I hope, always remember me.'

'Remember you? What are you talking about – you are my wife! And I need you here! I need you, Rae!'

She picked up the knapsack and tied her hair into a ponytail before walking down the stairs one last time.

Howard followed her.

'Can you at least go and say goodbye to Dolly?' He pointed towards the dining room. 'She is going to go nuts! What should I say to her, to the family?'

Rae carefully pulled her wedding ring from her finger and placed it along with her phone on the hall table next to her house keys. She smiled at the man who had broken her heart and stolen her years and to whom she knew she would not give one more day.

'Tell her goodbye.' Her voice was thick with emotion. 'Tell her it's time for me to step out from her shadow and that I will be in touch eventually. And tell her – fun fact – that I am funding my travels with the proceeds from selling that disgusting diamond you tried to bribe me with. And tell her – second fun fact – that I have found my voice and I have found my feet and there will be no stopping me!'

Rae stepped outside into Lawns Crescent as darkness bit. With her knapsack on her back, she lifted her hand in a wave to Mrs Williams, who stood in the kitchen window, watching the world pass her by.

◆ ◆ ◆

'Good morning.' The man smiled at her.

'Good morning.' She smiled back.

Rae handed him her passport and answered the security questions as he stood officiously behind his counter at the Eurostar station.

'Can I get an upgrade? I want to have sex with your brother.'

'Excuse me?' He stared at her, open-mouthed in surprise.

'Never mind.' She grabbed her passport and boarding card and popped them into her red knapsack. 'It was worth a try.'

BOOK CLUB QUESTIONS

1. Which character did you most closely identify with and why?

2. What advice would you have given Rae-Valentine at the beginning, middle and end of her marriage?

3. How did you feel about Dolly, her nature and the part she played in Rae-Valentine's life?

4. Did you recognise any aspects of your own family in *The Girl in the Corner*?

5. What do you think the overriding message of the book is for women?

6. Is there anything you think Rae-Valentine should have done differently?

7. Which bits made you laugh or made you cry?